Redemption

James K Burk

Sky Warrior Book Publishing, LLC

Published by Sky Warrior Book Publishing, LLC.
PO Box 99
Clinton, MT 59825
www.skywarriorbooks.com

Cover by Mitchell Davidson Bentley
Editor: Carol Hightshoe
Publisher: M. H. Bonham

Printed in the United States of America
0 9 8 7 6 5 4 3 2 1

In Memorium to Brad Beeson who started the ball rolling and to four masters from whom I learned to write; Roger Zelazny, Poul Anderson, Gordon R. Dickson, and Walter R. Brooks.

Chapter 1

The two guards opened his cell and gestured for him to stand and walk out into the corridor. Captain Li was too enervated by his captivity and the oppressive heat to even make his usual observations about their parentage or sexual proclivities. As he stood and limped out of the cell one of the guards preceded him while the other followed.

Even if he had been in better condition he doubted he could have taken on either guard, much less both of them. They stood just under two meters tall and he'd never been sure whether the chitinous plates that covered their torsos and limbs were battle armor, a uniform, or even part of their bodies. More such armor covered their heads, coming to a point between their deep-set eyes and flaring to form heavy cheekbones and pronounced mandibles. Their noses were short and sharp-edged and their mouths were lipless.

The guard before him stopped and gestured to an open door. Inside, on a table, lay a bucket of water and some folded gray cloth.

Li tried to keep his features composed as he reached into the bucket, cupped his hands, and drank. It seemed these creatures knew just how much water the human body needed for survival and withheld even a drop more than that. This was the most water he'd seen in what he guessed to be two years. He drank until he felt full, and even the tepid water seemed cool and sweet, then washed his face, using his fingers to comb back his matted hair and sparse beard.

One of the guards motioned at the cloth and Li unfolded it to discover it was a one-piece jumper. More gestures indicated he was to put on the clothing. For the first time since the day after he'd been captured, he was able to cover himself.

As soon as he'd dressed himself more gestures ordered him out of the room and down the corriodor.

Again he had to control his face, even his body, as he was directed to the door of the torturer. More than once he'd been broken and been dragged, sobbing and fighting a futile battle against the guards, afraid of finding more things worse than death.

The torturer entered the other door of the cubicle as Li was being ushered in from the hall.

"Captain Li, it is a pleasure to see you again." It always surprised Li that a species whose own speech sounded like high-pitched chittering, could cause a computer, translating into Trade Common, to have such an oily voice. Perhaps that was what all human speech sounded like to them. "This is the last time I will be pleased to speak with you."

Li simply stared at the thing facing him. He'd never learned to distinguish between them except his tormenter had patterns engraved on his helmet, breastplate, and upper arm guards and these were highlighted with red paint.

"Speechless again, Captain Li?" The alien turned his right hand palm down and waved it from side to side, perhaps an alien version of a shrug. "We are returning you to others of your species." A pause. "It has been fascinating to study you and you have given me a great gift."

"Whatever it is," Li said, "it isn't the present I'd most like to give you."

The other's eyes widened in what Li had come to guess indicated amusement. "I'm sure it isn't what you'd like to give me, but it is the best gift you can give me." A sigh. "You humans are very interesting—and surprisingly hard to kill. When we first encountered you, we took you for grubs and wondered why a species would crew their vessels with immature forms.

"Ah, well, in some ways you're quite immature. Your gift to me is that you will remember me until you die. You will hate me for the rest of your life, and it is better to be hated than to be forgotten."

"That's another gift I'll happily give you."

The eyes widened again.

Li fought to keep his voice steady. "You might want to remember me, too. Someday I hope to see you again, and then I'll give you a very different gift."

The eyes remained wide. "I don't think so, Captain Li. I have to consult my records to remember your name now. I'm sure there are differences between you humans, but you all look the same to me. And after you're gone I will have other matters to absorb my interests.

"The best thing about the gift you give me is that you'll always be giving it to me. Even after I've told you what it is, told you how much I appreciate it, you will continue to give it to me. I find the irony—delicious."

The torturer nodded to the guards, who seized Li's arms and hauled him out of the cubicle and down the corridor. They stopped at another door and one pressed a lighted stud. The door sighed open and Li faced the first humans he'd seen in at least two years. He could only recognize Lieutenant Bachman by his blond hair. It looked as though the man had been broken several times. Tears ran down the man's cheeks and it was impossible to guess whether the man's hunched posture was from a broken spirit or a broken body. Perhaps both. The other ragged, bearded man, probably Lieutenant Singh, stared at the guards with an eye that should have burned them to cinders where they stood. One eye was missing and the other harbored more than a trace of madness.

Li wondered what he looked like to his brother officers and straightened his shoulders, suppressing a wince at the pain.

The door to the outside was opened and the three men squinted. The sun hung just above the horizon and they had no way to know whether it was morning or evening. The hot, muggy air scarcely moved but they were able to catch a sort of tidewater odor.

A heavy vehicle drew up just outside the building and the guards led them out. The driver or pilot sat in a small cab at the front. Three guards took their places in seats facing the rear, the prisoners were seated in three rows, a guard on either side of each man, and three more guards occupied the last row of seats. As soon as the last guard had taken his place the vehicle moved smoothly forward.

Li had been given the prisoner's seat nearest the front

and simply stared straight ahead. He could, at the edge of his vision, see they were being driven along a road bordered by dense vegetation but wouldn't give his captors the satisfaction of seeing him curious about their world. In less than half an hour they arrived at a shuttle which looked very like the vehicle but for a heavy engine at the rear and a locking ring surrounding the single large door. The whole process of disembarking and reboarding followed the same pattern but he observed the shuttle seat had straps. He fumbled with them until a guard became impatient and strapped him into the seat.

With a whine that rose steadily in pitch, the engine started and the vessel lurched forward. Again, he simply stared at the guards facing him but could see the interior brighten as they rose into more direct sunlight then darken as they rose above the planet's atmosphere.

Li supposed he should be rejoicing at the nearness of freedom but he was numb, emotionally drained. He had been lied to so often he'd learned to expect nothing, certainly nothing good.

The shuttle slowed, then finally, with a clangor from the locking ring, shuddered. The guard to his left pulled the releases and the straps retracted, then the guards gestured for him to get out. Bachman and Singh followed him into the featureless airlock and the heavy door closed behind them.

Li remained stoic. He wouldn't have been surprised if the door behind them opened again and vomited them into space. Instead, the door opened to a large room nearly filled with men and women wearing Solar League uniforms. Li almost broke down at the sight but ignored the pain to straighten his shoulders and tried to stride forward, although he realized it was little more than a shamble. Still, he marched forward to face a Solar League admiral and snapped a salute.

The admiral returned the salute then turned to the woman beside him, who wore the insigniae of the medical service. "Get gurneys for these men and get them to the infirmary at once." To Li, he said, "I'll be in to visit you men in half an hour."

From behind him Li heard a sob, then the sound of someone

weeping. For a moment, he was annoyed. The sounds were making his own stoicism more difficult to maintain. Pushing himself to his limit, he stared at the admiral. "With your permission, sir, I will walk to the infirmary."

The admiral seemed to have problems maintaining his own composure and simply nodded, a single curt declination of his head.

The crowd parted and men in white uniforms entered as he made his way to the door. He glanced at the first man to approach him and asked, "Would you please escort me to the infirmary, corpsman?"

After a heartbeat's pause, the man nodded as the admiral had. Two more corpsmen moved past him for Singh and Bachman. A dozen paces carried Li through the door and he ignored the three gurneys and the men beside them and followed his escort to the lift.

The drier, cooler air helped to reinvigorate Li, although his bare feet were beginning to chill. He moved to the back of the large cubicle and turned. Singh was also walking, a man beside him, but two men secured Bachman to a gurney while another administered an injection. The racking sobs faded as the men drew the cart to the lift.

Despite his resolve, Li swayed as the lift moved up two levels to the infirmary. He waited while Bachman, now unconscious, was wheeled out, then followed his escort to a room. A woman stood, waiting, and, after a cursory examination, she asked, "Is there anything you need?"

"Yes. A shower."

The woman opened a folding door and showed him how to operate the shower and how the seat could be unfolded. After assuring him she would return as soon as the imaging equipment arrived, she left the room.

After stripping off the gray prisoner's jumpsuit, Li flung it into a trash receptacle and stepped into the shower. The needles of hot water stung his skin but made him feel more alive. After the water stopped he applied the cleansing lotion, rubbing vigorously everywhere he could reach, before pressing the tab for another fifteen seconds of hot water. He seemed to feel not only years of accumulated grime washing away but his humiliation as well. Fifteen seconds of cold water finished refreshing him and he stepped out of the shower, dried himself, and put on the gown provided by the infirmary.

While he searched for a depilatory, he heard a knock at the door before it slid open and the admiral stepped into the room. Li snapped to attention and saluted.

"At ease, Captain Li." The admiral glanced around at the room, large enough only for a bed and whatever medical equipment needed to be wheeled in. "Please, sit."

"I'd rather stand, sir. In the interrogations I was always seated while the lobster stood over me."

"Captain Li, I am Admiral Tsung. I'm sure you have many questions for me, as I have for you. There'll be an official debriefing later but I'm anxious to know what happened."

Li had relaxed his posture to 'parade rest.' "Admiral, we'd just discovered what appeared to be a habitable planet, rich in resources. We'd assembled the exploration team when another ship appeared in normal space. After assuming a defensive position, we sent an all-bands message identifying ourselves and requesting identification of the other ship.

"The alien ship reminded me of nothing so much as a horseshoe crab with a club-like tail. Our sensors detected a heavy power-flow and ascertained the gasses in the ship were largely the same as our own and in nearly the same proportions but the interior temperatures of the ship were somewhat higher than our own. We were not able to count the other vessel's crew but the computer extrapolated at least a hundred fifty lifeforms. We were also able to detect that we were being studied as well.

"Apparently, our computer and theirs were able to reach a level of understanding sufficient to translate our communications. There was, of course, no visual communication."

"Interesting," the admiral said. "Our communications with them have, for the last two years, been both auditory and visual."

Li raised his eyebrows. "How long have we been ... missing?"

"The *Leap Forward* was destroyed almost three and a half years ago. Commodore Weiss sent a message bottle shortly after contact was made with what we know as the ChiTseTsi. Assuming about a month's travel time to the nearest hub, you've been held for approximately forty-one months."

Li lapsed into silence, absorbing the information, then roused himself and managed a wry grin. "Or, subjectively, about forty years." He paused, then continued his report. "After perhaps four hours we were able to communicate. We identified ourselves and learned we'd encountered a previously unknown species. After a few preliminaries we agreed to use the shuttle to send a delegation to their vessel while they sent a similar group to ours. Our technologies were similar enough to manage such a transfer.

"As Commodore Weiss' second-in-command, I was chosen to lead the delegation. There were eight of us; Lieutenants Singh, Bachman, Sadar, and Chin as well as ensigns Ling, Volokov, Borde and myself. Just as we reached the alien ship we saw a flash. I can only assume their shuttle contained a bomb. The alien ship immediately opened fire with some sort of beam and the *Leap Forward* was slashed apart."

The memories, even after so long, were so powerful Li was forced to pause. Horror, shame, and rage were as twisted around each other as snakes in a nest. When he could trust his voice again, he continued. "Our shuttle had no weapons and, of course, we wore none. The voice of their communicator demanded that we proceed, in a line, into their airlock. We did so, and that's how we first saw the lobsters." He desribed them; symetrical, bipedal, and both tall and powerfully built. "Their average mass is probably about a hundred fifty kilos, perhaps heavier because of their armor. They all carried bladed weapons, something like a cross between a heavy-bladed knife and a hatchet. Once they had us lined up, they ordered Ensign Borde to step forward, then they decapitated her." He again had to struggle to bring his feelings under control and when he spoke the fury still thickened his voice. "You can't imagine how often I've wanted to do the same to their entire race."

Admiral Tsung studied his face. "I understand. Then what happened?"

"We were all placed in a small room. One of the lobsters took cell samples from us. After nearly a day they delivered a bucket of water. We all took turns drinking and, after about an hour, they removed the water. The next time they brought water, they brought less of it.

"They never tried to speak to us. In fact, I don't recall ever hearing them speak to each other. The only reason I know what their language sounds like is because the torturer spoke so their computer could translate it into Trade Common."

Tsung's eyebrows rose. "The torturer?"

"That's how I thought of him. The ship carrying us docked in some sort of station then we were sent to a planet and we were separated. I never saw another human until they brought us together before delivering us to your ship."

"The name of the ship is *The Glorious*. I gather it was a compromise." Tsung turned at another knock at the door. "I will speak with you again, later. I'd rather wait until you've been examined." He raised his arm to salute and, as Li quckly brought up his own arm and hand, the admiral said, "No, I salute you."

The admiral strode past the cart carrying a scanner and an analysis computer. The tech nodded toward the bed. "Would you please lie down, captain?"

When Li had lain down on the bed the tech pricked his forearm and deftly swept up a drop of blood on a small, clear plate, which she inserted into the analyzer, following it with a single hair plucked from his scalp.

The imager was guided into a track and its wheels retracted so the machine moved up the bed, humming softly, guided by the grooves in the floor.

"Please lie still and close your eyes," the tech said.

Li closed his eyes and waited. He could only tell the imager was over his face when the insides of his eyelids darkened and by the sound of the humming, then the humming stopped and he barely heard the machine retreat down its tracks.

"You may open your eyes again," the doctor said. "I'm

sure you'd like a good meal but, according to the analyzer, an ingestion of more than small amounts would cause sickness. You are also dangerously low on zinc and potassium. We're going to administer drugs and sound therapy to allow you to sleep peacefully."

Li heard a faint hiss and tried to say he wasn't sleepy but the words came out slurred and it didn't seem worth the effort to try again.

* * *

When he woke he found the edge of his hunger and thirst had been dulled. Within moments a nurse knocked at his door and entered the room. After a glance at the monitors she detached a tube from the saline lock on the back of his wrist.

"Are you ready for breakfast?"

Li considered a moment. While the desperate need for food seemed to be gone, his stomach still grumbled. "Yes."

The nurse left the room to return moments later with a small, covered tray. Reaching under the bed, she swung out and raised an arm that held a small table. Setting the tray on the table, she pulled off the cover to reveal a small cup of tea, a thumb-sized piece of tofu, and a dollop of something green and shapeless. "You received hydration and nutrients while you slept. We have to get your stomach used to processing food again. If we give you too much food, you will become sick. We'll allow you to digest this, then allow you fifteen minutes of light exercise. You'll receive small meals and light exercise every two hours until your system is ready for larger meals and more exertion."

Li sipped the tea, then sampled the foods. To him, they were delicacies. "What about the men with me?"

"I'm sorry. Both of them will have to be sedated until we reach a hub, perhaps even until they've returned to Earth. The damage they've received, both physical and mental, is too extensive for shipboard facilities to deal with." She covered the tray with its now empty plate and cup. "Would you rather rest or may I bring you something to occupy your mind?"

"I have nearly three and a half years of news to catch up on."

"We also have messages from your family. If you're comfortable viewing them, I'll provide you with a card and screen."

"I would be very comfortable doing so."

The nurse left and returned with a small card-like control pad and a screen on a frame. "If you need anything you can use the control. In the meantime, I'll see you aren't disturbed."

"I appreciate your discretion," Li said.

After the nurse had gone, he keyed the card for contents. He'd be able to use the same card and screen for news archives later but he saw a message from his mother, another from his elder brother, and even one from his estranged wife. He was at first disappointed that there were no messages from his father, then became worried. He selected the message from his mother first.

"Eaglet, we've been told you're still alive and I hope you may see this message. Your father has gone to rest."

Li paused the message and stared at the screen. Again, his emotions were stronger than they were coherent. His father had been a stern taskmaster, sparing in his praise, but Li had respected him and now he realized he'd also loved him. Tears he'd fought back so many times stung his eyes and ran down his cheeks. He grieved silently for a time, remembering episodes both painful and warming; an odd bit of praise, a shared joke, times when the older man seemed made of stone. Finally he touched the "continue" key.

"Among the last things he said was to ask me to tell you how proud of you he was. The learning was not always easy, but you learned well."

Li had to pause the message again as tears flowed. When he'd finally dried his face with his hands he resumed the message.

"I cannot imagine what you've experienced. Some things I will never know, but I want you to know I have always hoped for your return, and I look forward to seeing my eaglet again, and I will hold you but not hold your wings too tightly to keep you from flying."

A soft chime from the card and a light in the upper right

of the screen announced the arrival of a new message and he touched for audial.

The nurse's voice said, "I hate to bother you but would you be ready for some exercise?"

"Thank you, nurse. I will be ready in a moment." He turned off the card and watched the screen darken.

Within moments the nurse, after a knock at the door, carried in a soft blue exercise suit and soft shoes. She helped him dress but hesitated a moment when she saw the missing and broken toes. Without uttering a word, she carefully helped him into the shoes. She led him into the corridor and Li felt an involutary shudder, then followed, glancing at the woman to see if she'd noticed. If she had, she gave no sign.

Only a little larger than his sickbay room, the exercise room already had two occupants. One crewman pulled at cords set for a certain resistance while another pedaled a stationary bicycle. "Please step onto the mat. You may hold the bar at the end for balance. We'll set it for an easy walk."

The mat was actually a belt which began to move, picking up a little speed and Li grasped the bar. While he was walking, Li reflected that his nurse had used almost no gestures and had spoken to him at each step of the treatment. Apparently they'd taken note of what he'd said, done some extrapolations, and instructed her on the proper way to behave to avoid upsetting him. It was a little like an insult but, he admitted to himself, a comfort. After being humiliated and isolated, the hospital staff were showing him he not only had value but they respected that value.

The brief walk was enough to leave him noticiably short of breath and with a fine sheen of sweat.

"Have you had enough?"

"Yes, nurse." He waited until the belt had stopped moving then stepped off the machine. "Back to the room?"

"Back to the room," she agreed. "I'll be bringing you another meal in about an hour."

"What's your name?"

"I'm Padmaju Patel. And, to answer the question you're

thinking of asking, if I'm related to Fleet Admiral Patel, it's so distantly that neither of us is aware of it. Patel is at least as common a name as Li." She flashed a smile and he felt his own lips twitch in reponse.

As she led him into his room she asked, "Would you like to put on your robe again?"

"Thank you, no. But I was wondering if I could take another shower."

"Captain Li, you may spend all the time you're not eating, resting, or exercing taking showers if you wish. And, if you'd like, I'll apply a depilatory to your face as well. You're our honored guest,"

"Ms. Patel, I'd be pleased to be rid of this beard, and the hair as well." For some reason, he found his own hair to be not only unclean but somehow related to his captivity.

"As you wish."

He sat in the chair as she carefully applied the cream to his head and face. The cool cream, as it warmed, tickled. After waiting until it had become a gel, the nurse wiped it away, and his hair and beard with it. Immediately he had a sense of his skin tautening.

As the nurse carried out the towel and his hair, Li undressed and entered the shower, repeating the sequence of hot water, cleanser, more hot water, and a last dose of cold water. After drying himself he opened the door of a cabinet which, on opening, drew out a toilet bowl. He urinated into it, washed his hands in a tiny basin, and returned to his room. After putting on the excercise suit, he lay on the bed and called up the message from his brother.

As boys, he and Chin had been close but over the years the shared childhood and parentage had provided only a weak glue and they'd grown apart.

"Wing, I've just learned you're still alive. I was pleased to hear it. When you can, I'd be very honored to have you as my guest."

Li deleted the message. He then debated with himself whether he even wanted to hear the message from Bao-Yu.

At last he decided the worst damage the message could inflict would be to bore him.

The face on the screen was a bit more plump than he remembered but the features were still attractive. "Wing, I was very happy to hear you're alive. I want you to know you will always be a friend I'll cherish. While we've gone our separate ways, I still think of you fondly and wish you well. Please call me when you return."

At least it was brief and hadn't bored him. They'd met when he'd just graduated from the academy and had enjoyed a torrid romance. Marriage had seemed to end the romance, although some of the heat had still spontaneously combusted. Even that had finally disappeared when he found himself, even in love-making, resenting her. The one unmixed blessing was that they'd had no children. Bao Yu had embraced a career in journalism, if that was the correct term for one who interviewed celebrities, while Li had made the service his life.

He deleted that message as well and had just begun to study the menu of news items when the chime sounded again and the light flashed.

"If you're ready, I'll bring you your next meal," Padmaju's voice said through the speaker.

This time the cup contained broth and the tofu had a sweeter flavor but the green blob on the plate seemed the same.

As soon as the nurse had carried out the tray he returned to the card's menu, then adjusted for voice command and said, "First contact with sentient alien species in the last forty-two months."

The first listing was, of course, the ChiTseTsi and he adjusted the reading speed to a comfortable two thousand words per minute. The *Leap Forward* had been the first contact with the lobsters and the service had lost half a dozen vessels in subsequent clashes with them, although they'd inflicted more damage on the ChiTseTsi.

First contact with another race, the Walawi, had been made during the war. A Commodore Sauvage had been investigating a new system when he found two ChiTseTsi ships bombarding a planet. He immediately attacked the ships, destroying both. They'd been able to retrieve two bodies, then landed on the planet. After some time they'd managed to make contact with the inhabitants and had provided some medical assistance.

The Walawi were advanced enough to have developed fusion power generators and had established scientific colonies on one of their moons and on another planet orbiting their star.

Nearly the entire population had been shipped out as part of the treaty between the Solar League and the ChiTseTsi, when the lobsters had claimed the planet as part of their sphere of space.

Li's eyes narrowed as he paused the script. Such a treaty was a bitter humiliation. He wondered whether Earth's negotiators had sold out the Walawi to get back human prisoners or whether he and the other prisoners were an afterthought. He tapped in two memos to himself. The first was to learn as much as he could about the treaty and the present political situation on Earth. The second was to try to meet Commodor Sauvage.

After his next exercise session, at which he requested a brisker pace, he received a request for his presence for an official debriefing. He asked for and received a uniform with his captain's insigniae and a pair of shoes. While the shoes were uncomfortable, he did not intend to appear at any hearing dressed like a prisoner or a patient.

Doctor Zhang, head of the medical staff, informed him he need not attend the debriefing, that she could submit a notice of her professional disapproval.

"Thank you, doctor, but I would prefer to return to normal duties as soon as possible."

"In that case, I suggest you let me remove the medication lock. The sensors will remain in your system so we can monitor your health. If the readings suggest you're being overtaxed, I'll end the debriefing."

Her removal of the medication lock was so deft he hardly felt it and she led him to the lift. Another crewman stood in the lift as the door slid open. The man stared at Li for a moment before stepping out into the corridor. After Li and the doctor had entered the lift and gone 'down' two levels and followed a hallway to a room two doors from the entry hall, the doctor nodded at the red light glowing above the door.

"I'll leave you here, Captain, but I'll be watching your vital signs." She knocked at the door then returned the way they had come.

When Li entered he observed the room was small, as were almost all the accommodations on a ship. At the opposite end of the room Admiral Tsung sat behind a table, flanked by a commodore, a captain, and two commanders. As Li stepped through the door the officers stood. In the three paces to the empty chair facing the officers Li had to fight down a smile as he remembered the end of an old joke, "Who's minding the store?"

He snapped a salute, which was returned, then Admiral Tsung said, "Please sit down, captain."

As Li sat , Tsung gestured toward a lens and a small grille set into the wall. "This meeting will be observed and recorded by the ship's computer. Have you any objections, Captain Li?"

"None."

Li recounted the story of the destruction of the *Leap Forward* and his captivity. After he'd finished, Admiral Tsung said, "We have verification of at least one of your observations. Analysis of the bodies recovered by the *Glorious Light* revealed the ChiTseTsi indeed have an exoskeleton."

"I should like to know," Li said, "what was offered the ChiTseTsi in exchange for my life and those of my fellow crewmen."

"Stop recording," the admiral snapped, "and delete the previous question from Captain Li."

After glances at the other officers at the table, Admiral Tsung stared into Li's eyes. "I regret to imform you that, had the decision been mine to make, you would still be a ChiTseTsi prisoner and we would still be at war with them. The decision was made by the Solar League Council."

Li and Tsung exchanged sardonic smiles. Despite the pompous title, the Solar League was dominated by the Earth government. Luna was only a scientific and commercial base of some four thousand scientists completely dependent on Earth, and Mars, which had been partially terraformed and settled by genetically altered humans who, beyond their own local interests, voted as the Earth government told them to. The colony worlds were all under the thumb of the League Council or economic interests, which amounted to the same thing.

"How did you even know we were prisoners?"

Tsung folded his hands. "The ChiTseTsi themselves announced it during negotiations. The war was already unpopular and a new Earth governement was trying to find a way to end it. The ChiTseTsi offered to allow the Walawi to emigrate, then added they had several human prisoners who would also be released. I am afraid you were used as a bargaining chip. It gave the Earth government a humanitarian fig leaf to hide behind as they ceded control of a huge volume of space to the ChiTseTsi."

Although Li's lips had curled , the expression couldn't have been mistaken for a smile. "I can't say I'm sorry not to be a prisoner, but I also agree the price was too high."

"If none of the others have any questions of you…" Tsung paused and glanced at the other officers, "I believe we're done here. If you have any questions to ask of any of us, this is the appropriate time."

Li shook his head, then saluted before pivoting and marching out of the room. Glancing up, he noted the light had been turned off.

Nurse Patel was already in the lift when the door opened. "I was just coming to wait for you. It's time for your next meal."

Li nodded and they rode the lift to the sickbay level.

"If you don't mind wearing the uniform a bit longer, we're having the exercise suit cleaned."

The rations were fractionally larger and included a bit of fish—or what tasted like fish—and a bit of sweet pastry. "You need fats to help you recover," Patel said, "especially if you're going to exercise."

* * *

The cycle of increasingly larger meals and more strenuous exercise assumed a rather comforting pattern. The doctor had prescribed a sedative along with sound therapy. After a week, Li decided he no longer needed the sedative but resumed taking it after waking up screaming.

In the meantime, he'd caught up on the news for three and a half years, then decided to study, in turn, the known space-faring races. His recent experiences made him very aware that man's place in the universe was a tenuous one. Man's first alien contact had been with the Huer, nearly sixty years earlier. Li realized comparing aliens to any Earth species was patently absurd. Genetically, he had more in common with a sponge than the Huer had with any Earth species, but they had always seemed faintly canine to him, with their short, pointed ears set high on the skull, their short noses ending in wide, flat tips, and the outward curving expanse between the bottom of their nose and their mouth. Their prominent lower jaws and teeth and their thick nails, which reminded him of claws, all added to the effect. They were almost hairless and most of they were colored gray-green or brown.

They were larger than humans, averaging about two and a quarter meters in height and, for being so heavily muscled, were very quick. The first contacts with them had been violent but, slowly, accommodations had been reached. When the Earth government had realized most of the reason for Huer aggression was fueled by desperation—the Huer homeworld lacked any substantial deposits of heavy metals—Earth had ceded a large volume of space known to contain several worlds rich in natural resources. The agreement, reached thirty years ago, had ended the conflict with the Huer.

Little was known of their culture or their history. They had some sort of caste system and, within each of the castes, septs. Most of the Huer the humans had encountered had been members of the Warrior/Explorer Caste, but eventually the humans had learned the Warrior Caste had little influence on the planet's government.

Learning their language was a challenge, and Li needed challenge, attacking the problem with hypno-lessons. The human vocal apparatus was ill-equipped for producing the rumbling sounds of much of their language and the coughings and exhalations were difficult to distinguish.

Their etiquette was subtle. In greeting, they spread their arms. They displayed goodwill by keeping their three fingers and thumb straight while crooked, claw-like fingers were a sign of challenge. They smiled but did so with closed mouth, because a display of teeth in a smile was considered another form of challenge.

He'd just begun to study the Valek when the doctor visited him.

"I just wanted to make sure you were getting enough rest. Nurse Patel tells me you've been studying very hard."

Li shrugged, then hid the wince of pain the movement caused him. "If I do nothing but rest, you will be delivering a fat, indolent, and still ignorant man to the hub. Besides, I need something to concentrate on."

The doctor nodded. "I think that's good therapy. New interests and new experiences will help you heal. Just don't assume your memories have lost their power. They will always be there, like patches of quicksand, but dealing with the world around you is just what this doctor ordered. Just be sure to get enough rest and exercise."

As the doctor left, Nurse Patel entered with his tray. His meals had become larger and with four hours between each meal. Food on a starship was, of course, recycled and reconstituted, but every effort had been made to make it palatable. Most of the protein was provided by tofu, or something resembling it, which had the advantage of providing an array of tastes. Since tofu had no real flavor of its own, preparation could make it taste like almost anything.

"How much longer will I have the pleasure of your company, Ms Patel?"

"We should be at the hub nearest Earth in the next standard week and, if they send you to Earth, another week after that." She gathered the bowls and utensils, placed them in the tray, and carried them out.

Li was surprised the prospect of returning to Earth didn't excite him and he wondered if the ChiTseTsi had killed his emotions.

He returned to his studies. The Valek had clashed with both humans and the Huer. Their drive was less desperation than expansionist, and they were very careful but fierce when they perceived insult or a danger to their interests. Unlike the Huer, their warrior class was intimately involved in their government. Their ships' commanders were usually capable but were also politically well-connected.

The truce between the Valek and the humans was still fragile, and their truce with the Huer even more so.

They were more open about their history and culture than the Huer and when humans learned the Valek had once been a subject race, some of their culture became more understandable. Their suspicion of other races and their apparent arrogance were a reaction to the humiliation of being a conquered people. The leaders of the revolt had become the political and military leaders. The Valek's apparent arrogance and the pride of the Huer Warrior Caste were a combustible mixture and their governments seldom communicated directly. The treaties between the Valek and the Huer had largely been the result of human intercession.

The Valek were about the same height as humans and slender. Although they were warm-blooded, they had nictitating membranes and their skin was covered with fine scales, the skin tones ranging from tan through dark brown. Their noses were broader between the eyes than at the tips, which were very thin and hooked which, with their large eyes protected by bony ridges, gave them the appearance of birds of prey. The impression was reinforced by their reserve. Their greeting was a curt nod, which had nothing but a passing resemblance to a bow.

Like Li's native Chinese, the Valek spoke a tonal language, which made interpretation more difficult, since the nuances were difficult for even the computers to translate.

After absorbing all the information he could find on the ship's computer about the Valek, Li took a day's break from his studies, He obtained permission to visit the bridge, the command center located near the middle of the ship and felt, pacing around the banks of instuments and monitors, as though he had returned home. The only discomfort he felt simply reflected his being a visitor and he resolved he would bend every effort to convince the government to give him his own command.

The remainder of the day was spent in exercise, rest, and meditation. He felt his place in the universe was faintly out of balance and it was time to restore the balance.

The Chadanor were the next subjects of study. Studying even the physical differences and similarities of the races was instructive. All were smymetrical and, with the exception of the Chadanor, all were bipedal. The Chadanor were four-legged and two-armed, rather like the old mythical centaurs, although the resemblance ended there. Their legs ended in clawed, padded paws. They were also the only race with six eyes; one pair mounted on the sides of their long heads, the other two pair on the front of the head, The upper pair of frontal eyes were apparently adapted for distant vision while the lower pair were specialized for close observation. Their bodies, except for their hands, were covered with a coarse fur that ranged in color from red-brown through many shades of tan to blue-gray, and many of them bore markings of two or more colors.

They seemed, to observers, to be very orderly and ethical among their own race but they had a reputation for keeping their own agreements with others only when the terms were enforced. The most common opinion was that, among aliens, the Chadanor would steal anything that wasn't nailed down, and anything they could pry or break loose wasn't nailed down.

Most of them had learned the pidgin that passed for a common trade language, which was a very good thing because about a third of their language was in stances or gestures. Li could imagine a computer trying to translate Chadanor emitting smoke and sparks before exploding in sheer frustration.

The ChiTseTsi he knew all too well, although he learned that, from the bodies recovered, they had vestigal gills, suggesting they were descended from an amphibian species. They seemed more comfortable with a slightly lower than Earth gravity but were as quck as humans. The general assumption was that they had developed in a very competitive environment which required quickness and ruthlessness.

This left only the Walawi. Their homeworld and the planets the Earth government had granted them had a higher gravity, nearly thirty percent higher, than Earth's. The Walawi were slender, usually a meter and a half tall or so, and possessed of remarkable strength and quickness. On a high-gravity planet, things fall faster so speedy reactions were a survival trait.

The Walawi had been an advanced race who'd developed space flight enough to have placed scientific communities on both of their homeworld's satellites and the two nearest planets in their star system. In another half-century they might have become a star-faring race. They'd advanced sufficiently that being forced to rebuild on other planets had been and remained an ordeal, even with occasional supplies brought from Earth.

In coloration they were similar to the Chadanor, athough the fur that covered most of their bodies was very fine. Their society was based on family units Earth anthropologists tended to describe as prides. Each group contained a dominant male and several females and their young. Observers had noted a ratio of ten to twelve females born for each male birth. Young males remained with the family or pride until they were prepared to mate. If the pride was wealthy in land, the dominant male might provide living accommodations for the younger male to let him establish his own pride, otherwise the young male could challenge the dominant male or strike out to find his own territory. The adaptation to an urban existence must have been trying.

The dominant male made decisions for the pride and defended the pride, but the females hunted or farmed. More recently, the females constituted almost the totality of the worker and engineer classes, with the males being directors. That was another reason human anthropologists had referred to their basic unit as a pride.

Their language was fluid-sounding except for an occasional growling sound. Like the Chadanor, most of them spoke the trade pidgin. A handful of them had been allowed to immigrate to Earth, where they frequently excelled. The number of Walawi immigrants was kept limited by the hostile immigration policies and the fact prides would only emigrate as a group. Young males had no incentive to emigrate since there were so few available females of their species on Earth.

The Martians weren't really an alien race, being genetically modified humans. They all spoke Trade Common in addition to dialects of their once-native languages. Earth had attempted to make Mars another Earth, with mixed results. Then it was decided it was easier to modify people and other Earth species than to terraform the planet. What had started as an advance into space had turned into a dead end with the invention of the Liang drive, which had placed habitable worlds within man's reach and the Martians had become a vestigal species, a sort of racial appendix.

At least another dozen species had evolved to using fire and crude tools and the general policy was to leave them alone to develop as they would. The disagreements between humans and both the Huer and the Valek had been about exploiting those worlds with native creatures not considered sentient. The human position was based on the premise a species could be sentient without producing signs of culture. The dolphin was most frequently cited as an example of a sentient race but one without technology.

Both the Huer and the Valek countered it was impossible to detect sentience and, even in the vast universe, hospitable planets were very few. A planet most likely to be habitable by the space-faring species was almost certain to have some lifeforms develop on that world.

The Huer were willing to allow human scientists to be members of their colonizing teams but their only functions were to record and classify indigenous lifeforms. The Valek simply claimed a sphere of space which the humans had ceded because of the proximity of the Valek homeworld.

* * *

Li had just wakened when he felt the subtle change from the ship's artifical gravity to the pull of momentun. As a ship dropped from the Liang drive into normal space it maintained the residual speed of its velocity before entering the wrinkle in time created by the Liang drive. A good helmsman could orient the ship in such a way an emerging ship would arrive 'bottom first,' using the deceleration as a form of artificial gravity until its speed dropped to a level when the true artificial gravity generators would take over.

Li found the card and turned on the screen. A man in the uniform of a rear admiral stared out of the screen. "Welcome back, *Glorious*. Please contact us when you're prepared to receive a supply shuttle."

The screen split and Admiral Tsung's face appeared on the left half. "Am I to assume we're proceed to Earth?"

"That is correct. We're to reprovision you. If you'll send a list of your requirements we'll ship them out by shuttle. We'll also send the latest news, only a week old. You should be able to proceed to Earth in approximately six hours."

Since he was already awake, Li dressed and waited for his first meal. Idly, he keyed up the information being transferred by the hub and was shocked to see his own picture, one taken about five years earlier, along with old pictures of Singh and Bachman. The news report accompanying the images seemed undecided whether to refer to them as victims or as heroes.

He paged Admiral Tsung and received a reply almost immediately.

"Admiral, I just had the disagreeable surprise of finding my picture and a rather fanciful biography on a news story."

"Captain Li, if you have even half the wisdom and cleverness I credit you for, you will use this for proper ends. The government needs you. Remember, you are their fig leaf. There are some who will try to have you retired and others who will want you assigned administrative duties. If, as I suspect, you want to go back into space you will need every tool and weapon that comes to your hand. I do not expect you to enjoy the celebrity, I expect you to use it wisely."

Li suppressed a sigh. "As you say, sir."

He'd just turned off the screen when Nurse Patel brought him breakfast. He was sure the yellow mass was supposed to be some sort of substitute for eggs, the bright yellow and pink strips that looked as though they might have been made out of a child's modeling clay were apparently in lieu of bacon. He still hadn't been able to guess what the green mass was supposed to represent. There was also tea and some sort of orange-colored drink with a faintly astringent taste.

Li finished the meal and said, "We'll be taking on supplies for the trip to Earth. Will those include something like food?"

"Something like it, I suppose, but you'll have to wait until you're back on Earth before you can enjoy anything like Shahi Khorma." As she covered the plate with lid of the tray, she added, "You've become more discriminating. You really seemed to enjoy ship's food at first."

"I suppose one becomes jaded very quickly. After captivity, everything seems better." He reached for the comcard. "Will you be taking leave on Earth?"

She smiled. "It should be diverting. I always look forward to leave—seeing family and friends, eating real food, being able to shop, and all the things I can't do now. Then, in two or three weeks, I'm exhausted and eager to get back to the ship and settle into a steady pattern again. And you?"

"I'm eager to see my mother again. And there are two or three people I'd like to look up. Beyond that, I'll be eager to be back aboard a ship."

As Patel left he studied imformation he knew was already over a week old. He was annoyed he was so prominently displayed and wondered if that had crowded out something more newsworthy.

He did learn the Solar League had approved a new Dicovery class ship. The vessels were to be enormous, and with the most potent weapons available although its stated mission was peaceful. It would patrol contested space and visit colony worlds and scientific stations on its way out to unexplored space, where its real work would begin. The greater capacity was needed for families, scientists, and laboratories. Because of the unknown dangers, the ship would also support a larger complement of fighting crew. The journey out and back would require eight years, so all the crews' personnel would be volunteers.

Li would be eligible for a twenty-year retirement in three years, which would mean extending his career to thirty years, but he'd already decided to remain in the service, and this news was only another incentive.

* * *

The *Glorious* docked at the station in Earth orbit. The ship did not actually settle under its own power. Tugs attached themselves to the vessel and they and magnetic fields drew the *Glorious* into the dock. The entry lock was then sealed and the crew took a tube leading from the airlock to the interior of the station. From there they were conducted to a shuttle bay.

Seats had been removed from the shuttle to make room for the wheelchairs for Singh and Bachman and the chairs carefully secured. The admiral and the doctor sat in the seats beside Li and Patel. Other officers from the *Glorious* and two nurses made up the rest of the passengers.

Unlike the ship and the station, the shuttle lacked artificial gravity so everyone was secured before a slight bump and the sensation of floating announced they were on their way to Earth.

Apparently, their shuttle was used for people the Solar League considered important, as screens lit up and showed them the blue and white world they were approaching. Gradually, as the planet loomed larger in the viewscreens, they began to feel the effects of gravity. A couple of mild lurches marked their entry into Earth's atmosphere.

Li watched the Earth grow geographical features and in a little over half an hour they settled down within half a kilometer from a massive building. A vehicle half the size of the shuttle sped out to them and stopped only a couple of meters from the opening shuttle door and platforms folded out of the vehicle's side to accommodate the wheelchairs.

As the bus delivered them to a reception hall, Li was almost overwhelmed by the crowd. Fleet Admiral Patel himself, along with a small battalion of other officers, waited for them and gravely returned their salutes. "Commodore Li, if my office or I can be of any assistance, please let me know."

"Sir, I'm a captain."

"Not anymore. While this is an informal setting for it, you've been given a promotion."

"Thank you, Admiral Patel." To himself, Li wondered how much of the admiral's offer of assistance was simply for the benefit of the vidcams mounted around the hall and carried by recorder crews. He suspected the promotion was part of a narrative being created.

"I'd like to request the men with me be given the best of care. I'm sure they endured far more than I did."

"That goes without saying, Commodore Li." The admiral nodded toward a man wearing the caduceus on his dress uniform. "For now, I'd appreciate it if you would accompany Commander Bennergee, who will conduct more tests to verify the reports we received."

Li saluted again and shook hands with the medical officer, then marched in step with his escort, Nurse Patel, following them. A brief ride on a moving walkway and half a dozen levels on a lift brought them to a complex of examination rooms. Patel waited outside while Li stripped off his uniform and, for the next hour, permitted himself to be subjected to batteries of tests. At the end of the ordeal he was allowed to dress again and he and Nurse Patel were ushered into an office.

When they entered they found Doctor Bennergee sitting at a desk and scanning readouts, not looking up until he'd apparently finished his files and only gesturing at chairs on the other side of the desk. Irritated, Li considered remaining standing but it wasn't enough of an insult to make an issue of, then he realized he was again thinking like a prisoner.

Bennergee glanced up. "That was a test. How did it make you feel?"

"Annoyed. I felt angry."

"But you dealt with it. That's a good sign." The doctor spread the readouts on his desk. "I find I deal better with printed matter than with information on a screen. Your physical health is something we can deal with. None of it is life-threatening. Your toes can be replaced and the badly-healed break in your clavicle and the torn tendon in your shoulder, which probably cause pain when you make some motions, can be repaired. That will take time, however, and if you should wish to be placed on leave for a month or two before the therapy, I'll be happy to sign the papers."

"Thank you, doctor. I will need only about two weeks."

Bennergee leaned forward. "Interesting. Most men would take all the liberty time they were allowed. Would you mind explaining why you're taking so little time?"

"I would like to see my mother. There are few other members of the family I wish to see, and most of my friends from the service will almost certainly be in space."

Bennergee made a mark on one of the papers. "You know, of course, that the com syndicates are all clamoring for the opportunity to interview you,"

"You may decline in my name or use whatever excuse the service provides."

"Your former wife," Bennergee said with a smile, "is most insistent and persistent."

"One of the reasons she is my former wife," Li replied, with his own smile.

"I suggest you spend the night here, indulge in a mild vice or two, and we'll arrange a flight for you tomorrow. I'm going to process your leave for a month. You can always report to the hospital before the time is used."

"And the men with me?"

Bennergee frowned. "I'm afraid both of them will require extensive therapy. Singh may respond, but I'm afraid Bachman is in such a state that any therapy that could hope to heal him would almost lobotomize him. It would require the complete destruction of his personality and replacing it. Ethically, we're damned no matter what we do."

"May I see them?"

"I'd suggest you wait until your leave is finished. I'd like to have time to sort out their likely reactions. At this point, I don't know whether your visit to them would help or harm. It's a chance I'd rather not take."

Li nodded. "As you wish, doctor. Is the Officers' Club near?"

"I was going to go there after our visit. If you'll wait until I've signed out, I'll take you." The doctor touched two places on his desk, then stood up. "Nurse, you've been commissioned. If anyone asks, you're Aspirant Patel."

Bennergee led them though a maze of corridors to the entry and the lifts. They rode two levels down to a hallway leading to a bloc of offices. The Officers' Club, located at the end of the corridor, was dimly lit and almost as quiet as the labs. They'd hardly seated themselves when a waiter approached their table. "Gin and tonic," Bennergee said and glanced at Li and Patel.

Li looked up at the waiter. "I would like a small glass of Scotch, if you have any, and ice."

"I would prefer mango juice," Patel said.

"Interesting choice," Bennergee said to Li. "How did you acquire that taste?"

"There was actually a Scot in my class at the academy. I was curious about his usual drink and tried it. I probably liked it because of the scarcity, the cachet of drinking something different, but it grows on you."

The waiter carried their drinks to the table and carefully set them on coasters. Li raised the glass to study the amber color, then sipped. It was, as he had remembered it, fire and smoke, the burn of the alcohol mitigated by a smoky flavor. He nursed the drink carefully, treating it with respect. He'd taken his last drink of anything alcoholic six years earlier and he had no wish to become drunk.

Bennergee sipped at his own drink and glanced at Li. "What plans do you have? Under the circumstances, I'm sure you could take early retirement without a penalty on your pension."

"And do what?" Li asked. "I'd always wanted to go into space. When I was a child I used to stare into the night sky and wonder what marvels were out there. I've since learned there's more tedium than excitement, and that not all the wonders are benign, but there's still more to see. I can't do it in retirement, nor from an office chair. And I've found I'm comfortable sitting in a command chair."

Bennergee raised his glass. "I can appreciate your passion and I hope you realize your dreams and avoid the nightmares."

"Thank you, doctor." Li raised his own glass. "And I hope you achieve your desires." He sipped the Scotch. "While I hate to darken the general sesnse of well-being at the table, what sort of minefield must I dance through to get what I want?"

After a glance at Nurse Patel, Bennergee leaned forward and lowered his voice. "You have some advantages. Many in the service want you to succeed, and many members of the Solar League council want to be seen with you, to build their own political capital, but some in the service would like you to be retired, either to keep you as an icon or because they consider you a loose cannon. And some in the council may see you as a reminder of their...shame isn't a good word, since they can't feel shame, but embarrassment. Watch your back, because even those who oppose you will try to use you."

"Thank you. And how do we get billets here at the base?"

After a last drink, Bennergee said, "I'll help you with that, as soon as you've finished your drinks."

Li glanced down at his small glass, still half full. "I'm finished, Nurse?"

Patel drained the last of her mango juice. "Ready when you are."

"Aren't you going to finish your drink, Commodore?'

For a moment Li paused, unaccustomed to answering to his new rank, then he replied, "I have. I've felt the burn and enjoyed the taste. That's enough."

They followed Bennergee to the lift, rode down another level, and stopped at a desk. "We'd like adjoining rooms for Commodore Li and his aide."

The lieutenant sitting behind the desk sprang to her feet and snapped a salute. When it was returned she sat behind the console and touched the lighted screen. "Please press your thumbs on this plate on the pad in front of you." After they'd done so a small green light flashed and two slips of paper were spat out of the computer,

Li glanced at the slip with his room number. "Which way to the rooms, and how do we find the Officers' Mess?"

"Your rooms are on the corridor to my right. If you follow the corridor to my left it will lead you to the Officers' Mess."

They stopped at the rooms so Patel could have her belongings delivered to the desk, then strolled to the messhall. At Patel's urging, Li took a portion of Lamb Rogan Josh, along with a cup of egg-drop soup, some sushi, and tea.

Taste buds Li thought had been killed by his prisoner's diet and ship food seemed resurrected, and he reveled in the aromas and the subtle flavors he'd almost forgotten. They ate in silence and, after finishing the meal, strolled to the desk where Patel claimed her bag and returned to their rooms.

Finally alone, Li turned on the screen in his room, checked the time, and placed a call to Tientsin.

His palms seemed damp as the screen chimed, then it was lit with the image of his mother. The lines around her eyes were deeper than he remembered, as were the lines bracketing her mouth, and her black hair was shot with gray. "Mother." It was all he could manage.

"My eaglet!" Chen-Chi cried. For a moment the joy in her face was hard to bear, like a powerful light, then she composed herself. "I'd heard you were returning. Do you know when you'll be here?"

"Not yet, mother. The service has certain requirements. I hope to know in twelve hours or so. It is evening here." He paused. "I was sorry to hear about father…"

"He went very quickly."

They both felt the awkward silence until Li asked, "Do you have a room for a guest? I will be bringing an aide, who is my nurse. I'm sure the service will want to keep me under medical observation for some time."

"Of course." Another pause. "Is she a friend?"

Li considered the question. "I'm not sure. She's someone who's been kind to me, and she can make me smile, but she's definitely someone who needs her own room. Would you have me rush into another marriage?"

Li's mother was the only woman he'd met who could show disapproval while smiling. "I'm not that greedy for grandchildren, and your brother Chin has given me two."

Li concealed his surprise. Chin would have had to either risen in his office or obtained the favor of a powerful man in government to be allowed two children. He would be insufferable. "I'll call you again as soon as I know more about my schedule."

"I look forward to your visit."

He broke the connection and undressed. The excitement of the day had tired him and the bed felt as soft as a cloud.

Chapter 2

Li woke suddenly, the dream already fading like fog in sunlight. He could remember nothing about it except it hadn't involved the ChiTseTsi. He'd survived his first full night without sound therapy. He fumbled for his card on the bedside table and touched the pad, it read 04:55.

He stripped and showered and dressed in his uniform. When he felt ready to face the day he used the card to call Patel's comcard. A surprisingly brisk voice replied.

"Are you ready for breakfast?" Li asked.

"Yes sir. I'll meet you at your door."

Together they stolled to the Officers' Mess and ordered. While they were eating, the card chimed. Glancing at the text, he saw he was requested to present himself to the Fleet Admiral's office at 08:00. After acknowledging the message he pocketed the card. "I'm to report to the fleet admiral in about two hours. After we finish here, I'm returning to my room to get caught up on the news. I'll meet you outside my room at 07:50."

The meal had left him feeling fortified. Returning to his room he activated the screen and set the alarm for 07:45, then pulled up a map and directions from his room to Admiral Patel's office and downloaded the information into the comcard. Next, he pulled up personal messages. Over three hundred messages had been left for him, most of them from news agencies, along with one from his brother and one from Bao. He deleted them all.

He was going to delete any news with any mention of himself but caught an interview with one of the council. The man had artfully coiffed hair and an expensive gray robe. Staring into the camera, the man said, "I'm delighted with the return of our men. This proves we can negotiate with the ChiTseTsi." Li listened only long enough to note the man's name, Madan Sharma.

The rest of the news was predictably dull and political. The colony worlds were demanding direct representation on the Solar League Council. The rest of it was simply white noise and

Li felt less guilty about the possibility coverage of his return might've kept something important from being reported.

He'd have tried to exercise some of the breakfast off but all the preparations and another shower would take more time than he had before his meeting with the admiral. Instead, he reviewed the information on the other races. The only new thing he'd learned was that the Valek had been helped in their revolt by the ChiTseTsi who, when the invading race had been destroyed, had attempted to seize Valk, the Valek homeworld for themselves. The Valek had, however, learned their lessons well and, using captured spacecraft and weapons of their defeated enemies, had beaten back the ChiTseTsi.

This explained even more of the Valek character and their suspicion of other races. He wondered why they hadn't warned the humans and the other races about the ChiTseTsi. Perhaps they'd believed all the other races were in league against them. Certainly, there was no love lost between the Valek and the Huer.

His reflections were interrupted by the alarm chime and he stood, adjusted his uniform, and paced to his door. Patel stepped out of her door at the same time and they followed the directions on his comcard to the Fleet Admiral's office.

An ensign sat at a desk beside an inner door. He snapped to attention and saluted as Li and Patel approached. As soon as the salute was returned, he said, "Please enter. The admiral is waiting for you."

"You may wait for me here, nurse." Li gave his uniform a last adjusting tug and entered.

Admiral Patel's large desk, made of some dark red-brown wood with black trim, appeared centered before a huge latticed window, then Li realized the window and the scene outside it was some sort of projection, although it was realistic enough to serve as a lightsource.

The admiral stood, accepted and returned Li's salute, then said, "Please sit down." The admiral sat and glanced at a screen inset in the top of his desk. Li took the chair facing the admiral's desk.

"I understand that while you require some corrective

surgery, you are generally in good physical health and mentally stable. I also see you've requested a month's leave. What are you using the time for?"

"To visit my mother and perhaps look up an old friend or two."

"Do any of those include your former wife?"

"No sir."

"I'm granting you the leave on one condition. I do not want to see you being interviewed. The media are as persistent as they are ubiquitous. The only answers I expect you to give is that you're very happy to be home. Is that sufficiently clear, Commodore Li?"

"Very clear, Admiral."

"Excellent. Please let the service handle your transportation arrangements. We have experience in moving important people with a minimum of fanfare. Dismissed."

Using the screen in his room, Li ordered a civilian comcard, then studied the directory, looking for a listing for Commodore Sauvage. The name didn't appear on the list of active personnel. On a hunch, Li checked the name against the list of retired officers and it immediately appeared. He pulled up the contact information and copied it into a file he could download onto the new comcard.

Next he ordered a civilian wardrobe. The styles had changed in the five years since he'd last visited Earth, with more vivid colors and both geometric and representational patterns. The military boots he wore were sufficiently nondescript that they'd be unnoticed and were more comfortable than shoes or boots he'd need to break in.

A chime and a message on the screen announced the arrival of his comcard at the reception desk. After obtaining directions to the exercise room and changing into a sweatsuit, he left a message on Nurse Patel's screen, claimed the card, and strolled to the gym where he worked up a satisfactory sweat. By the time he was ready to return to his room the comcard announced the arrival of his civilian clothing.

After another shower and a change of clothing he took

Nurse Patel to lunch. She'd also acquired civilian dress and he noted the newest styles tended to turn her curves into angles. Most fashion, he was firmly convinced, was designed to make humans look ridiculous.

As they ate, he realized that on the base he was being treated to anonymity, something he found very precious when not in a position of command. Here, he was cloistered, away from prying eyes and inconvenient questions.

They'd hardly finished lunch when the card chimed again. After a glance at the tiny screen, he said, "We have forty-five minutes to prepare. Bring everything you need for a week's visit."

* * *

The apartment in Tientsin was as Li had remembered. Li found his hands clammy and his heartbeat raced, a strangely pleasurable feeling after too much emotional numbness. His mother answered his knock at the door and caught Li in a hug. "My Eagle."

After returning the embrace, Li turned to Patel. "Mother, this is my nurse and aide, Padmaju Patel."

His mother bowed. "Please, accept our hospitality."

"There's gray in your hair, mother."

Chen-Chi smiled. "At least I have hair," she replied, with a long stare at his bare head. "Your brother is here. I took the liberty of calling him when I received your call."

"You are convinced we can be as close again as we were when children."

"Ah," Chen-Chi said, "your formal tone, the one you only use when you disagree with me and don't want to say so directly."

Li chuckled. "Your perceptiveness isn't new but your directness is."

"Time has become too precious to waste on being inscrutable or oblique. And there's always the danger you won't catch my meaning, Eaglet."

"What happened? With father?" Li's throat felt tight and his eyes stung, feelings that surprised him. He thought he'd dealt with the loss.

"A brain aneurism. He went very quickly."

Li and Patel left their boots at the entry and walked into the living room where Chin stood as they entered. The two men nodded to each other. Li smiled at the thought that for two Valek, it would be a proper greeting.

"You are quite the cynosure, Wing."

Li smiled again. "If I'd known that was one of the hazards of command, I might've looked for another career. I'm sure you appreciate the irony that the celebrity is occasioned by failure. I perceive you and Mei-Li prosper." Padmaju sat on a couch and Chin returned to his chair.

"I'd have brought Mei-Li and our children but wanted to be sure they would not make you uncomfortable."

"While I thank you for your concern, children do not upset me, and neither have I started eating them." Li sat down in the guest chair.

The flicker of expression on his brother's face told him his reply had hit near the mark. "I promise to treat them with cool courtesy and avoid reminding them that they're children."

"I regret our family will be very busy for the next week," Chin said stiffly. "Actually, I'm here to resolve our father's estate."

Li leaned forward in the chair. "It's unseemly to speak of this, since our mother still lives."

"I felt it would be better to resolve any issues now." Chin had assumed the manner of a government functionary.

Li accepted the cup of tea his mother handed him. "Very well. We in the service must travel light. A couple of holoprints and maybe some small momento. A favorite pen, perhaps."

"It hardly shows respect for one's family to take so little," Chin said.

Li sipped the tea, remembering with fondness the other spices his mother always added. "I've come to believe we should respect our ancestors but it's more important our descendants be proud of us. In the unlikely event I have a child or children, I will pass the momento to them, but to make them proud of me I must excel as a man and in my chosen career. More than what

I've asked for would be a hindrance."

Chin stood, his face emotionless but his eyes cold. "As you wish, Wing." He nodded again to Li, who returned the nod without rising. "I'm afraid, mother, there are matters elsewhere requiring my attention." He walked stiffly from the room. In the silence that followed they could hear him drawing on his shoes and the sound of the door opening and closing.

The corner of Li's lip twitched and he said, "That was very well done. He didn't even slam the door."

"Why do you goad your older brother, Eaglet?"

"Would it have been better to ask for more so we could have something to argue about?" Li took another sip of tea. "I do not regard my father's possessions as carrion to be fought over. And what sort of creature fights over carrion? Chin takes himself much too seriously. He needs to believe he is an important man. Or worse, he needs to believe his work is very important because he believes his work is the total of what he is."

His mother had sat down on the couch beside Padmaju, her face sad. "I think it's envy. I think he lost his own dreams to live up to the expectations of others, and you've kept your dream and achieved it." She glanced sidelong at Padmaju. "I am a poor hostess. You are uncomfortable."

Padmaju looked serene despite the tension leaking from the room. "It will pass. My own family has its own disagreements."

Chen-Chi stood. "You've both been on a long flight. May I get you something to eat?"

* * *

On the first night of their visit Li and his mother spoke late into the night, or perhaps early into the morning. His uncle Deshi, his mother's brother, visited late the next morning. Deshi had been working on refinements to the Liang Drive and they discussed recent advances. Deshi was very familiar with the new Discovery class ships, of which two were being built.

"How soon will the first ship be ready?" Li asked.

"Perhaps two months. The new technology takes time. System redundancy, accommodations for safety, storing the anti-matter, the effect of the anti-matter field on other equipment.

This has been a long project. Sometimes I think the Great Wall was built quicker than a new starship."

* * *

Five days passed pleasantly. Without an exercise room, he returned to the tai chi exercises he'd learned as a child, and he supposed Padmaju was practicing yoga in her room. They seldom left the apartment. Twice the women went shopping for food and the first time they were swarmed by men and women with camcorders. Li simply called the police.

After one of the trips, Patel made a rosewater lahsee, a liquid yogurt concoction that was sweet without being cloying.

On the fifth day he called retired Commodore Rene Sauvage but a recording instructed him to leave message. He left his name and the code for his comcard and severed the connection.

The visit was a balm to his wounds. The familiar quiet surroundings let him rest and restore himself, unlike the enforced idleness of shipboard. Several times he sat beside the freshwater aquarium and found repose in watching the fish. He resolved, when he was again stationed on a ship, to purchase a holographic aquarium. His head nodded as the lassitude became drousing, then his comcard chimed.

"Commodore Li Wing Hua." He was still getting used to the new rank.

"This is retired Commodore Rene Sauvage." Li thought he detected a trace of irony in the word "retired." "I was hoping to contact you. I'd been told you'd taken a month's leave." Sauvage had a deep, rich voice.

"I've been given a month's leave but I doubt I'll take more than half that. I'm presently in Tientsin, old China. I'd very much like to meet you. I'll be leaving Tientsin the day after tomorrow."

After a pause, Sauvage said, "Excuse me. I had to look up the difference in times. I'd like to meet you the second day after you've returned. Go to the Noram Norwest base. You can take a hovercar from there. Let me feed my coordinates to you, including the best route. My home is rather remote."

Li listened to a series of tones indicating numbers being fed into his comcard.

"I'll see you in the early afternoon, between thirteen hundred and fourteen hundred hours."

"I'll be pleased to meet you," Li said.

Sauvage laughed and his deep voice replied, "I'll hope so." Then the connection was broken.

"A friend?" He hadn't heard his mother enter the room.

"I hope so. He's a retired commodore. I don't believe we've ever met, unless it was at some social function where you barely remember the name of the person to whom you've just been introduced."

"I hope you've enjoyed your visit as I have enjoyed seeing you and Ms. Patel."

He couldn't keep a smile from curling his lips. "I hope you haven't taken up match-making. Ms. Patel and I hardly know each other and I'm her senior by over a dozen years."

His mother smiled back then waved her hand as though dismissing his objections like so much dust. "Trifles. She's a very good woman."

"She's a very good person, and we're on our way to becoming friends. For the present, I think that's good for both of us. Besides, I thought you weren't greedy for grandchildren."

"Eaglet," his mother poured a cup of tea and handed it to him. "There's a big difference between need and greed. Your brother's children are too well-behaved. I worry about them. I don't know if I worry more they'll someday explode and take most of Tientsin with them or they will remain boring until my dying day. So I need his children to worry about and yours for excitement." She poured another cup and sipped.

"What will be, will." Li finished his tea and stood up to set the cup on the sideboard. "I've learned not to hurry."

"Will you come for another visit, before you leave again?"

"I don't know. I've learned not to hurry but the service has never learned anything but to hurry and wait. I will if I can. You seem very certain I'll ship out again."

Chen-Chi finished her tea and reached up to place her cup beside his on the sideboard. "I know you will. You may sit here for a time, nursing your wounded wings, but you'll spread them and fly again. It's as much a part of you as breathing."

Padmaju entered the room, her face grave. "Commodore Li, I've been reassigned. They're training a crew for the first five-year ship. They're calling it *The Long March*. I've been ordered to report to the Baikonur base."

Li nodded. "I wish you well, Padmaju Patel. I believe I've recovered enough to manage on my own. I do thank you for helping me with the transitions."

"That was in my report to them, that your transition was complete, or very near it. Your monitors show no undue stress levels. I wanted to thank you and Chen-Chi for your hospitality."

"I'm just sorry you never really got to go shopping."

"Baikonur is a major base. It's been surrounded by merchandisers. If I really want to go to stores, there will be more than enough of them to take my money."

"How soon must you leave?" Chen-Chi asked.

"Immediately after lunch."

Li asked, "Do you know who will be your commanding officer?"

"I believe it will be Commodore Wing."

Li nodded. "I've heard of him. He has a good reputation. If the rest of the crew is of the same quality as you, it'll be an elite group."

Padmaju smiled. "Do you want me to deliver that message for you?"

Li chuckled. "I don't think it'll be necessary."

They enjoyed a salad and soup and within a quarter of an hour a military hovercar arrived. Li carried one of Padmaju's bags for her and he and Chen-Chi watched the car until it was out of sight.

As they walked back into the house, Chen-Chi said, "That's the worst part of the service. One has to come and go at the whims of others."

"Agreed." Li set up the table for a game of Go." But it's the worst part of life. If we aren't at the beck and call of others, we still have to answer to fate."

* * *

Li wasn't surprised he missed Padmaju's company but was surprised at the strength of the feeling. She had the ability to lighten his mood. Worse, his mother noticed it as well.

"You should have asked that she remain with you until the end of your leave, at least. You smiled more when she was with us."

"She would have to leave, sooner or later. And I think she sensed it was a good time to go. Had she wanted to remain she could've given excuses they'd have accepted, or she could've turned down the assignment. While the service is an impersonal master—or mistress—members of starship crews are volunteers." He grinned. "Believe me, it is difficult enough serving on even a large ship with people, even when they want to be there. I'm sometimes astonished there are so few 'accidents' and assaults on starships as there are.

"When I was an ensign, one of my fellows had a habit of humming tunelessly. It was completely unconscious. Most of the time I doubt he was even aware he was doing it, but I had occasional temptations to brain him with the nearest blunt object or to find a way to strand him outside of the airlock." He nodded. "I believe Padmaju will do well."

"She's one of those people who carries sunlight with her. She will do well wherever she goes. It's a shame you couldn't bask more in her light. I see a darkness in you that needs light."

"It'll pass. And life should have both light and dark. It's what gives us depth."

They set up their stones and began the game. For a mother who was nurturing and giving, Chen-Chi was both cunning and ruthless at the game. Li was no novice, and he'd studied strategy and tactics, but within two hours his mother had soundly beaten him. He smiled at her. "And you say I'm dark."

* * *

As he packed for the trip to Noram Norwest Li felt, as he had whenever he prepared to leave home, a curious mixture of loss and excitement. Home was not only a refuge, it also held a treasure-trove of memories. The sense of loss was as much for his lost youth as the realization that he was preparing to go out alone again. And that was the source of the excitement; there were challenges to be met and victories to be achieved, and the shadows of possible disasters added spice to one's endeavors.

His mother stood waiting for him, another cup of tea in her hands. "I'll miss you, Eaglet. The few days we've had together have been a tonic, and an exciting one."

"I'll talk to you often, even if you can't hear me. And I promise, unless I'm assigned to one of the deep space ships, to speak with you more often than I did in the last five years."

They embraced and Li felt again as he had when he'd left for the university, reluctant to go and a little intimidated but exhilerated.

The driver rapped at the apartment's door and carried Li's bag to the car and Li limped after him.

On the way to the airport he scanned the latest news. The Huer seemed to be allying themselves with the humans, which seemed to create more tensions with the Valek. Japan had suffered another earthquake but with little destruction and no loss of lives. Apparently, humans could live with almost anything and eventually adapt. He was relieved to find his name absent from the news releases although he wasn't sure the celebrated singer who'd had a child by his own daughter was an improvement. He supposed most news was generated by failure.

At the port he was able to avoid the crowds in the civilian area and the smaller military terminal held only a couple of dozen men and women, most of them enlisted and most of them on leave. He'd been careful to wear civilian clothing although he found the nearly ankle-length robe to be a nuisance. Fashion for men, he realized, was no less ridiculous than fashion for women.

Since he was not in uniform he was saved from the bother of returning salutes and he was able to spend nearly an hour expanding his vocabulary and grammar skills in Huer. He'd already discovered there were no similar lessons for the language of the ChiTseTsi, since human vocal equipment wasn't up to the task. A shame. The only thing more important than learning the language of a possible ally was learning that of a certain enemy. Language reflected thought, and learning a language gave one entry to thought patterns unusual to one's own processes.

The flight to the Noram base took almost three hours, during which he continued his studies of the Huer language and their customs. Their language revealed a fatalism that had nothing to do with inaction. Perhaps that was why they had no religion and he wondered if they'd ever had a religion or whether their acceptance of a whimsical fate had precluded religion. To the Huer, luck was important to success but not a measure of it. One had a store of luck and when it ran out, one was doomed. Since a Huer never knew whether fate smiled or laughed, they might behave boldly but the true test of the Huer came when he'd exhausted his store of good fortune. The measure of a Huer was less how he dealt with success than the courage he displayed in failure. He recalled in the early days, when humans had fought the Huer, a damaged Huer ship would often try to ram its enemy.

To a Huer, living well was important but dying well was essential.

A chime announcing their approach to the port interrupted his reverie. As he strapped himself into his seat he looked at the image on the walls. Sensors in the hull "saw" the ground below, converted the images into streams of information which, transmitted to the walls of the cabin, were retranslated into images.

The base was located near the ocean and the islands and the landmasses were lined with moored boats and with clumps of ships and massive cranes, although they looked, from his vantage, like children's toys. Beyond and scattered among the clumps and clusters of buildings were masses of dark green, which must be dense patches of fir. In the distance he could barely see what appeared to be ghosts of mountains.

The view magnified as the plane neared the airport and slowed. Landing and taxiing seemed to take nearly as long as the flight across the Pacific and he was grateful to be out of the plane and able to move freely again. The military terminal at which they'd landed was more compact than the much larger civilian field a few kilometers away.

He stopped for a cup of coffee and a bit of sushi at the canteen before he claimed his bag. Following the directions of the flowing lines of script, he joined the crowd and rode down to the underground express that delivered him to the base terminal. At the security gate he handed over his identification card, passed his hand over the faintly glowing plate, and submitted to a retinal scan.

Rooms were available for visiting officers and he interfaced his comcard with the desk unit to get directions to his room, the mess hall, and the exercise room.

His room was, like all the other service facilities he'd stayed in on any base, utilitarian and without character. It did have a screen and he used his comcard to set up his schedule. He reserved a hovercar for his visit to Sauvage then arranged a flight and made appointments for the medical work on his feet and shoulders. A quick scan was enough to warn him his recovery would last at least two weeks.

He dreaded the surgeries almost as much as he anticipated them. Memories of the pain when the toes were smashed before they were cut away were still sharp enough to make him wince, but the benefits were that he'd again be able to walk without discomfort and the pains in his back and left shoulder would be gone. He could now hardly remember a time when he hadn't been plagued by the ache and the sudden stitches of agony.

Carrying a small bag with his workout clothes, he walked to the exercise room and spent thirty minutes working up a sweat and another thirty in the pool, working those parts of his body which could still be flexed without having to clench his teeth.

Back in his room he returned to his study of the Huer. The hypnoconditioning speeded his absorbtion of the language but also made it more difficult to detect differences between the human and Huer cultures. The Huer placed a heavy emphasis on responsibility and he began to realize it wasn't just for the Warrior caste. To the Huer, a worthy menial Worker had the same standing as a worthy Director or Warrior. He suddenly realized their word for "worthy" could also be translated as "honorable" or "virtuous," which meant it carried the force of religion as well as a secular meaning.

The more he studied the Huer, the more he found to admire about them. He decided, as an experiment, to study the Valek to see if the effect were the same.

After several hours of study, interrupted by breaks for exercises and for meals, he decided the Valek were actually more like humans than the Huer. At first the Valek religion was almost invisible but the more he learned the language, the more it seemed to permeate the culture.

They believed in a supreme being which was honored less with words than with action. Over the centuries the religion had been secularized so that religious references were inflected or implied. An example was a twenty-day period each Valek year. The first ten days were spent in fasting and reflection, followed by two days of military parades and exercises. The last eight days were spent in feasting and works of solidarity. Human scholars had suggested that, in this instance, "solidarity" was synonymous with "charity."

The same scholars had suggested it was an adaptation of an earlier religious custom but now referred to the conquest by the extinct alien race and the Valeks' eventual self-liberation. They had so thoroughly obliterated every vestige of their conquerors that only conjecture existed about the species. Valek ships tended to have high ceilings, suggesting that if they'd simply copied the alien ships the species might've been over two meters tall, and they were known to be bipedal.

To the Valek, to live well was virtuous, suggesting their behavior was influenced if not dictated by at least a semi-religious set of mores. Of course, some study revealed that, like humans, in some the display of virtue simply masked a drive for personal and familial advancement. Perhaps because of the hypocrisy, the Valek were very touchy about their personal honor and duels, while uncommon, were not rare.

Li went to sleep wondering what his own life might have been like had he been born Huer or Valek.

* * *

Riding to Sauvage's home was a different experience for Li, with unexpected sensations. The country over which he flew was almost barren of any signs that humans had ever found the place, and it reminded him, in a way, of deep space. Instead of spires and towers and blocks of buildings or curving walls of windows, he rode over dense forests with trees and even bushes on a gargantuan scale. He recognized one plant as holly, but the bush was taller than many trees he'd seen, and the trees loomed high over it. Setting the hovercar on autopilot, he relaxed and gazed at what seemed to be a green city.

Everything, almost everything he corrected himself, seemed to be ying and yang. It was a little disturbing for one who had always lived in cities or in ships with crews to be alone in such a wilderness, where a stray microerror could leave him totally lost, but he also found a restful pleasure in the scenery around him. Few emotions seemed unmixed and he wondered if emotional purity were at all desireable. The strongest emotions , those with the least qualifiers, were desires. His hatred of the ChiTseTsi was a desire for revenge, while his ealier obsession with Bao-Yu was a desire for sex. It made him wonder if the Buddhists weren't right about desire being a bane of the human race. His hatred of the ChiTseTsi was unalloyed but letting it rage would only injure him and, perhaps a ship's crew.

Singh and Bachman were both at the Ramstein/Landstuhl medical center, where his own treatment was scheduled. He'd see them while he was there.

The engine almost inaudibly rose in pitch as the car climbed higher. It had been following a sort of depression in the trees that might've been an overgrown highway but now the machine rose and turned and, within a minute the artificial voice announced that Li was approaching his destination.

He saw a flash that might've been reflections from solar panels and soon saw a house which appeared to be partially built into a hillside, with a landing pad just large enough for three cars, with one silver-black vehicle parked at the end of the pad nearest the house.

A glance at his hovercar's clock told him it was 13:10 and Li took back the controls and set his machine down beside the other car. Releasing the harness, he pressed the button that swung the door up and out of the way.

A tall man strode out of the house toward him. Former Commodore Sauvage was tan-skinned with dark brown hair streaked with gray and tightly curled, suggesting African ancestry. He wore a thick, dark gray shirt and faded black trousers that had obviously been chosen with an eye to hard use rather than fashion, and military ankle boots. As the man approached, Li observed he was still slender, which emphasized his height, over a head taller than Li.

Within two steps of Li he smiled and extended his right hand in the western fashion. Li shook the hand, then Sauvage turned and gestured at the buildings. "Welcome to the House of Sauvage." His Trade Common had an unusual, almost slurring accent.

Li followed the taller man down the path to something he'd heard of but never actually seen, an enclosed porch made mostly of some sort of screen with a light door made mostly of the same material. At one end of the porch stood a table flanked by light chairs, and on the table rested a dark green bottle and two glasses.

Sauvage sat in the chair farthest from the door and said, "Please, sit down. Would you care for a glass of wine?"

Li smiled. Apparently this was going a contest of courtesies. He'd worn his civilian suit to avoid reminding Sauvage he was no longer in the service and Sauvage had sat, diminishing the difference in their height. "I'd enjoy trying it."

Sauvage picked up the bottle and a corkscrew, removed the cork, and poured a little into Li's glass.

While not as formal as a Japanese tea ceremony, this was obviously some sort of ritual. Li sniffed at the glass, found the scent light and fruity, and sipped. While he'd seldom drunk wine, the taste matched the smell, smooth and not overpowering. "It's very good. Thank you."

Sauvage half-filled Li's glass, poured the same amount into this own, and sipped. "It's from my half-brother's farm in

Europe." He sipped again. "I'd been wanting to speak with you and I gather you'd also been wanting to contact me. How may I help you?"

"I understand your ship destoyed two ChiTseTsi ships. What did you learn about them?"

"*The Glorious Light*," Sauvage replied, "destroyed six ChiTseTsi ships. The first two were apparently too absorbed in killing Walawi to notice us until we fired on them. We were above atmosphere and our lasers crippled them. From the copies of their transmissions, they panicked when they detected the missiles but their anti-missiles were easy to pick off, both by ship's laser and the warheads' defence missiles.

"Unfortunately, we were unable to recover any wreckage that would give us the location of their homeworld.

"Two more ChiTseTsi ships were destroyed in major engagements inside our solar system. Apparently, they have knowledge about us that we lack about them. The other two ships we destroyed in single engagements. They didn't use lasers, at least then, but seem to use a lot of autocannon. These can be very unpleasant, as they're hard to destroy and a long burst of them would probably break down a repulsor field. The explosions against the repulsor field also play hell on instruments, so you're practically fighting them blind. They're generally aggressive only when they have the upper hand."

"From my experience with them," Li said, "I'd say they seem to take pleasure in causing pain."

"Which explains why we were able to destory the first two of them," Sauvage replied. "They were bombarding the Walawi."

"This is very good," Li said, and took another drink of wine. "Why did we sign a treaty with them?"

Sauvage refilled their glasses. "Mostly because the war was unpopular. One of their ships managed to fire a nuclear warhead at New Delhi. Once upon a time, that would've caused a demand for revenge but—how much do you know about Prime Minister Xo Deshi?"

"One of my resolutions I failed to keep was to study recent history and become current on members of the Council. I'll be 'enjoying' two weeks or so of convalescence and should have plenty of time then."

Sauvage nodded. "Xo was elected on a platform of peace in the universe. He convinced most of the population that war with the ChiTseTsi would be beyond Earth's resources and cost even more lives. His given name means 'virtuous man' but he and his ally, Madan Sharma, have apparently worked tirelessly to turn cowardice into a virtue. They opened negotiations with the ChiTseTsi and used their authority to interfere in the command of the fleet. When Admiral Gro resigned in disgust, they appointed Patel.

"They're the sort who convince themselves that their solutions are the only ones possible and can be ruthless in carrying them out. I advise you to beware of them and many of the commanders they've promoted."

"Did you resign in digust or—"

Sauvage's smile was more teeth than humor. "The or. I was told to retire 'for the good of the service.' I suspect it was one of the unwritten agreements in the treaty. No other ship killed more than three ChiTseTsi ships. Which brings me to my reason for wishing to see you. Will you be given command of another ship?"

"If I can convince my superiors."

"If you're careful and if you're calculating, I believe you will get another command. I would like to ask you to consider Gyanashwar Singh for your First Captain. He was my second in command on *The Glorious Light* and a gifted commander. When I 'retired' I took the full responsibility for our actions against the ChiTseTsi but Gyan hasn't been offered a command position since then, unless you consider piloting a freighter to Luna and back a command. I'd hate to see a good man ground under the heels of cowards with power."

"I can't promise to choose him but I will look up his service record and, if it's as good as you say, I'll recommend him. Your endorsement will also be a strong consideration."

Sauvage stared into his eyes a moment, then asked, "Are you hungry?"

"A little. It's been several hours since breakfast."

"If you'd care for an omelette, I can provide you with a lunch." He led the way into the house.

Following, Li glanced around the rooms they walked through. The center room was large, with one wall almost completely occupied by a screen for viewing. Two other walls were bookcases holding more of the old bound paper volumes than Li had seen in one place. The fourth wall was occupied by paintings and photographs. The only furniture was a pair of chairs flanking a table on which rested a lamp. "Are you an antiquarian?"

Sauvage's laugh was explosive. "No, but I'm sure some would call me an antique. I enjoy the sensation of reading a real book and I'm comfortable with two-dimensional art and photographs." He led the way into the kitchen, setting his glass on a counter. A range and a refrigerator stood side-by-side against one wall, facing a sink and cupboard. Opening the refrigerator, he assembled the ingredients for omelettes and nodded to another small table with two chairs. "Please have a seat."

When the first omelette was finished he carried the plate and a fork to the table, then returned to the counter under the cupboard and made his own meal. While it was cooking he returned the unused ingredients to the refrigerator.

Li sampled the omelette, then fell to the meal with an appetite. When Sauvage joined him at the table, Li glanced at him. "I take it you're not married."

Sauvage smiled, somewhat ruefully. "I married the service. I don't know if I'd have made the same choice if I'd known what a fickle bitch she is." He paused. "Actually, I can honestly say I regret nothing. I met and worked with some very good men and women. I achieved a position of command, and I've fought some opponents I respected and some enemies who needed to be killed. It's not a bad record, and it wouldn't even be a bad epitaph."

"Do you ever worry the lobsters might have you killed?"

Sauvage finished chewing a bite of omelette and swallowed before he answered. "No, I don't think they could do it or have it done and, if someone tries, they will have to earn their thirty pieces of silver."

"What do you think of the Huer and the Valek?" Li finished his meal with another sip of wine.

"The last battle with the Huer had been fought before I was an aspirant, and I'd just been promoted to captain when we fought the Valek. I found both of them to be brave and resourceful. I wish I could say the same about all our leaders. Did you know they tried to get me to admit to having committed war crimes? That was part of their leverage in convincing me to retire, and that was when I knew I had to leave the service. When the only feeling you have for those who give the orders is contempt, it's time to get out."

Li nodded. "Sometimes we have to bear it. We choose to serve, even when it's onerous."

"If I were needed, I'd go back into uniform, but I'm not needed. I've fought my wars. There's no war now and I'd be an embarrassment to the commanders who gained their positions by political favoritism."

"For what it's worth, I'd have liked serving with you." Li stood. "It's time for me to return to the base. I'll be taking a red-eye to Europe tomorrow. And I will study Captain Singh's service record. If I get a command, I'll certainly consider him."

"Thank you." Sauvage got to his feet. "I noticed you're limping. Is that the reason for the trip to Europe?"

"Part of it. My men from the *Leap Forward* are there and I want to see them." He keyed his comcard and the door swung up and forward. "It's a good thing this vehicle can drive itself. The wine has left me a bit tipsy."

With another smile, Sauvage said, "There's an old saying, 'The horse knows the way home.'"

Li closed the door, harnessed himself in and, after Sauvage had stepped back, started the hovercar. He simply touched the "return" key and relaxed in the seat. The wine had been dangerous. He'd enjoyed it too much and was still enjoying the effects. Sauvage had given him many things to think about, one of them being one of the greatest ironies of command. You needed men and women you could trust and a good commander like Sauvage was loyal to those under him, but command sometimes required that you sometimes place those who trusted you in situations of mortal danger.

He was unaware when musing had become drowsing but woke with a start as the car chimed at their arrival over the base and he again took control to land the vehicle. He could trust it on the ground or in the air, but when he made the trasition from air to ground he much preferred being in control. It was, he realized, irrational; the car had electronic reflexes hundreds of times faster and more precise than his own, but he still wanted control at the most critical moment.

Using his comcard, he signed the vehicle back into the pool and paced to his room. He'd change into his sweats, exercise off some of the effects of the wine, and have dinner alone. On a whim, he first drew up Gyanashwar Singh's record. Within a few lines he realized Sauvage had been right. This was too good a commander to be sitting at a desk managing inventory or piloting a scow.

Singh had been in the top five of his class. He'd excelled at fencing and martial arts and his infractions were the sort one could expect of a high-spirited young man with a sense of humor. From aspirant he'd risen to captain faster than any of his classmates and he'd done it without help from anyone, and while making no enemies. Until after the treaty with the ChiTseTsi. None of his commanders since then had been able to find any real fault with him but damned him with faint praise. The preferred report had apparently been "Not suited for this assignment."

If he got a command, he'd be sure Singh was his second in command.

He exercised, showered, ate, and turned in.

* * *

The base at Ramstein-Landstuhl in what had been Germany reminded Li of an anthill. Thousands of workers rushed to and fro, each of them apparently on some urgent mission, few observing anything but rank badges. The hospital was enormous, a small city in its own right.

Barely glancing up at him, the receptionist informed him Doctor Liu would see him as soon as possible. Li took a seat in a waiting room with a dozen other men and women, most absorbed in the displays on their comcards. He simply waited.

Li's name was the third one called and an orderly led him to an office where Liu sat waiting. The doctor had a thin face dominated by piercing black eyes.

"Do you understand the procedures we're going to undertake?"

Li sat in the chair across the desk from the doctor. "Not very well. I trust you to do your job." He hid a smile. "Will I be able to play the piano?"

Liu's face didn't change. "That's an ancient joke. And the answer is, yes, you'll be able to if you played piano with your feet." He leaned forward. "When you were examined after your release, they took some cells from you. Those cells were used to grow new toes for you and more were replicated for an injection in your back. We'll do that when we make fresh cuts and attach the toes. The injection is to "remind" your system how it's supposed to be and function. Are you concerned about the pain?"

"Not especially. I doubt it will match the sensations when they were smashed, then cut off."

The doctor raised his eyebrows. "It's our job to cure you, not to cause unnecessary pain, but I will tell you there'll be some discomfort."

"When do you want to start?"

"I'd prefer you fast the rest of the day. Nothing but water and clear liquids, nothing at all after midnight. Unless you have something you need to do, I can have you assigned a room immediately. It'll let us better monitor you in preparation for the procedures. We'll do it tomorrow at oh eight hundred." The doctor stood. "Is there anything else, Commodore Li?"

"Yes, sir. Will I be able to see my men before the procedure?"

"I'm afraid you have the advantage. I presume you know what you're talking about. I do not. If you have men formerly under your command at this facility, I don't know about it."

Li inclined his head. "My error. I'm used to dealing with smaller groups. On a ship, everyone knows everyone else." He opened the door and closed it behind him.

He'd thought it common knowledge he'd tried to arrange visits with Singh and Bachman. Apparently, hospitals were more airtight than military installations. In the military, there were always ways around a problem. With a different system, he'd have to continue trying to scale the slick stone wall.

The receptionist fed directions to his room into his comcard so he could find his way. Admissions had already been notified and a room assigned. He was in no hurry so he strolled through most of the building on his way to the walkway leading to the hospital proper. He found nothing of interest in his amble and he cut short his investigation when walking became increasingly uncomfortable.

His hospital room was nearly three times the size of the sickbay room on the ship, and he shared it with another patient. Captain Manuel Sanchez had been brought to the hospital after passing blood.

Sanchez saluted, although neither man was in uniform. "I've heard about you, Commodore Li. Your visit is because of your time spent with the lobsters, no?"

Li simply nodded.

Sanchez, a large, heavy-set man with black hair and startling gray eyes, glanced away. "I meant no offence. I'm here simply because my gut sprang a leak. My penance is that I won't, for a while, be able to indulge my taste for spicy food and a good beer. It wasn't a scar I earned."

Li waved a dismissal. "I didn't take offence, I just don't wish to talk about it."

"Fair enough." Sanchez sat on his bed. "I've always envied you who had the courage to brave the deep space. Most of my runs are in a ship that doesn't have a Liang drive."

"What do you do?"

"During the war, I was in command of a defence ship. I never fired a shot or a missile. Never even saw a lobster ship.

Since then I've been making milk runs to Luna and Mars."

Li sat on his own bed. "What's Mars like? Strange to say, I've never visited the planet."

Sanchez had a booming laugh. "And you've missed nothing. It was almost a completely dead world when humans landed on it five hundred years ago and it's a dying planet now. It could probably never have been completely terraformed even if we'd had the resources, but the Liang drive killed it.. The Martians largely stopped breeding two generations ago. Now, a Martian child is as rare as a red-headed Indian. It's a sad place."

"I'm sorry to hear it. A couple of decades ago there was a nostalgia fad and I read some old stories about Mars." Li started to shrug then remembered the pain he'd pay for the gesture. "Another case where the dreams were far more attractive and interesting than the reality."

"Sometimes," Sanchez said, "I think reality is what we've settled for when we stopped dreaming. Sometimes, reality rubs me the wrong way."

Li chuckled and poured icewater from the pitcher into two cups, handed one to Sanchez, and raised the other in salute. "Captain Sanchez, if I weren't ordered to drink only water I'd stand you to a drink."

Sanchez raised his own cup and drank half the water. "And if my gut didn't forbid it, I'd accept."

Li lay down on his bed and a question occurred to him. "Have you ever served with a Captain Gyanashwar Singh?"

"How did you know? Yes I did. A good man being wasted. He was always very pleasant and friendly but if you looked closely you could see the sadness in his eyes. He usually hid it and he never spoke of it, but it was there. He reminded me of a bird with a broken wing. He'd once been in deep space and you could tell that was where he belonged."

"Have you ever been to deep space, Captain?"

Sanchez shook his head. "I don't like being gone for so long. My cruises last a week or two, then I have a day or two off to spend with my wife and daughter. During the war, we were on alert for nearly six months. Got supplies from a lighter once a week. I hated it. I don't know how you deep-space people can bear to look at the same yellow and gray walls for years at a time and not go crazy."

Li chuckled again. "Maybe we are crazy. Or, maybe, after the first tour or two, we become crazy."

The room had two screens and Li used one with his comcard, noticing he'd received a message from the hospital director. The communique suggested he wait until after his recovery from his own procedure to see Singh. It also hinted that it would be better for Bachman if Li didn't see him at all.

Li considered his reply before typing it in and sending it. He would like to be able to speak personally with the director after his procedures so he could understand why it was so difficult to see his men. He would have to submit a report to his superiors and would need to make the report complete. He smiled grimly as he signed the message. He'd couched his response in the most courteous tones possible while still making his threat clear. He doubted the director had reached his position without understanding subtlety.

"Anything important?"

"I haven't seen the other men the lobsters released since we reached Earth."

"I'm sorry," Sanchez said. "If there were anything I could do…"

Li smiled. "Only if you had an incriminating vid of the director with a small child or a barnyard animal."

Sanchez chuckled.

The time passed slowly. Sanchez didn't play chess or go and the conversation largely died until Li asked about Sanchez's family. Apparently, the daughter was a prodigy. Time was marked only by nurses carrying in fresh pitchers of icewater and, for Sanchez, clear liquids.

"I must be guilty of some terrible wrong," Sanchez said as he spooned up red gelatin, "because I'm doing great penance. And once I'm out I'll have to watch my diet for the next month or so. They expect me to graze like an ox."

Li turned on the screen again and they watched the news,

most of which was about the budget, although they did show a piece on the new class of starship. They showed a view of the ship in the shipyard where the final additions were being made and another ship, half-completed, lay beside it. Computer-generated images showed the scale and Li was impressed by the sheer size of the vessel.

Most of the crew would be housed in a gigantic sphere which, like the intake and the engine nacelles, was polished to a mirror-like brightness, relieved by occasional loading ports and ports for weapons. Two pinnaces were mounted below the engine intake and it looked as though they were winged, although the wings lay along the tops of the pinnaces.

The ship could be crewed by as few as a hundred fifty men and women, although it had been built to accommodate seven hundred more. The first ship had already been christened *The Long March* and the second was to the called the *Krishna*.

"That's not a ship," Sanchez said softly, "that's a shell around a small town."

"That's the idea. The purpose of that ship is to go deeper into space than we've ever gone before. It'll have hydroponic gardens for food and oxygen. Its mission is to be self-sufficient for five years or more."

Sanchez shook his head. "You couldn't get me on that with a gun to my head, and after five years you'd have to take me off in a straitjacket."

"That's how I'd feel about doing your work. It's a good thing people differ."

The light in the room gradually dimmed and Li finally changed into the hospital gown and went to sleep.

Chapter 3

The sun of Huerda hadn't cleared the horizon when Brod stepped out of the barracks to find his brother, Shkogar, waiting. Shkogar was lean and half a head shorter than his older brother. Together they squinted up at the sun, a disc of red.

"A bad omen," Shkogar said. "A red sun at dawn means blood will flow by nightfall."

"Worry is just the future robbing the present," Brod replied. They strode to where two others of the sept waited with their mounts. Brod's animal grumbled at him and shook his head at the reins but accepted a handful of bread.

The four Huer climbed into their saddles and, leading a pack beast, followed the track along the bank of a stream. After an hour they crossed at a ford then rode into rolling grasslands. Springs and streams were marked by stands of trees. To their left towered a huge black fang of rock and they used it as a marker. By late morning they'd reached the treeless plains where the three-horned cattle grazed.

At Brod's signal they dismounted and hobbled their animals. Brod stripped off his clothing until he wore only a thong around his waist with the harvest knife in its sheath. The others took up spears and shields. Making sure the breeze was in his face, Brod led the way to a small spring, where he covered himself with gray-brown mud.

A quarter of an hour's march later they approached a hill and the other Huer remained a dozen paces behind him as he dropped to his hands and knees and crawled to the crest of the hill.

A herd of the cattle milled and fed in a dale below. They were not the domesticated beasts common on Huerda but the original breed, wild and wily. Brod picked out a large bull and backed away, going around the crest of the hill rather than over the top. With his coating of mud, as long as he stayed on all fours or crouched, the beasts would pay him no more attention than the occasional lone plainstalker. Three-horns had no fear of a single plainstalker; only a pack of the animals would cause the cattle to either run or form their circle with the females and young in the center and horns pointing outward.

Brod slipped the knife out of its sheath and began to stalk the herd. For a feast for the local sept hall, the animal had to be hunted and killed the old way.

The grass came almost to his eyes as he crept forward on all fours. Every sense alert, he moved carefully, hardly making a sound. Approaching the herd, he saw a colony of four-legged beetles. An ancient ancestor would've noted the place so that had he failed to kill a three-horn his belly wouldn't have to stay empty.

The bull he'd chosen suddenly looked up, its ears spread, and Brod froze, even suspending his breathing. After a long stare in the direction of the hunter, the animal lowered his head to graze but almost immediately looked up again. Brod let his breath slowly leak out and inhaled just as carefully, still not moving. He saw the ears drop and the beast turned its side to him, grazing again, its tail sweeping back and forth.

Only moving when there were no heads raised, he crept closer. The horns were wicked weapons, two sweeping back and the central horn thrust forward, but he knew the animal's hooves were almost as dangerous; sharp enough to lay flesh open to the bone.

Closing the distance to his quarry, he gripped the knife tightly and tensed for the rush.

When he'd stalked to within the animal's own length, he sprang. The bull's head swung up but he'd slammed into its body before it could either spring away or turn toward him. His left hand caught the opposite horn and he threw his weight down while driving the knife into the beast's neck. Bright blood geysered from the wound as he twisted the blade and cut a wider wound.

The bull's legs folded and the beast fell, and Brod clung desperately to the horn and the knife, trying to keep his legs and body clear of the feebly kicking legs. Hot blood gushed out over his hand, making the knife's grip slippery.

Brod staggered to his feet and stood facing another bull, this one with head lowered to charge. Most of the herd had pounded away, the females and the young led and flanked by bulls, but one had stayed behind. The beast turned its head to see him more clearly and pawed the ground. Brod braced himself for the bull's charge.

Then Shkogar raced up, shouting and waving his spear. For a moment the bull faced them as though trying to decide which of them to attack, then it turned and dashed after the herd.

"Well done, brother." Brod cleaned the harvest knife as best he could on a handful of grass, then returned it to its sheath. Shkogar handed him his claw and he used it to cut open the body and carve out the liver. Carefully, he sliced it into four pieces, one each for his brother, the other two shield-bearers, and himself. As he ate, Brod seemed to feel the strength and speed of the beast become his.

Shkogar grinned. "Usually we only protect you from the plainstalkers, but that bull was impressive. I didn't know whether I'd be carrying my shield back or being carried back on it."

Brod and the other two chuckled softly, then Brod said, "There was only one. We'd have had more meat for the feast."

As soon as they'd finished their morsels of raw liver, the hunters skinned and cut up the carcass and loaded the meat on the pack animal. The entrails they left for the plainstalkers. In less than half an hour they were riding back to the hall. When they reached the stream, Brod washed away the dried blood and mud and dressed again, then remounted for the ride back to the hall.

Shkogar, riding beside him, asked softly, "Are you nervous, brother?"

After a pause, Brod admitted, "A little. It's the first time I've seen my oldest son since before he went away to school. Of course I hope he chooses the Warrior caste, but the choice is his." He paused again before he added, "Our father was a great captain until he fell fighting the Valek and his father is one of the sept's elders. It would seem a shame to break the family tradition."

"Passion must follow talent." Shkogar recited, and added, "Even so, you have two other sons."

"Lagobrod is my first son. 'Hopes ride the highest on the first attempt.' I can quote the book, too, brother."

As they approached the hall and the barracks Brod noticed a strange hovercar, a red machine, which was the favorite color of the Thundermaker Sept, sometimes called the blooddrinkers. As they delivered the meat to the master of the hall, he asked the old Warrior about the car.

"That's the car of a guest. Hyot, a classmate of Droz's, although Droz doesn't seem particularly happy to see him."

"Why not?"

"I don't talk about a Huer behind his back except to praise him." The old Warrior took the hauch from Brod and carried it inside.

When the last of the meat had been taken to be prepared, Brod asked, "Has my son arrived yet?"

"Not yet. Dorr took the car to meet him at the station. He left nearly an hour ago. He should be back in about half an hour."

The hunters handed the mounts over to the master of the stables and filed into the barracks where they stripped, showered, and dressed in trousers, soft boots, and the dark gray tunics of the Stormbringer Sept, finally buckling on their belts with their claws.

By the time Brod had stepped out onto the barracks porch the sept hovercar drew to a stop over its marked space and settled. The pad was concrete, so the car's downwash only blew up the dust that had drifted onto the space. Shkogar beside him, Brod marched to the car. While they were still a dozen paces from it the door swung upward and driver and passenger stepped out.

Brod studied his son, not yet Huer but too big to be called a cub except in jest. The young one's eyes and lips reminded him strongly of Kee, Lagobrod's mother. He wore the light blue tunic of the northern school.

"Father?" The young one advanced toward him.

"Lagobrod, greetings." A storm of emotions struck him like an incoming tide as he stared at his son. He spread his arms, fingers straight, and watched his son do the same.

Shkogar stood beside him, hands on hips, clearly assessing the young one as though he were a sept cadet. "He has the look of our father about his chin, jaw, and the cheekbones." He spread his arms and then stepped past his nephew to release the traveling chest mounted on the car's back end. He swung the chest clear and caught it by one of the handles on the ends. As he walked by the young one he smiled. "Greetings, nephew. Don't mind your father. He's one of those serious Huer who even scowl in their sleep."

In spite of himself, Brod barked a laugh and looked his gratitude at his brother for relaxing them all. "Lagobrod, this is my brother, your uncle, Shkogar. If he weren't so brave and so capable, I'd warn you against him as a bad influence."

Lagobrod seemed unsure whether to laugh or not.

Shkogar carried the chest into the barracks and Brod said, "Lagobrod, will you walk with me?"

Together they strolled between the fence of the pen for the mounts and the barracks. Lagobrod wrinkled his nose at the scent, which had always seemed pleasant to Brod. "How is your mother?"

"She's well. And she's gotten permission to keep my sister for another half-year. She seems happy with both her mathematics and with her students. She was pleased I could understand some of the equations she's studying."

They'd reached the grove kept for meditation and sat down on two of the low stools facing each other. "How long can you visit?" Brod asked.

"I have three days of leave remaining, and it will take most of one of them to return to the school."

"I think of you often. Do you see your brothers now and then?"

"We're seldom granted free time. The director is very stern, so most of my time is spent with others in my group. I can only see them about three times a month."

"In my time they were a little more lax, so I was able to see your uncle five or six times a month."

"You had no other brothers or sisters?"

"Your grandfather, Lagobrod, was killed after only mating twice. We were fighting the Valek then, and it took three of their ships to destroy his. I've heard he destroyed one of the Valek ships and one had to be abandoned. His father, Brod, is one of the leaders of our sept."

"Are all our family on your side Warriors?"

"Of course not. One of my uncles is a Director, another a Teacher. Shkogar has sired two daughters and a son but they are still in school."

"Do you ever see your uncles?"

"Only when someone in the family dies, then we gather to howl their souls into the afterlife. They both seem accomplished Huer."

Lagobrod released a breath. "So you would not be offended if I chose another caste than Warrior?"

Brod paused, considering his answer. It was hard to be honest and still not take away his son's choice. "I would be disappointed, but you would still be my first son. I'm sure whatever caste you chose, I would be proud of you."

They sat sharing silence for perhaps a quarter of an hour, then Brod stood. "Unless you're already as hungry as a plainstalker, we should probably at least walk up an appetite. We'll be feasting on three-horn meat. We'll also be drinking beer, and you want to take care. After the second cup—perhaps even after the first—I advise you to drink only water. There's time enough for you to learn how to drink."

Together they walked to the stream and followed it until the barracks and hall were out of sight and they could only see the tops of the trees in the meditation grove.

Lagobrod stared at the trees along the banks and at the rolling hills with their sea of grass with its foam of yellow and pale purple flowers. "Why does the Warrior Caste have these remote outposts? Those fields could be producing crops."

Brod tried to order his thoughts. Some concepts seemed hard to put into words. "The Warriors, as warriors, are only the claws of the Huer. We do not choose who or what to cut, and we hope and trust to be used well, for the good of the Huer, but we're also keepers of the old ways. The Huer domesticated most of the three-horned cattle ages ago and now we have many breeds, some for meat, some for milk and cheese. We've done the same with many of the plants and animals of Huerda but here we keep the old breeds. If a plague broke out among the domesticated breeds, we would still have the parent stock. We could adapt. We take what we need from the herds and we share them with our cousins, the plainstalkers—"

"I've heard," Lagobrod interjected, "that many think we're related to the plainstalkers, that they and we are branches of the same family."

Brod frowned. "Were you not taught not to interrupt your elders?" His tone was sharper than he'd intended.

His son looked down and waited until he was sure Brod had finished speaking. "I make no excuse, father."

"You have a good mind, Lagobrod, and it's natural you should think quickly, but you show respect by letting others finish their thoughts before you speak. Or is it different for the other castes?"

"You were right to correct me. It's one of my weaknesses."

"We all have them."

Lagobrod stared out at the land around them. "Aren't you ever afraid, out here in the empty places, with the plainstalkers so near?"

Brod chuckled. "Less afraid than I am on those rare occasions when I visit a city. As for the plainstalkers, they tend to avoid us and we them unless they become so numerous they endanger the herds. The plainstalkers are as valuable as the three-horns, and we protect them as well."

Lagobrod's brow furrowed. "From what do they need protection?"

"Some of the Huer of other classes sometimes hunt them. They consider it a great story to tell how they hunted and shot a wild three-horn or some of the other things we protect. We only allow hunts when herds or packs must be culled."

As they turned to walk back to the outpost, Lagobrod said,

"I see you wear a knife. Do you always wear it?"

Brod chuckled again. "No, I take it off to bathe, sleep, and mate, but it's always within reach. It's the claw of a Warrior. I would have thought they'd have taught you that."

"The school doesn't teach us much about the Warrior class."

Brod frowned. He'd need to ask the sept leader to register a complaint. The custom had always been to respect all the classes, to realize all were useful, all were needed. To neglect the Warrior Caste was not only an affront to the class, but to the whole Huer culture.

"May I look at your claw?"

Brod drew the claw and, with a flip of his wrist, extended it, hilt-first, to his son. Lagobrod studied it from its curved bone handle secured by two ornamented brass studs to the decorated brass guard and the laminated downward-curving blade with the inner edge of the curve, down to the point, showing a thread of mirror-bright edge.

"It's a work of art." The young one handed it back, hilt-first.

"You learn quickly." Brod drew up his tunic sleeve and made a small cut on his forearm before he wiped the blade on his trousers and returned it to its sheath.

Lagobrod's eyes widened. "Why did you do that?"

"Some knives are only tools," Brod replied. "The knives the old Warriors use to cut the meat, for instance, but a claw or a harvest knife must never be drawn without drinking blood before it's sheathed. It's to remind us of the great responsibility we bear in wearing them."

They continued in silence to the barracks where they washed their hands and faces and walked to the sept hall. A double row of tables ran the length of the hall with benches flanking the tables. The lighting was concealed so it was only a series of glowing arcs on the ceiling. Brod glanced about and saw Shkogar sitting opposite a Huer wearing the dark red tunic of the Thundermaker sept.

Brod and his son were among the last to arrive and he sat between his brother and his son.

Each place had a platter of flatbread, almost as tough as

leather, covered with three-horn meat, roots, and vegetables, and a large, handled, clay cup filled with beer.

Shkogar gestured across the table. "Brod, this is Hyot, our guest from the Thundermaker sept."

"You livereaters throw a fine feast." Hyot refilled his cup from the pitcher near the center of the table.

"We prefer 'Stormbringers' as the sept name," Shkogar said softly.

Brod glanced at his brother. The soft voice was, to anyone who knew him, a warning, and the battle light was dancing in his eyes. Brod guessed he and the blooddrinker had been talking before he'd arrived with Lagobrod.

Hyot stared at Lagobrod. "A little young to be a novice, isn't he?"

Brod had just bitten off a morsel of meat and he chewed and swallowed before he replied. "My son hasn't chosen his caste yet."

"There's only one caste for a true Huer—the Warrior class. And for a Huer of strength and ability, the Thundermaker sept."

"My son has not yet decided," Brod repeated, and took a long drink of beer.

The silence was broken by Lagobrod's voice, still a little high-pitched. "I'm thinking of becoming an engineer."

The visitor almost sprayed his mouthful of beer over the table. "Cubs play with blocks. A real Huer masters weapons."

Again a pause. Lagobrod obviously waited to be sure he wasn't interrupting. "If it weren't for engineers, you'd be trying to walk to the stars. Ships aren't carved out of wood or grown like a crop."

Hyot raised his arm as a threat. "I've never been on a ship as fast as your mouth."

"Put your arm down," Brod said softly. He turned to Lagobrod. "I would talk to you about not respecting your elders, but you gave this boor just what he deserved." To Hyot he said, "If you have a disagreement with my son, you may direct your remarks to me."

Shkogar laughed. "You're the older brother. You should deal

with matters of greater importance. I can swat this gnat for you."

Raising his voice to a bellow, Hyot shouted, "The Warriors' blood must have cooled and thinned in the livereaters sept if you cannot even sire Warriors."

Chattuck, the local head of the sept, stood up at the head of the table. "Is it the custom of the Thundermaker sept to abuse the hospitality of others?"

Hyot roared back, "It's not my custom to pretend respect for females who wear claws and can't even produce Warriors."

Chattuck scowled at the Huer beside Hyot. "Droz, this blooddrinker is your guest. Do you stand with him?"

Droz stood. "Not when he shames himself attempting to shame others." He stalked from the hall.

"So, this is the 'hospitality' of the livereaters sept—to try to silence a true Huer who says what everyone is thinking." Hyot flung down the bone he'd been gnawing. "My remarks were for this female who carries a claw," he gestured at Brod, "and his whelp."

Shkogar began to get to his feet. "Brother, you provided the food for this feast. It's only fair I should provide the entertainment by gelding this loudmouth."

Brod caught Shkogar by the arm and drew him back down. "I'm the one he seems to have the quarrel with."

Shkogar grinned at Brod, then at Hyot, but when he grinned at the blooddrinker his teeth flashed. "Whichever one of us gelds him, it's no honor claimed. Perhaps we should let one of the old Warriors have him."

Hyot showed his teeth in a snarl. "If there's to be a fight, I can gut you after I've cut up your sister here."

Chattuck slammed his fist on the table so the cups danced. "Hyot, if you do not leave this table and this hall this very instant, there will be a fight. And if you lose the fight, no compensation will be paid for you and no one will avenge you."

Hyot shot to his feet. "I will not leave until I've cut my mark on this female."

"What weapons do you want to use, gnat?" Brod stood and grinned.

"A Warrior's weapon—claws." Hyot wiped his hands on the cloth covering the table then, bracing his hand on the table, sprang over it. As soon as his feet had hit the floor he whipped out the claw at his belt.

The Warriors in the room moved the tables back against the walls to leave more room for the fighters.

Brod drew his own claw. "Now we'll see how hot and thick *your* blood runs."

Hyot dropped into a crouch, his arm well in front of him, the curved blade parallel to the floor. Brod stood with his feet only a little wider apart than his shoulders, knees slightly bent, his blade vertical.

"A dancer, eh?" Hyot snarled. "In a minute we'll see how you sing."

Brod laughed. "Are you going to use that claw or just try to win the fight with your mouth? You won't talk me to death."

Hyot sprang forward, his blade slashing to his left then he turned his hand and slashed right.

Brod evaded the first slash, stepping to Hyot's right and, as the arm holding the knife swept back past him, he slashed downward. The claw cut deeply and Hyot roared and dropped the weapon but caught it in his left hand. "Blood is drawn, honor is satisfied," Brod said.

"I call that only a scratch," Hyot snapped, "a lucky hit."

Brod moved his claw to his own left hand to show he wanted no advantage. "Luck is better than skill, and you have neither."

Hyot feinted and Brod circled to the right but the blood made the floor slick and he slipped. Hyot rushed him and Brod twisted to avoid the blade but it gashed a deep furrow in his outer thigh. "Did that one bite or not?" Hyot asked.

Pretending to have trouble standing on his right leg, Brod seemed to slip again but, as Hyot stepped in, he slammed his right forearm against Hyot's left arm and slashed across.

Hyot stumbled back, using his wounded right arm to hold his guts in and slashed again, but Brod caught Hyot's blade with his own, deflected it downward, and cut for the neck. The claw cut deeply and Brod drew it across, blood spraying from the wound. Brod sprang back and watched his enemy fall.

The hall suddenly resounded to the wails as they all howled his spirit into the next life.

Shkogar had already cut a strip from the tablecloth and used it to bind the wound to Brod's thigh. "He died well," Shkogar said. "It's a shame he was too overbearing to learn to live well."

"I accept responsibility for this killing," Brod said clearly.

Chattuck left the table to contact the nearest Thundermakers' outpost.

Brod dropped onto the bench and raised his beer, let Shkogar refill his cup, and drank deeply.

One of the old Warriors approached and took off the binding and cut away Brod's trouser leg, sprayed an antiseptic that burned like fire on the wound, then, with needle and thread, stitched the wound. Brod finished his beer and accepted another cupfull. Making a stone mask of his face was easier than avoiding flinching as the needle pierced him, again and again, and the thread drew the wound closed. The beer helped.

Chattuck returned to take his place at the head of the table. "They will be sending a car for his body in the morning."

The Warriors drew the tables out again, all but the one at the end of the row. Old Warriors placed the corpse on a tablecloth, wrapped it around him, and carried the body to the table against the wall while novices cleaned the blood off the floor.

As soon as the old Warrior finished sewing the wound in his leg, Brod downed another cup of beer and began to eat again.

Lagobrod stared at him. "How can you eat so soon after killing another Huer?"

Brod gestured with his cup at the blood-stained cloth wrapped around Hyot's body. "He chose to fight, so he chose to bear the consequences. The food and beer both taste better to me now. Facing death reminded me how good life is." He swept the cup around, indicating everyone else in the room. "Do you see how few old Warriors are here? Those of us who live to die in our beds as old Huer are rare, but life goes on." He tapped his brother's shoulder with the cup. "Shkogar, what would you have done if he'd killed me?"

"I'd have killed him. But I'd have taken longer about it than you did. I'd have cut him a dozen times before I'd have seriously hurt him. And, after I'd finished him off, I'd have eaten until I could hold no more and I'd have gotten magnificently drunk."

"You see, son, that's our way. We grieve losses but we know life goes on until it stops. You are a part of me and I a part of you. When you have sons and daughters, you will be a part of them, and so will I, even if I've died. Family and those closest to us will always be in us, here," he tapped his upper belly with his fist, "in our core."

* * *

The hovercraft from the Thundermakers Sept arrived an hour after dawn and two Huer stepped out. Chattuck strode out to meet them, Brod limping beside him. The Thundermaker who'd been driving spread his arms, fingers extended. "Where is the body?"

After returning the greeting, Chattuck inclined his head. "In the hall. We'll help you carry it to the vehicle."

"We carry our own dead." The two strode into the hall and picked up the wrapped body, which was already stiff. With one holding the shoulders and the other the lower legs, they hauled the corpse to the craft. The rear door slid open and they moved their burden into the vehicle, the door closing as they stepped back.

The driver approached Brod and Chattuck. "The meeting will be tomorrow at the Windwalkers' Sept hall." Without waiting for a response, he walked to the driver's door of the vehicle while the other entered the hovercraft Hyot had driven. After a few seconds both vehicles started with a whine, rose in unison, and swept away, side by side.

"I'll attend the meeting with you, Chattuck," Brod said.

"Not necessary. You did nothing to disgrace yourself or the sept. The head of the Thundermakers Sept will lodge a complaint but it is only to be expected. The honor of his sept requires it, but he knows Hyot was in the wrong and will not be eager for a full report. I suspect Hyot was as overbearing to his sept brothers as he was here, so there will be no question of compensation, and I doubt Hyot had any friends to seek vengeance." Chattuck glanced at the porch where the local members of the sept stood, along with Lagobrod. "See to your son."

Brod gestured assent and limped toward his son. "Are you ready to go on a hunt?"

Lagobrod paused before he said, "Yes," and his voice was soft and unsteady.

Shkogar stepped off the porch. "Are you sure you're ready for a hunt with that leg?"

Brod grinned with his lips closed. "Even with this leg I could ride faster and farther than you on your best day." Turning to Lagobrod, he said, "This hunt is just for food, not for a feast, so I won't need to make the kill the old way. You'll need to draw clothing, though. Your school uniform is too pale." He waved an old Warrior over. "Hgar, could you find a cadet's hunting uniform my son won't lose himself in?"

Hgar led Lagobrod to the barracks and Brod and Shkogar followed. The brothers changed into tunics and trousers of broken and uneven stripes of purple on green and both took gauss rifles from their racks. Shkogar also strapped on a holster and checked the charge of a projectile weapon, making sure the projectiles were the solid brass loads rather than the frangible bullets used on shipboard.

Brod said, "We're only hunting three-horns, not making war on them."

Settling the belt around his waist, Shkogar replied, "I find the weight and feel comfortable."

Lagobrod emerged wearing a hunting suit like the brothers', still tugging and tucking it in and followed Brod and Shkogar to the pen where the mounts stood drowsing. The two older Huer caught, bridled, and saddled three mounts and they set off for the three-horns herd.

Lagobrod seemed nervous of his mount and the animal was apparently aware of his rider's uneasiness, occasionally stopping to crop grass.

"You must remember," Brod said, "you are the one in control, and your mount must remember it as well. Keep the reins in a firm hand and keep pressure on him with your knees."

"He's a lot bigger than I am," Lagobrod said.

"Not where it's most important. It has to be your mind and determination that rules you both."

Lagobrod frowned but gradually became more comfortable in the saddle by the time they crossed the ford. "You said something about my uncle being very capable. You've served with him?"

"I have," Brod replied. "We've both served as captain. When he is the captain I am the Weapons Master. He's a very daring captain—better than I am, although I'm a better Weapons Master than he is."

Shkogar barked a laugh. "Still trying to convince yourself of that, eh, brother?"

Brod grinned ruefully. "I'm the older brother. I have to be able to claim superiority at something. You've proved there are few, if any, better captains among the Huer."

Lagobrod glanced at his uncle, then at his father. "How did he do that?"

"It was two years ago, before our truce with the Valek. We were on a ship called *Freedom* and were visiting one of our colony worlds. One of the things you need to know about the Longstride drive is that it cannot be activated within five planetary diameters of an object in space. It cost a lot of lives to find out that within five diameters of even a small moon, the field generated around a ship will collapse, and it crushes the ship within it.

"We were no more than two planetary diameters from the planet when three Valek ships appeared. The Valek do make impressive ships, and they crew and arm them well. Our repulsor fields were beginning to fail and it was only a matter of time before one of their missiles or shells got through. Even diluted by the field, the energy beams were heating the ship. It must've glowed like a blade in the forge." He clasped air, making a fist. "They had us."

"What happened?" Lagobrod stared with wide eyes, obviously captivated by the story.

"Your uncle called for our helm to bring us within a heartbeat of the Valek lead ship. He told the commander, Flightmaster Falk, that if his men did not cease firing, he'd ram the Flightmaster's ship. At the same time, he'd had me reverse the repulsor field so the Valek ship was being drawn ever nearer. The Valek couldn't fire at us because we were so close to their flagship that any missile that damaged us would also damage their ship.

"Then he ordered the Flightmaster to send his ships out far enough to engage their Longstride drives. He told the Flightleader if he did not do so, he would engage our Longstride drive, which would draw in and crush their ship as well as the *Freedom*."

"What happened?"

"The Valek did as they were told. And the *Freedom* and the Valek flagship climbed out far enough to let us use the Longstride drive—after Shkogar had me again reverse the repulsor fields to fling the Valek ship a safe distance from us. We returned to Freehall base to gather reinforcements to go hunting the Valek when we received word of the truce. I've heard the Valek Flightmaster cut his own throat out of shame."

"You see, cub, you need not face an enemy with your weapon bare in your hand to defeat him," Shkogar said. "Cunning and skill mean more than brute force."

Brod chuckled. "I wasn't sure we were going to win that one, brother. Had the Flightmaster chosen to risk his ship, we'd have been lost."

Shkogar laughed. "I wasn't sure, myself." He leaned forward to look past Brod at Lagobrod. "You see, cub, sometimes you have to risk much to gain much."

Brod drew his mount to a halt, dismounted, and hobbled him. The other two did the same but Brod had to show his son how to use the hobble. He led them down a draw, downwind of the herd. The three-horns were grazing, just near enough they could distinguish individual animals. Brod lowered his voice to a murmur. "Do you want to make the kill?"

Lagobrod considered a moment, then turned his hand down. "I've never killed anything, and I've never used a weapon."

Brod kept his face impassive but his brother scowled. "This

is not the time to learn, then. But stay with us." Brod took a projectile from his pocket and slipped it into the rifle's chamber. As he closed the lever, the red light appeared on the sight screen. "Close enough, brother, or should we stalk nearer?"

Shkogar had just armed his own rifle. "I can hit from any range you can, but you have older eyes. We'll move up until you can see clearly."

Brod crept almost to the mouth of the draw before taking a shooting stance. "Do you see that young bull with the light-colored throat? I'll take him."

"Good," Shkogar replied. "I'll take the old cow to his left. She looks to be barren."

Brod raised the gauss rifle, sighting with both eyes. The sight in front of his right eye held a dim red light so as he studied his quarry a red dot was superimposed over the three-horn's shoulder. He raised the rifle higher. The beast stopped grazing and looked in the direction of the hunters, his ears spread.

As Brod squeezed the trigger the rifle hummed softly and they all heard the racketing sound of the heavy slug breaking the speed of sound. Shkogar's rifle had hummed almost before Brod's had stopped, and mist shot from the heads of the bull and the cow and both dropped. The herd milled for several moments, then retreated.

"It seems a shame to kill such a noble-looking creature," Lagobrod said.

Brod and Shkogar reloaded their rifles and Shkogar said, "Would the meat taste better if it came from something uglier? We shot them in the head because we don't eat the heads. We Huer are just as much a part of this world as the three-horns. Are we to go hungry because they're good to look at?"

They'd cleared the mouth of the draw, which was actually a fork in an ancient, long-dry creekbed, and had covered almost half the distance to their kills when Shkogar turned, raised his rifle, and shot a plainstalker creeping out of the other branch of the draw. He threw the lever, loaded another projectile, closed the action, and handed it to Lagobrod. "You may need to learn quickly, pup. Keep both eyes open and, when the red spot covers what you want to hit, squeeze the trigger." He'd drawn his pistol as he'd spoken.

Brod shot a second plainstalker and worked to reload as quickly as possible. A dozen more of the beasts dashed out of the draw and Shkogar leveled his pistol and fired five shots; sharp, explosive barks. Five of the plainstalkers tumbled and a sixth beast screamed and thrashed, its shoulder shattered. The sound of the pistol had an effect the humming of the gauss rifles hadn't, and the remaining beasts howled and raced back up the draw.

Followed by Lagobrod, the brothers walked carefully toward the dead and wounded plainstalkers. One of the animals Shkogar had shot with the pistol whined and Shkogar whipped out his out his claw and cut its throat.

Brod and Lagobrod approached the beast Lagobrod had wounded, which was snarling and thrashing, showing its fangs. Brod set down his rifle and drew his claw and slashed, cutting its throat. They watched as the eyes dimmed and glazed and the mouth relaxed.

"That should have been yours to do, son," Brod said, "but I wanted to end its suffering. I was afraid you wouldn't have been able to cut deeply enough for a quick kill. The killing stroke has to be made without hesitation and without fear."

Lagobrod looked as though he was going to be ill. "Why does there have to be so much killing?"

"Because we were both hungry for three-horn meat." Shkogar took his rifle back from his nephew. To Brod he said, "This was an outlier pack. All of them were male."

"What does that mean?" Lagobrod asked.

"It means, son," Brod picked up his rifle, "that they were not a family pack. Young males leave the family pack to start their own. If they find no females, they form packs with other outcast males. Such packs are more dangerous than families. Each of them strives to lead, and so that desperation makes them bold."

Brod started back toward the three-horns they'd shot. "As to why there's so much killing, it's because Huerda was a stern world, and in some places it still is. The Huer are not grazing beasts like the three-horns or other plant-eaters. We've learned to eat grains, roots, and parts of plants but we're still primarily meat-eaters. Did you think the meat you eat comes from trees?"

When they reached the three-horns Brod drew out his communicator, called the outpost, and gave the coordinates that appeared on the communicator's face. After the brothers had cleaned the plainstalkers' blood off their blades, they began to butcher the three-horns' carcasses. By the time the hovervan appeared, they'd cleaned the entrails out.

When the old Warrior climbed out of the hovercraft he nodded toward the sky. "I didn't need the coordinates. I could've found the place by the gathering of bloodbirds." Several broad-winged shapes hovered above, waiting for the Huer to leave.

"They'll feast until they're too fat to fly," Shkogar said. "There are two hands of plainstalkers out that way." He pointed toward the draw with his chin.

They helped the old Warrior stow the meat in the vehicle, then walked back to their mounts. As they left the draw they could see the bloodbirds beginning to settle. "You see, son, we are part of it all. We're as much a part of Huerda as the plainstalkers and three-horns we've killed and the bloodbirds we've fed."

The mounts were as they'd been left and the Huer mounted and rode back to the outpost. Lagobrod was silent on the ride and Brod glaced at him anxiously. His son was obviously deep in thought and Brod tried to remember what it had been like to be a cub. He couldn't remember a time when he hadn't wanted to be a Warrior. To him, the life was harsh but rewarding. He couldn't imagine living in a city, doing the same thing day after day. To him, it would be like being dead and buried, but his son seemed to see only the starker side of the Warrior class.

Shkogar was uncharacteristically quiet, too, and Brod glanced at him. Shkogar noticed and leaned toward him and murmured, "My nephew has enough on his mind without my prattling on." After a sharp glance at Brod, he added, "Better a worthy Builder than a reluctant Warrior."

* * *

Brod ate but without his usual appetite and the beer tasted flat. His son again wore his school uniform and Shkogar hadn't regained his usual explosive laugh. After he'd finished the meal Chattuck caught his attention and nodded toward the corner of the room where the body had laid last night.

"I know your son must return tomorrow. There's no reason for you to attend the meeting at the Windwalkers' Sept hall."

Brod turned his hand down. "I'm responsible for Hyot's death. I should be there."

"I want you to handsell this death to me," Chattuck said. "That way, the obligations will have been met and you'll be able to see your son off."

"Thank you." Brod handsold the death to Chattuck, then said, "I also have to speak with you about my son. The Director at his school has decided to wish away the Warrior caste. The cubs are taught nothing about our class. I should like to lodge a protest."

Chattuck's eyes blazed. "The sept will lodge that protest, and the other septs as well. We'll have that she-plainstalker's hide on the wall. Now, go back to your son. Old Shmar's beginning to recite the Epic of Kolmar."

Brod returned to the table. Shkogar had just poured his fifth cup of beer and Lagobrod was sipping water, and both were watching the dais where Shmar stood, flanked by Warriors with tambours, the drone bow, and pipes. As Shmar began his recitation the tambours kept the meter, the drone bow gave the counterpoint, and the pipes waited for the important pauses.

The epic was recited in the poetic old form so Brod had to translate for his son. The tale began when the old council had almost ruined Huerda with their bickering and struggles for power. The old chieftain class ruled, with the warrior and merchant classes serving the families, and the other classes little better than slaves. Kolmar had led an uprising that broke the power of the families and personally read in public the charges against the members of the council. The list of charges of corruption and secret murder were impressive, and he'd had them all banished to an island in the Brown Sea. He'd established the new order of castes and septs and was interviewing leaders of the castes to establish the new council when he'd been assassinated by a warrior who felt the warrior class should rule.

Lofang, Kolman's son, had led the warriors under his command and many others who joined him, as well as Huer who were not warrior-born but from the other classes. That was the last war on Huerda between brothers. When Lofang finally won he had killed all the men of the families and clans of the Huer who'd fought for a caste hierarchy, and the children were adopted by the council, and the school system had been established. The family names of the defeated were stricken from all stories, records, even to defacing names on graves. Then he'd finished the work his father had started and the new Council was born, with all castes regarded equal and voluntary septs replacing the clans.

Lagobrod had paid close attention to the recitation and when it was finished he joined the others in pounding on the table.

Shmar strode to the head table and drank deeply from a pitcher. "Reciting builds a thirst." He drained the pitcher, then filled his cup from another ewer.

"How much of the story is true?" Lagobrod asked.

"Most of it, at least," Brod replied. "Some of the feats may have been exaggerated, but the important parts are as they happened. Kolman and Lofang exemplified the greatest qualities of the Huer; courage, ruthlessness, and the strength to put the good of the Huer above their own interests. Lofang could've ruled, but gave the power and his support to the Council. He founded the Stormbringer Sept and died an old Huer, on a hunt. It was he who made the Warrior caste the keepers of the wild places and the upholders of tradition."

* * *

By an hour after dawn, Brod, Lagobrod, and Shkogar had gathered by the hovercar pad. Shkogar wore half a grin and carried a sheathed claw, which he handed to his nephew. "You can't wear it unless you become a Warrior, but you can keep it to remember this time."

Lagobrod's eyes widened as he studied the glossy black horn hilt and the guard, on which were engraved the names of his father and uncle. He slowly drew the weapon, admiring the wavering patterns of the differently colored steels flowing from guard to point, and the bright edge. Wordlessly, he drew up his left sleeve and drew a fine line of blood across his outer forearm before he wiped the blade on his trousers and returned the claw to its sheath.

"That was well done," Shkogar said. "I'd say you'll always be part a Warrior and all Huer."

Lagobrod beamed at the praise. "When will I see you again?"

Brod turned his hand palm-up. "Who can say? As I said, there are few old Warriors. That's another thing that makes life sweet. Each parting may be the last, so each time you bid farewell you must leave out nothing of importance. I want you to know that whatever choices you make, I'll be proud of you."

Shkogar had kept his half-grin. "And if I weren't proud of you, I wouldn't have given you the claw. Whether you wear it or not, it's now an experience we've shared. Whatever you do, I wish you success. The honor you have to earn yourself." He turned slightly as Dorr approached. "See my nephew is at the station early."

Brod helped his son with the travel chest, securing it in the rear of the vehicle, then all three extended their arms, fingers extended. Lagobrod slipped into the passenger's seat, buckled in, and closed the door but stared at his father and uncle, who stared after the hovercraft until it was out of sight.

Shkogar glanced at Brod. "Perhaps you should spend time with me at the pistol range."

"Still trying to find a way to embarrass me, brother?" Brod said it with a smile.

"No, but with your leg, you can use some training that won't tax you. If I'd wanted to embarrass you, I'd have challenged you to a footrace."

They spent the morning at the pistol range. Brod hadn't used a pistol in nearly half a season and he was surprised at how much skill he'd lost. Firing a pistol, even at stationary targets, had to be practiced frequently. By noon Brod was pleased that he could almost compete with Shkogar.

They'd just washed for lunch and were taking their places in the hall when Chattuck strode in. As he passed Brod, he said, "See me outside after the meal."

Chapter 4

Appetite is often the first victim of worry, and Brod ate sparingly, wondering if the sept would be penalized for his killing Hyot. The fight had been a fair one, and Brod had accepted responsibility for the killing but he wondered if Hyot hadn't been strongly supported by the Thundermaker Sept.

After finishing the meal, Brod paced outside to the pen for the mounts and Chattuck joined him. "We have a mission for you," Chattuck said."You are known to be reserved. Some would even say cautious."

Brod made a mask of his face but Chattuck had apparently perceived his stiffness. "It was not an insult, only an observation. And for this mission, your reserve will be valuable." Chattuck leaned on the top pole of the corral. "How much do you know about the humans?"

Brod set his right foot on the bottom pole and leaned on the top, studying Chattuck's face but the old Warrior was a master at revealing nothing by his expression. "I've met a few of them. We had several of them on our ship when we explored Silverlakeworld."

"What did you think of them?"

Brod held his hand palm up. "I didn't spend much time with them and I don't speak their language. They're only a little taller than my son, and the ones I met spent most of their time with each other. I gather they were excited about some of the discoveries we made."

"Are you aware we may become allies?"

Brod repeated the hand gesture. "I know humans and Huer have worked together and haven't fought for over twenty years." He stared at the mounts. "They don't seem to have many Warriors among them."

Chattuck glanced at him. "Like us, their Council isn't made up of Warriors, but don't assume there are no Warriors among them. We would like to find out what their other classes think and feel. We already have someone to speak with and deal with their Council, but we would like to find out whether they would be worthy allies or if they're made of straw."

Brod scowled. "Are you asking me to become a spy?"

Chattuck turned his hand palm-down. "No, that is not worthy work for a Warrior. We would like you to work with the humans on one of their ships. Ambassador Ruhl has committed the leaders of their fleet to accept a Huer to serve with one of their crews. We are only waiting for a ship's leader to accept."

Chattuck stared at Brod's face. "We have, of course, our own secrets, but you don't know the technical details and I trust you not to give away any information that isn't common knowledge."

Brod smiled. "Like the new repulsor and attractor gear, or the fact the attactor field can make our ships effectively invisible?"

Chattuck returned the smile. "I'm sure the humans will find out about the effects sooner or later, but there's no reason to excite their curiosity any sooner than we'd like.

"Beyond that, most of our equipment is very similar. We both use similar repulsor fields and the humans have learned enough from us they're also learning to reverse them to serve as attractors, although our new system is different enough they're still a long way from being able to match it. Their small arms, lasers, missiles, and anti-missile systems are quite similar to our own. We will send you with a gauss rifle, an autorifle, and a pistol because theirs would be awkward for you to handle. We will agree that they be kept in the ship's armory."

"And my claw?" Brod's fingers curled around the haft of the weapon at his belt.

"That's one of the reasons we'll have to wait for a commander to accept you. Human crewmen are seldom armed but we are making it a condition of your joining a crew. Also, you will not be going alone. Kee, your chosen mate, will join you in a few months."

Chattuck wrinkled his face as though he'd caught some unpleasant scent. "Humans don't have a mating season. I understand their ship discipline and some cultural traits keep them from screwing whenever and where ever their whim strikes them, but even on ships there are times when they do so. I gather they're generally discreet about it, but don't be surprised or offended."

Brod barked a laugh. "I hope someone has also warned Kee about this."

"She was informed. In addition to her other work, she's also studying Trade Common, something you will also have to learn. The ship that will deliver you to a human ship will leave four days from now. You will leave here tomorrow. The voyage to Earth will take approximately two months, which should be more than enough time for you to become fluent in Trade Common."

"How long will I be gone?"

"I don't know. Commonly their ships' tours last about a year and a half of our years, about two human years, but there are rumors the humans are constructing a new class of ship for deep exploration and their tours are estimated to last around five of our years. You may be gone six years or more."

Brod's lips twisted. "This leaves me to wonder if I'm not being punished for killing Hyot."

Again the palm-up gesture as Chattuck replied, "You aren't. And you and I both know that. Does it matter what the blooddrinker Sept might think?"

"It's never mattered to me before." Brod drew in a deep breath. "I shall miss this place, and the sept."

"How's the leg?"

"It won't interfere with my boarding a ship and it'll be fully healed in less than two months."

"Good. Now see to your preparations." Chattuck turned and strode back to the hall.

Preparing his travel chest would take Brod less than half an hour. A Warrior wasn't burdened with possessions, but he knew Chattuck hadn't been talking about packing.

* * *

Brod found Shkogar, as he'd expected, on the practice field, sparring with another Warrior. It'd taken less than a week after Shkogar's arrival at the sept for his sparring opponents to learn to wear all the protective gear they could. While shorter and slimmer than most Huer, Shkogar was very fast, impressively aggressive, and he learned quickly. Brod watched as his brother slipped outside an attempted punch, drove his elbow into the other Warrior's ribs, and back-kicked with his heel into the back of the other's knee, then threw him to the ground.

The downed Warrior groaned, then laughed. "You're getting slow, Shkogar. It took you at least half a second longer to knock me on my ass than to do the same to Fomorr." He reached up to accept the hand Shkogar extended. By the time the other Huer had been drawn to his feet Brod had reached them.

"Shkogar, I have a mission. I leave tomorrow. Would you get your gear for a ride?"

Shkogar peered at his brother, then turned and walked with him to the barracks where they gathered filled canteens, rations, and their leather sleeping sacks. Both of them strapped on pistols and took autorifles from the rack. With saddles and reins over their shoulders they walked out to the pen, chose mounts, and saddled them.

They rode in silence until Brod chose a site on a hillside that showed the remains of campfires and a small pile of wood.

After they'd set up camp and started a fire, Shkogar glanced at Brod. "Where have you been assigned?"

Brod managed a laugh. "To the human navy. I suppose the humans need to see what a Warrior looks like."

"Then that's what they'll see." Shkogar had just finished gnawing and swallowing a strip of dried meat. He overturned a rock, caught a grub, and popped it into his mouth. "I always prefer something fresher than dried meat." He took a sip from his canteen. "How do you feel about it?"

Brod drank from his own canteen. "As Warriors, it's our duty and honor to meet challenges. This should be a challenge."

"Spoken like a true Huer Warrior," Shkogar said. After a pause, he said, "I've just received orders as well. I leave at the end of the week to take command of the *Challenge*. So. We both have our own challenge."

"Isn't that a new ship?"

Shkogar took another sip of water and grimaced. "You'd

think they'd fill these things with beer, so we could celebrate properly. Yes, the old *Challenge* was the first of her line, and her name will be used for the first of a new line. I'll have the new attractor/repulsor gear."

"It couldn't have a better commander."

"I'll miss you at the weapons controls. It'll take time to find another weapons officer I can work with as well as we did."

"How long will you be gone?"

"The first tour will only be a break-in run. I should be back in less than six months, in time for mating season, then we sit while the techs try to fix everything we find wrong with her. Then a two-year voyage. I don't know whether they'll let us bring mates or drug us to stop the cycle."

Brod chuckled. "I've heard they were going to geld the crew."

"Not even as a joke, brother," Shkogar growled. "Besides the fact I'd kill any Huer who came near my private parts with a blade, the race couldn't afford to lose our bloodline."

"Now that's a true statement."

Shkogar sniffed the air and turned his head, slowly turning his body to make a full circle. "Plainstalkers are cunning. I've heard they'll send one of a pack upwind, then have the rest circle around to come in from another direction. I thought I smelled one, but heard nothing." After a pause, "How long will you be away?"

"Up to five years. I'm sorry I won't be able to find out what choice Lagobrod has made before then, and by then his brother Shkogar will have chosen his caste."

"One of the burdens of a Warrior. I've heard it was worse in the old days."

Brod sipped more water. "Everything was harder in the old days. I'm not sure about worse. Sometimes I think we've become pampered, lost our hard edge."

Shkogar grinned. "Not as long as you and I are Warriors. You rest first and I'll waken you."

As Brod crawled into his learther sleeping sack he said, "'Bare is the back without brother to guard it.'"

* * *

Brod woke sometime after the middle of the night. He crawled out of the bag and said, "You were supposed to wake me for my watch."

"You'll be leaving tomorrow, so you need your rest more than I do. And you do scowl in your sleep."

"I'm awake now, so get some sleep. We'll need to ride as soon as it's light enough for the mounts to see the way back."

After waiting until Shkogar had crawled into his sack, Brod prowled the perimeter of the site, looking, listening, smelling the air, and checking the mounts. Although they were already dozing they would likely sense a plainstalker before he could.

He found the stone Shkogar had been sitting on and sat down, gazing into the darkness. After a moment he tilted his head back and stared at the stars. Soon he would be among them again but, at the moment and from where he sat, the stars seemed a part of Huerda. How many generations of Huer had looked up at the stars and felt they belonged to this world? He supposed some human was gazing up on his world and thinking the same thing—that the stars were his.

Once one had been among the stars, one learned they belonged to no one. The space between the stars seemed to hate all life, as though the space itself was the jealous owner and determined to keep Huer and human alike bound to their own worlds.

He wondered how much discipline their navy had, decided it didn't matter; he'd show them a Huer Warrior could bear anything a human could, and more. He'd earn their respect for his race. He just wondered whether he'd respect them.

He repeated his circuit of the camp. This was really why he'd come out to the open plains. Leaving these things he knew best and loved most was hard, but this time with them was a chance to store memories like treasure to be taken out and studied in times of trial or boredom. He wished Lagobrod and his brothers and sister were here too, to share it with them as he shared it with his brother.

The sky began to lighten and Shkogar stirred, then crawled

out of his sack. Walking to just beyond the camp's perimeter he relieved himself then waited while Brod did the same. Saddling the mounts took only moments, though Shkogar's beast growled and showed his teeth. They rode back to the outpost in silence. They'd said all they needed to say last night and both were aware some things couldn't be said, that words sometimes turned gold into lead.

As they strode to the hall Chattuck stepped out onto the porch. "You need to be ready to leave in an hour and a half." He paused as if to say something more, then turned and re-entered the hall.

"I'll miss that old plainstalker," Brod said.

He and Shkogar showered and ate a late breakfast, then Brod assembled everything he wanted to take with him that wouldn't be issued. He had a tri-vid of his mate and the young ones, a few items of dress that he wore for comfort, including an extra pair of soft boots.

As he stepped out onto the barracks porch he found the other Warriors of the Stormbringer Sept standing in two lines, each one holding his claw upraised. Setting his face, he strode the open space between the lines and the Warriors began their chant, "We will remember you! Remember us!"

Chattuck himself was the last Huer in the right-hand file and he stepped out of line and walked beside Brod to the car. "I'll take you to the port."

Brod took the passenger's seat and drew the restraints tight around his waist and chest. "All this is not necessary. I'm not going to a battle."

"Perhaps not." Chattuck strapped himself in and started the car, "but you are still going to face a trial, and you will be doing it alone. The Huer are like the plainstalkers—we are pack animals . You are going where no one from your sept can help you."

"I will not disgrace my sept or the Huer."

Chattuck smiled. "I trust you not to. If I hadn't, I'd have sent someone else." He touched the lift control and steered with the levers at the sides of his seat. "I think you will find human

Warriors more like us than the human scientists you've met. Even, perhaps, more than the Huer scientists you may have met."

"Do you think this is a good thing—allying ourselves with the humans?"

"'Bare is the back without brother to guard it,'" Chattuck quoted. "we are no longer at war with the Valek, but we're not truly at peace with them either. The Chadanor are no one's friends. We haven't yet met the ChiTseTsi but, from what I've heard of them, they're not promising allies. The only good thing I've heard about them is that the Valek hate them. From what I've heard of the Walawi, they might be good allies but their Warriors are all females. They're also practically a subject race, totally dependent upon the humans. Your mission is to find out if the humans would actually guard our backs."

"Trust is not easily come by," Brod said. "Even if I find humans I trust, it'd be a mistake to believe the race can be trusted."

Chattuck released the right-hand control to make the palm-up gesture. "We do what we can. More depends upon Ambassador Ruhl's judgement and actions. Still, it's better to reach some sort of understanding with the humans."

They rode in silence until they saw the spires of a city and Chattuck set the car down until they rode less than a meter above the pavement. "We also need to know how likely the humans are to need our assistance…but they will need to realize that if we fight beside them, it is as allies, not as subjects or mercenaries."

Brod started. That last word, "mercenaries," was a word seldom used in Huer and recalled a curse from ancient days, when each holding was only as safe as its Warriors could make it and warlords with armed bands roamed the countryside.

To Brod's relief, it wasn't necessary to go deeply into the city. The sept maintained a level of a building at the port and Chattuck led him to an old Warrior sitting behind a desk.

"Brod."

The old Huer placed a mark beside his name in a book. "Choose any room with an unlocked door. The doctor will see you in less than half an hour."

Brod and Chattuck faced each other and Brod spread his arms, fingers extended . Chattuck responded the same way and walked out of the building.

The building impressed Brod more than he wanted to admit. The structure was of permastone, glossy black with trim of silver-colored ceramic, and the doors seemed a solid sheet of a dark red wood. He tried two doors before he found one that swung inward. The room inside had space for a cot, a toilet, a shower, and a tiny closet to hold his traveling chest.

Within moments an old Huer entered, gave him a quick medical examination in which the stitching on his thigh was noticed and dismissed as barely workmanlike, and administered a series of injections. "These should protect you from the most common human diseases. Report to the desk and they will assign you a chit for meals. Or, you can choose field rations."

"I'll have the field rations," Brod said.

"Most Warriors would rather have a meal and beer."

"Having to mix with crowds in the port is a higher price than I want to pay, and beer isn't as good if you're not sharing it with your sept brothers."

"As you wish, but report to the desk for your rations and for the time you need to be ready to board. You also have to be tested."

Brod did as he'd been ordered and ate the dried rations sitting on his cot. At sixteen hundred hours he reported to another old Warrior who tested his balance, strength, and coordination and finally sparred with him.

"You'll do," the old Warrior finally admitted. "I understand you're going to live with the humans."

"For a time."

"I've fought them. Most of them are small and slow and soft, but some of them have spirit." He stroked a scar that ran from his forehead to his right cheek.

"I'll remember that." Brod spread his arms . When the old Warrior spread and lowered his arms Brod lowered his arms and returned to the room. After evening rations and water he became bored and strolled to the desk where a different old Warrior sat.

"Do we have access to computers? I need to learn all I can about humans."

"The last door on the left down that hall." The old Warrior pointed with his chin.

The room held thirty computers in three rows with only two other Huer working. Brod stepped to the nearest computer and sat before it. When he pulled up "Human" a list of options appeared. He chose "History" and spent the next three hours in a mixture of amusement and disbelief. Apparently, humans had spent ages concerned with the color of each others' skins or something called religion. In many places they'd replicated parts of Huer history. They'd had holdings ruled by force, roving Warriors who were often thieves, and some parts of their world were still being ruled by leaders who would've profitted centuries earlier.

Their present government was ruled by heads of corporations, what seemed a class of Administrators but with little apparent training for the work, and men who were elected. This last group was a mixed lot. Some were idealists trying to make their ideals into reality. Others were apparently ideologues who believed fervently in their own rightness. The most disturbing were those who seeemed to have no principles, no goals except their own advancement, and Brod wondered that any supposedly intelligent race could be so gullible. While those scavengers might pretend to be idealists or ideologues, their drive for self-interest always betrayed them.

The history was, of course, an overview and Brod had no way of knowing what prejudices had skewed it.

He had a more immediate need so he typed in "military behavior." The computer suggested an odd phrase, "Military Courtesy." He chose that option and learned humans were apparently more conscious of military rank than the Huer. Whenever a human saw another of superior rank he saluted, touching the backs of his fingertips to his forehead while standing stiffly at "attention." The word seemed to have a very different meaning, for a human or Huer standing in such a position would be very vulnerable. He resolved to practice this odd custom if he found time alone.

Humans had other strange customs. A superior officer was always addressed as "sir" or "ma'am" depending upon whether the superior was a male or a female. He hoped he could tell the difference. It was very confusing. Apparently humans believed in displays of deference to superior officers, while a Huer knew who his commander was but showed his respect by doing his own work well. He'd been a weapons officer but had relied upon the Techs who maintained the weapons as much as he'd relied upon his commander to make the proper decisions. The commander, for his part, relied upon his weapons officer, his Navigator, his helm, and all the Techs and Warriors under his command.

When it was necessary to visit a strange planet, each Warrior had to be constantly alert, for himself and for the pack, for his survival and that of the pack depended upon each Huer doing his work well.

Apparently the human customs worked well for them but it would require some adjustment for Brod. His work was going to be harder than he'd thought. He'd assumed that it would be enough to do his assignments well, but now he had to carry them out while remembering all the odd alien traditions that made up so much of what humans called "military courtesy."

Chapter 5

Li's upper back was sore and his feet itched terribly. Glancing around, he saw the medication lock still in his arm. He'd just located the control that raised the bed below his upper body when a gray-haired nurse carried in a tray.

"We don't want you moving around much," he said. "We especially don't want you using your left arm."

"Is there any way to stop the itching in my toes?"

"We can try acupuncture but the sensation should pass in a day or two. The doctor should be in to see you within an hour. He's still working on another patient."

After glancing at the empty bed, Li asked, "Where is Sanchez?"

"He was released his morning."

"What time is it?"

"It's about thirteen hundred hours."

The nurse raised the upper part of the bed until Li was sitting up and set a tray on a table he moved over Li's lower body.

The meal was actually quite good; tea, sushi, and a seaweed salad. As he ate, Li discovered he also felt a tingling sensation in his upper back and chest, a feeling that became almost painful the time or two he tried to move his left arm.

The doctor arrived as the nurse carried away the tray. He nodded to Li and sat down in the chair facing the bed. "How are you feeling, Commodore?"

"Fine, except for the itching in my feet and toes."

"You're one of the two worst types of patients. The worst are those who complain about everything. Conversations with them never contain any useful medical information." The doctor leaned forward and poured himself a glass of icewater. "In fact, conversations with them make one wish for the occasional medical misadventure. You stoic types are no more informative but at least you aren't as annoying. Is the itching more like a tingling, a burning sensation, or somewhere between?"

"Not really painful, just a really irritating, itchy feeling. I'd like to be able to scratch them."

"We could drug you or use acupuncture to relieve the discomfort but if you're able to deal with it I'd rather be able to follow the healing progress. Let the nurse know if the discomfort becomes worse. Now, how about your back and chest?"

"Just more discomfort. I only experienced anything like pain when I moved the arm."

"We had to break your clavicle and re-set it and injected you with a sort of genetic reminder to your clavicle and the tendon. The clavicle should heal pretty quickly but there's no reason to strain it. The same is true with your tendon. Both should be ready for light exercise in the next week or so."

"That long?"

"We've been spoiled. Your father, in his teens, would have worn a sling and taken longer to heal. Perhaps your son, at your age, will be able to go into an office, have the same thing done as a minor procedure, and walk out fully healed. Or, perhaps not. Medicine continues to advance but the human frame hasn't changed noticeably in thousands of years. Until you're better I want you to stay off your feet and to move the left arm as little as possible."

After the doctor left Li returned to his study of Huer. The hypnoconditioning had the added benefit that he became less aware of the itching.

* * *

Early the second day after the operation he began to study Valek. Again, learning a language was a look into the minds of the speakers. Even among human languages there were words or expressions that could only be translated with difficulty and a few not at all. Huer, he found was a very straightforward, rather plain-spoken language. Valek was more subtle, with much ambiguity. While capable of great precision, it more commonly was used in areas of imprecision, which had to be intentional. It was the sort of language a subject people might use to communicate ideas and information as a sort of subtext.

Three days later they removed the dressings from his feet and he could clearly see where the toes had been grafted – the new toes were paler than the rest of his feet but he was able to flex them. The sensations in his left chest, back, and shoulder had also vanished but he was told to wait another two days before exercising his left arm and hand.

For his first trips to the exercise room he wore very soft boots. The new toes would take a little extra care, since they had no calluses. Even so, he was still left more time than he needed.

A week after his surgery he received a note from the hospital director. He would be able to see Singh and could talk to Bachman's doctor. He let the computer feed the layout of the hospital into his comcard. Since it was already sixteen thirty-five when he received the message he would wait until the next day. He quickly fired off a message: Should he be in uniform?

The response was immediate: He should wear civilian clothing.

Frowning, he set the comcard on the table. Apparently, Singh and Bachman had experienced so much uniforms might trigger painful memories. He'd considered the possibility but hoped the men could recover.

* * *

Ghopal Singh stood when Li entered the room and probably would've saluted had either man been wearing a uniform. He looked fit and he had both eyes again. "Good morning, Commodore. Congratulations."

"Let's sit down," Li said, "I've just walked a good three kilometers. How are they treating you?"

Singh dropped into his chair. "Rather like an armed bomb. I presume you know I've been retired?"

"I hadn't known. They made it difficult to see either you or Bachman." Li sat in the chair facing Singh's. "I thought you'd become regarded as a planetary treasure."

Singh snorted. "More like the insane uncle. I'm afraid that's a fair assessment. You know the worst part of it?"

Li shook his head.

"The worst part is knowing I'm mad and there's nothing I can do about it. Rationally, I understand everything but I still want to see every lobster in the universe torn apart and their twitching body parts set afire. I'm subject to sudden fits of rage. They disturb me as much as they frighten the doctors and nurses. I wish I had your strength."

A nurse entered with cups of tea. Both men accepted a cup and waited until the nurse had left the room.

After a sip of tea, Li stared into Singh's eyes. "I have no more strength than you. I have no idea what you endured, but I'm sure it would have done to me what it did to you. Have you seen Bachman?"

"No, the doctors told me it would be bad for both of us. I was able to speak to his doctor. He's a totally broken man. The doctor told me some of what he'd endured, and I suspect either of us would've wound up the same way."

Singh stared into some middle distance for over a minute before he blinked and said, "I understand you're hoping to command another ship."

"Hoping for one, but I don't know if they'll permit me."

"I'll hope for it, too. And I hope you get to kill lobsters. For all of us."

Li nodded. "We'll first have to see if I can get command of a ship."

"If anyone can, you're the one," Singh said.

"If there's anything I can do for you—"

"I've already told you the only thing I want."

Li stood. Singh had also gotten to his feet. "I wish you well, Ghopal Singh."

As Li walked out of the room he glanced at his comcard. At least Bachman's doctor was in the same building, although he should probably have worn more comfortable shoes for the walk. He followed the directions to the end of the corridor to a cross-corridor and a lift, which carried him two levels up. Turning left, he followed the corridor to a cluster of offices.

He reported to a young man behind a desk and was asked to wait. Waiting rooms bore a dreary similarity to each other. The furniture was nondescript and barely comfortable. He shared the room with half a dozen men and women and no conversation, everyone studying his or her comcard. Li took out his own comcard and checked the news.

Before he could initiate a real search the door to the office opened and a nurse called, "Commodore Li."

Li followed her down a corridor to an office lined with books. The doctor was either an antiquarian, a sensualist like Sauvage, or pretentious. After staring at the spine of one of "the books" he drew it out and opened it; six crystals lay clamped inside the cover.

"I've learned most people expect to see books," said a voice at the door. A slender man with graying hair walked around the desk and sat down. "I'm Doctor Bose. I take it you're Commodore Li and you'd like to see Erich Bachman."

Li sat in the chair facing the desk. It was a notch up the comfort scale from those in the waiting room. "That is correct."

Bose clasped his hands and leaned forward. "Commodore, I don't want you to think I'm keeping Bachman hidden away to add isolation to the other torments he's survived. The only word that approaches an adequate description of his torture is 'diabolical.' It would be pointless to say his treatment was inhuman because his captors were't human, but only the most vile, twisted human could have conceived of such a torture.

"The effect was to destroy almost entirely his self-image. We're using drugs and sonotherapy just to keep him from killing himself."

"What did they do to him?" Li urgently needed to know and desperately needed not to know.

"They took you and Singh away but kept the others together. Each one was interrogated and each was given a password. They were to tell no one else the password. Then, little by little, they were provided less food and water. When the crew were sure they were going to die, they were told to choose among themselves who would be taken away. Volokoff was the weakest and she volunteered. The rations increased and they were even given meat. Then it started all over again.

"The next time, they chose lots. Ensign Chin was taken out and the rations improved again. The pattern kept repeating but your crew kept their discipline. They didn't fight among themselves and each who died went bravely. Finally, it was only Bachman and Sadar. During all this, the interrogations continued and they were asked, again and again, for the paswords of the dead crew memnbers.

"Sadar had contracted pneumonia and finally she asked Bachman to kill her, certain the ChiTseTsi would kill her as painfully as possible. Bachman stunned her with a blow from his fist and choked her to death."

Li had trouble speaking through a strained throat. "I can understand how Bachman might feel but it would have been a mercy to Sadar. Both Singh and I can attest that such a death would've been welcome."

"You and Singh were the 'controls.' They used different approaches on you. You survived simply because you had such a strong instinct for survival and endurance. Singh fought them with his rage. He never stopped wanting to inflict pain on them, to avenge himself and the rest of the crew. It's ironic that what saved his life drove him mad. But the other five were the group the ChiTseTsi were most interested in.

"After they'd hauled Sadar's body away, the rations improved again. Finally, Bachman was taken in for interrogation and asked the passwords of the others again. When he couldn't give them, the interrogator showed him the preserved faces of the dead. Their skulls had been broken and the brains removed and served to the remaining prisoners along with the rest of their bodies."

The doctor opened a drawer in his desk, took out two glasses and a bottle, filled the glasses, and replaced the bottle. "You look as though you need something medicinal, and I know I do. I'm sure hearing this story is like watching some sort of catastrophe. You want to look away but you can't. And telling it is like explaining to someone how their loved ones died painfully." Bose took a deep drink of the colorless liquid.

When Li followed suit he felt liquid fire race down his throat and he almost gagged but after a few minutes he felt at least slightly numbed.

Bose cleared his throat and went on. "It reminds me of some

experiments done nearly seven hundred years ago. Psychologists were trying to find if learning could be ingested, so they would maze-train worms, then kill them and feed them to other worms. That seems senseless today but the investigation of intelligence was in its infancy. But to do the same things to a sentient, sapient species—" The doctor finished the liquid in his glass.

Li observed Bose had begun to sweat and Li couldn't tell if it was from the alcohol or from tension. "I feel partially responsible. Not for what the ChiTseTsi did but for condoning it, even if I didn't know what I was permitting. I voted for the Peace candidate in the last election. I won't bore you with my justifications, but I believed every species was amenable to reason. Now, I'm far from sure of that."

Li finished his own liquor and placed the glass on the desk.

"If you still wish to see Backman, I can let you see him through a one-way wall. I'm afraid the sight of you or Singh would cause a setback, force us to increase the drugs to even more dangerous levels."

"What's his prognosis, Doctor Bose?"

"I'd like to believe in miracles, Commodore, but I'm a skeptic. His system has already begun to shut down. He must be fed interveinously because he refuses to eat. Just the sight of food causes him to start screaming unless he's so drugged he can't safely be fed. We can exercise his muscles electronically but what's the point? He has no quality of life. All we can do is use the drugs and sonotherapy to keep him from pain. Sooner or later he will suffer a fatal episode and all we can do is make his passing as painless as possible. I've already given orders that if he suffers an infarction or a stroke he not be revived."

"Yes, Doctor, I'd like to see him."

Bose took two ampules from his desk. "You might want a taste of ginger and mint." He handed one to Li then twisted the top off the other and squirted the liquid into his mouth. "I almost never drink, and never did at work—until this case. I'd prefer it not become general knowledge."

Li shot the liquid into his mouth and guessed, from the taste, it would hide more than a drink or two of alcohol.

Both men stood and Bose led the way down a hallway to what appeared to be another hospital room. Inside, however, sat only a nurse with a computer, watching the left wall.

When he turned his head, Li could see the next room. He barely recognized Bachman to be the figure sitting and staring at the wall as though he could see through it. His blond hair had been cleaned and combed but his pale blue eyes were vacant, lifeless. His posture revealed nothing and the features of his face were slack, without a trace of animation.

"Good morning, nurse," Bose said. "Has the patient shown any signs of agitation?"

"No, Doctor. He hasn't moved in the last hour."

Li stared at Bachman's empty shell. With a pang he remembered how the man had been a stickler for protocol but with a wry sense of humor. He'd been looking forward to getting married at the end of the cruise. It was like looking at a dead body, except the body still lived but the spirit had died, and it seemed sadder than seeing the remains of a body in repose. "Thank you, Doctor."

Deeply effected, Li paced the long way back to his own room. He was sure the service had contacted the families of each of the officers who'd been with him, but he felt more was needed.

To each of the families he composed and wrote a letter. In each case he thanked the family for the service of their son or daughter, or their partner, in each case remarking on some quality he most appreciated and recalling some incident he found memorable. He simply wrote the letters in Chinese for Chin and Ling. He was forced to use a translation program to convert Borde's into Hindi, Sadar's into Arabic, and Volokoff's into Russian.

The letters to the families of Singh and Bachman were even more difficult. At least Singh's family could see and even visit with Singh. He expressed his admiration for Singh's courage and sacrifice and expressed the hope he could recover enough to return to them.

Bachman's letter was the most difficult of all. He was sure

the family had been spared the details of Bachman's ordeal and he had no desire to throttle hope, no matter how futile. He simply expressed his pride in having served with him, again adding some personal remembrances. That letter had to be translated into German.

Few items or communications were actually shipped. The letters would be sent electronically to the nearest express office where facsimilies would be printed and delivered, Copies would, of course, be read and perhaps censored by the security office.

He still had time to call his mother, who answered on the third tone.

"Eaglet! How are you?"

"Very well," he lied. What had happened to his crew was his burden and not to be borne by his mother. "They repaired my feet, and my back and shoulder have never been better. Tomorrow I fly to Delhi to report to Rear Admiral Tamaguchi to see what the service has in store for me. How are you?"

"Enjoying my time. It seems that your niece, Chu-Hua, like the chrysanthemum for which she is named, is spreading her petals. Perhaps we may expect another age of miracles. She has discovered gymnastics, so perhaps she is spreading wings. You should see her fly. Unfortunately, her brother doesn't seem destined to disappoint your brother."

Li chuckled. "I'm glad the family has another eaglet. Now, perhaps, you'll stop calling me that."

"I suppose you've gotten your wings back and now you're an eagle. Did the man you wanted to speak with turn out to be a friend?"

"He did. And I think he's done me a great favor. If I'm able, I'll visit you again before I'm reassigned."

For a moment they endured an awkward silence, then Chen-Chi said, "I'm sure you have things you must be doing. I'll look forward to your next visit."

* * *

The ship was one of the old Huer Starstrider class that had been converted to a freighter, with cramped quarters for the crew and, unlike a ship of the first-line, had no name but only a number. The commander knew of Brod's mission so he kept the air slightly thinner and the gravity slightly greater than usual. This would give Brod a temporary advantage on a human ship. Brod's major task was to learn Trade Common well enough to easily converse, and he spent hours each cycle at the hypnoconditioner and its crystals. The hard part wasn't replicating the sounds, although he had trouble with some of the softer noises, but understanding new concepts.

The hierarchical structure of the humans seemed so illogical they were hard to digest, while the implied behavior between males and females seemed scandlous. Sometimes, to get away from beating his head against alien concepts he relieved the weapons officer. While, as a freighter, it lacked the heavier armament of a warship the old hulk still carried a laser and a dozen missiles.

Sometimes the voyage seemed very quick, as he realized how much he had to learn and how little time he had for that part of the mission and other times, when he tried to make sense of the noises he was hearing and learning to make, it seemed interminable.

The journey was nearing its seventieth cycle when the ship's alarm sounded and they dropped into normal space. Brod could always tell when they went into or came out of the time wrinkles the ship created; the sensation was like a sudden fall in the dark, lasting only a split-second but still disagreeable, and it always made his ears twitch.

By the time he'd reached the berth for the shuttle he'd felt it twice more as the Navigator and the helm adjusted their position. A pilot and two Warriors met him at the entrance to the shuttle. As they took their seats, Brod stowed his travel chest and sat behind the pilot to watch over his shoulder at the display.

The shuttle lurched as it was ejected from its berth and Brod scanned the blackness ahead until he could discern the human ship, which was not a deep space vessel, lacking any drive engines but those for sublight traveling. It was a plain ship, almost ugly, a column of spheres held together by a rigid metal framework. As they neared the second sphere from one end

Brod could see the ring to which the shuttle was being drawn, felt the shock as the rings were energized and clamped together with a clang. He slapped the release on his harness, retrieved his traveling chest, stood, and walked back to the opening, which dilated.

Three humans wearing their gray uniforms stood inside their ship. Brod studied them closely. Two of them had long noses and were a tan color, the other was brown, and all of them were shorter the Shkogar. He'd forgotten how small their ears were and how low they were set on their heads. He also hadn't remembered they had four fingers and a thumb rather than the three-fingered, thumbed hands of the Huer. He searched their collars and shoulders and saw no badges of rank, so he didn't need to salute them.

One of the Warriors with him handed one of the humans a guass rifle and a pistol, the other handed over an autorifle and a case of ammunition. The third human held out its arms for the traveling chest, which Brod handed to him.

The brown human, who held the chest with what appeared to be some effort, asked, "Are you Commander Brod?"

"I am Brod."

"Please, follow me."

Brod followed the humans through a door out of the airlock and, through a port, watched as the opening to the Huer shuttle closed. The humans led the way along a passage and Brod was aware of a strange smell. It was neither pleasant nor the opposite, simply different. At the end of the passage the door opened into a circular room. Brod had to lower his head at the doorway.

Another human in uniform, much smaller than his escorts, stood in the middle of the room and Brod quickly observed the small metal tabs at the human's collar. He strode to just outside arm's reach of the human, halted in the awkward position required, and touched his forehead with the backs of his fingertips.

"At ease," the human replied in a high-pitched voice as it returned the salute. This was another deceptive human expression. It meant he could place his hands behind his back and spread his legs slightly.

"I am Captain Ai-Li Gupta. I presume you are Commander Brod."

Brod kept his face expressionless. Apparently he had either been given some rank by the humans or the Huer ambassador had claimed the rank for him. He fought a smile as he realized the captain's attention had been drawn to the claw at his side. "I am Brod."

"Welcome aboard, Commander Brod. Have you eaten?"

"No, sir."

The captain smiled. "It's no, ma'am. I'm female. I'd be pleased to have you share breakfast with my officers and I." She turned and led the way down another corridor to a small room with a table and chairs that looked flimsy. Three other humans followed them into the room and took places in the chairs around the table, leaving an empty chair beside the Captain's. Brod sat down in it carefully, relaxed a little when it seemed capable of bearing his weight.

A crewman without rank badges entered carrying a flat piece of metal with five small cups filled with some steaming liquid. The crewman set a cup before each of the officers and Brod, then left, returning moments later with plates of food on the flat plate.

Seeing the humans sip from their cups, Brod raised the cup to his lips. The liquid was hot, but not unbearably so. He sipped at it and wondered if the bitter liquid was some sort of medicine, although the humans seemed to find the taste pleasant.

Captain Gupta introduced him to the other humans at the table but the names meant nothing to him and the ranks almost as little. He sampled the different colored foods. Like the smell of the human ship, they were simply different.

The human introduced as a commander asked, "Have you ever been on a Terran ship before?"

It took Brod a moment to realize 'Terran' was another word for human. "No, this is my first time." After a moment, he asked, "What is the name of your ship?"

"It's *SLC 603 Hanoi*," the captain replied. "We may have to put two beds together for you for docking. I'm afraid we have no chairs your size. The head and neck support would be too low."

The female who wore the lieutenant's badges said, "You don't seem to be wearing any insignia of rank."

"They aren't needed on a Huer ship," Brod replied.

The captain smiled again. "Are all Huer so talkative?"

Because the comment was in a still unfamiliar language, Brod considered the question before he saw the humor. He smiled back, lips closed. "Some."

The captain and the lieutenant commander both grinned broadly and Brod stiffened for a moment.

Apparently sensitive even to foreign reactions, the captain asked, "What's wrong?"

Brod paused before he answered. "A Huer who shows his teeth risks losing them." After another pause he added, "It's a little difficult to adjust to different ways."

The captain smiled, carefully keeping her lips closed. "I'll remember that the next time I meet a Huer."

Brod held out his hand, palm up, then realized the humans probably wouldn't understand the gesture. "This would probably mean the same as a shrug does to many humans. I was just going to say I doubt it matters. Most Huer who thought about it for a moment would probably be amused."

The commander nodded. "It's easier to expect and tolerate cultural differences from someone who looks very different from us than someone who looks just like us."

The captain drew out a card and looked at it. "We should be ready to dock at the station in about twelve hours. Would you like a tour of the ship?"

"Yes, ma'am, I would."

The captain let each officer display their specialties. The biggest surprise was the amount of space given each crewman. While the Huer were larger, the human passages were wider than those on a Huer ship and almost as high. Brod seldom had to crouch to avoid bumping his head and never had to turn sidewise. Even more surprising was that each officer on the ship had his or her own small room and there were two barracks, one for males and the other for females. To Brod, this suggested humans could not bear to see the opposite sex without a desire to mate, leaving him to wonder how they could work together without being distracted.

The laser batteries and missile launchers were almost the same as those on a Huer ship and the repulsors reminded him of older Huer models but developed in a different way. When he entered the command room the commander, who was the weapons officer, showed him the screens and sensor arrays. He stood beside the human and watched him constantly recheck weapons readiness and watch the sensor indicators.

The screen was similar to that on a Huer ship but the symbols were different and the numbers meaningless to him. He'd learned the meaning of human numbers but hadn't yet adjusted to their use of a base ten rather than base eight system.

He pointed to each symbol in turn and learned the meaning of each. The functions were the same as those on a Huer ship and the symbols were easy to memorize but the numbers still frustrated him. Besides the difference of a base ten system, the distances measured were unfamiliar to him. Their kilometer was, for instance, was about two thirds of a *shoka*. His only consolation was that part of the difference could be absorbed through hypnoconditioning and he already knew the basics as he knew his own hands.

The commander glanced at him. "Are Huer ships' instruments laid out like ours?"

"Very close. We're not so different."

"No offense, Mister Brod, but you look very different from the people I serve with."

"Just Brod. And we both have two arms and two legs, a pair of eyes, and only limited attention. We both place the most critical indicators and controls in the most accessible places."

The human moved his head up and down, which Brod guessed to be an affirmative.

By the time the human was replaced by another officer, Brod had largely mastered the new system. As the commander turned the controls over to his replacement, he said, "Time to rest. We work in eight bour watches. I was already on duty when we picked you up. We should be at the station just before the lieutenant, here, is ready to go off duty."

"Would the lieutentant be offended if I remained here to learn?"

"Don't you Huer ever tire?"

"Our days are twenty-seven point three of your hours and we work in two watches on our ships."

"We adjusted our schedules because we've learned that after eight hours the loss of efficiency and judgement increases the risk of accidents."

"That may be true of humans but we are not human and our cycles are different."

"As you wish. Lieutenant, please help Brod become more familiar with our systems."

Brod silently watched the lieutenant monitor the power flow to the weapons and the repulsor field. After an hour he said, "You are a female, are you not?"

The lieutenant looked closely at his face and finally smiled. "I was the last time I looked. Why?"

"It isn't easy to know the differences between you humans. Many of you cut the fur on your heads very closely and, while you are proportioned differently the differences are subtle to another species. I doubt if you could tell the difference between a female Huer and myself, in most cases. But you do smell different."

The lieutenant's coloring changed, reddening. "I hope I smell better than the commander."

"Not better, not worse. Just different."

"I doubt you're going to flatter many women with your conversation."

Brod frowned. "I don't understand. Why would I want to flatter anyone? The use of conversation is to convey information." He thought about conversations he'd had. "Sometimes to share humor, but that's information of a sort, too."

After a few moments the lieutenant asked, "Are Huer ships like ours?"

"Similar. Our ceilings are slightly higher but the crew

quarters smaller. We have a single barracks. Equipment is stowed much the same way and we have similar weapons and sensor systems. I'm not an Engineer but I suppose the engines are also very similar."

"Does that mean your ships have an all-male crew?"

"No, Warriors are typically all males but many of the Techs, Navigators and most of the best Pilots are female."

"Then…how do you…?"

"Humans are among the few species we've encountered who have no mating season. Except in mating season, the females are simply shipmates."

"But if you have a mating season, how do you keep ships…?"

"There are drugs that will delay the mating season. There are even drugs that stop it completely until the drug is withheld. We prefer not to use them because there are certain penalties. They interfere with concentration and sometimes affect mood."

"If I may ask, have you seen combat?"

"Yes, with the Valek."

"Are their ships as formidable as I've heard?"

"I don't know what you've heard." Brod glanced at the boards, reassured himself all systems were functioning properly. "They look different but they function much like ours. Their sensors and armament are very similar. I've heard they're introducing a new class of ship, the Stormbird class, which is a dedicated space-fighting vessel. Most of their commanders are able but unimaginative."

"What about our ships." Even from an alien throat Brod recognized a bit of tension in the question.

"Human ships tend to be larger but well-crewed. I'd rather fight with a human ship than against it. Some of your commanders are very capable."

The lieutenant glaced up. "You seem familiar with the weapons console. Was that your position?"

"Usually. I did command a ship twice. On my first few cruises I was, of course, apprenticed."

"Don't you have an academy?"

"No, we go to schools. At first, we are taught basics then, as we progress, we are introduced to other areas of study. After six years we choose those studies which interest us most, We spend most of our time on those pursuits, although we must allot at least a minimum to other studies. At twelve, we apply to the sept of our choice in our chosen caste."

"What's a sept?"

"It is similar to what you humans call a clan, but it is voluntary. But within the sept are the same bonds of—almost family—as your clans."

"What if the sept you've chosen doesn' t accept you?"

"There are at least four septs in each caste. If none of them accept you, you apply to some other caste. If you are unable to join a caste, you are assigned a caste for which you are suited. Within many castes are septs which must accept you."

"But it must be hard to give up your dreams. If you really wanted to be a Warrior and have to accept something less, it would be terrible." The lieutenant made a gesture Brod couldn't interpret.

"We believe passion leads the spirit. If you do not have enough passion, you must then do your best work at whatever you have been assigned to do, and no caste is less than another. The compensation you will receive is similar and you can gain the respect of others by being worthy. A worthy Farmer or Factory Worker has the same standing as a worthy Warrior or Director. Do you humans all have what you want?"

"Of course not." The lieutenant studied the board very intently. "It's just that your system is so different from ours." After a pause, she said, "So, you only have basic training for your first few cruises?"

"That is correct, and a Warrior is expected to be able to do all those things a worthy Warrior is fitted to do. I have an aptitude for weapons, while my younger brother is most suited, by ability and temprament, to command a ship. But we are also expected to be ready to replace any other Warrior on the ship. Both my brother, Shkogar, and I have been on exploration teams on new worlds."

"What's it like?"

"It can be dangerous but it's always exciting. The smallest organism can be the most deadly—bacteria, spores, incredibly small parasites. Larger organisms can be seen and fought, but it's the ones you can't fight that are the most lethal."

* * *

The ship was drawn into its berth at the hub and Brod joined the crew as they disembarked, carrying his traveling chest. A human wearing the markings of a captain met him and directed him to a shuttle.

The seats in the shuttle were small and Brod was seated in the first row and granted an extra seat and given extenders for the safety harness. The flight started with a small bump and Brod wished he could see outside the shuttle. The sensation of motion built up slowly until they experienced some turbulence, meaning they'd entered Earth's atmosphere.

Less than two dozen Huer had actually visited Earth and Brod was disappointed he couldn't see the planet grow in a port. Finally the shuttle settled and slid to a stop.

A light flashed at the front of the cabin and the others began to unbuckle their harnesses so Brod freed himself and took his chest out of the bay in the front. When the door opened he blinked at the brilliant sunlight. The skies of Earth were blue, with none of the greenish tinge of Huerda. A structure was wheeled to the door and he trod down the steps to see old Ruhl waiting for him. Both Huer spread their arms, fingers straight, and Ruhl smiled as broadly as possible without showing teeth. "Welcome!"

"It's good to see you."

Ruhl gestured at a car half again as large as most of the vehicles around it. "I thought I'd meet you here, take you to the embassy, and get you fed a good Huer meal and let you get some sleep before I take you to the base. How are things on Huerda?"

"The same." They walked briskly to the hovercar and Brod stowed his chest in the back of the car, his eyes constantly scanning. From what he could see of the buildings in the distance, human architecture was generally similar to that of the Huer, although they used more metal and, off the black, slightly resilient surface on which they walked, Earth seemed to have more trees than most parts of Huerda.

"I'm afraid Earth beer has little flavor or body, and most of it is pale, but it's better than water." Ruhl opened the door and gestured for Brod to enter. As soon as their straps clicked the engine started and the car rose and moved forward. Through a glass, Brod could see the human driver lean back in his seat.

"The car is operated electronically," Rhul said. "The driver is only there in case something goes wrong."

"What does the human military need to teach me?"

"I don't think they know, themselves. They will want to see if you're disciplined. I will warn you—they will try to humiliate you. They will probably give you absurd orders. They may even attempt to intimidate you. Humans are very strange. They will also want to be sure you're familiar with their measurements of time and distance, and with their military customs."

* * *

Wearing a new uniform and boots and with his hospital discharge papers in his pocket, Li reported to the office of Rear Admiral Tamaguchi. The receptionist appeared not to know he'd been assigned to Tamaguchi's command and seemed to have trouble finding his records. He was left sitting in the outer office an hour and a half before the receptionist announced Rear Admiral Tadashi Tamaguchi would be delighted to see him.

"Commodore Li Wing Hua," Li said, as he saluted the rear admiral, "reporting as ordered, sir."

Tamaguchi was shorter than Li but stocky, with coarse black hair cut short and a scowl the man probably cultivated. "I'm sorry for the confusion and the delay, Commodore. What may I do for you?" Despite the courteous words, he kept the scowl and his voice came out in a growl.

"I'm reporting for duty, sir." He drew the discharge papers from the hospital out of his pocket and set them on the desk. "I've been released and my leave is ended."

Tamaguchi stared at the screen on his desk. "I see you posted letters to the families of the men and women who were captured with you. That was quite unnecessary."

"Sir, it was necessary for me. There was nothing in the

letters that could remotely be considered confidential, but as the commanding officer of the group, I was responsible for those men and women and it was my duty to inform the families I shared their sense of loss, that those people had been exemplary."

Tamaguchi stared at Li as though this was some novel idea that had never occurred to him. "I saw nothing in the letters I would call indiscreet but I suggest that, in the future, you clear any such communications with your superiors first. I've permitted the letters to be posted."

He returned his attention to the screen. "I see you're qualified to command deep-space craft. We have no vacancies at either the command or second-in-command levels. You are probably qualified to teach at the academy but we'd have to have you cleared by a psych evaluation."

The admiral stared at Li as though dissecting him with his eyes. "I'll put you on detached duty. Check with my office weekly to see if there is an opening for you." Another quick study of the screen. "I see you have several requests for interviews from the media and invitations to gatherings held by government officials. We can dismiss the media requests but it might benefit the service if you were to attend some of those gatherings. You realize, of course, your experiences and those of the men and women under your command are considered secret."

"I do, sir." Looking at Tamaguchi, he suddenly knew the man had never been in deep space and, quite probably, had never commanded a ship. Tamaguchi was only another cog in an impersonal machine and, quite possibly, someone's political lapdog. "If that is all, sir…"

The admiral tapped the screen. "I'll forward a list of invitations from members of the Council to your comcard. "Yes, Commodore, that will be all." He didn't stand to return the salute.

Walking away from the meeting, Li felt the need for exercise. He supposed that, during the war, the service had been forced to expand and some officers had risen past their level of competetence. Tamaguchi would probably remain a rear admiral until he retired.

In the gym, Li warmed up with Tai Chi exercises then

attacked a punching bag, taking out his frustration on something that couldn't feel pain. When he worked with weights he noticed his left arm was weaker and needed more attention than his right. After putting ten kilometers on a stationary bicycle he showered and swam ten laps, allowing himself to slow steadily. By the time he'd showered again and changed into his uniform he'd developed a healthy appetite.

He ate in the officer's mess, sharing little more than a table with other captains and commodores.

He preferred a small apartment at the base to the housing available. Most of the officers who were assigned houses had family. He had no one with whom to share his quarters and few possessions to take up space, so an apartment was more than sufficient.

In his quarters he used his comcard to activate the screen on the wall and scanned down the list of invitations. One immediately caught his attention. One of the leaders of the Social Egalitarian party was holding a reception for Ruhl, the Huer ambassador. That, at least, should prove interesting. Noting the reception was to be held in three days, he sent an acceptance.

With little else to do for the next three days he kept fit, purchased a formal dress uniform, and studied the files on the Huer. Even with the hypnoconditioning there were details to study and social protocols to learn. He was less worried about Huer customs than the minutiae of human social customs. He also had to arrange for the use of a car.

Another treat was taking long walks through the base housing complex. Long walks were, of course, almost impossible on a ship and the exercise machines, although they measured everything from vital signs to the number of steps he took, were less relaxing than actually traveling on one's own two feet through a maze of streets and the occasional haven of a park. The weather was crisp but not cold and he took pleasure in again inhabiting a body capable of walking painlessly.

On the evening of the party he dressed carefully, then drove to the government complex in which the reception was to be held. The line of cars seemed to stretch to infinity, then he was asked for his identification and given a retinal scan and a full-body scan. Apparently, security was intense and he wondered whether they were more concerned about weapons or recorders. Finally he was able to turn the car over to a valet and walked through the huge double doors of the building.

Palaces, it seemed, were still in vogue for powerful people. Just inside the door he was met by a tall man wearing very traditional formal attire. "May I introduce you, sir?"

"I'd rather you didn't."

"As you wish, sir." The man stepped back to wait for the next guest, nicely hiding his irritation.

Strolling from the antechamber into a much larger room, Li glanced around. The place had a high ceiling and a marble floor and the walls seemed covered with velvet and punctuated with portraits. A handful of chairs that looked both fragile and uncomfortable were scattered about the room, but Li hadn't come to look at the room or its furniture. The Valek ambassador had already arrived and stood alone near one of the walls, wearing a short black jacket over a rust-colored shirt that looked like silk, black pants, and highly polished black shoes or boots. The Valek held a glass of some clear liquid in one hand and an expression on his face that suggested everyone else in the room smelled bad. He noticed Li and they exchanged curt nods.

Further along the same wall stood his host, Madhavdas Nair, dressed in a dark blue brocade robe with a collar and cuffs of lace. All the men he saw wore similar robes ranging from sedate colors and simple weaves to some that suggested their wearers were color-blind and most wore some sort of ornate collar or neckwear and plain boots or shoes. His own plain black uniform with the knee-length jacket, decorated only with his rank insignia and decorations stood out in the crowd.

In the ebb and flow of the human tidal pool, Li drifted nearer the Councilor until they stood facing each other. "Thank you for your invitation."

Nair nodded. "I thank you for attending. You are not an easy man to reach."

"Service business and a few minor repairs. And I was most

anxious to meet the Huer ambassador."

"Ambassador Ruhl tends to arrive fashionably late." Nair looked at his decorations. "I'd hoped the Council would award you another medal but the Peace party seems to want as few reminders of the war as possible."

"Being back and in uniform is all the award I could want."

The man who'd asked to introduce him walked out of the antechamber. "His excellency, Ambassador Ruhl of Huerda," he announced.

Ruhl stepped through the door to a torrent of applause and Li glanced at the Valek ambassador, who maintained the same pose he'd adopted earlier, and Li noticed the liquid in the glass was still at the same level it'd been when he first noticed the Valek.

The Huer was surrounded by humans, few of whom spread their arms and even fewer kept their fingers straight. Ruhl responded to each of these greetings, mimicking the greeting and returning their smiles, often showing teeth. The ambassador seemed to be amused.

Li excused himself and accepted a glass of fruit juice from one of the men carrying trays. From a distance he watched until the crowd around the Huer had finally thinned.

Ruhl had made his way to the corner of the wall opposite the Valek ambassador, near a table. Like the Valek, the Huer had made no concessions to human fashion, wearing a dark red tunic bound by a wide leather belt and dark gray trousers bloused into boots that extended to mid-calf. He'd gotten a mug of beer, which he sometimes remembered to drink and appeared to be studying the humans with mild curiosity.

Li finished his juice, set the glass on the nearest table, and walked toward Ruhl. It was hard not to be intimidated. The Huer was over two meters tall and broadly built. His skin was the grayish color that suggested stone. Li approached and held out his arms, fingers extended, and smiled without showing his teeth.

Ruhl's eyes widened almost imperceptibly and he set his beer on an table then returned the greeting.

"I am Commodore Li, and I'm proud to meet you."

"I thought you looked familiar. The pictures they showed of you on the vid was of a younger man." Ruhl's voice was a rumble. "Will you share a drink with me?"

"I'd be pleased."

Ruhl raised his mug and held up two fingers to one of the men scurrying through the crowd carrying a tray of glasses. In under a minute the man approached with two mugs of beer. Li noticed that in the Huer's massive hand the mug looked like a cup.

Li took a deep drink while Ruhl drained his mug. "What you humans call beer is but a pale shadow of a good beer, but you mean well." He studied Li. "You look like a Warrior."

"I'm flattered."

Ruhl held out his right hand, palm up. "More importantly, you look like a worthy human. Warriors are only a caste, but a worthy human or Huer deserves respect." He'd moved so his back was against a wall, leaving a space beside him for Li.

"I would seem to be the dancing bear at this party," Ruhl rumbled.

"I don't understand."

"Ages ago, it was the custom of some of your peoples to have social gatherings and often they would bring dancing bears for entertainment. I seem to be the dancing bear here."

Li smiled. "I suspect I am another dancing bear. I just hope they don't expect us to dance together."

It took a moment for Li to realize the sound like distant thunder was Ruhl chuckling. He nodded toward the crowd. "I noticed you didn't take offence at the improper greetings."

Ruhl smiled. "I was amused. These people mean well, they just lack knowledge. Also," he gestured out at the men milling and gathered in clumps, "I found it amusing. Can you actually imagine them challenging me? I'm just a fat old Scholar but I could snap most of them like dry twigs."

"The only one who might think of challenging you is standing over there." He nodded toward the Valek ambassador.

"He's also about the only one who might stand a chance. But we're opponents, not enemies. We're too old to entertain the love of confrontation, unlike our younger Valek and Huer."

"I've been trying to learn about the Huer. You seem to have many qualities I appreciate."

"Do you have a command, a ship?"

"Not yet, but I intend to have a ship."

Ruhl studied his face, his shoulders, and his hands. "You will have a ship. Everything follows where passion leads. And when you get that ship, you may have a chance to learn the Huer better. We have a Warrior who is supposed to serve with your navy. I would want a worthy commander for him. I should warn you, however, that there are some qualities you might have trouble with."

"What would those be?"

"Unlike you humans, we Huer have a mating season. This is repeated about every eighteen of your months. During that time, he will not be available for service. He and his mate will have only one passion, and that one intense. It will last for about three of your weeks. Obviously, if you accepted him for your crew you would also have to accept his mate, but she's a teacher and a highly-regarded mathematician. The other possible difficulty will be that he will always wear his claw. It's what you'd call a knife. To a Huer Warrior, not to be able to wear his claw would be like denying what he is."

"If I'm given another command, I'd be honored to have such a Warrior as part of my crew. What's his name."

"He's called Brod."

"I'll keep that in mind."

Ruhl waved again at the waiter. "You humans are either very weak or very strong."

"How so?" Li took another drink of beer.

"You had an enemy and you made peace with it. Either you're too weak to destroy it or you're certain enough of your strength you did not need to defeat it."

"I'll have to consider that. Possibly both."

The shoal of people had begun to shift back and several approached the Huer and a few moved toward Li. He immediately recognized Madan Sharma.

"I'm pleased to meet you, Commodore," Sharma said. "You've made yourself more socially desirable by being difficult to reach. There will be a dinner at Prime Minister Xo Deshi's residence in two days. Will you be able to attend?"

Li's polite smile hid his thought that while one should meet one's possible friends, one must meet one's certain enemies. "I'd be pleased to attend. Will Ambassador Ruhl be there?"

"If he'll attend. I shall have to ask him. I regret we were late in sending out some of the invitations."

The Huer's hearing seemed to be uncanny and he said, from half a dozen paces away, "I'd be pleased to attend," He smiled, showing his teeth.

"As I said," Sharma tugged at the lace cuff of his left arm, "some of the invitations have been delayed. I'm sure, Ambassador Ruhl, that you understand how social errors can happen, even in the best-run offices."

"Of course, of course," Ruhl replied. Li observed Ruhl seemed to enjoy Sharma's discomfort almost as much as Li did.

Sharma's smile seemed to hurt his face as he said, "I'll look forward to seeing you both there. For now, please excuse me, I have to thank our host." He moved away in the direction of Nair.

Ruhl smiled at Li with his lips closed. "Neither he nor Xo had ever intended to invite me, and now he's wondering if he wanted to invite you. You know, of course, he intends to use this to garner favor and take away some of the gleam the opposition gained by your appearance at my reception."

"Of course. Someone once said politics is the art of the possible. It's also the art of using others. But I believe they may find the same breath can blow hot or cold."

Ruhl stared at him a moment and smiled again. "Yes, Commodore, I believe you will have your ship."

* * *

Li spent the next two days preparing. It was possible he could persuade Prime Minister Xo to use granting him command of a new ship as an easy way to curry public favor, but confrontation was more likely and he needed to be ready for either possibility. He rented a security box and left some worthless papers in it.

He also made a number of calls and sent a blank crystal to Bao-Yu. He also set up a program which was disseminated through hundreds of computers should his death or disappearance be announced. He also studied videos of the ministers of the Solar League and many of their supporters.

Certain he'd left enough false trails and little to chance, he dressed for the dinner and drove to the Prime Minister's residence.

While somewhat smaller, the residence was even more palatial than the hall in which he'd attended Ruhl's reception. The security at the dinner was even more obvious and thorough than it'd been at the reception, and actually stepping inside the building seemed an accomplishment.

Ruhl had arrived before him and they greeted each other in the Huer manner, then Ruhl gestured toward a corner. "I'll watch you from here. In a place like this, I prefer to keep my back to a wall."

Li nodded and strolled to the bar, accepted a glass of juice, and studied the crowd. Most of them were career officials or leaders of the Peace party. He saw few members of opposition parties, certainly no one in a leadership position. He also noted Rear Admiral Tamaguchi scowling at a conversation with the Minister of Education and a woman Li took to be the minister's wife.

Li found himself exchanging inane pleasantries with the Security Minister and a woman who appeared to be too vacuous to be the minister's wife. Li'd learned the difference. Most political wives were as canny as their husbands—sometimes more so—and usually had a keen grasp of the issues. The Security Minister was a flat man, with a flat face, flat hair that clung to his head, and flat, dead eyes which revealed nothing of what he was thinking but marked him as a man who would kill without the faintest qualm.

He glanced around just in time to see a gray-green figure enter the room, then felt his stomach fall and his blood turn to icewater.

The ChiTseTsi was communicating with the Prime Minister.

He was like the other lobsters Li had met but this one wore the patterns carved into his exoskeleton painted black.

Li deliberately raised his glass and poured the juice on the floor, set the glass on a table, and stalked from the room.

He'd reclaimed his coat and hat and was waiting for the valet to bring his car. When he saw a movement at his shoulder he turned, taking a step to his left.

Ruhl's rumbling chuckle was strangely comforting. "That was well and boldly done. Since I left immediately after you, I doubt we'll be disturbed."

"We have a treaty with them, but I don't have to drink with them."

"I'm pleased by your integrity, but it won't have endeared you to the Prime Minister."

* * *

Li understood, waiting outside the Prime Minister's office, that he was preparing to step into a battle and he found himself calmer, colder, and thinking more clearly than he had since before he'd been a prisoner.

At the receptionist's nod he walked into Xo's office, closed the door, marched to the desk, snapped to attention and saluted. "Commodore Li, reporting as ordered, sir."

Xo stood, walked around his desk and glared into Li's eyes. "What you did was inexcusable. You've brought disgrace on yourself, the uniform you wear, and on the entire Solar League."

Li controlled his voice, keeping it quiet but still steel-edged. "What you did was worse than inexcusable." He watched Xo's mouth fall open and continued. "You signed a treaty with the blood of better men than you could ever aspire to be. You may 'discipline' me but I doubt you'll win the next election. And if the people learn what happened to our men and women, with what sort of creatures you've dealt, you might not be in the next election. Even in a decadent culture, some things can inspire revolt.

"I have very carefully kept away from some subjects in conversation and I have not granted a single interview. How badly do you want me to continue that course? If you're thinking of having me hustled out and hauled before a star chamber, I should let you know I have introduced a virus to much of the media which, if I do not delete it in a certain length of time, will give them more than enough information to shake your government."

Sweat broke out across Xo's forehead and upper lip. "You were saved because we made peace with the ChiTseTsi. Are you forgetting that, Commodore?"

"I forget nothing, including the fate of the men and women who were with me. Perhaps you should ask the other 'survivors' how grateful they are. We can, however, reach an accommodation. I won't have time for interviews or to hold extended conversations if I'm busy preparing to take command of the new ship to be launched in five months, and I won't be available for interviews if I'm on an eight-year cruise."

"Are you threatening me, Commodore?"

"Not at all. I'm only suggesting a way to keep me far too busy to very publicly remember some facts neither of us would want revealed, though for different reasons. And I thnk you're even more inclined to let sleeping dragons dream."

"What you're doing is blackmail."

"Do you have a guilty conscience? Let's just call it extortion." Li smiled. "You give me a ship and let me choose my own crew and I will continue to avoid certains topics and the media in general. If, on the other hand, you consult with your Security Minister, I've already ensured if anything untoward happens to me or to anyone I care about, you will never recover politically. I am mildly curious. I really don't know whether you are deluded or a simple opportunist."

Xo's face twitched and his eyes seemed to burn with his fury. "I don't expect you to understand. Strategically, we were in a terrible position. We'd already lost one major city, but we were able to get very favorable terms. We saved almost all of the Walawi and we rescued you and your men."

Li glared back at the Prime Minister." You mean you surrendered to merciless destroyers and salved your conscience by consigning most of the Walawi to worlds where most of them would be thrust back into the stone age or die. What have you left to offer the ChiTseTsi the next time they want to expand?"

"You're one of those pig-headed imperialists." Xo spat out the words. "Human expansion is the only expansion allowed, and you judge other races by human standards. You don't take account of differences in cultures or other drives we can't understand."

"You're wrong," Li snapped. "Have you actually learned anything about the other races? I've found much to admire about them. I don't expect them to be humans wearing costumes, but I do judge by whether or not a race is civilized. There are minimum standards of civilization and the ChiTseTsi do not begin to meet them. Ask the people treating poor Bachman if they've found anything to admire about the ChiTseTsi. They enjoy inflicting pain. Because I accept my duty, I did not attempt to kill the one at your party. I simply showed my contempt and left."

Li leaned forward. "I assure you, the ChiTseTsi have not nearly exhausted my store of contempt."

"What do you want?" Xo tried to stare him down. "Do you want war with the ChiTseTsi?"

"Not especially. I suspect it will develop at its own pace. The ChiTseTsi are not allies. As soon as they think they have the upper hand, they will make very clear to you what they think of treaties. We can both hope I'm wrong, but you need me to be wrong."

"Commodore Li, you will make a misstep and I will personally see to it you will pay more dearly than you can guess."

"But until I do, Prime Minister, I will have my ship. If there's a problem my memory will suddenly improve and the mute man will speak."

Chapter 6

Brod stood at "attention," staring straight forward over the head of the human in the gray uniform. The man bore no badges on his collar or his shoulders but several stripes on his arm.

"Sir, you will not salute me. I'm not an officer, I work for a living. You will call me 'sir' and I will call you 'sir.' The difference is that you will mean it. Behind me is an obstacle course. You will go over, under, or through everything between you and a red flag planted five kilometers away. Do you understand?"

"Yes, sir."

"Then, sir, begin."

Brod raced forward, moving easily in the slightly lower gravity of Earth. He sprang for the top of a wall, drew himself up, and rolled over the top, keeping as low as possible. After another long dash he confronted a web of ropes not as high as his knee. Another human gestured for him to go under the web and he threw himself onto his belly and propelled himself by fingers and toes. Clearing that, he faced a series of offset cylinters. Apparently he was expected to run setting his feet in the circles. The extra motion tired him and he became aware of the slightly thinner air of Earth as he began to breathe heavily.

The marked path led up a hill and down again until he faced another wall, this one too high for even Brod to jump, but a rope dangled from the top. Brod caught the rope and drew himself, hand over hand, using his feet against the wall until he was near the top. Clutching the rope with one hand, he caught the top of the wall with the other, drew himself up, and again rolled over. As soon as his feet hit the ground he broke into another run.

The air began to burn his nasal passages and his throat, down to his lungs but he forced himself to run up the next hill where he could see the flag. By the time he reached it he was afraid he'd vomit and the strength seemed to have run out of his muscles.

Another human stood beside the flag. "Are you ready to run back to the starting point?"

Brod turned and began to force himself down the hill.

"Stop!" the human called, "I was joking."

At the word "stop," Brod immediately halted.

"You'd have done it, wouldn't you?" The human's face and voice revealed stress. "We're not trying to kill you."

Brod fought his muscles and nausea and forced himself erect and walked back up the hill. "I must prove myself worthy."

"You're obviously physically fit. I'll be your next trainer. Your next test will be more cerebral." The human walked beside him to a large building that looked like a huge, half-buried barrel. As they entered, Brod saw it held a series of what looked like command rooms. The inner walls were transparent and officers stood peering into the rooms as cadets, in their green uniforms, responded to orders from trainers in gray and to the screens and streams of numbers on instruments. Brod had recovered his breath and swallowed several times, pushing the nausea back.

His new trainer led him into one of the empty rooms. From the inside, the walls the officers looked through seemed to be banks of more instruments. Brod paced to the controls and studied them. They seemed similar to the ones on the *Hanoi*. Suddenly the screens and some of the controls lit up and Brod realized they depicted the command station of a deep space vessel. Without thinking, he gave his first attention to the power flow to the repulsor fields and to the weapons. He noted power was low on a rear repulsor and used the controls to correct the flow.

Seeing a movement on the left upper part of the screen he directed the screen to focus on it and to magnify. The tiny dot resolved into a Valek ship. Glancing around the board, he detected movement on another screen and repeated the process. Another Valek ship. They were moving into positions where they could bracket the human ship. He set the instruments for maximum range detection and wasn't surprised by finding a third Valek ship.

He punched the control for the warning. The human ship used a deep, hooting sound, unlike the Huer warning, which sounded like a battle song.

He ramped the repulsors up to full power and caused the ship to emit a fine mist of water vapor. The mist instantly turned to ice crystals and between the crystals refracting the light and the repulsor fields disrupting it, the laser beams from the Valek ships hardly warmed the hull.

He launched warheads at the first two ships. Missiles streaked out of the Valek ships and he fired a salvo of defensive weapons and decoys. One of the Valek ships was engulfed in an explosion and disappeared.

"Good shooting, sir," the trainer said.

Brod switched the repulsor field off for half a second, firing lasers at the two remaining ships, who adopted the same defense he had, then he launched a missile at each. Another Valek ship vanished while the third turned slightly, presenting the minimum surface.

Red lights flashed across the board. Power had been cut to the repulsor fields. With his shield gone, Brod parried with his sword. Using all the lasers in the front of the ship he created a quick-moving grid that cut through the salvo the Valek ship had launched, then used one laser after another to strike out at the other ship. He knew he had to be wearing through their repulsors and launched another warhead, aiming it at their sensor array.

Effectively blinding them with the explosions against their repulsor field, he brought three lasers to bear on the command module of the Valek ship. Holes appeared, black edged with glowing red until the wreckage sparkled with small explosions until only parts of a hull were left.

"Sir, you've fought battles," the trainer said. "That kind of thinking and shooting doesn't come to someone still green from the academy."

"Sir, it's a Warrior's duty to fight and to know how to fight well."

The trainer leaned forward and tapped rapidly on a small screen, and the words appeared, "I'm damned glad you're on our side."

Brod realized what he'd forgotten in the excitement of the simulation; he was being observed. Obviously, the trainer had put the message on the screen so it wouldn't be overheard. Using his own keys to blank the screen, Brod asked, "Are there any more simulations programmed into your system?"

"Perhaps after lunch, sir" the trainer said. "I'll walk with you to the mess hall. I'm Sergeant Men."

For a moment Brod had trouble with the translation of mess hall, then realized it was a place to eat. "Thank you, sir."

Together they walked outside the building, then the trainer jerked his head in the direction they'd come. "Some of the people back there aren't pleased you're doing so well. Some lost fathers or uncles when we fought with you Huer. They'd like to think you're some sort of animal or devil."

"The war was long ago." Brod walked slowly enough to let the human keep up with him without having to trot. "Both the humans and the Huer have other enemies. We may need each other."

Sergeant Men apparently considered Brod's remark before he asked, "How accurate is that simulation?"

"Not very, The Valek ships would've launched missiles at the first sight of us. The three-point tactics were correct, if the Valek had enough ships to use it. Like us, they tend to use single-ship and two-ship elements."

At the mess hall Brod took a tray and sidled down the row, piling it with selections. He and Men, whose tray looked bare by comparison, sat across a table from each other. Brod ignored the stares and sudden silences of the humans in the mess hall and began to eat.

As Brod finished his meal he said, "I don't understand why you are using the Valek as your enemies in the simulations. It's always possible you're going to have to fight the Valek again but it's more likely your conflicts will be with the Chadanor or, most likely, the ChiTseTsi."

Men leaned forward and lowered his voice. "I don't understand it either. The orders for these exercises come from the top. I'm not at all sure we're done with the lobsters, and the Chadanor are nobody's friends." Glancing around to make sure no one was listening, he asked, "What do you think is the best way to fight the lobsters?"

Brod had to think about the question. The only definition he had for "lobster" was a crustacean, usually consumed, but apparently it was also a derogatory term for the ChiTseTsi. "I've never fought them. Your area of space is between theirs and ours. From what I've heard, they have the same or similar weapons and defenses."

Men stood. "Let's go back to the training center. They'll want to find out as much as they can about your abilities."

On the walk back, Men said, "I think we quit too soon with the lobsters. Sooner or later, we'd have discovered the location of their homeworld and taken the battle to them. You know, they had three of our men prisoner for over four years. I have a friend on the ship that retrieved them. He said two of them had to be kept in a coma all the way back, and nothing's been heard of them since. He wasn't even sure they were still human. And two of them are still in the hospital."

Brod could think of nothing to say, so he said nothing.

As they approached the door of the half-barrel building, Men said, "I'll be your trainer for the next couple of sessions, I wanted you to know I'm glad I got to work with you. You're a veteran and a damned fine trooper. I'd be proud to serve with you."

Brod smiled at Men, lips closed. "I've noticed many humans call themselves soldiers. You are a Warrior."

"Thank you," Men said, as he opened the door and stood aside to let Brod enter first. They walked to another unused room and Brod was required to plot, in human distances and measurements of time, the trajectories of incoming and outgoing ships and missiles. After over an hour of answering questions, plotting, and directing return fire, another trainer entered the room and led Brod outside where a number of mats had been placed edge-to-edge. A barefoot human in a loose uniform stood at the other end of the mat, stretching muscles in an exercise.

"Sir, take off your knife," the trainer said.

"No, sir. I was told I could wear my claw." Brod kept his voice quiet.

"Sir, you are here to assess your ability at unarmed combat. Take off your knife."

"No sir. If my opponent is unarmed, I will not draw my claw, but I will not take it off."

"Sir, if you draw that weapon I will be forced to kill you."

Brod smiled at the human, showing teeth. "Shall we begin, sir?"

As Brod approached, the human in the loose uniform moved into a defensive posture, then tried a whip kick at Brod's knees. The human was quick, almost as fast as a Huer, but Brod sprang up and forward and shoved at the human's chest. The human was flung back, rolling with the fall, and was almost instantly back on his feet, although his eyes seemed to have lost some of their focus. Brod had no desire to hurt the human so he responded to the other's punches or kicks with simple blocks, evasions, or light pushes.

The human continued to try to break through Brod's defenses but Brod simply blocked or avoided, never really striking back. Idly, Brod wondered at some of the feints the human used, so he threw out a hand as though he'd attempted a push and missed. The human seized Brod's wrist with both hands and spun, trying to use leverage against him. Brod simply jerked his arm back and the human was tossed onto his back.

"Sir, I believe that's enough," the trainer called and Brod walked back to face him. Brod studied the human's face. The eyes were very intense and the corners of the mouth were drawn down. He took the expression to mean the human was not happy.

"Sir, if you have another test—"

"No sir, I haven't," the trainer replied, his voice deeper than before. "You are dismissed for the rest of the day. Report to the command training center at oh-eight hundred hours tomorrow."

Brod realized he was going to have trouble adjusting to the Earth day. His next meal was hours away and if he wanted to sleep soundly he'd need to wear himself out. He returned to the obstacle course and received permission to run it again. This time he took it at an easier pace, trying to accomplish with skill and rhythym what he'd done with power when he'd first run it.

After he finished he explored the area, ignoring the stares of most of the humans he met. One of the buildings contained a large room where humans strained at machines which were apparently designed to make them exert themselves. After watching the operations of some of them he tried several of the machines but found they represented small challenge.

Physically, the humans were weaker than he was. Shkogar would probably dismiss them as cubs or females but he was becoming comfortable with them. Some were very difficult to understand, like the last trainer, but most of them, after their first shocked reaction to seeing him, seemed friendly.

Most of the buildings were offices, which held no interest for him. He did notice humans used much more metal in their buildings than did the Huer, but the functions of offices were not his concern. He did find a field with benches and mats. The grass on the field was kept trimmed and was bordered, opposite the benches and mats, by dirt berms. He could guess it was a shooting range. The distance from the mats to the berm was about the same distance the Huer used to practice with a gauss rifle; in human meassurement, about three hundred meters. All the targets had been removed, so he couldn't see how well humans were able to use a rifle.

His stomach grumbled and he knew it was time to appease it.

Most humans didn't seem to appreciate their food as much as the Huer did. They didn't seem to mind using food as fuel instead of an opportunity to share with their sept-brothers enjoying time and life, fleeting things that disappeared. He'd noticed they seemed to have no beverage except juices and two rather bitter drinks they consumed hot. And water, of course.

When he entered the mess hall the usual silence fell, interrupting even the low murmurning that was usually the only human conversation at meals. Picking up a tray, he joined the line of humans choosing morsels from rows of pans. He hadn't become sufficiently used to human foods for the scents to entice him. He filled his platter with meat and vegetables and took two of the sweet pastries, choosing to drink water because he'd learned the hot drinks agitated him too much for easy sleep and the darker one sometimes upset his belly.

He'd just finished selecting and turned to face the tables when he saw movement and recognized Sergeant Men, sitting at a table with two other trainers in the gray uniforms, waving at him. Taking the motion as a possible invitation, he carried his tray to the table where the trainer and his sept-brothers sat. Men gestured at the empty chair at the table and said, "Please, join us."

Brod set his tray on the table and carefully sat down.

Men laughed. "You don't need to worry about the chair. I took it from the officers' mess. It's meant to hold someone broader and heavier than us."

Brod guessed the remark was intended as humorous and smiled.

"I was telling my friends part of our conversation today," Men said. "Have you ever had any dealings with the Chadanor?"

Brod paused in his eating to reply. "Once. My brother was commanding the *Courage* and we found a planet to land to re-provision. The place was worthless for anything else. It rotated at the same rate it circled its primary, so one side was always high summer and the other deepest winter. The only place nearly habitable was what we called the twilight lands, on the border between hot and cold, and it was subject to violent storms. When we approached the planet we detected a ship. On visual, we saw it was a Chadanor vessel. We identified outselves and they responded. We told them we were going to put down a shuttle to take on water.

"Their commander tried to tell us it was their planet and we'd have to pay in metal to land there."

"What happened then?" asked one of the trainers.

"My brother laughed and told them the only metal we'd pay would be warheads. Then he told them if they had a party on the planet to recall them and get out." Brod took several bites of food.

"Well, did they?"

"About as quickly as I can eat this meal. Their ship's

commander tried to suggest we could share the planet and both re-provision. Shkogar told him that was an excellent idea and if he'd proposed it in the first place, that's what would've happened."

"Then you got the water."

"Just barely. We'd just gotten enough to fill our tanks from the purification equipment when we had to scramble to get the apparatus on the shuttle and get out before a circular windstorm swept the area. It left most of the area stripped bare. Even massive stones were picked up, spun, and flung like pebbles."

"Have you ever fought the Chadanor?" Men asked.

"We've never had to. They posture and bluster but they seem to lack confidence."

"There's a danger in overconfidence," one of the other trainers said.

Brod washed down food with a long drink of water. "True, but there's also a danger in being too cautious. Shkogar realized we'd never fought the Chadanor and there was always the chance their weapons might be better than ours or their luck better than ours, but Shkogar knew the worst that could happen to us is that we might die as Warriors, and that's nothing to be feared."

Brod gave his attention to the food until his platter was empty. As he drank the last of the water in the pitcher he'd taken, he asked, "Do you have any idea how long I'll be here?"

"I'd guess at least a month," Men said. "I told them how you performed on the battle drill and Kai tells me Sergeant Tan is still growling about how you wouldn't take off your knife and then beat Sergeant Huang without breaking a sweat."

"You humans move a little slower than we Huer," Brod said. "Your gravity is less than ours. Heaver gravity means we must be well-balanced and quicker, to avoid falls."

"I don't think I'll tell either Tan or Huang that," Men replied. "Just let them think you're harder than diamond and better trained than Huang. Some people need a little salt rubbed into their wounds. It might make them realize they aren't the toughest beings in the universe."

Brod laughed. "You might let them know my younger

brother Shkogar is far more fierce than I am. He'd probably have broken every bone in Huang's body at least once."

"How much family do you have?" Men asked.

For over a human hour they talked about their families and Brod learned humans had no septs and no castes. Apparently, human society was far more chaotic than that of the Huer. On Earth, extended families were common. Unless a family had prestige and wealth, the parents usually lived, in their old age, in the homes of their children, and many families lived in homes with four generations.

"Home" was another alien concept to Brod. A Huer lived with his or her mother for the first year, then was sent to the first school. From that time forward, a Huer lived in barracks with the rest of one's class or, later, sept. Solitude was always possible, even in the cities, he supposed, but a Huer was part of a school or a sept.

Humans were even more chaotic in their mating. Sergeant Men had a chosen mate and had undertaken a ritual to formalize the relationship. One of the other trainers seemed to take pride in mating with any willing female and boasted of some of the improbable places in which he'd mated. The third trainer's chosen mate was a male. If the trainer was as capable and worthy as he seemed, Brod regretted the loss of his genes to the human race. Such relationships were rare among the Huer and any mating outside of the season was prohibited and punished.

The humans were as surprised by Huer customs and seemed not to understand how the Huer could be content living as they did. They offered to take him to a place called a club where he could drink beer but, to Brod, beer without a meal seemed as wrong as a meal without beer.

"Very well," Men said. "Meet us here tomorrow night but don't take any food, and we'll go someplace where you can both eat and drink."

* * *

Brod's newest trainer wore a lieutenant's insigniae and watched as Brod responded to a variety of simulated disasters. In some of the drills, Brod sat with arms crossed because the catastrophes could only be dealt with by engineering. The final simulation showed a Valek ship on an attack vector and, inexplicably, the power died. Glancing at the other boards, Brod saw all had become dark, all the normal lighted displays dead. Brod attemtpted to redirect power but his instruments didn't respond. Brod looked at the lieutenant then sprang to the helm position but the controls there were also dead. An alarm hooted, warning the hull had been breached.

"Do you have explosive charges on the ship to destroy it? Sir?" He'd almost forgotten to add the "sir"

"No sir, we do not."

"Sir, is there a lifesuit in my size?"

"No, sir, there is not. What would you do with one? You are without help."

"Sir, I would do everything I could to destroy anything that might help the enemy. If the enemy were to attempt to board, I would kill as many of them as I could."

"Sir, you do not have any of those options. What would you do?"

Brod stood and took a deep breath. "Sir, this is what I would do. A Warrior should die standing on his feet. I would take a deep breath and hold it as long as possible. When I exhaled, I would expect to die."

The lieutenant smiled, showing teeth and Brod did the same.

"Do Huer ships have explosive charges on their equipment?"

"Yes sir, they do. They're kept stable by a trickle charge. When the charge stops, a mechanical timer begins. When the time expires, so does the ship."

"How long are the timers set for, sir?"

"Sir, I would prefer not to answer." Brod stared into the trainer's eyes.

"Very well, sir, that concludes this training session."

Brod was dismissed for lunch, which he ate at the mess hall, and returned to find one of the sergeants be'd met the night before. Sergeant Kai was carrying Brod's gauss rifle and his holstered pistol. "Sir, we're going to the range."

Brod walked beside the human to the firing range he'd seen

earlier. He was allowed three test shots to adjust the sights, which had been set to deal with Huerda's greater gravity. Humans fired from four positions; standing, sitting, kneeling, and prone while Brod had only learned two, standing and prone. Firing from the unusual positions affected Brod's accuracy but Kai seemed to find it adequate, and from standing and prone he fired groups Kai acknowledged with "Very good shooting, sir."

With the pistol, firing at twenty-five meters Brod simply aimed a little low. He was required to fire from the same four positions used for the rifle but it was easier with a handgun.

"Sir, do you want to tell me how heavier gravity makes you a better shot?" Kai said with a smile.

"Sir, I've been using weapons since I was four years old," Brod said. "I suspect few humans handle rifles or pistols at that age, or as often as I did. It's all a matter of familiarity."

"How young were you when you knew you wanted to be a Warrior, sir?" Kai watched as Brod disassembled both rifle and pistol and gave them a thorough cleaning using the materials in the butt of the rifle.

Brod looked downrange without seeing it. "Sir, I can't remember a time when I didn't want to be a Warrior or wanted to be anything else. And when did you realize you wanted to be a Warrior?"

"Sir, I grew up on a farm. Even with mechanized farming the work is brutal. They were still consolidating farms and I would have become just another laborer. I had the opportunity to join the service. I've found contentment in doing what I'm good at. It's not perfect but it's still better than farming, especially as a hireling for someone else."

"Is there anything else you'd rather be doing?" He caught himself and added the "sir."

"Perhaps working in a library, sir." Kai watched as, with an economy of motion, Brod reassembled the weapons and put the pistol in its holster. "I never particularly wanted to be a Warrior. I'm content being a soldier."

"Sir, there's honor in that," Brod said.

* * *

Sergeant Men had removed the front passenger's seat from his car so Brod would not have to sit with his head between his knees. They'd gone off the base to a nearby town to a building that that looked archaic. The structure had too much useless decoration to be modern. Brod had observed all the buildings on the base looked old but utilitarian. This building had towers and ornate windows and what appeared to be much wasted space.

Men set his car on a pad and Sergeant Kai, with the other sergeant, set his machine on a neighboring pad and they walked to the building in a group.

Just inside the door they were met by a human wearing an elaborately patterned pale blue robe from neck to ankles. The human stared at Brod, his gaze fixed on the claw.

"Diplomatic immunity," Men told the man and the other human finally turned and led them to a table. At least twenty other humans sat at the tables and six more, dressed in the same elaborate robes as the one who'd met them at the door, moved among the tables carrying trays. Most of the humans sitting at the tables wore similar robes, although they seemed to have many different colors, patterns, and decorations at neck and wrists. Most of the others, who Brod guessed were females because they wore the fur on their heads longer, wore short jackets and trousers.

Brod was accustomed to the sudden silence that descended upon the rooms he entered. He and the sergeants were led to a table and one of the humans in the pale blue robes brought them folding sheets of rough paper with leather covers. "Bring us your best beer," Men said. The man lowered his head and walked away.

"Do you mind if I choose your dinner?" Men asked.

"I would prefer it," Brod said. He'd learned to read human writing but most of the things printed on the paper seemed in some other language entirely.

The man in the robes returned with a tray holding four glasses and placed them on the table, then the sergeants listed the foods they wanted prepared. Brod sipped the amber liquid in the glass.

"What do you think of the beer?" Men asked.

"I think it was water that wanted to be beer but changed its mind."

The sergeants laughed and it seemed like a signal for the other humans in the place to return to their murmured conversations. Men told them about his latest trainee, a cadet who apparently didn't remember the simulator was only that. He'd ignored the screen and the Valek ship centered on it, fixed on the instuments, stabbing at the repulsor key without looking to see whether power was being routed to the repulsors.

"Finally, I just said 'Look up at the screen.' The Valek ship was all but filling the screen. The trainee looked up, his eyes got about this big," Men held up both hands, making a circle, "and I was afraid I was going to have to call the medic or the janitor. It probably didn't help that I screamed in his ear." They all laughed at the story. "As he left the room, I silently wished him good fortune in his future career as a finance officer."

Kai made an exaggerated frown. "With our luck, he'll be in charge of our pay and we and our families will all starve to death."

The man in the robe walked to the table. "More beer, gentlemen?"

"Do you have a heavier, darker beer?" Men asked.

"I believe we have some porter."

"Bring my friends and I" Men gestured at the other two sergeants and himself, "another glass of what we had and bring my other friend," he indicated Brod, "a pitcher of the porter. And you might add an ounce of alcohol to it."

"As you say, sir," the human said, bobbing his head again.

With the second tray of glasses and the pitcher, the human Men told Brod was called a waiter brought each of them a bowl of leaves with bits of raw vegetables. Brod sampled it and refrained from remarking that it looked like a meal for a three-horned cow.

The beer was better and he'd drank half the pitcher before the waiter brought them plates of food. Two of the sergeants had ordered something that looked a little like pale meat but didn't smell like it. Sergeant Kai told him it was fish and offered him a taste.

Brod had learned humans frowned on spitting out bad food so he swallowed it, but it took determination. He attacked his own meat, which was quite good if a little overcooked. The green things on the plate were somewhat bitter so, after a taste, he ignored them. He did like a small mound of something white with a brown sauce. After Brod had finished, Men ordered him another plate and ordered the steak very rare. The meat wasn't as sweet as three-horn but acceptable.

* * *

Li spent a week studying records of officers and enlisted personnel. He wanted his crew trained to work on the ship before it was finished. Actually seeing the structure and installations was better than the best training manual.

At the end of the week he was visited by the Walawi ambassador, who was dressed in human fashion. The Walawi was half a head shorter than Li, with smoke-gray fur and dark eyes. "Commodore Li, I am Hesha Jontal, the ambassador representing the Walawi. We have mutual friends and, perhaps more to the point, a common enemy."

Li had stood as the ambassador entered. "May I offer you a chair?"

"Thank you." The Walawi sat in the chair nearest the desk.

Li immediately sat down again. "Could you be more specific about our friends and enemies?"

"Commodore Sauvage and Ambassador Ruhl both speak highly of you. As for our enemies, they are, of course, the ChiTseTsi." Jontal's accent was soft but obvious and he seemed almost unable to pronounce "ChiTseTsi," although the reason might've been more than linguistic.

"I'm honored the Commodore and Ruhl hold me in regard. As for the ChiTseTsi, we have a treaty with them."

"Commodore, you're too wise to believe a scrap of paper makes an enemy a friend. It simply means you're no longer engaged in open war. I do not expect you to go hunting their ships but I doubt you will lower your guard around them."

James K. Burk

"Ambassador, we both know you didn't visit me to discuss our friends or our enemies. What can I do for you?"

"I have a friend who is now a citizen of Earth and his daughter is graduating from the academy next month. She has been trained to be a ship's helm. I would like to see her in a position of respect with a commander and crew who will demand excellence of her."

"I don't wish to offend you, but we're going to have some… interesting social dynamics. Most of the humans will have their families with them. If I accept a Huer for my crew, I shall also have to accept his mate. I know nothing about the mating season or customs of the Walawi."

"I'm not offended. We have a rather complex mating pattern. The female must be in the presence of a Walawi male before she comes into season, then her hormones change her body chemistry and create pheromones that attract the male. With no males present, the female does not go into season. It is a survival trait. If a female is separated from the pride she would be more vulnerable while in season. Not going into season improves her chances to return to her pride or to join another pride."

"Do you understand she'll be the only one of her species on a ship for eight Earth years?" Li poured a glass of water and placed it across the desk for Jontal.

Jontal ignored the glass. "Do not underestimate the self-reliance of a Walawi female."

"What is the name of your friend's daughter?"

"Aspirant Isharra Shanni."

Li tapped the name into his card. "I'll look at her records and interview her. I can't make any promises until I've satisfied myself she would be the best choice."

"I do not ask any more than that." Jontal stood. "I have enjoyed meeting you."

"And I, you." Li got to his feet. "I regret, in one way, that I'll be leaving so soon. One leaves behind so many people one knows well and people one has just met who might become friends. I wish I'd been able to spend more time with you."

"I will see you again in about eight of your years."

As soon as the Walawi had left Li checked the time and called his mother. He'd reminded himself he'd become so immersed in achieving his goals he'd neglected to treasure the time he had with those most important to him.

After he'd finished the conversation he checked the time again and called Sauvage. He assured him Gyanashwar Singh was most likely to be his second in command and he'd be interviewing him the next day. He also passed on a greeting from the Walawi ambassador. While brief, Li found the conversation pleasant.

He was nearly finished for the day but pulled up records for Isharra Shanni. Her test scores were solid but not excellent, but her ability to handle a ship was an academy legend in the making. She was athletic and excelled at gymnastics and martial arts. Her disciplinary record was flawless but several instructors had noted that she never engaged in conversations or developed friendships with other cadets. Interesting, Li thought. An interview with her might give him a better sense of her.

On his way back to his apartment he stopped at the Officer's Club for a meal and a very small glass of Scotch. He'd have to remember to lay in a supply of a few bottles for special occasions on the mission.

* * *

Captain Gyanashwar Singh saluted. "Reporting as ordered, sir."

Li studied the man critically. Singh was of medium height but seemed taller because of his slenderness, although there was nothing frail about him. His complexion was dark, with black eyes and hair. He was also opaque. Li was a little surprised he was unable to read the man better. "You come highly recommended, Captain Singh.

"If I were to make you my second in command, what would your first response be?"

"Sir, I would want to assist in choosing the crew."

"You're very direct, Captain. What about the ship and the mission?"

"Sir, it's common knowledge you'll be taking command

of the *Krishna*, the second Discovery-class ship and like *The Great March*, the *Krishna* will be going deeper into space than any human ships have gone before. In an eight-year cruise, we will need to depend even more on each member of the crew, not only to do their duties but to work together. I would point out to the Commodore I have more recent experience with most of the available crews."

"Please sit down, Captain. May I offer you tea?"

"Thank you."

As Li brewed the tea he considered what Singh had said. The nagging doubt about the Walawi now had a name. "I'm considering a few crew members. After the ship is completed we'll have at least two months for testing. That should be ample time to know whether the crew can work together." He poured tea into two cups.

"If I might ask, who were you considering?" Singh accepted a cup and carefully sipped.

"I have been asked to consider a Huer commander and a Walawi aspirant. And I believe a doctor is available who I'd like to put in charge of the ship's medical section."

Singh's cup stopped halfway to his mouth. "You realize, of course, some of the crew may have difficulties working with non-humans, particularly a Huer. Some may have lost relatives in our conflict with the Huer."

Li sat and leaned forward. "If the problem with the Huer or the Walawi have to do with their competetence or their abilities to work with others, then we'll know and deal with it. If the humans have other problems, then the humans will have to go. We must make it very clear all the members of the crew are one community. Anything else will leave us at the mercies of the most prejudiced officers."

"Very well." Singh's black, expressionless eyes stared into Li's. "And we will each spend some time working with them."

Li studied Singh a moment longer, then said, "I'm requesting your transfer to my command, effective immediately. I'd like a list of your recommendations in three days. We'll get together then to compare lists. I've simply been working off records, as you say, which won't tell me the things I most need to know. I'd prefer that we meet out of uniform. The command structure has a formality about it that discourages frank discussion."

"Very good." Singh placed his cup on the desk and stood. "And I want to thank you very much for the opportunity."

Li smiled. "Don't thank me yet. You've earned it and I'm afraid you'll continue to earn it."

Singh flashed even, white teeth in a broad smile.

"Just don't do that around the Huer. Showing teeth is, to them, a challenge. And if their ambassador is the fat old scholar he claims to be, a member of the Warrior caste should not be unnecessarily annoyed. Good captains are hard to find."

* * *

Just before Li cleared his desk for the day he received an order to present himself in Rear Admiral Tamaguchi's office.

The trip required ten minutes of walking corridors and riding lifts, and Li was grateful for the repairs to his body. Before the procedures, such a trip would've taken twice as long and would've cost real pain.

He gave his name to the receptionist and took a chair. After waiting twenty minutes he became angry. Tamaguchi was trying to remind him who held the higher rank, and Li wondered if he was more annoyed at the rudeness or the childish waste of both their times. After another ten minutes the receptionist told him he might enter Tamaguchi's office.

He strode into the office, snapped to attention, and saluted crisply.

Tamaguchi glanced up at him and, without rising, tossed a negligent salute to him, then returned his scowl to the computer screen in front of him. "I see you have chosen Captain Gyanashwar Singh as your second in command. I assume you did not know he was associated with a Commodore Sauvage. He is considered suspect."

"I know that you know I've met Commodore Sauvage and I'm also aware Captain Singh was his second in command, a post he filled to the commodore's satisfaction." Li carefully kept his face expressionless.

"I do not know how you gained the patronage of the Prime Minister after insulting him. I do not enjoy subordinates going over my head or behind my back. Did that salute when you entered mean anything?" The voice was again a growl.

"The salute means I respect your rank—"

"But not the man?" Tamaguchi's narrowed eyes smouldered.

"I am always careful to be totally honest and fair with those I respect—and some I don't." Li glowered back at Tamaguchi. "You were only an obstacle. And if you do anything more to impede me in crewing my ship, I suspect you'll dicover Prime Minister Xo can be very persuasive. If he can cashier a man like Sauvage, he can easily deal with you. I don't suggest you test him."

The frown on Tamaguchi's face deepened, as did the color.

"If the Admiral has nothing else to discuss—"

"You are dismissed, Commodore."

* * *

Li answered the door chime and gestured Singh into the apartment. Singh wore a silver-gray shirt and dark gray slacks and carried a folder under his arm.

"I have my files on the kitchen table. May I offer you something to drink?"

"Do you have fruit juice?"

"Several kinds, What would you prefer?"

"Mango, if you have it." Singh smiled. "Out of uniform my friends call me Gyan."

"I'm Wing." Li poured a glass and handed it to Gyan. "I'll want a list of at least five candidates for each major position. I'd like to have Doctor Zhang in charge of the Medical Section. She was on board *The Glorious* and she had an excellent staff. A good staff is the mark of a good leader. A lot of her teams have been assigned to *The Long March*, but she'd taken a leave. Her sister was getting married and she wanted to spend time with her family."

"Not a bad recommendation by itself," Gyan said. "Who do you have for Weapons and Communications?"

"My first choice for Weapons would be the Huer, He's

equivalent to a commander in the Solar League Navy. We'll want two alternates for the first choice in each command position. Once the command positions are filled we can consult with the candidates.

"We also have to consider the families. We'll have teachers for the children but the spouses must also be able to contribute. That also creates some interesting social dynamics."

"I've anticipated that. My suggestion for the second-watch commander is Captain Manoucher Amin-Madini. It's partially based on the fact that his wife, Sirna, is an excellent nurse who could actually head the second watch medical staff. Both are good people to work with."

"Lin Ju-Long is an exceptional commander."

"He is," Gyan agreed. "I've worked with him. His name means 'Powerful Dragon,' but his wife is called the 'Petulent Dragon.' She has no skills to speak of and she's a very difficult woman. I'd recommend, for third watch, Wu Ming-Hoa. His wife is a first-rate communications officer."

For over two hours they worked at assembling a crew. Gyan's personal experience with and knowledge of possible crew members proved more useful than the files Li had studied.

Li leaned back and rubbed his eyes. "We still don't have any recommendations for the science staff."

"Or for the landing details. We can get enormous information from orbiting a planet," Gyan said,"but there's nothing like having people on the ground. That will mostly be the function of the science staff, but we'll need some Marines to protect them. There are also other reasons for having a Marine complement. One of the first rules of command it to expect the unexpected."

"I'm going to leave that to you." Li stretched, a luxury he could now enjoy without pain. "Tomorrow I'm going to schedule appointments with Commander Brod, the Huer, and Aspirant Isharra Shanni. If I tentatively approve them, I'll have you interview them as well."

"It's pleasant to be working with you, Wing."

"And you, too, Gyan, but tomorrow we'll again be Commodore Li and Captain Singh. We should try to find some time to take off our rank badges and talk."

* * *

The training and testing continued. Brod was taught new medical procedures and how to use medical equipment humans carried. Much time was also spent on the structure of the service and what humans called a "chain of command." Their structure made their crews more rigid and less enterprising than Huer crews, most of whom were expected to learn at least two other specialties.

Every seven days the sergeants took him to dinner. Men's chosen mate joined them twice and Kai's partner joined them once. Each time they ate at a different place, trying different foods. Some Brod regarded as merely fuel for the body but some he found to his tastes.

He'd risen the morning after one of the meals with the sergeants to find a message to report to the base commander's office. After putting on his dress uniform and enjoying a quick breakfast, he entered the office at the appointed time. He'd mentally rehearsed the required formula so often that it was almost habitual. After halting in front of the desk he saluted and said, "Commander Brod, reporting as ordered, sir."

The admiral stood, returned the salute, then sat down, gesturing at a chair. "Commander, I have your performance reports here." He nodded toward a small screen on his desk. "You seem to be qualified to be a Marine Commander and, at the very least, a Commander in the Navy. I do, however, see a few problems. The first is that on two occasions you have refused a direct order to hand over your knife. Most of our personnel are never armed and even those who are allowed to carry a weapon will turn it over under the command of a superior officer."

"Sir, would you strip off your uniform at a command from an officer with greater rank?"

"They would never issue such an order."

"Yes, sir. And they should never have ordered me to take off my claw. It is not merely a weapon, it is a symbol of what I am. Your uniform speaks for you. It says 'I am a human and an officer in the Navy.' My claw says 'I am a Huer Warrior.'"

"You have also been spending a good deal of time with enlisted personnel. This is not the way an officer should conduct himself."

"Sir, most of your officers seem eager to see me fail or perhaps they're afraid of other officers who do. I am not only a Huer, I am Brod. Those sergeants accepted me. We ate and drank and laughed together. They are all worthy humans."

"They are also enlisted personnel. Our custom is to remember that they are enlisted, not officers. You are a guest here—"

"No, sir, I am not," Brod snapped, "I am here as an observer. I am here to determine whether humans are worthy allies."

The admiral's eyes bulged and his cheeks reddened and, for a moment, Brod feared the man had swallowed something. "That is not the way agreements are forged. You have an ambassador for those sorts of decisions."

"No, sir, you humans make your agreements that way. Ruhl has dealth with torrents of words. Words are only that. An ambassador is all but a prisoner. I was chosen to observe, to understand your navy and your people and determine whether I consider them worthy."

The admiral had composed himself and his voice was icy. "And what is your assessment of the human race, Commander Brod?"

"I have only seen very little of it. Far too little to have made an informed decision."

"And why would we want the Huer as allies? We're at peace with the other races."

Brod laughed. "Admiral, you don't believe that any more than I do. You have largely become comfortable with the Huer, you're uncertain about the Valek, and you have no idea how numerous and well-equipped the ChiTseTsi might be. You are not at peace with them, you're simply not at war with them."

"Are all the Huer as straightforward?"

"All the worthy ones."

The admiral sat staring at Brod, his face unreadable, even had Brod been more adept at reading human facial expressions.

As it was, he understood the human, for whatever reasons, had put on an impassive mask and he simply stared back.

Finally, the admiral spoke. "I'd rather wondered what you were made of. I'd heard stories and read reports, of course, but the only way to know someone is to meet him face-to-face. I will say you didn't disappoint me. However, the main reason for calling you here was to let you know you are at liberty for the next twenty-eight days and the Huer embassy is sending a car for you. It should be here in about two hours." He stood. "Dismissed," he said, and returned Brod's salute.

Brod returned to his quarters, left messages for the sergeants, and packed his traveling chest. He realized he'd become more exciteable as mating season neared and now it was almost upon him. He strode to the landing pad and paced until the embassy car appeared, hovered, and set down.

Ruhl stepped out, his arms spread. "I think I have found a worthy human commander for you. He's taken the time to learn Huer speach and customs and he seems to have boldness and ruthlessness. He is a human I respect and, to be honest, rather like."

"Very good." Brod returned the greeting then stowed his traveling chest in the back of the car and took a seat in the passengers' compartment. "I was afraid I would have to wait longer. What class of ship will it be?"

Ruhl sat beside him. "It's the new Discovery class. You'll be in space for five years. He already knows he must also accept Kee as part of the crew. Speaking of Kee, she arrived yesterday." He handed Brod a mug. "It's real Huer beer. I doubt you've had anything like it for a while."

Brod took a deep drink and thought he could guess how a plant would feel at the first drops of rain after a drought. Already he could see Kee in his mind's eye. He caressed the memory then carefully put it away. He was already becoming excited. Better to wait. Still, he could taste the coppery flavor of the beginning of mating season.

Chapter 7

Li had tried to call the Huer embassy only to find it closed. A recorded message informed him the embassy would remain closed for another two weeks. Apparently, it was the mating season for the Huer. Then he drew up a list of personnel and verified Isharra Shanni was unassigned, He left messages for her and for the personnel officer that he wanted her to meet him in his office at thirteen hundred hours.

Consulting the list he and Gyan had prepared, he sent in the personnel requests. Three of their choices were on cruises but would return before the *Krishna* would be prepared to ship out. He listed alternates for the three, then tapped his desk. He still had no leaders and few members for the science staff. After a moment's thought he called his uncle, Deshi.

"Zhin Deshi here."

"Greetings, uncle. I'm looking for advice. You may have heard I'm to take command of the *Krishna*. I'm trying to assemble a crew and need suggestions for the science team. We not only need professional excellence, we also need a team that can work well together."

Deshi paused. "Why don't you ask the ship's computer?"

"The ship isn't finished yet."

"No, but the computer is already up and they're finishing 'teaching' it. It's an AI—artificial intelligence. It will be assigned a senior commander's rank and will be in charge of the science team. By the way, congratulations on your new command. Your mother had said you were ready to spread your wings again."

"Thank you, uncle. And thank you for the information about the computer. I wasn't aware computers were being used except for computation, navigation, and recording."

"This one is the first of a new generation. If the system works as well as intended, future ships may not even have a human crew."

Li chuckled. "Another reason for me to be grateful for my mortality. I'd rather not live to see the day when humans are simply passengers. If I'm part of the last generation of human ships'commanders, I'll savor it even more,"

He turned off the comcard and stared across the room, not seeing the door. To be able to access the computer he'd have to visit the shipyard. Clearance would be required, which meant he'd have to provide fingerprints and retinal patterns and establish voice recognition. Once he'd done that, he could use a password to communicate. If he finished his interview with the Walawi early enough, he could start the process later in the afternoon. Otherwise, he'd have to wait until morning. Time wouldn't matter to a computer but the human techs would need to verify his indentity and provide clearance and, knowing the service, only the first watch would have the authority. He was able to book a seat on the shuttle to the station.

After lunch he had time to review the Walawi's records before she tapped at his door.

"Enter."

He hadn't known what to expect, so it was no surprise to see what appeared to be a child with fine powder-blue fur and pale blue eyes wearing a naval uniform. The ears were set a little higher on the skull than a human's and were larger and shaped like those of a cat..

"Aspirant Isharra Shanni, reporting as ordered, sir."

The voice was surprisingly deep. Li stood and returned the salute. "Please, sit down, Aspirant. Do I call you Aspirant Isharra or Aspirant Shanni?"

"Aspirant Isharra, sir. That is my first given name. Since I am not part of a pride, I have no pride name."

"Very well, Aspirant Isharra. Do you know why I've asked to see you?"

"I believe so, sir. It's rumored you're to command the *Krishna*." Her accent was slight, mostly softening hard consonants.

"I have some concerns. Your grades are not as good as those of some of your classmates."

"Sir, it would not be proper to embarrass most of my male classmates."

For a moment, Li couldn't believe what he'd heard. "Why not?"

"Because, as males, they will be heads of prides. A female does not shame the head of a pride."

"I see that doesn't keep you from excelling at either gymnastics or martial arts."

"I do not compete against males in either sport, sir."

Li stared silently at the Walawi, who stared back. There was no challenge in her gaze, only an impressive self-possession and calmness. Somehow he couldn't doubt what she'd said. "The other most common criticism of you is that you are aloof, not part of a group. Why should I expect that to change?"

"I am not a member of a pride. If I become a member of a ship's crew, I will be part of a pride."

"I will choose you to be the *Krishna's* first watch helm if you will excel at your test scores. It does not show respect for the males who can't match your performance. And when you become a member of the crew, I will expect you to always do your best work. Do you understand and do you agree?"

"Yes, sir. Now I am part of a pride."

* * *

Li sat fuming in a chair. The security team had taken his fingerprints, checked his retinal patterns, and had even drawn a drop of his blood. He was expecting them to tell him to urinate in a bottle before he'd be allowed to interface with the ship's computer. He wondered if the commander of *The Long March* had been subjected to the same scrutiny, then realized the other ship might not have had a computer like the *Krishna's*. Deshi had said this was the first of a new generation. He'd said nothing about a similar system in *The Long March*.

A stocky man with a grim face and the black rank badges of Security on the shoulders of his uniform stepped into the room in which they'd left Li. "Commodore Li, please follow me."

Keeping the annoyance out of his face, Li stood and followed the Lieutenant Commander to a moving walkway. The trip to the unfinished ship's control room required a quarter of an hour until he at last stood before a wall largely featureless except for an inset figure with treads and a pair of lenses and a speaker grill on its chest.

"You may speak to the computer."

More lenses and grills were spaced across the otherwise blank wall. Li stood where at least two of the lenses seemed to be focussed. "I'm Commodore Li. I'll be your commander on the *Krishna*. What should I call you?"

A very precise voice replied, "That question provides the possibility for a number of humorous answers, but you can call me Commander Able."

"Well, Commander Able, humor is probably the last thing I would expect of a computer." Li stared into the lenses nearest the grill from which the voice had issued.

"My programming, training, if you will, has to be more extensive than that of any previous computer. Humor is largely the perception of a series of options combined with an appreciation for irony. For example, one of the optional answers to your question would have been,'Call me master.' This expanded programming and training is necessary for me to carry out all my functions, including that of a crewman."

"I'd hate to think," Li said, "that you would find some delightful irony in having us drop into normal space in the heart of a star."

"Astrogation involves choices but only within certain parameters. Since I will often be dealing simultaneously with multiple tasks I recognize that each task has certain parameters. My interaction with fellow crewmen has more options and fewer parameters except I may not harm or offend a member of the crew."

"Very interesting. Are you ready for your first order?"

"Yes, sir."

"I want you to select, from the available personnel, the science and support crews for the *Krishna*. I already have a list of eight names. The personnel you select must not only be capable but able to work with each other and with the eight people on my list, with a minimum of friction. If any of them are partnered, their partner must also be able to contribute to the ship's community."

"If you have the list on your comcard, please forward it to me."

Li submitted his list. "All those selected must be able to start training for the mission in two months and be ready to leave in no more than four months from today."

"A most reasonable order, sir. I believe I can verify the status of the crew within two hours."

"I'd prefer you handle the notifications, Commander Able. I would also like to have some way to contact you without having to use the shuttle and to identify myself each time to the Security forces."

"Easily done, sir." A comcard was thrust out of one of the crevices in the wall. "That is a scrambled unit. I already have your voiceprint.. If you activate the card you may contact me without fear of being tapped and I will compare any voices I hear to your print. That will be all the password you need."

"You're as good as your name, Commander Able."

"Thank you, sir." Apparently, the computer could appreciate a compliment, even delivered as a pun.

"When I return to my office I'll send you a tentative list of the command crew. I'd appreciate your input on the choices and also to make it easier for you to fill in the rest of the crew. I'll be consulting with the staff to fill in those same slots, so we'll have a pool to choose from."

"Yes, sir."

Li returned to the walkway, then gestured at the wall nearest the ship. "I'd like to take a look at her."

"Sir, that's not my decision to make."

Li had to work to keep a growl out of his voice. "Then contact whoever has the authority. I've seen videos of it and, since I'm the one who will be commanding it, I can assure you I'm less of a security risk than the people who took the pictures for the video."

"Yes, sir." The stocky man stopped, drew his comcard and keyed a message.

Li also stopped. Obviously, some Security personnel were

more intelligent than others. Just his luck to draw the one who apparently couldn't walk and talk at the same time.

"The admiral says we can go to the command center." The Lieutenant Commander led the way to a lift, up seven levels, and down another hallway to a heavy door guarded by two Marines. The name was archaic since these men stormed no beaches, but they were still the soldiers on naval vessels and protected landing parties. The officer with him displayed his card to them and drew open the door.

Except for computer banks, comminications gear, two screens which displayed men at work, and metal girders, the room was transparent. A commander, two lieutenants, and a sergeant all snapped salutes which Li returned. The three civilian techs in white jackets ignored him.

Li paced to the wall and stared out at the *Krishna*. Several sections still stood naked, exposing their framework and the equipment between the inner and outer hulls, while most of the ship was already sheathed in polished metal. The most important parts were the globe of the body and the immense intake at the bow. As a ship approached lightspeed the repulsors were needed to protect the ship. Space was not truly a void. While they were widely scattered, hydrogen atoms existed in space and, if one ventured near lightspeed, a hydrogen atom was a silver bullet that could kill the biggest ship. The intake was lined with repulsors and, at the base of the intake, other repulsors slowed the atoms but allowed them to be passed into the ship to be used as fuel.

Someone had once tried to explain to Li how the Liang drive functioned but had only succeeded in making him feel dizzy. Essentially, the Liang drive created its own wormhole burrowing through time and space and drawing the ship after it.

Rows of plates covered missile bays, and lasers were mounted in pods that, at this distance, looked tiny. Short, thick tubes jutted from other places on the hull and the small jets for spraying vapor into space were invisible at this distance. Two long tubes with rounded ends attached to opposite sides of the globe were the shuttle bays and a shorter tube was the container for ships' bottles.

Since the fastest means of communication were the ships themselves and other vessels capable of wrinkling time, each ship carried a number of what had come to be called "ships' bottles." These were computer-controlled, unmanned vessels designed to deliver messages to the nearest hub. Because of the immense distances and the movement of the universe, they had to be reprogrammed for the location of the nearest hub after each jump. There was simply too much navigational information required to preprogram them for all the locations a ship might need to launch a bottle and still have it arrive at the nearest hub.

Another tube and a framework ran aft to a smaller globe, which was the power generator, a small fusion reactor that directly provided power for the entire ship and indirectly provided the rest through the batteries it charged. This section would also be given a protective coating , complete with its own defence missiles, repulsors, and vapor jets. The jets could also be loaded with nitrogen and used to manuever a ship in normal space.

Li gazed at the ship. His ship. He loved it already.

Finally looking away from his ship, Li faced the other men in the room. "Carry on, gentlemen and ladies." He returned their salutes and strode back to the corridor, the Security officer at his heels.

On the shuttle trip back to Earth, Li called Gyan and arranged another meeting and used the rest of the time to anticipate problems and look for possibilities. One thing he'd already decided was to see if Commander Able would be able to more quickly program the message bottles, which was usually a time-consuming task.

Reviewing the team he'd assembled, he was aware of how many he had yet to meet but, of those he had met, he was pleased with the choices he and Gyan had made. The day was near enough gone the offices would be closed and that left only his meeting with Captain Singh at nineteen hundred. Tomorrow he would start scheduling interviews.

* * *

Gyan arrived as Li was setting up the screen for his comcard.

"We will need a bigger view than available on the comcards. I've already got a password to the computer and we can download and send everything on my card."

Gyan set his comcard to display on the screen and said, "Command structure."

A graph appeared on the screen and Li was gratified to see his name at the far left of the column and lines running to the right, the top line ending at Captain Singh, the other lines turned downward then right, toward Captain Amin-Madini and Captain Wu.

Other lines branched and continued right. Looking over the graph, Li noticed gaps in the lines and some names in lighter print.. "Those are provisional appointments," Gyan explained.

Li slid the sheet toward himself and tapped in Ensign Isharra for helm. "I've met her and I'm very impressed. She still has a month in the academy to finish but I trust her. I'll have you interview her as soon as she's graduated." After a moment's thought, he tapped in Commander Brod for weapons and added another line to put him in charge of the Marine complement.

"That's two large hats for one man," Gyan observed.

"It would be if he were human. I've been reviewing his records at the training center. He's experienced, he's learned our systems as well as his own, and he is physically amazing."

Gyan stared at the screen. "How well does he work with humans? It doesn't matter if he's all you say if he can't be part of a team."

"Perhaps a third of his trainers used every superlative they could think of while the rest gave either grudging respect or resentful acknowledgement. From what I can tell, the problems were with the humans rather than Commander Brod. We'll both interview him, of course, but if he's as good as he seems to be, I want him for our crew. We'll also interview his mate: she's a mathematician and a teacher. We do need to start thinking about our civilian crew."

"I'd like to propose another command position," Gyan said. "Someone who will be a bridge between the military and the civilians. I believe we need a chaplain."

"I didn't know there were that many devout believers in the Navy."

"There are some," Gyan replied, "and the chaplain need not be a member of any church but be prepared to deal with problems for all faiths—or lack of them. People will tell a chaplain things they'd never tell a psychologist."

Li considered the matter. "Very convincing. Do you have a candidate?"

"I do. Lupe Moreno. She was the chaplain on the *Glorious Light*."

"What's her rank?"

"She's a lieutenant."

Li pursed his lips, then nodded. "We'll see if we can't have her promoted to lieutenant commander. If she's really good at what she does, I'd like to have her attending staff meetings."

After adding the chaplain to the graph, Li uploaded it to his comcard and contacted Commander Able. "I have that list of personnel for you," he said, and sent a copy of the graph.

Able's voice asked, "How soon would you like a response, Commodore?"

"In about twelve hours."

* * *

Li had risen and prepared himself for the office when his card chimed. He immediately recognized Able's very modulated voice. "I'm preparing to put your list and mine together, which should help fill some of the gaps in the service section."

"Excellent," Li replied. "Please forward the information to my desk unit. I'll check it out as soon as I arrive. I need to schedule more interviews."

When he arrived at his office he found Able was indeed as good as his name. He'd not only provided names but comcard numbers as well as the comcard numbers of their superiors.

He began the interviews that afternoon and realized Gyan had chosen well. The men and women he met were obviously intelligent but, more importantly, he could sense their excitement. They realized they'd be serving on a new ship with unforeseeable problems to correct and they'd be in deep space for eight years, most of that time so distant from Earth they could only rely upon themselves and each other, but they were men and women who welcomed the challenge as an adventure. Like him, they wanted to see and experience things they'd never known before.

Added to the exhileration was the knowledge he was not only choosing a crew but creating a community.

Lieutenant Lupe Moreno was another addition to the group. While excited, she was composed. A small woman with large, dark eyes, she radiated warmth that invited confidence. Her credentials were good, having served on the *Glorious Light* and two other ships.

"If I," Li asked suddenly, "trusted you with a confidence, how would I know it would remain a secret?"

"Sir, you would have my word."

"And if I asked you for information about another member of the crew, perhaps even a criminal matter?"

"Sir, they would also have had my word. And I'd change the subject."

"And if I brought you up on charges for concealing the facts of a crime?"

Lieutenant Moreno showed her dimples in a smile. "Then, sir, I would hope to find good civilian employment after I got out of the brig."

"Good answer, Lieutenant. Would you care for some tea?"

"I'd like that, sir. Thank you."

Li spent the next few minutes busying himself with making tea. To the Japanese, it was a ritual and he could understand why. It was an opportunity to think while still expressing your appreciation of another person's presence.

When he'd set the two small cups on the desk he sat down and watched as the lieutenant sipped tea. "Do you realize four members of the crew will not be human?"

Moreno set her cup down. "No, I hadn't heard that. Should it make a difference?"

"I'm glad it doesn't. I have no idea what religion any of them have, or even if they have a religion, but I've met two of them and think you'll be able to work well with them." He sipped at his own tea before adding, "Captain Gyanashwar Singh has recommened you highly."

Her smile was as enigmatic as that of a sphinx. "Captain Singh and I have become good friends."

He waited until she'd finished her tea, then took the cup. "Welcome to the crew of the *Krishna*, Lieutenant."

"Thank you, sir."

After Moreno left Li observed the room seemed a little darker. Like Nurse Patel, Moreno seemed to bring her own light. Gyan's suggestions had all been excellent. He could only hope the man's reservations were less accurate.

He had no more interviews for the day so he began preparing requests for transfer of the personnel he'd approved.. Most of the command positions were now filled, for all three watches. This left mostly the support staff and techs. The weapons section and engineering were the next most crucial part of the crew, and the Marines who would protect the science teams as they explored new worlds were nearly as important. After a brief reflection he reminded himself all were essential, no section was disposable. They were as interdependent as fingers on a hand and they needed to be able to work with the same coordination.

On his way back to his apartment he bought ten bottles of the best Scotch he could find, which was all the store had in stock. These bottles would be saved for special occasions.

* * *

When the Huer halted and performed a perfect salute, Li returned the gesture then extended his arms, fingers straight. Commander Brod responded without any sign of surprise. Li guessed Ruhl had told the Huer a human had at least a rudimentary grasp of Huer etiguette.

"At ease, Commander." He took some moments to study the alien. The commander was even taller than Ruhl but not as massive, although he'd still make two large humans and his complexion had a dark green tinge. "I've heard some impressive things about you but don't have access to your Huer records. At a guess, you're a veteran. Did you have any trouble adjusting to the ships' controls we use?"

"No, sir."

"Do you understand that if your are accepted to join the *Krishna's* crew your cruise will last eight human years?"

"Yes, sir."

"Welcome aboard, Commander Brod. Cabins will be assigned within the next week. Once I've satisfied myself the ship's ready and the crew integrated, we'll take her on a shakedown cruise to the Neil Armstrong Hub. You and Kee will be interviewed by Captain Gyanashwar Singh. This is to help determine if you have any other useful skills."

"Yes, sir."

"Dismissed, commander." Li returned the salute and watched Brod stride from the room. Whatever flaws the Huer had, being overly talkative wasn't one of them.

The next interview was with Kee, the Huer's mate. She was nearly as tall as Ruhl and built nearly as strongly as her mate. He wondered how the Huer could distinguish between the sexes. To him, they were as indistinguishable as penguins.

After she'd responded to the open-armed greeting he waved her to a seat. "What do I call you?"

"Kee."

"As a teacher, we need a little more formality. If you don't mind, we'll refer to you as Ms. Kee. What ages do you teach?"

"Three-year-olds through college in mathematics. I've reviewed your language on my trip out. My grasp would be adequate to teach language to up to ten-year-olds. I do not understand your society or history well enough to teach but I would be able to teach ethics to the three-year-old to the eight-year-old level."

"What sort of ethics?"

"To respect yourself and others. To earn the respect. To understand differences and appreciate them. To tell the truth. To show respect for others by respecting their property as well as their persons." She leaned forward. "Unless the lessons of ethics are learned, none of the other lessons have any meaning. If success is the only measure of worthiness, some individuals may prosper but at the expense of others and of society as a whole."

Li permitted himself a smile. "You are most convincing. Welcome aboard. Do you think you can teach young humans as easily as you teach young Huer?"

"Are young humans polite, considerate, and patient?"

Li's smile broadened. "Not that I've heard."

"Then there's no difference."

"I'll have Commander Able set up appointments for you, the children, and their parents. It was a pleasure meeting you."

Using his comcard he called Commander Able and added the two Huer to the list of the ship's confirmed personnel and ascertained he'd gotten appointments to interview the crew recommended by the computer. His next act was to call up the latest test scores of Isharra Shanni. As he'd expected, her scores had shot to the top of her class. Mutual need was an unusual but rewarding experience. The Walawi needed a pride and he needed the best possible helm.

As he pocketed his comcard it chimed again and he saw a message from Gyan inviting him to the Captain's residence for a meal and a meeting tomorrow night. He acknowledged the message, closed the office, and returned to his apartment.

He wondered if he'd ever again feel completely satisfied. Ghopal Singh and Eric Bachman were more obvious casualties but the ChiTseTsi had seemed to have killed any sense of unalloyed joy he might feel. Everything seemed to have a faint trace of dissatisfaction. To the extent he could be pleased, however, he was pleased with his crew and, from what he'd seen of the ship, the vessel was as good as his crew.

* * *

After spending the day interviewing techs, science crew, and Marines, he was looking forward to conferring with Gyan. When he arrived, Gyan offered him a beer, a meal of Rogan Josh, and paneer naan.

After sampling the meal, Li remarked, "You're a man of many talents."

Gyan grinned. "True, but cooking is not among them. I picked this up on the way home."

"Well, what do you think of the Huer?"

"Commander Brod will not annoy me with needless conversation." Gyan grinned. "My only worry is that he may be intimidating to some of the crew. It's the first time I've ever personnally met a Huer. I think we've all heard stories but few of us really know very much about them. As for Ms. Kee, she impressed me."

"Very good. I have a lot of men and women for other empty slots in our table of organization. Let me know if you want to interview any of them. Have you seen the ship yet?"

"I'm still trying to get a clearance."

Li frowned. "I'll take care of that tomorrow. I suspect the reason you were denied was because the high command is afraid of annoying the Prime Minister, who seems to be afraid of offending the ChiTseTsi. The only thing worse than a coward is a coward who makes a virtue of cowardice."

As they finished eating, Gyan pulled up the organizational chart. Very few empty spaces remained. Li gestured at them. "I hope to have those slots filled by the end of the week and, by the end of next week, I want everyone actually on the ship and becoming familiarized with the systems. I also want two lifesuits for each member of the crew. That includes Brod, Kee, and Ishara."

Gyan grinned again. "The material they save on the suit for the Walawi will be more than used up on the suits for the Huer. Somehow, I don't think Ms. Kee is going to have trouble maintaining order in her classroom."

"Then you underestimate children. I'm waiting to see if any of the parents object to having their children studying under a Huer teacher."

* * *

The flat features of the Security Minister stared at him from the screen, wearing the expression of a man watching microbes on an electro-microscope.

"Minister Kim, I'm preparing to have my crew become familiar with the ship's systems and I require security clearances for all of them. I'm sending you a complete list."

Kim's voice was as flat as his face or hair. "Security clearances sometimes take time. I'm sure you understand."

"I understand. I'm sure you understand if it takes too long—more than two hours for Captain Singh and forty-eight hours for the rest of the crew—I'll find myself becoming bored. If bored, I might entertain myself with an interview. You might want to mention that to the Prime Minister. I'm sure he can find a way to relieve my boredom. Keeping me busy working on the *Krishna* with my crew would be an excellent antidote."

Flat, almost dead eyes stared into his from the screen. "If someone shows a gun very often, others might wonder if he actually intends to use it."

Li stared back. "I only have to fire it once. You may gamble it will not cause a revolution. It doesn't matter to me. If I can get my command by dealing with the devil, I can do it, but if your opposition gains the upper hand, you might find Mars more habitable than most places on Earth, while I will still get my command. Your only hope is that the supine posture you've adopted with the ChiTseTsi will be accepted by the people, something I doubt. I might be wrong."

The face staring at him might have been a snake's trying to fascinate its prey. "If you pick up a gun, you might expect the other party to pick up their own gun."

"I'm sure you didn't intend that as a threat. I'm also sure you're not naive enough to believe in a completely secure transmission." Li smiled but without warmth. "But I'm keeping you from matters more important, such as getting those clearances resolved." Li broke the connection.

Li fumed until he realized it simply wasted energy. He'd made no effort to be transferred from Tamaguchi's command simply because any commander he transferred to would either be another of the Prime Minister's puppets or a good man who might face reprisals to his career. And, if he had to deal with another puppet, than man or woman might be less transparent than Tamaguchi.

Within two hours, as he'd nearly finished his interviews, he received a message from Gyan. *Clearance received, leaving to examine the ship.*

* * *

Li returned the salute of the figure facing him, then studied it. It appeared to be a human male wearing the uniform and insignia of a commander. The features were nondescript and the coloring could pass for most nationalities. The black hair was worn short and the figure was only about a centimeter taller than Li.

"Very impressive, Commander Able, but why create an image?"

Through some electronic ventriloquism, the voice seemed to come from the figure. "Humans are less comfortable conversing with a panel than with another human. I noticed you had trouble staring into screens when we spoke earlier. The holographic image is completely without substance. If it appears to operate a control, I move the control. I've even set it up to make the sounds of footsteps as it 'walks.' Silence except for a voice would be a nagging anomoly to you. And it lets you focus your eyes on a face as you converse with me."

Li sat down in the command chair. "Please take your place at the console," he said to the figure. The holographic image did as he'd ordered and stared at him, awaiting further orders. "This seems an almost prodigal waste of your power and abilities."

"Not at all. The image is only available on the bridge or in the command room. It actually requires only the tiniest fraction of my power and approximately the same portion of my—attention, I suppose you could call it. And it makes your job easier, since humans are uncomfortable speaking to a disembodied voice. Anything that makes your job easier makes mine easier as well."

Li leaned back in the chair, which was apparently designed for comfort. "Have you and Captain Singh become comfortable with each other?"

"Yes, sir."

"Any observations?"

"Yes, sir. I would not have chosen him for his position based on available files. That's an area where you humans have a distinct advantage. Files are compiled by other humans, with all their prejudices and misunderstandings. The ancient wisdom is true—garbage in, garbage out."

* * *

A sudden gust caused Rasak's nictitating membranes to cover his eyes. A summons from the Vice Fleetleader hadn't alarmed him but it had made him curious. As he strode the walkway he idly wondered if having a live father was as useful as having one who was a dead hero. As it was, being his father's son had helped him get into the academy. Certainly, a live father couldn't have made his rise through the ranks since graduation any easier.

Presenting his right wrist, with its embedded chip, and the summons to the guards just inside the door, he submitted to electronic examination and was directed to the door at the end of the corridor.

Entering the room, he stopped at the assistant's desk. The assistant was obviously another guard. He accepted the summons, and rapped at the door, then opened it for Rasak.

Vice Fleetleader Dagher looked up as Rasak saluted, his right forearm across his chest, fist clenched.

Dagher returned the salute but remained in his chair. "Captain Rasak, you live a charmed life." His expression and his tone made it an observation rather than a challenge. "You've been selected to command the third of the new Stormbird-class ships. You will have a picked crew." He paused a moment. "You will also be assisted by Security Officer Batagar." His face and tone were carefully neutral, as even the office of a Vice Fleetleader was not sacrosanct to the cameras and electronic listening devices of Security.

"My mission, sir?"

"You will patrol our space nearest the human-claimed worlds. Your ship will have the new crystal-based tracking system. If any human ships enter Valek space, I want them stopped. I'll leave the question of 'how' to you."

"I am honored, sir."

"Dismissed," Dagher said. He again returned the salute without rising.

Rasak had to restrain himself to keep a determined expression and a purposeful stride when he wanted to leap and laugh. Older Valek warships had used the design and dimensions of the former overlords but the new Stormbird-class vessels were severely functional and as lethal as anything any race had. It was mostly engines and weapons. What it lacked in crew comfort it more than made up in superiority to any ship Rasak had seen, and he was an ardent student.

The hardest part of not having a father had been learning to choose advisors. He'd learned it was better to have advisors who were too cautious. They always gave reasons for why a solution to a problem was impossible and warn of the consequences of failure. When he'd formed a plan for success and an escape from the untoward results, he was ready to act.

He mistrusted those who flattered and those who were reckless. Boldness was a weakness of his and he saw no reason to compound it.

While pleased with his new command, Rasak wasn't surprised by it and had already prepared for the possibility. He wondered if Dagher had also found a way to read the reports of Ambassador Velnik. The humans were also launching a new class of ship, and he'd heard the Huer were as well. Velnik had no information on the Huer ship, although they'd probably refined the engines. Velnik had been able to provide vids of the new human ship in the shipyards and they were impressive. The engine alone was the size of most Valek ships and techs had enhanced the vids to show several sorts of armaments being installed. The ship was huge; a large ship for large dreams. This class of ship was to explore the universe beyond known space. It should be an embarrassment to the Valek Council that they hadn't even contemplated such a mission.

The commanders of the first two new human ships had been chosen. Commodore Wing had fought as an underofficer in the war with the Valek and had distinguished himself in the war with the ChiTseTsi. Rasak wondered why they hadn't appointed Commodore Sauvage to the ship. He'd been the most famous fighter on the line. If the humans were like the Valek, the reason for ignoring him was probably political. The other ship was to be commanded by a Commodore Li. Li had a solid if undistinguished career then, about five years ago, had been taken prisoner with some of his crew by the ChiTseTsi.

The fact he'd been given such an important command gave Rasak pause for thought. Being a prisoner for so long would've marked him, even under the best conditions. Being held captive by the ChiTseTsi would have been far worse. The Valek had settled their score with the shellbacks even before they'd encountered the humans, but there were still stories.

If the human had survived and been entrusted with a command he had to be either very tough or the appointment had been political. He'd learned enough about the humans to know they frequently considered their surviving prisoners heroes. So, he was a live hero or he had political support, possibly both.

Rasak's steady walk had carried him to the officers' dining hall. He exchanged nods with fellow officers and spied Satar eating with two other officers. Weaving his way through the maze of tables he sat in an empty chair at the table, nodded, and asked, "Do you have any plans for the next year to keep you from being my aide on one of the new ships? It's called the *Tercel*."

Satar stared at him a moment, then shot to his feet and saluted. "No, sir, I'd be more than pleased. And congratulations."

Rasak permitted himself a smile. "The rest of the crew has been chosen. We'll look over the list and meet with them beginning tomorrow." This was not the time to mention the turd on the banquet platter, the Security Master.

"Now that's news to make an old man young again," Satar said, although he was only ten years Rasak's senior.

The server stopped beside Rasak.

"Just a serving of whatever you have the most of," Rasak said. To Satar he added, "It's only fuel and I don't want to tarry over my meal."

From the next table came a voice. "Yes, congratulations, Rasak. Again, politics triumphs over ability."

Rasak recognized Karas' voice. They'd been rivals since

their first meeting a ten-day into their first year at the academy. He ignored it.

"Didn't you hear me, Rasak?"

Rasak had already computed the friends he'd make as well as the enemies. The difference was paltry. "Yes, Karas, my hearing is excellent. Fortunately for you, I'm too well-bred to point out if your father weren't on the council you'd probably be serving my dinner."

The server returned with a tray, set the dishes on the table in front of Rasak, and hurried away with the platter.

As Rasak had said, to him food was simply fuel. Hungry, he could down rations as easily as a banquet and hardly notice the difference. With the food was a small glass of brandy. Rasak took a sip, then ignored the drink as he ate. He'd never developed a taste for either alchohol or sugar. He anticipated Karas's next move.

"Notice," Karas' voice boomed, "Rasak has some sense of honor since he can't even drink to his own unearned success."

Rasak held out the glass to Karas. "Here, Karas, I'll let you drink to your earned failure."

The room had become deathly still. Karas was trying to provoke him into challenging Karas to a duel. The Valek who offered the challenge was legally liable for any deaths or injuries received in a duel, while the one who simply accepted was not. And the one who accepted had the choice of weapons. They were about equal with pistols but Karas was the better fencer. "If you're so overwrought with my success, why don't you issue the challenge, or are you hiding behind the law as well as behind your father's rank?"

His barb had struck home. Karas said, "I challenge you. Within the hour. What weapons do you choose?"

"Ships' command sims," Rasak replied, smiling.

"I challenge you to a duel and you want to play games?"

"It seems appropriate." Rasak replied. "The question was which of us could better command a ship. A simulation duel would answer that nicely. Since no wounds, mortal or otherwise, would be dealt I suggest we add spice to the contest by agreeing that for the next five years the loser will uphold the honor of the winner, although you'll find it far easier than I would."

Karas' face had darkened and his voice grew harsh. "Very well, an even match, you against me."

Rasak hid his smile. He'd manuevered Karas into a position where the other had much more to lose and any additional anger would tip the scales in his favor. "I didn't say it would be an even match. Perhaps you should bring your friends—both of them. It would bring me no honor to shoot down your mother but she'd probably give me a better fight than you will."

Karas was quivering with his rage and his hands clenched. Rasak stood and led the way to the training room. Duels in this fashion were not unheard-of but the facilities were usually used for training new pilots and new first officers. Each entered a cubicle in which sat a chair and a bank of controls. Rasak settled the headset over his ears. "Ready?"

"Ready."

For thirty seconds no instruments would function except the speed controls. The 'ships' were theoretically placed stern-to-stern and would move apart from each other in opposite directions. If Rasak's barbs had done their work, Karas would've thrust his speed control to the stops. Rasak set his own control on the slowest setting and waited. As his screens flashed on, announcing he now had full control, he used the steering jets to point the ship back the way it had come and fired a missile even before consulting the targeting system.

Using the engine, he slowed the ship then, with his nose pointed at Karas' 'ship' he advanced the speed control. He saw the image of Karas' ship at the edge of his missile's range executing a turn. A beginner's mistake, trying to turn the ship at high speed instead of using the steering jets. Karas' vessel shuddered as his instruments detected the incoming missile and he tried to evade, then spun his own ship and launched a defense missile and two decoys. Karas was still having to orient himself after the spin.

Rasak's first missile hadn't been an attempt to hit but to create more tension. With the distance between them beginning to narrow he took careful aim and fired his laser and launched another missile. The laser's function was to destroy or to blind. The condition would be temporary in the simulators but, with luck, it would burn through the repulsors and damage the ship.

The warhead bloomed like a flower of light in the darkness and Rasak fired the laser again. Using the steering jets, he slowed his ship and moved, crabwise, to one side. When his viewscreen was dark again it was an utter darkness and his instruments detected only wreckage.

Rasak touched the 'off' key, took off the headset, and stepped out of the cubicle. Karas was slower to emerge and Rasak observed their contest had attracted a crowd of young officers who'd been able to watch the action on an overhead screen.

With a curt nod to Karas, he lied, "You gave me a good fight. Thank you." Rasak had learned offering one who'd been beaten a consolation either made them allies or festered inside them more than would another insult. Either way, he won.

As he walked out of the building with Satar to their barracks, Satar said, "You won that fight handily."

"I'd won most of the fight before we stepped into the simulators. That's what makes facing aliens so fascinating. It's far more difficult to get inside them and have them hand the victory to me."

Chapter 8

Ensign Isharra was the last member of the crew to sign onto the roster. Despite the improvement in her grades she would probably have been assigned to some near-space scow, but she seated herself at the helm with the air of someone who'd found a home.

Three days later the *Krishna* lifted from her berth and as Isharra's quick, deft hands caressed the controls the lift-off was executed so smoothly Li could only tell they were free by the instruments and the viewscreen. Moving the ship five planetary diameters, she pressed the key that turned control over to the AI.

As they 'wrinkled time,' Li felt a weight lifted. While the vague sense of dissatisfaction remained, he was now free. He had his ship and his crew and all the machinations and intrigues were behind him. With the new versions of the Liang drive installed in the *Krishna*, no human ship was faster.

* * *

The Neil Armstrong Hub was, like all deep-space hubs, built into a natural satellite. Ensign Isharra set the *Krishna* in her berth like a mother placing a baby into a crib, with almost no magnetics necessary to guide it. Li called for a final systems check before releasing the crew who wished to leave on liberty. The trip had been flawless, with all systems performing at peak efficiency and the crew had operated without friction. He was just congratulating himself when Commander Able leaned toward him and murmured, "Commodore, may I speak with you in the Command Center?"

"Of course." Li stood and strode to the room, about a quarter of the size of the bridge, to find the image already waiting for him. "Is there a problem, Commander?"

"Yes, sir. Just before lift-off I detected a mechanical timer on one of the charges around the main power line to the Liang drive. It would've exploded once we'd 'wrinkled.' I disabled the timer with one of my maintainance units."

Li glared at the image. "Why didn't you notify me when you found the timer?" He dropped into the chair at the head of the table.

"Sir, because nothing more needed be done. Had I alerted you, you'd have been able to do nothing but worry."

"Is there anything else you neglected to tell me?" Li controlled both his face and his voice.

"No, sir. There was another matter I did not report but it had nothing to do with negligence. Someone tried to tap into my system. After creating a maze program that let them think they'd accomplished their ends, I followed the line back to its source. This was not as easy as it seems. The operative was working for someone else, with several safeguards in place. The source was Security Minister Kim. I then made copies of the records, with citations, and forwarded them to the six major news outlets, the leaders of the opposition parties, and to Prime Minister Xo. The copies were to remain dormant for twenty-four hours before appearing.

"At the very least, Prime Minister Xo will be forced to denounce and discharge Security Minister Kim and the effects will weaken the Prime Minister considerably. His coalition will collapse and his appointments will be given much greater scrutiny."

Li's laughter surprised him more than it appeared to surprise the image but he forced himself to adopt a stern expression. "Commander Able, I appreciate what you've done but, in future, I expect you to report such matters to me. I am in command of the ship and I'm responsible for the ship and crew. If you require that I issue you a direct order to do so, I give that order now. Do you understand?"

"Of course, sir."

"Commander Able, you have committed a breach of military protocol, something I trust will not happen again. I will personally inform Captain Singh. The rest of the crew need not know. We'll send the re-call from liberty in twenty-four hours. I'll want the command staff available for a meeting an hour before then." He paused. "Have you observed any problems with the ship's systems?"

"No, sir. Aside from myself, all the systems are evolutionary rather than revolutionary, so any problems are well within League Navy parameters."

Li started to stand, then dropped back into the seat. "What is your assessment of the crew?"

"I could, of course, take over the functions of any of the crew besides yourself but Ensign Isharra is an excellent helm and the rest of the crew seem very capable."

Li stood. "Thank you. I'm very glad to have you as part of my crew."

When Li returned to the bridge he blinked, a reaction to seeing Commander Able already standing by the status board. With all the obvious proofs the image was only that, a projection of a computer, it was still unsettling to have it appear ahead of him without having to walk from room to room. Li was sure he'd become accustomed to it, but it was still a novelty.

Brod was still at his weapons board, monitoring.

"Commander Brod, you may stand down. You have permission to leave the ship."

Brod stood and saluted. "Sir, I would prefer to become more familiar with the system."

Li returned the salute. "Commander Able, please notify all officers at the beginning of their next watch that saluting will not be required on the bridge. Commander Brod, if you become any more familiar with the system, it will be bearing your cubs."

"Commodore, I doubt Commander Brod is sufficiently conversant with the language to be aware of the alternative meanings of the term 'familiar.'" Able said, then, to Brod, "It was a joke essentially commending you for your diligence and dedication to duty."

"And," Li added, "suggesting you take some time off."

"Sir," Brod said, "a Warrior is always on duty."

"Very well. I'm considering giving you an additional responsibility. Have you tried out your lifesuit?"

"I tried on both of them when they were issued, sir."

"I want you to practice wearing it until it's like a second skin.

I also want you to study our Marine tactics. You're individually formidable but you have to learn to operate as part of a unit. After you've learned our tactics I'd be grateful if you'd also propose any improvements to them. Commander Able will program the screen in your quarters."

"Very well, sir." Brod strode from the bridge.

Only Commander Able and Captain Singh remained on the bridge. "Captain Singh, I'd like to see you in the Command Center, Commander Able, you have the bridge."

After pacing to the Command Center Gyan took his accustomed seat and Li dropped into his own chair. Li reported what he'd learned from Able. When he'd finished, Gyan laughed louder than Li had.

"And I was afraid a computer would lack initiative." Gyan laughed again, then asked, "What do you want to do next?"

"Whatever happens on Earth has nothing to do with our mission. We'll stop next at the Yuri Gagarin hub, then visit the three colony worlds between that and the Liu station. From there we'll be skirting the area claimed by the Valek. The Huer sphere ends near the Liu station. Beyond the station we'll be moving into places no human has seen. Then we can simply set course for the next likely star and outward."

* * *

Lupe had met most of the crew but the ship's liberty provided her an opportunity to meet more of those who'd also remained aboard ship. On the few occasions she'd visited the bridge, she'd apparently been invisible to the Huer commander, whose complete attention had been directed toward his instruments and displays.

Not at all sure her visit might not be considered an intrusion, she paused before touching the membrane of the door chime.

The door slid open and she stared into a room so sparsely furnished it might almost have been vacant. The Huer wearing the uniform with the commander's insigniae sat facing one of the walls, apparently scanning information from the screen, while the other sat staring at the screen on the opposite wall.

"Commander Brod and Ms. Kee, I'm Lieutenant Commander

Moreno, and I hadn't had the chance to meet you."

Something that was almost a smile flickered across the male Huer's lips and he replied, "In this place, we are Brod and Kee. What should we call you?"

"If we're dispensing with formality, please call me Lupe."

Kee spoke, her voice almost as deep as Brod's. "What do you want, Lupe?"

For a moment Lupe was confused by the directness of the question coupled with the courtesy of using her name, even with the strange accent, then she remembered she'd been told the Huer were very direct. What, to a human, would be rudeness was, to a Huer, a simple question. "I just wanted to meet you and find out if I could help you become more comfortable with the rest of the crew."

"All the crew I've met have been very pleasant and helpful," Kee replied.

"How have your classes been going?"

Kee gestured at her screen. "I'm just becoming familiar with them. Most of them seem eager to learn. I'm still having trouble telling them apart, but it's an opportunity for me to learn, too."

Lupe turned to Brod. "And you?"

"Your ships are more comfortable than Huer ships but you are more…private. It's something I'm having to learn."

"I hope it's not a difficulty."

"No, only different."

Lupe smiled, lips closed. "If you have any problems, please let me know. One of my functions is to help establish a sense of community." She stood and Brod opened the door for her.

Standing in the hall outside the Huers' room, Lupe was troubled by a sense of relief. Troubled, because she'd been trained to deal comfortably with awkward situations. She'd felt like an intruder but she'd also felt intimidated, not only by the sheer size of the Huer but by their sense of self-reliance. Both Huer seemed prepared to deal with any situation. They'd lacked the air of mutual support common in partnered couples. Instead, they'd reminded her of two crewmen, sharing the same space. They might like and respect each other, but each had his or her own interests and pursuits.

She'd skimmed the available information on the Huer but now realized how little she knew about them. She needed more intense study.

Drawing out her comcard, she pressed the number for Commander Able. When Commodore Li had told her there'd be four non-humans on the crew he'd failed to mention one of them was an AI.

"Commander Able, could you please tell me where I might find Ensign Isharra?"

"Yes, Lieutenant Commander Moreno, she is in the workout room on deck four."

"Thank you." For some reason, it didn't seem to be ridiculous to be thanking a machine.

Taking the lift to deck four, she found Ensign Isharra working at an exercise machine against as much resistance as a strong man might. The Walawi was panting heavily and wore a sort of mask over her lower face, with some sort of valves near the top. Moreno sat on the seat of an exercise cycle and waited. Despite the panting, it was almost impossible to see the play of muscles under the fine but thick coat of fur.

After another minute of working out, Isharra stopped, said, "Excuse me," and walked to the shower, still panting.

When she returned she'd taken off the mask and her fur was still damp. "How may I assist you, Lieutenant?" Although the words were more polite, the tone was cooler than the Huers' "What do you want?"

"Actually, I just wanted to meet you. You're the first Walawi I've seen."

Isharra stared at her with pale blue eyes that seemed calculating, then she coughed into a towel. "Then you may be surprised to learn we don't sweat like humans but we do use water to help lower our body temperature, just as you do. Again, how may I assist you?"

"I'm partly here in my function as a chaplain and partly because I'd like to become your friend."

Isharra sat on the seat of another exercise cycle. "Becoming friends takes time. Something given too freely has little value. We have eight of your years for friendship to develop. And what is a chaplain?"

"Just as a doctor concerns himself or herself with the physical and mental well-being of others, a chaplain is concerned with the spiritual well-being of others. I have a few problems because I know nothing about the gods or spiritual religious beliefs of the Huer or the Walawi."

The pale blue eyes narrowed almost imperceptibly. "We Walawi left our gods on our world. Gods unwilling or unable to protect their world and their people do not deserve to be worshipped or respected, and none of the human gods care about the Walawi." Despite the soft voice, the bitterness was plain.

"I'm sorry if I've offended you."

"You haven't. You had no way to know. I'm still learning about humans, too, and I've lived my whole life among them. Or, at least, around them." She dismounted from her seat, walked to a water fountain, and drank.

Moreno stood, followed Isharra to the fountain, and also drank. "I'll try to learn about the Walawi and, if you wish, try to help you understand humans."

Isharra's eyes opened wider. "Then perhaps we will become friends." She walked from the room gracefully, although she didn't move like a human female.

Moreno sat back down on the exercycle. She was steeped in dozens of human cultures and understood human beliefs but realized she was totally inadequate at understanding the aliens. To her, this was an unusual and unpleasant sensation. She was as familiar with human atheists as with any other system of belief or disbelief and was comfortable with all of them, but she wondered if she could ever see the world through other than human eyes.

She tried to imagine what Isharra might feel. She'd been isolated from the humans around her. Moreno had been quick enough to notice the distinction between "among" and "around," as the Walawi had so aptly phrased it. She had no way of knowing the degree of closeness of a pride, whether the Walawi had any sense of family or what form it might take. It didn't help that she couldn't read Walawi expressions. The narrowed eyes might've indicated anger, bitterness, or simply hurt, while the widened eyes could have meant amusement or acceptance.

Moreno strolled back to her quarters, seated herself before the screen, and keyed her comcard. "Commander Able, I'd like to access all the available cultural and social information on the Huer and the Walawi."

* * *

In all the old vids he'd seen and the electronic books he'd read, Li had been lured by the romance and adventure of spaceflight. Sometimes it even existed. He sometimes experienced a thrill seeing new constellations or in seeing the old ones from a different perspective, or seeing a planet that had never before been seen by humans. He was sure there had been excitement in the first tottering steps to exploring Earth's own Solar system and in the first few years after the Liang drive had been installed in the first starships, but most time spent in space was simply incredibly tedious. Systems had been invented and refined and, in deep space, most of the time was spent fighting only boredom. On those rare occasions when he'd felt real excitement, it'd often been tinged with fear.

On the first planet they visited, ironically called Tientsin, they sent down a shuttle with medical personnel and equipment. A form of mold native to the world was a nuisance potentially even more dangerous than plague. If it made the leap to attacking Earthborn lifeforms as it did native ones, it could possibly wipe out the colony. Samples had been sent to the Lunar laboratories and treatments had been developed as well as a means to destroy the mold.

Commander Able uploaded all the available information on the planet that had been collected since the first landing, an exercise he'd completed before the shuttle had touched down. Other ships would take the data back to Earth but Able would retain a copy on the principle it was better to have worthless information than not have information that might prove crucial.

At the second colony world they didn't even send down

a shuttle. Able uploaded information from the planet and downloaded the most recent news.

In some ways, Li realized, the human race had returned to an earlier time, despite all the technology. Man was again settling into remote villages which became more parochial and the Navy was both the roving patrol and the minstrels and peddlers, whose real stock was in news of other places as much as songs or papers of pins. Somehow, he found the thought comforting.

The delivery for the third colony was certainly more exotic than papers of pins; it was horse semen. Through an accident, they'd lost the supply from the ship that had settled them. Earth grasses and grains grew readily on Bramha, had all but completely replaced the native ground cover and the native herbivores had adjusted to the new diet. Several strains of native species had disappeared with the original vegetation but most either tolerated or even thrived on the imported grasses and grains.

More of the return to an earlier time. Much of the land surface of this planet was rolling plains, ideal for raising cattle as well as farming. If the settlement ship had left them vehicles, they'd only have lasted until major repairs and spare parts were required. At the planet's present stage of development, a factory to produce vehicles was out of the question. Establishing those factories would have also required mining and smelting, both for raw materials and for fuel. It was far easier to bring a handful of horses, or even elephants, as a renewable resource. The small breeding population would've quickly resulted in inbreeding with the inevitable results. But semen from half a hundred stallions took up little space and had the effect of increasing the breeding population.

The *Krishna* sent down one of the shuttles and remained in orbit most of a standard day.

Li stared at the turquoise world. It would be settled as man had always settled, with primitive implements and agriculture. Until a planet could feed its population and have surpluses, all other activities such as mining and manufacturing would have to wait. Those few planets mined for rare elements were the exception and were expensive to maintain. Subsequently, they were only established in those few cases where the scarce elements were easily mined.

When the shuttle returned it brought with it fresh meat, vegetables, and fruit. The native herbivores, it turned out, tasted much like lamb but sweeter. Fresh food was a delicacy and Li saw to it the mess hall would serve at least one fresh meal to each of the three watches.

Their next stop was the Yuri Gagarin Hub where they delivered the news as it had been when they'd left the Earth and allowed the crew to spend a few hours off the ship. As the crew trickled in from their leaves, Li and Singh met in the command center.

"On to the Liu Station?" Gyan asked.

"I think not. There's a quarantined planet between here and there, and I'd like to take a look. We can remain out of visual sight of the planet and still observe. Several odd things stand out about the natives. From all we can tell, they're the only vegetarian life-forms known to achieve a complicated social structure and the use of tools, and the first we've discovered that haven't developed the use of fire."

"Interesting," Gyan said. "I still remember one of my teachers pointing out that a grazing herbivore is unlikely to develop real intelligence. Her point was it doesn't take much in the way of brains to creep up on a blade of grass."

"The species we're going to observe wouldn't change your teacher's mind. They're not grazing herbivores, they're bipedal and symetrical. From what we can tell, they have at least rudimentary language skills and they're territorial. They're like humans in at least one respect; their greatest technological advances are the result of war."

"What do they look like?"

"They're fur-covered and about a meter tall on those occasions when they stand erect," Able said. "They're a brachiating species with opposable thumbs and a prehensile tail. When they walk on the ground, they tend to travel on all fours. They actually seem in a state of transition. Since they've discovered stone implements, primarily weapons, they spend more time on the ground. They tend to be very curious, which is often an adjunct to intelligence. While some of them have built shelters on the ground, they usually nest in trees."

"It sounds as though the transition might be more of a divergence," Li observed. "Commander Able, I'd like to put an observation satellite in orbit."

"Yes, sir."

When the planet appeared on the screens it looked blue with green and purple patches and small polar icecaps.

"Commodore," Able said, "instruments detect a Chadanor ship in low planetary orbit. Central screen." The planet disappeared from the central screen to be replaced by the image of a ship. Lit by the yellow sun, the ship glowed with a golden hue. Its "outrigger" design was apparent, with two massive tubes separated by an equally huge rectangular box.

Li leaned forward in his chair. "Hailing frequency, Commander Able."

"No response."

"Keep the hailing frequencies open, Commander Able. Commander Brod, establish a targeting solution on that vessel."

"I've already done so, sir."

The left screen was suddenly centered on a Chadanor staring at them with its upper frontal eyes, the other eyes closed. "I sorry, human ship. Communicator not working good." The Chadanor was gesturing rapidly. As if to punctuate its statement the screen flickered and the speaker transmitted static.

"Commander Brod, I've heard transmission difficulties can sometimes be fixed with a laser beam that lights up the ship's repulsor field."

Immediately the Chadanor's image reappeared on the left screen and it was, if anything, gesturing even more frantically. "Not necessary, human ship. All fixed now."

Li leaned forward, staring intently at the screen. "I am Commodore Li Wing Hua of the *Krishna*. Identify yourself and your ship."

"I am Shipleader Tagarth of the *Happy Fortune*."

"Perhaps, Shipleader Tagarth, you could explain why you're in low orbit over a quarantined planet."

"Trouble. Ship needed repairs, and we have sent down a team for water."

"I detect no malfunction of the ship's systems," Able said.

"Shipleader Tagarth, you seem to have resolved any problems with your ship. Recall your team now."

"Not long enough. Water-cleaning gear take time." The eyes shifted to something over the screen. "Eight of your hours."

Able said, "Commodore, any reasonable water purification system can be loaded in two hours."

The Chadanor shot Able a glare that should have at least crippled him.

"Shipleader Tagarth, you have half of one of our hours to retrieve your shuttles."

More rapid gesturing as the Chadanor's voice rose. "Your follower say two hours."

Li leaned back in his chair. "Shipleader, you can abandon the gear in half an hour. I might've accepted the two hours but you told me something that was not true. You showed your disrespect for me by telling me an untruth." Li lowered his voice and spoke slowly and distinctly. "I am going to show my disrespect for you by telling you the absolute truth. If you do not recall your shuttle and rise to escape altitude in three quarters of an hour, I will blow your ship apart. You can try to claim the planet with your wreckage and whatever remains of you."

After a glare at Li, the Chadanor turned its long face to the side and, with gestures, rattled off a short phrase in its language which the computer couldn't translate before glowering again at Li. "I will lodge protest with Earth," the Chadanor snapped. "Will remember you."

Li smiled slightly. It did feel good to know he'd be remembered. "Just so long as you remember the message as well. If you tell a human something that is not true, you annoy him."

Brod glanced a question at Li and Li nodded. Brod stepped back from his instuments so he was in the screen the Chadanor was watching. "That is also true of the Huer."

The Chadanor glared into the screen. "Will remember all of you." He muttered something under his breath and the center screen went dark, the view of the Chadanor command deck replaced by the image of the ship, now all dark blue but for a golden rim.

"Helm, stay above the Chadanor ship but open the distance. Commander Brod, keep your targeting solution current."

"Done, sir."

The *Krishna* rose smoothly, always maintaining the advantage of altitude, even as it moved away from the other vessel. They watched as the shuttle returned to dock in one of the tubes.

"Power is increasing on the Chadanor ship but they seem to be directing it to the drive engines," Able reported, then the *Happy Fortune* rose to five planetary diameters and disappeared.

"Let's go down for a closer look, helm."

"If they return—" Gyan said.

"If they return, I suspect Commander Brod will have prepared a welcome for them."

As the *Krishna* lost altitude, Commander Able nodded to Li. "Commodore, I observe you follow some regulations rather stringently while, with others, you take a more liberal interpretation."

"True, Commander Able, and when you learn to correctly choose which are flexible and which are not, you'll be that much more prepared to command a starhip." Li winked at him.

Gyan asked, "Why are we descending, Commodore?"

"Captain, I'm not sure our work here is done. We saw a shuttle dock on the *Happy Fortune*. How many shuttles could dock in that outrigger bay?"

Able replied, "Four more shuttles in that bay alone, and both outriggers looked the same."

"Precisely," Li said. "We know one shuttle returned to the ship. We don't know how many landed. We don't know how long the Chadanor have been here, and we don't know what they were taking off-planet. How many of you actually believe the

Chadanor only sent down a water crew?"

The command staff looked at each other, all but Isharra whose attention never left the controls.

"Commander Able, scan the planet, beginning where that shuttle lifted off. Full magnification."

The central screen flashed into a vivid splash of color, primarily green. The vegetation was lush, with trees heavy with fronds. As the screen moved they could see that only meters away the surface had been devastated, with downed trees and black burned-out areas rippled with gray ash. "It would appear," Li said quietly, "the Chadanor have been on the planet long enough to make themselves obnoxious. Those aren't landing strips, that's battle damage. Commander Able, can you find any of the shuttles?"

The screen shifted, following the ship's search. They were able to visually acquire two shuttles covered with fronds cut from trees and the ship's computer placed glowing outlines over two more that were hidden by the heavy forest canopy. "The scanners detect at least one more shuttle inside the entrance of a cave in the mountain. There is a huge vein of gold in that mountain, apparently only a dozen or so meters from the cave's entrance.

After a pause, Able added, "The sensors also detect at least two hundred lifeforms. Unfortunately, the instruments cannot distinguish between Chadanor and natives."

Li frowned. "They seem to have set their shuttles in a defensive arc around the cave, with one parked inside. And I'm looking at what appear to be several lifeforms on the opposite ridge of the mountain, covering the rear. Do I hear any suggestions?"

Able was the first to speak. "Whatever we do, we must first warn the Chadanor and request their surrender. The regulations are very specific on that point."

"I could argue I met that requirement in the first confrontation with the Chadanor, but we will follow the protocols scrupulously. Prepare a skimdrone with a recorded message in Chadrian to move up the slopes of the mountain. They can maintain cover from the trees but they must be exposed to aerial observation."

Gyan, staring at the scanner, said, "Sir, if we lose enough altitude to be able to support a landing party, we will be vulnerable to the Chadanor ship if it returns."

"When it returns," Brod said.

Gyan gestured at the glowing outlines of Chadanor shuttles. "We could destroy them all with missiles."

Li shook his head. "How many natives would die in the explosions? The Chadanor have already contaminated this world. I'd prefer we not add to the damage they've done."

"Leave war for Warriors," Brod said. "It is almost time for the second watch to take over. I trust Lieutenant Commander Feng to deal with the Chadanor ship. I should lead the landing party."

"With the Commodore's permission," Isharra said, "I'd like to join the landing party. I'll need to eat first, but I may be useful. I was given Marine training at the academy."

Li stared at her. "Just be careful. You're the best helm on the ship and we can't afford to lose you."

Isharra gestured at the others in the room. "We can't afford to lose anyone, and I believe I have the best chance of surviving."

Li stroked his chin. "You make a good point. Very well, but be careful."

Able said, "I'll call for the landing party to assemble in the shuttle bay with their equipment." The message rang through the ship, followed by the order for battle stations.

Within half an hour the second watch had taken their stations and Brod reported the landing party ready to depart. The skimdrone was launched, followed moments later by the shuttle.

The skimdrone dropped, then its antigravity slowed it enough to let it spread its mylar wings and it began broadcasting. Flashes from some of the Chadanor positions warned it was under fire then the visual feed to the left-side screen flared and went black. "So much for warning them," Li said. "Helm, take us up. I want to be at least six planetary diameters from here."

The ship rose, slowly at first but accelerating. As they escaped the atmosphere and the gravity lessened, the perception of gravity remainded as the vessel shot away from the planet. In a short time the screen showed two of the world's five moons between them and the planet and still they drew away.

The artificial gravity was activated as the *Krishna* began to slow and the laws of inertia battled with the applied science of the artificial gravity, so the effect on the crew was to feel a lighter than normal gravity until the system stabilized.

"Now," Li said, "we wait to see if Commander Brod was correct."

* * *

Brod studied his memory of the Chadanor positions. If they landed too far from the site, they'd almost certainly encounter natives who would not likely welcome more aliens, no matter how different they appeared from the first invaders. To bring the shuttle too close to the site would bring it under heavy enemy fire. That still left an excellent opening. The shuttle carried cannisters of fleschettes and minigrenades, and he had the perfect target for them.

"How many of you are drop-trained?" he asked the shuttle crew.

All nodded or raised a hand. "Excellent. We will follow the flaschettes and grenades by ten seconds. Strap yourselves into the harnesses." He turned his head to the front of the shuttle. "Pilot, I want you to bring the shuttle down to one hundred meters from the surface and just above the rearguard arc. At that altitude, drop grenades and fleschettes and the landing party will jump. As soon as we're clear, move behind the peak. That should protect you from enemy fire from the major Chadanor formation. I'll summon you when we're ready to evacuate."

Despite a sudden pallor, the pilot managed a "Yes, sir."

The shuttle, riding its antigravity field, bucked and pitched. The vessel was a cylinder with pretentions of stability and the pilot was adding to the movement, trying not to present a straight-running target, then it dropped as though the bottom had fallen out of the universe.

Brod hoped the tech who'd adjusted his harness and its anti-grav pod had taken into account his added weight. Even as the shuttle fell he heard the weapons being dropped then the shuttle shot upward twenty meters and the ports sprang open. Brod leading the first team, they were all falling toward the broken ridge.

The rapid crackle of exploding minigrenades rattled below them, mixed with screams, and Brod looked down. Between the grenades, not much larger than the ball of his thumb and the fleschettes, small steel nails with vanes, not a Chadanor below them was still alive, then he was clutched by his harness as the sensors triggered the antigrav.

His fall slowed and he studied the rocky ridge below. The area was littered with rust-colored smears and body parts of the Chadanor rearguard. He landed on his feet, hitting with the same impact as if he'd dropped from his own height, and he managed to avoid the nearest messes. Unslinging his autorifle, he glanced about, noted everyone who'd jumped was unhurt and moving to their assigned positions. Two teams of five each moved to flank the rounded peak while his team fell in behind him as he moved diagonally around the mountain and nearer its base.

The gravity on this planet was slightly less than that of Earth and the air, heavy with humidity, was oxygen-rich but smelled of mildew. By the time he'd reached a vantage, the two shuttles below him were bathed in the glow of plasma almost breaking through the vessels' repulsors. One of his squad settled the heavy barrel of his gauss rifle on the rock and the weapon hummed, then the nearer shuttle disappeared in an explosion. Shifting his aim, the man targeted the second shuttle and it, too, exploded as the shaped-charge penetrator round punched through the weakened repulsor field.

Return fire, most of it directed up the mountain, flashed in the dense jungle and Brod and his team suppressed it ruthlessly.

A heavy autorifle stuttered below and rock chips from the mountain became shrapnel. Something glanced off Brod's helmet and something else hammered his right ribs then Isharra fired a short burst that ended the staccato pounding of the heavier rifle.

Brod shook the mist from inside his head and glanced down. A rock shard had broken the stiffening plates of his armor but hadn't apparently penetrated. "Keep moving," he shouted, and continued to lead the way downward around the mountain.

The two teams above continued to provide fire support and Brod and his team had just reached a position where they could observe the other two shuttles. The fire from autorifles seemed to be eating through the repulsor field on the nearer vehicle, which glowed brightly before a pillar of flame shot upward and the vessel exploded. The man with the gauss rifle took aim at the other shuttle and it disappeared in a flash and a roar.

As the sound and concussion of the blast rolled away Brod keyed his com. "Teams two and three, descend."

Squinting at the mine entrance, Brod saw the defenders there were either dead or had been driven deeper into the hole. For a quarter of an hour he waited while the other teams moved into flanking position then, when they were clear of the top, he directed fire at the upper face of the mountain until a heavy sheet of stone dropped, roaring, into the mouth of the mine. Dust belched from the entrance as the walls collapsed.

Brod considered having the teams search for any Chadanor weapons but this increased their risk of confronting natives, something he wanted even less than a native finding a weapon it couldn't understand. Instead, he keyed the com again. "Shuttle, there's some level ground just below the mine entrance. As soon as possible."

In less than five minutes the shuttle had descended and the assault teams had boarded. Despite a burn scar on the upper right corner of the rear hull, the vessel was sound. As the shuttle rose, Brod stipped off his jump gear and his armor. He'd have to wait for decontamination before he could remove his lifesuit but with the armor off, he ascertain it was intact. With his fingertips he gingerly explored his ribs. He doubted anything was broken but even deep breaths were uncomfortable.

After reaching seven thousand meters the shuttle simply waited to be recalled.

* * *

"The Chadanor ship is returning," Commander Able announced. "It'll reappear on bearing one-eight-seven by zero-nine-three, range eighty-seven thousand kilometers."

Hardly had the words been spoken when the ship's blocky shape materialized.

"Fire!" Li leaned forward, staring intently at the forward screen.

Lasers lanced out, bright spears in the darkness, and the missiles streaked after them.

"Chadanor ship hailing," Able reported.

"No response," Li snapped.

The two lasers flared as they struck the repulsor field then the first missile became an expanding globe of light. Within a second the other missile struck and a much larger ball of light expanded until it disappeared, leaving less than an afterimage.

"Let's pick up the shuttle." Li shoved himself out of his chair. "Captain Amin-Madini, you have the bridge. Commander Able, meet me in the Command Center."

When he reached the conference room the image of Commander Able stood waiting beside the chair adjacent to the head of the table. At least some of the novelty had worn off—he'd expected Able to precede him. Li sat in the chair at the head of the table and nodded, watching the image take its seat. "Commander Able, I want you to send a recording of our contact with the Chadanor by ship's bottle. We will send another report by ship's bottle as soon as we've had a chance to debrief the assault crew. We'll do that at the beginning of the first watch, in appoximately fourteen hours."

"Yes, sir."

"Commander, you are very difficult to 'read.' You do not give the usual cues humans give to express feelings and I suspect you're too discreet to question my judgement in front of your fellow officers. In this room, we're simply part of a team and I prefer honest criticism to false praise or silence."

Able stared into Li's eyes. "Not criticism but curiosity. You chose not to give a final warning to the Chadanor ship, nor did you respond to their hail."

Li returned the stare. "I had already warned them, in no uncertain terms. Another warning would have been taken by them as a sign of weakness. At best, we would've left a Chadanor ship's crew with a false impression. It's possible they might have chosen to fight and I will not risk the *Krishna* to a preventable mischance. I'm sure the records will be forwarded to the Chadanor, and it may prevent similar incidents from occurring."

"Or it may mean the Chadanor will simply fire on any ship not their own." Able continued to stare into Li's eyes.

"It's a learning experience for both sides." Li clasped his hands on the table. "Other ships will be more vigilant in dealing with the Chadanor. One possible outcome is the Chadanor may try to ally themselves with either the Valek or the ChiTseTsi. The Valek are unlikely to deal with a race they despise while the ChiTseTsi would not negotiate with the Chadanor in any better faith than the Chadanor with them. I suspect the Chadanor are sufficiently intelligent to learn to behave themselves."

Li unclasped his hands and placed them, palms-down, on the table. "How did you know when and where the Chadanor ship would reappear?"

"I'm sorry," Able said. "I thought you would have already anticipated it. The sensors and other instuments on *The Long March* and the *Krishna* are the very newest and most sensitive. It's possible *The Long March* wouldn't have detected the entry point simply because the readings are so slight a human operator might not notice them but, since I'm part of the computer, I was instantly able to recognize them. There may be other phenomena I can detect that a human would not."

"Very good, but how did you detect the point of re-emergence?"

"The short answer is a projectile moving through an object always forces part of the object ahead of itself. It's been theorized for decades a ship in hyperspace is actually in motion and the eruption of hydrogen atoms preceding the arrival of the Chadanor ship would seem to bear that out. That was also included in the report we sent by ship's bottle."

Li frowned at Able. "Do you mean there's still some question how the Liang drive operates?"

"Of course. Professor Liang's genius wasn't in creating a comprehensive theory but in taking some theories and using them for a practical application. The practical application didn't actually prove the theories, of course. Other theories and even theories derived from the application would be equally possible. There are even theories that suggest the Liang drive has no effect on space, that it only 'telescopes' time. The most widely accepted theory is that the drive creates a moveable wormhole in space with the ship either moving like a bubble in a hose or that the ship remains stationary while the wormhole itself is the bubble. And either theory accounts for the passage of perceived time while the ship is in transit from one point to another.

"'Perceived' is the operant word," Able continued, "since all our experiences are perceived. A mystic might hypothesize hyperspace is actually sentient and aware and simply wishes us to that other place. There's no way to disprove such a speculation."

Li realized his hands had curled into fists. "But the classes at the academy...."

Able's voice was soft. "Theories to support the practical applications. Some men are driven to explore the irrational, and some of them become mystics. Many more attempt to provide a rational explanation for everything, either ignoring or theorizing around those areas not amenable to quantification, which is the favorite tool of the rationalists. They are, in their way, materialistic mystics. 'There are more things in heaven and earth, Horatio, than are dreamt of in your philosophies.'"

"But how could we use something without understanding it?"

Able smiled and continued in the soft voice. "Mankind has a tradition of that. How long do you think it took men, using gunpowder, to understand the chemical and mechanical processes? And electicity was used for decades before a real understanding developed. The great majority are neither mystics nor rationalists but somewhere in between. Many otherwise rational people believe in angels or ghosts or something called luck."

"If luck exists," Li replied slowly, "I hope it's riding in the

Krishna."

As the figure of Able disappeared Li levered himself out of the chair and trod around the table. He was tired. During the confrontation he'd been too involved to notice fatigue but now he had more than enough time to think, to reflect, and to feel drained. After trudging back to his room he glanced at the bare table beside the recliner. He'd never taken the time to turn on the hologram but now he felt the need to relax.

Sitting in the chair, he pressed a small button under the table and a shape flickered then resolved itself into a lit aquarium with ten colorful fish swimming in the illusion of water. It even had a column of rising bubbles at one corner and the sound of a bubbler. As he'd discovered at his mother's house, the grace and serenity was restful.

He wondered if the Captain Li, before his capture by the ChiTseTsi, would have dealt as harshly with the Chadanor. There was no way to know, of course. Like the bubbles, time moved in only one direction. Still, he wondered if he hadn't been hardened by his captivity and by the ChiTseTsi's treatment of himself and his crew.

Memory was also untrustworthy. It seemed to him the younger Li believed all could be clarified and resolved by reason and negotiation. They were still his preferred course, but when negotitiations were only lies and evasions, one had to change the playing field or the negotiators. He had changed the Chadanor negotiators, not by reason or persuasion but by the application of naked force. He supposed he should feel guilt or regret but he felt neither. Actually, he seemed to feel nothing at all, as the tension of the confrontation had apparently drained him of emotions as well as energy.

Finally he rose and undressed for bed and realized one thing he felt was a deep concern for the *Krishna* and her crew.

* * *

As Brod touched the entry pad to his quarters he remembered what he'd thought as he'd pulled on his lifesuit; that he missed his sept brothers but returning to the quarters he shared with Kee was comfortable and comforting. When he entered the outer room, Kee looked up from her screen.

She nodded to him. "I'd heard you'd been injured."

Brod made a mask of his face. "Merely inconvenienced. Nothing is broken or cracked and the bruise will heal." He paused as he remembered what he'd told Lagobrod, that one should always say everything that needed be said. "It gives me pleasure to see you each night in our quarters. It reminds me of why I picked you to be my chosen mate."

"I've sometime wondered about that. Your brother, Shkogar, has chosen a different mate each season."

Brod eased himself into a chair and settled himself so the bruise was only a minor discomfort. "Perhaps Shkogar is more Huer than I am. He's a creature of the moment. He has goals, of course, but he lives much more in the moment than I do."

Kee turned to face him. "No, I think you're more Huer. More primitive, perhaps. I understand the plainstalkers, to which we're related, most often choose a single mate for life. That's why I accepted you as my chosen mate. A few other cubs in our class were stronger but you would never allow yourself to be beaten. You felt deeply and you remained true to your passions. That seems a primitive thing to me but a thing of great value. I was sure your cubs would have that same quality." After a moment's thought, she asked, "Why did you choose me?"

Brod stared at her and wondered how he could have ever kept from telling her. "Your beauty, of course. Your strength. Your intelligence. But, mostly, I think, because I saw your patience with cubs and the way you could encourage them, help them grow. I wanted those qualities for my cubs and to help those cubs grow." He smiled. "It seems to have worked. We can be proud of our cubs."

Kee smiled in response. "And they of you. I saw Lagobrod and his brothers just before I boarded the ship for Earth. Lagobrod told me all about his visit. He was uneasy about you at first, afraid you would disapprove of his joining any but the Warrior Caste. He was impressed that you allowed him to choose for himself. The argument in the hall frightened him and he was terrified you might be killed. The hunt was a new experience for him and showed him things he'd never thought of—what it really meant to be Huer. He'd never really thought of where the meat he ate came from and you helped him see we are responsible for our world and the things in it. And when you and Shkogar sent him on his way with warm wishes and more besides, he was overwhelmed."

Brod stared down at his hands. "He and his brothers are worthy sons. They'll do well."

Kee turned off her screen and stood. "Shall we share dinner and, perhaps, more conversation?"

The human rations were only fuel for the body—even the humans ate them without relishing the taste, and Kee drank a cup of some hot gray-brown substance favored by some humans. Brod drank water.

"How fierce was the fight on the planet?"

"None of our party were seriously hurt, but the others were only Chadanor. Had we been facing the Valek, the battle would have been more desperate."

As he finished the meal, Brod felt a pleasant weariness, partly made of contentment, wash over him. He showered and prepared for sleep, then Kee took the other bunk. He found he wanted to continue the conversation but had no idea how to begin. His interests and Kee's were so different. Finally he asked, "How do you feel about teaching young humans?"

"Teaching the young is something I enjoy. And, when you open yourself to them, you learn too. It helps keep my mind young, something a mathematician needs. Mathematics is not all formulae and theory, it's also something that rewards a fresh perspective with insights. And some of those insights can be turned back into teaching." She chuckled. "At first, I think they were afraid of me. Perhaps they thought if they misbehaved I would eat them. But we have become much more comfortable with each other."

* * *

Brod stood as he delivered his report, keeping it terse but providing all the necessary information. The rest of the command staff sat at the conference table.

When he finished, Commodore Li asked, "Did the team perform as well as you thought they should?"

"They were very competent, and Ensign Isharra was excellent. Her quickness and her strength is matched by her courage. If she had not been with us to stop the heavy autofire, we'd have lost some of the team."

"Are you suggesting she become part of the exploration team?"

Brod turned his hand down then shook his head from side to side, the human gesture that meant the same thing. "No, sir. Exploration teams seldom encounter armed resistance and even in most of such cases, it would probably be a waste of her abilities. If I were in command of a Huer ship I'd feel very fortunate to have one such as her at the helm."

Li smiled. "That's high praise."

"It's deserved."

Li glanced at the others at the table. "I'm submitting recommendations for both you and Ensign Isharra to receive the Bronze Star."

"I thank the Commodore, but I only did my duty."

"But you did it very well," Li replied. "Something tells me there will be a day when you will command a Huer ship." He glanced again at the other officers. "Does anyone have any other questions or observations? No? Then I believe we can seal this hearing and send a copy back in a ship's bottle. We should be at the Liu Station in ten standard days and can file a copy there, as well as replace our ship's bottles."

As the officers stood to leave, Captain Singh leaned toward Brod. "Well done. See me when the bruises are healed."

Chapter 9

Five days later, when the bruises had become only an ache when he remembered them, Brod approached Captain Singh. "The ribs are healed, sir. Why did you want to see me?"

"How would you like a little exercise after our watch?"

"Yes, sir."

"Then meet me in the gym after we're relieved."

The watch was boring. When one travels 'between,' one only has the instuments to watch and few of them functioned with the Liang drive activated. Brod had no way of knowing if their path led them through a planet, or even a sun. The screens remained blank and it wasn't possible to contact or even detect another ship. He remembered a Huer tech had once told him that going 'between' was like being the only ship in existence or, perhaps, the ship didn't exist, that the universe was real and the ship only a collection of perceptions. While Brod had found the concept fascinating, the experience was one of tedium.

When the watch finally ended he strode to the gym and found Captain Singh wearing a loose-fitting exercise suit and performing stretching exercises. Brod undressed and pulled on an exercise suit in his size, then also began stretching.

"I'd heard stories about your time at the academy," Singh said, "and I'm by nature curious. Are you ready?"

"I'm ready," Brod replied.

Singh moved forward, almost stalking, light on his feet and combining caution with aggressiveness. Using his greater length of arm and leg, Brod threw a kick to the human's legs but Singh managed to spring up and he lashed out with both feet. Brod caught one of his legs and pulled, slipping out of the way. Caught off-balance, Singh barely managed a fall he could roll out of.

When he'd rolled back onto his feet, Singh began another advance. Brod drew back his right arm, then shot his left, the palm open, to Singh's chest. Twisting, Singh managed to slip most of the push and drove his left hand at Brod's face. Brod moved his head aside and caught Singh about the body and tossed him away.

Again the human rolled into the fall and was instantly on his feet. Curious, Brod simply deflected the punches and kicks . Singh was very fast for a human, perhaps quicker than the trainer at the academy, and he was deceptively strong.

Both were sweating and Singh seemed to lose power in his blows and seemed to have slowed but when Brod allowed him within the human's reach he responded with a flurry of punches, one of which landed solidly in Brod's midsection. Suppressing a grunt, Brod swept a leg to his right while swinging an arm to his left. Singh was caught and tumbled in the air, managing to land on his back, striking the mat with his right arm to redirect some of the impact.

Singh hauled himself to his feet then he grinned. After a moment he seemed to realize the expression could be misread and closed his lips but kept the grin. "If anything, I'd say your abilities were understated."

Brod smiled. "You rather remind me of my younger brother, Shkogar."

"He's not a scholar, I hope," Singh said, his grin broadening.

Brod stood, momentarily confused, then he perceived the humor in Singh's remark and laughed. "No, he's a Warrior, and perhaps the only one I could never best at anything."

"I find that hard to believe. At any rate, when we reach the station, let me buy you a drink. And when we're not on the bridge, I'm called Gyan."

"Honored. You are very impressive for a human."

Gyan smiled again. "It sounds as though that bar isn't set very high."

"You haven't seen Isharra move when she feels the need to be quick. I've watched her move her fingers over the controls and there's no way I could be as quick or adept, but I've also seen her fight. If I were one to feel shame at someone else's prowess, she would shame me. But we are all what we are and each of us can only be the best we can be. That is the center of being Huer and, perhaps, being human."

Gyan gathered together his uniform. "To be honest, I wasn't sure about the wisdom of having a Huer on the *Krishna* but you and Kee have convinced me. I've only known the Huer as a species we'd once fought. Now I find much to respect about them."

Brod flashed a half-smile. "I shared your reservations and not every human has earned my respect, but this is a good crew. I'm honored to be serving with them."

Gyan paused at the door. "Remember, I owe you a drink."

* * *

The *Krishna* emerged into normal space within less than a light-minute of the station, which was a tribute to Able's navigation, and they used their drive engines for the next two hours. The emergence had occurred during the third watch but the bridge quickly filled with officers of all three watches. While still at twenty thousand kilometers they could see two ships docked at the outpost and at ten thousand they could discern one was the older Explorer class human ship but the other had the greyhound lines of a new Huer vessel.

Brod was both pleased and surprised to see the ship, whose sleek lines made the *Krishna* look like a scow. The *Krishna*, on the other hand, was built to support a massive crew and to explore while the Huer vessel was a warship.

Gyan glanced at Brod. "That ship is all business."

Brod had to consider the statement before he understood it. "That's the new Challenge class ship. Design was started on it while we were still at war with the Valek."

"Do you suppose there's any way I could get a closer look at it?"

Brod smiled with half his mouth. "Were you going to invite the commander of the Huer ship aboard for a tour of the *Krishna*?"

"Good point." Gyan was obviously studying the lines of the ship. "I wish I could, though. Like him, my government limits my actions."

The *Krishna* had already begun deceleration when the center screen lit up with the image of a square-faced woman wearing a Navy uniform with rear admiral insigniae. "This is Admiral Long of the Liu station. Identify yourselves and your ship, please." The 'please' may have been added to make it sound more like a request than an order. It failed.

"Commodore Li of the *Krishna*. I see you already have company."

"Yes, the *Challenge*, a Huer ship, requested permission to dock. The ship's commander, Shkogar, was interested in meeting with you and several of your crew." The admiral paused. "So, this is the new Discovery class ship. Very impressive."

"Thank you, Admiral. Please tell the Huer commander my crew and I would be delighted to meet him. With your permission, I'll clear the channel for docking instructions."

As he cleared the screen he glanced at the ship's clock above the central screen. "Time for the first watch to relieve the third watch. Are you ready to take the ship in, Ensign Isharra?"

"Yes, sir." Isharra took over the helm and keyed her earset to the station's channel.

As Brod took his place at his controls, Gyan leaned over as if to look at the board and murmured, "I don't know how common a name Shkogar is but…."

"Yes, sir," Brod said. "The *Challenge* is my brother's ship."

* * *

Li pursed his lips then glanced at Able. The image seemed intently studying the screens before it. It was an interesting game Able played. While the human crew realized Able was only a hologram, a manifestation of the ship's computer, they had come to expect and take comfort in having the image go through the motions.

"Commander Able, as soon as the ship docks and before we open the bays, I wish to speak to the crew."

"Yes, sir."

Li sat staring at the blank screen. He'd never spoke Huer with Brod and, while it probably wasn't necessary, it was always better to keep some of your knowledge hidden.

The ship eased into the berth so gently he couldn't tell when the magnetics had taken over but he noticed Ishara's hands resting on the platform on which the helm controls were mounted. Moments later a chime sounded, announcing they had completed docking.

Able nodded at him and Li spoke, knowing his voice was being carried throughout the ship. "This is Commodore Li. I want to commend all the crew for their service. Before you are released on leave I should let you know a Huer ship is docked at the station. Many of them will be wearing knives. This is not to intimidate but is a part of their identity. The correct way to greet a Huer is with arms outspread and fingers straight. It is important to remember this detail, and it is equally important never to show your teeth to a Huer. That, in their culture, is considered a challenge. I want every courtesy extended to the Huer. Anyone not prepared to follow these orders is advised to remain on the ship. Dismissed."

Li stood. "I want the command staff to take their comcards. I believe there will be a couple of times when I will wish to contact you very quickly." He glanced again at Able's image. "Please request a meeting with the Admiral. I presume you've downloaded the latest news and entertainment to the station's computer."

"Just finished, sir." Able paused, then added, "The Admiral wishes to come aboard."

"Very good. Detail a Marine honor guard to meet her."

By the time Li had reached the ship's main entry, half a dozen Marines in spotless uniforms and highly polished boots stood in a row, their autorifles across their chests.

Rear Admiral Long Min-Hoa was square of face and body, a stocky woman with an intense gaze. "Commodore Li, I'd heard we were building a new class of ship but this is the first one I've actually seen."

"Welcome aboard, Admiral. Let me give you the guided tour." Long was most interested in the new engines and the hydroponics and finished with a visit to the bridge.

"It's as impressive on the inside as on the outside," she said. "My compliments on your command, Commodore Li."

Li nodded at the praise. "If I might have a word with you in the command center, Admiral?"

"Of course." Long followed Li into the smaller room and sat in the chair at the head of the table. Li reported on his encounter with the Chadanor, detailing the actions of Brod and Isharra. "I believe, Admiral, their actions merit the Bronze Star. And I would like to see Ensign Isharra promoted to lieutenant."

Long stroked her jaw and leveled her piercing gaze on Li's face, then flashed a smile. "I agree, and it wouldn't hurt to invite the Huer crew to the ceremony to let them see one of their own being honored. We'll do it at the end of the next first watch."

Li lowered his voice. "What's your assessment of the Huer, Admiral?"

Long leaned back in the chair. "They're very...correct and they have one hell of a navigator. We didn't detect them until they were thirty thousand kilometers from the station. They identified themselves and requested permission to dock. Since we aren't at war with them, I gave them leave to take a berth. I've only seen one of them since then, their captain—about a kilometer tall, like all Huer—met me to tell me that he was waiting for your ship."

Li sat in the chair to the Admiral's right. "Very interesting. The Huer seem to be magicians. They know where we're going to be and appear out of nowhere. Have you tried scanning their ship, Admiral?"

"Of course, but any ship you can scan isn't carrying anything worth looking for." The admiral stood. "I'll see you at the ceremony in—" the admiral glanced at her card, "—twenty-one hours."

After he'd escorted the admiral off the ship Li strolled to the Marine duty station, wondering whether Admiral Long was one of Xo's creatures or if she'd been sent to the station as a form of banishment. He suspected the latter, as she seemed very capable and outspoken. After accepting and returning the salute of the lieutenant on duty, he said, "I will require an honor guard at the end of the next first watch. Admiral Long will be presenting Commander Brod and Ensign Isharra with the Bronze Star. All the other Marines are welcome to attend."

When he returned to the bridge, only the first watch crew remained. "Commander Able, I wish to take most of the first watch staff with me. I'm releasing on leave all non-essential personnel. How big a crew will you need?"

"Commodore, I need only one person in Engineering and one in Hydroponics. If you wish, I can relieve them as well but I prefer to keep those two."

"Then, Commander Able, you have the bridge. I intend to meet the commander of the Huer ship. Captain Singh, Commander Brod, Lieutenant Commander Moreno, and Ensign Isharra, I'd like you to accompany me."

"Commodore, the admiral wishes you to know the Huer commander and four of his crew will meet you in the mess hall at your earliest convenience."

Li's lips twitched. "At least we know the Huer commander doesn't waste time. Let's go see them."

* * *

Li knew Brod had to walk slowly to maintain his pace three strides behind Li and beside Captain Singh. From the airlock they followed a long corridor to a large octagonal room with double doors on each wall. Tables had been laid out in rows and the Huer group stood beside a table at one end of a row. The Huer were an impressive sight—one was as tall as Brod, another half a head taller, and the other two half a head shorter than Brod, although one of them was half again as wide in the shoulders and torso. The man he guessed to be the leader was the shorter, slender Huer.

"Commander," Li said softly, "I'd like you to translate for me."

"Yes, sir." Brod increased his pace momentarily to fall in beside the commodore and they stopped across the table from the Huer.

Li spread his arms, fingers straight and the other humans and the Walawi did the same. "I am Commodore Li and these are my officers, Captain Singh, Commander Brod, Lieutenant Commander Moreno, and Ensign Isharra. How should I properly address you?"

The Huer returned the greeting and, after Brod had interpreted, Shkogar said, "Greetings, brother. Tell the commodore to call me Shkogar. You know Clell, Hkai, Thom, and Geir."

"He says to call him Shkogar," Brod said, and gave the names of the others.

"Shkogar, I'm honored to meet you and your officers. Did you have some special reason for wishing to meet us?" He spoke directly to the Huer as though no interpreter was needed.

Brod spoke then translated the reply. "Shkogar wished to see me, his brother, again and to meet my commander. He wanted to know what sexes you are to properly address you."

"Tell him, then ask him how he knew we would be here."

After Brod had spoken and asked the question, Shkogar laughed. "Old Ruhl told us which ship accepted Brod as a member and there were only two likely directions your ships would take. The other long-step ship went one way so we assumed you would go the other and this is your deepest hub, so it was likely you would come here. This hub is closer to Huerda than to Earth so we were able to arrive before you." He laughed again. "Your ship is impressively large. Some of the crew thought you humans would make we Huer look like cubs."

Li observed Brod translated with faultless honesty, even explaining the reason for Shkogar's laughter.

"Shkogar," Li said in Common, again speaking directly to the Huer leader. "Our ship is so large because our voyage is so long and requires so many people. The crew actually make up only a part of the humans on board." As soon as his reply had been delivered in Huer he added, "I am not only pleased to meet you and your officers, I'm happy to be able to invite you to a ceremony where Brod and Ensign Isharra will be honored by the Navy for their exceptional services. It will be held in—" he glanced at his card "approximately nineteen of our hours and will be held in this room."

For the first time, Brod deviated from the precise wording as he told Shkogar, "The commodore wishes to honor me simply for doing my duty but Isharra fought fiercely and with great courage. He is inviting you and your officers to attend the ceremony," and stated the time and place.

Shkogar laughed again. "Your modesty is almost human. Of course I will attend, and many of the crew as well. You brought honor to the sept and the family."

In Trade Common Brod said, "Shkogar will be happy to attend, and many of his crew, too."

Li kept his features an unreadable mask.

Brod made a gesture to his brother and said, in Huer, "Our fight was with the Chadanor, not a worthy enemy."

Shkogar's lips curled but he did not show his teeth. "But, as they say, even a striped scavenger will show its teeth when it's trapped."

Brod turned to Li. "I was just telling my brother our fight was with the Chadanor."

"Very good. Please ask him if there is anything we might offer him and his officers to eat or drink."

Brod asked the question in Huer and Shkogar held out his hand, palm down. "While we appreciate the offer we find human food and drink not to be to our tastes. But would you like to visit the *Challenge*?"

"May I bring Kee?"

"I'd be offended if you didn't."

Brod reported the exchange to Li.

Li smiled. "Neither you nor Kee have any duties until the end of the first watch tomorrow. But you will have to be in top form, so treat the beer with respect."

When Brod translated Li's reply, Shkogar laughed. "He's not so innocent, that old man, but it's good advice. I'll see you and Kee on the *Challenge*." He spread his arms, fingers straight, first to Li then to the other officers and the Huer with him did the same, then they turned their backs and strode away.

"Commander Brod," Li said, "you are dismissed. If I don't see you before then, I'll see you here at the end of the next first watch."

As they watched Brod stride back to the *Krishna*, Gyan said, "I wasn't sure, at first, whether we could trust him. Now he's a shipmate."

Li led the way to the dispensers against the wall where he and Gyan took tea, Moreno chose coffee, and Isharra took a cup of a heavily-sugared drink. As they returned to the table and sat down, Li glanced at Moreno. "What are your impressions of our Huer friends?"

"The Huer leader is exceptional, if the Huer are anything like humans. We tend to expect the tallest to dominate but he was among the shortest and the slightest built but his followers obviously respect him. Unfortunately, I wasn't able to intuit much more than that, except they are less formal than we." She sipped at her coffee. "They seem to laugh very freely but I get the impression they have little physical contact with each other."

"What do you mean?" Li asked.

"I didn't know Brod and the Huer leader were brothers until it was mentioned. Granted, in some human cultures there would be no great display of emotion but, in others, we might have expected them to hug each other or at least to rest a hand on the other's arm. They obviously have affection and respect for each other but there was no physical contact at all.

"I can't even tell whether theirs is a guilt culture or a shame culture."

Gyan frowned. "I don't understand what you mean, but neither culture sounds very healthy."

Moreno shrugged. "Both have their strengths and both have weaknesses, but they're the primary method of enforcing the mores of a social group. In a guilt culture the group's members behave properly to avoid feeling guilt. This is a self-motivating system. While others might not realize you've violated the mores of the culture, the individual is very aware of it and feels it deeply.

"In a shame culture, there is less personal sense of guilt but, if one is found out by others, one feels a much greater sense of shame. People behave properly in such cultures because they don't want to be shamed before others. Interestingly enough, some human cultures that set great store by pride and honor also reward incredible deviousness. Most human cultures are a mixture of the two."

Isharra stood and saluted. "If I may be dismissed, sir."

Li stared up at her. She seemed a little larger and her eyes stared intently into his. He stood and returned her salute. "Of course, Ensign." He stared after her as she stalked away. "She seems upset," he remarked to the others.

Moreno nodded. "Her fur was standing out. With most Terran fur-bearing species it's a sign of either fear or anger, and there's nothing here to pose a threat." She also stood and saluted. "If you've no further need for me here, sir…"

"Dismissed, Lieutenant Commander Moreno." Li returned the salute and, as Moreno walked after Isharra he glanced at Gyan. "Are you going to want to leave, too, Captain?"

Gyan smiled with half his mouth. "No sir. I'm very comfortable here. At least I'm off the ship. Do you have any idea what offended them?"

"Moreno wasn't offended, she was curious. I suspect she's going to find out what set off Isharra. What's your reaction to the Huer?"

Gyan sipped his tea and stared into some middle distance until he finally replied, speaking slowly as though weighing each word. "I'm wondering if they aren't asking each other the same thing about us. You must remember I've only met members of the Warrior caste. While we can't guess at their motives I believe they'd be steadfast allies or implacable enemies. Come to think of it, they probably aren't asking each other what they think of us. That would imply our opinions matter to them. They'll decide whether we're worthy or not based on their own values."

"I'd hardly call them implacable," Li said. "After all, we once fought them and they don't seem to have nursed any resentment."

"Sir, I don't think they regarded us as enemies, only as competitors. There's a very real difference. For instance, I don't think they regard the Chadanor as being worthy of being either friends or enemies. I'm not even sure they regard the Valek as enemies. But I know we humans need to be considered worthy, and I really don't want them as enemies."

* * *

Moreno found Isharra in the gym, punishing a heavy bag, and the speed with which she struck and the power behind the blows and kicks clearly showed her anger. Moreno simply waited until Isharra had finally stopped and had returned from the dressing room carrying her exercise clothes and the mask before she approached. "Isharra, could you explain to me why you're so angry?"

Isharra hesitated a moment, staring into Moreno's eyes, before she replied. "One is not permitted to speak ill of the pride or its members."

"Humans have different customs," Moreno said, "but most of us have learned hidden anger is the worst sort. Without knowing what has angered you, we can't either mollify the anger or avoid causing it again. Please, speak plainly."

Isharra studied Moreno for a long moment. "Commander Brod is not only part of the pride but a very important part of it but you were speaking of him almost as a thing. You humans want to measure everything—using human rules to judge— when you should learn to measure less and accept more. I have served with him. He is prepared to lay down his life for this ship and this crew. He is even willing to risk the lives of those serving under him, which is harder for him than risking his own life. And you still wonder about him."

Moreno lowered her gaze. "There's some truth in what you say, but there was no disrespect intended to Commander Brod." She raised her head and stared into Isharra's eyes. "But you are doing the same thing to us. You are judging we humans by Walawi standards. I won't say you're wrong to do that but we all look for answers and all of us use the measures we know. It's impossible for you to pretend to be human and look at us through human eyes.

"Perhaps you Walawi are more accepting but we humans strive to understand. It's easier for us to accept what we understand, but I want you to know both you and Brod are accepted." She smiled. "After all, if we can accept Commander Able, it's very easy to accept you."

Again she was struck by how utterly opaque Isharra was to her and she wondered if the Walawi themselves could read each others' expressions, then Isharra said, "I told you before that making friends is a long trip. I think we have taken the first steps."

"If I may ask," Moreno said, "why do you wear the mask?"

"I told you once we Walawi do not sweat as you humans do. We sweat through our tongues. It seems to bother humans to see me with my tongue out and sweat dripping from it. And the mask keeps me from getting my sweat on the equipment."

"Thank you." The gratitude was less for the information than for the budding friendship.

* * *

Shkogar met Brod and Kee at the *Challenge's* airlock. "Welcome. Kee, you are either very devoted or a little crazy to be my brother's chosen mate. Will you have beer?"

"Perhaps a little of both," Kee replied, "and beer is a Warrior's drink. I'll have some fruit juice, though."

Shkogar smiled. "I keep forgetting you're a Scholar. You have a Warrior's bearing."

He led them to the dining hall and poured a pitcher of fruit juice and one of beer. Another Huer carried mugs to the table then walked away.

Kee took a deep drink of the juice. "I've missed this. No Earth fruit juices have this tartness."

Brod downed his mug of beer in one long swallow and refilled the cup. "And I've missed this." He sipped, savoring the taste.

"Well, brother," Shkogar drank deeply and asked, "what do you think of the humans?"

"Ask what I think of the Huer. Like us, they have good and bad. The crew I'm serving with is very good."

"Why are they honoring you and—I forget the name?"

"Isharra. She's the Walawi you met with the others. If I had a crew of Walawi, I could give even you a real fight." He took another drink of beer, seemed to feel it washing away dust in his throat. He described the encounter with the Chadanor.

When he finished, Shkogar barked another laugh. "The Chadanor thought they were dealing with someone softer than the Huer. Your Commodore Li might almost be Huer. And for one so small and furry...Isharra" he stumbled over the name, "sounds like a worthy Warrior. If they are all like her, I'd be ready to fight the whole Valek fleet with one good ship crewed by Walawi."

Brod finished his beer and poured another. "An alliance between Huerda and their worlds might benefit us both. It might lead to war with the ChiTseTsi, but the Walawi would be worthy allies and we could give them back the stars."

"I'll put that in my report and send it back by ship's bottle when we're away from the station." Shkogar drained his own beer and, seeing the pitcher was empty, strode to the tun to refill it.

When Shkogar returned to his chair, Brod asked, "Any news from Huerda?"

"No, only that the *Challenge* performed so well on its test flight more will be built. They were laying out three hulls when I left. The attractor offers one surprising advantage. It draws in, among other things, inter-ship and even intra-ship communications. We could actually listen to any communications broadcast on the station and on the Huer ships we tried it against. We can program the computer to turn on the attractor even as we deactivate the Longstride drive. And, of course the computer has to find the proper frequencies to convert it to audible. Besides the new attractor, it has new engines that make it the fastest ship in the Huer fleet." He sipped more beer. "Will you stay and eat with us?"

Brod turned his hand palm-down. "Ship's food, human or Huer, is almost never a delicacy. I was thinking of taking Kee to the diner in the hub."

"There's still time enough to see some of your other friends." Shkogar held up his arm and nearly a dozen Huer, most of them Warriors or Techs, carried their pitchers and mugs to the table. They greeted Brod and Kee in the Huer fashion then all sat down. Brod had served with Clell, a Navigator, and Thom, a Helmsman, and he'd heard of Geir, the chief Engineer. Most of the others he knew by name. The Engineer and several of the Techs knew Kee and they answered questions and shared reminiscences for over a Huer hour before Brod's stomach grumbled.

Clell had just asked if the stories about the humans mating almost constantly were true.

"I couldn't say," Brod replied. "The *Krishna* is so huge each couple has their own quarters. I haven't seen them act other than properly on duty but humans seem to touch each other a lot. Friends will sometimes clasp hands or clap each other on the shoulder or arm, sometimes even embrace, but it seems to have nothing to do with mating. It seems more a reassurance of affection."

"You mean you and Kee have your own quarters?" Thom was incredulous.

"Yes, humans seem less comfortable sharing quarters. But Kee and I must leave for dinner."

"You've grown soft, Brod," Clell said with a smile. "You need some good Huer food. Shkogar, here, has set aside some three-horn meat harvested the old way for a feast. This seems an appropriate occasion."

Brod glanced at Shkogar, who turned a hand palm-up. "The old ways have to change. Now we can preserve the meat and hold a feast aboard ship."

"It sounds very good," Kee said.

Brod tried to hide a smile, failed. "Perhaps you're right, Clell. Maybe some three-horn meat and more Huer beer will turn me back into a true Huer."

As he ate three-horn so rare it still bled, drank Huer beer, and joked with other Huer, Brod almost felt that most of the last few months had been a dream. Here, he felt completely at ease. He could respect his human crewmates, even like them, but, in many ways, he was still a stranger. Here, he was with his sept-brothers and other Huer. And he wondered if, on the human ship, he was truly Huer.

"Why so grim, brother?" Shkogar asked. "You've fought well, even with a female Warrior, you will be honored tomorrow, and you share quarters with your chosen mate." He leaned forward to look past Brod at Kee. "He still scowls in his sleep, doesn't he?"

That wrung a chuckle from both Brod and Kee.

"I was just realizing how much Huer I am even after spending so much time with humans, but sometimes I feel… somehow…less Huer."

Shkogar downed his beer and refilled the mug. "Someone once told me worry was the future robbing the present. You will always be truly Huer. You are Huer to your core and you couldn't change that if you wanted to."

* * *

Admiral Long was resplendent in her full-dress uniform, with a glittering array of awards on her chest. Li and most of the other officers of the *Krishna* also wore dress uniforms, although the Marines wore their chameleon battle-garb, as did Brod. The Huer all wore their own chameleon battle dress, which was darker than the human version. A section of the mess hall floor had been raised to form a dais and the admiral and Li stood facing the crowd, directional microphones ready to amplify and translate their remarks.

Brod and Isharra stepped onto the dais and paced toward the ranking officers, halted, and saluted. The salutes were returned and the admiral accepted a small box from an aide, opened it, and took out a bronze twelve-pointed star which hung from a v of black and silver silk attached to a bronze bar.

Brod had to lean forward to allow the admiral to pin the medal to his uniform. "For courage and excellence in leadership, Commander Brod, you are awarded this decoration."

"Brod! Brod! Brod!" The Huer started the chant and it was quickly taken up by the Marines, then by the rest of the humans.

Brod saluted then turned, grinning, and raised his arms. The Huer immediately stopped the chant then the humans fell silent. Brod turned back to the admiral and saluted again.

The admiral took another box from the aide. "Ensign Isharra, you are receiving this award from a grateful service for your courageous action above and beyond your duties." This time the admiral had to lean forward to secure the decoration to Isharra's chest. "In addition, I want to announce your promotion from ensign to lieutenant." She handed Isharra another box which contained the new silver bars.

Isharra and Brod saluted and as the admiral returned the salute she said softly, "Dismissed," and gestured for the microphones to be turned off.

As they turned to face the crowd, Brod roared, "Isharra! Isharra! Isharra!" The Huer, then the others took up the chant until Isharra, her face as inscrutable as ever, raised her arms.

Li leaned toward the admiral. "Having the Huer at an awards ceremony adds in enthusiasm what it takes away in formality."

The admiral smiled. "Perhaps we should make it a custom to invite them to these things. You are dismissed, Commodore Li."

After returning Li's salute, Admiral Long walked off the dais to the door opposite the tables. Li nodded to an ensign, who ducked out of the room to return with two large bottles of Scotch.

Taking one of the bottles, Li approached the table lined with Huer. Asking Brod to interpret, he told them it was a human custom to drink a toast to those who were decorated and the glasses should not be raised until he raised his hand. He poured a dollop of Scotch in each Huer's cup, doing the same with the Marines and the ship's crew. Only Amin-Madini and his wife and another Muslim couple declined, preferring to drink their toast in fruit juice.

After putting a finger of whiskey in his own glass, he raised the glass and said, "We have honored two of our number, Commander Brod and Lieutenant Isharra, and we wish them to know we are all honored to call them comrades. To Commander Brod and Lieutenant Isharra!" He raised his hand then shot back the Scotch, appreciating the sudden fire and lasting warmth.

Shkogar roared something and Brod said, "My brother says that's a real Warrior's drink."

"I hope they like the meal," Li said to Brod. "Somehow, Lamb Vindaloo seemed the best idea. You seemed to enjoy spicy food."

Two Huer left the room to return in minutes with a tun of Huer beer and started filling glasses and pitchers. Li accepted a small glass and sipped. While not as potent as the Scotch, the drink had enough punch for him to treat it with respect. The color was very dark, almost black, and he could taste the yeast, a flavor that faintly reminded him of caramel, and a slight bitterness. He wondered if Huerda had something like hops.

The meal was delicious, although very spicy but the Huer seemed to enjoy it and the talk at their table was loud and raucous. Finally, Li took out his comcard and checked the time, then stood and raised his voice to be heard. "It's been a pleasure to see you all here, to meet the Huer crew, and especially to honor our friends but the first shift of the hub will be coming here in less than thirty minutes." He raised the glass of Huer beer and said, "To our Huer friends," then finished the beer in a swallow.

The Huer leader sprang to his feet and his voice filled the room, even without the benefit of a microphone. He spoke very briefly in Huer and Brod translated. "To the crew of the *Krishna*." The Huer crew all tossed back their drinks and began to file out of the room while Shkogar approached Li.

They exchanged the Huer greeting, which was also used for departures, then Shkogar said, in strongly accented but quite good Trade Common, "Thank you for honoring my brother and for sharing it with my crew and I."

After recovering from the momentary surprise, Li said in Huer, "You speak Common quite well. You are a person of... surprises."

Shkogar grinned, lips closed. "In some games it is a good practice to keep a piece hidden until you know who your friends are. I see you also observe the same custom. It is probably better Brod not know what we both know." As Brod approached, Shkogar said, in Huer, "You humans know how to feast, although you don't laugh enough."

Li waited for the translation and replied in common. "We have much to learn from the Huer."

"I will look forward to meeting you again, Commodore Li."

* * *

By the end of the third watch the next day the reprovisioning of the *Krishna* was complete. The Huer vessel had left during the first watch and disappeared.

Li took the command chair. "We have one more errand to run. Commander Able, I believe you have the coordinates for the *Copernicus_*science station. We're to deliver supplies and transmit all their data back by ship's bottle."

Gyan glanced at him. "I thought the Liu Station was the farthest any human ship had gone."

"I thought so, too, but apparently the *Indra* left a science station very near Valek-claimed space. An astronomer on the Liu saw what she thought might be conditions for the birth of a black hole and someone was convinced to leave a station to observe it. They may have wanted to be discreet, since an observation station so near Valek space would have been very controversial. They're too small to carry a ship's bottle and it would've taken a very dedicated crew to live on recycled everything."

"Coordinates input and ready to jump at your command," Able said in a monotone. "Expected arrival in one hour, twenty-seven minutes of perceived time."

"Now."

* * *

The globular station seemed to float, motionless in the void and the klaxon sounded a moment or two before Isharra began to slow the *Krishna* to match speeds with the station. As they neared it they could see sections had been torn away by energy weapons.

"Battle stations," Li snapped, and the klaxons hooted again, this time in rapid bursts of threes.

Brod's attention was fixed on the screens and the instruments before him. No other vessels were within range of the instruments.

Able's clear, precise voice announced, "No other ships within sensor range, although I detect a small anomaly aft." After a pause, he added, "There are no major life-forms on the station. Atmosphere and gravity within the central life pod and the observatory are normal."

Li stared at the science station at full magnification as though trying to see inside the *Copernicus*. "Captain Singh, would you care to lead the boarding party?"

"Yes, sir," Gyan replied. "Commander Brod, please choose a team to go with us."

Drawing and activating his comcard, Brod said, "Lieutenant Jeroskaya, assemble a boarding party. Everyone to wear lifesuits." He strode with Gyan to the shuttle bay and pulled on his own lifesuit, complete with the helmet and oxygen tank. "Relax before you go to oxygen," he said to Gyan. "You don't want to hyperventilate."

Gyan nodded, then the Marines, already suited, trotted down the corridor to the shuttle. Finally, a small machine with treads and cameras mounted on swivels whined out to the shuttle.

Brod recognized the pilot as the same man who'd piloted the vessel into a storm of Chadanor fire. The Huer smiled and said, "This trip will likely be less eventful than the last one."

The human smiled back and the shuttle lurched into space even as the crew finished securing themselves. The robot had clamped itself to the inner hull with metal rods that matched depressions in the formers. In less than a quarter of an hour their vessel had attached itself to the *Copernicus*' airlock. As they'd approached, Gyan had pointed out to them the slag from whatever had cut sections from the hull were on the outside of the station, meaning the weapons had been fired from inside. He reported the observations to the *Krishna* and Able had replied the only life-forms were the crew of the boarding party,

Breaching the airlock, they discovered the corridor leading to the crew's quarters were still largely intact and the station's artificial gravity still functioned.

Brod entered first, a light in one hand and his pistol in the other. Reaching the end of the corridor he paused at the door to the crew's quarters but the door opened at the turn of the wheel. Glancing back, he noted the Marines had set up another airseal on the near side of the hole in the corridor wall. Opening the door, his instruments sensed breathable air rushing out into the corridor and he opened the visor of his helmet and turned off his oxygen. A single deep breath told him what remained of the science team were in the observation section. A quick glance into the observatory was enough to inform him all six of the team were dead, the bodies so mutilated he could barely determine they had once been human.

Chapter 10

Hearing a racking sound, Brod turned and saw one of the Marines being violently ill. The already-pale faces of the rest of the party seemed to turn a faint greenish shade as the smell of death and vomit twisted their stomachs to another degree of nausea. Brod stepped in front of the stricken crewman. For a moment, he had trouble matching a name with the face, then he growled, "Rivera, you've disgraced yourself and your commanders. Return to the shuttle."

Rivera was barely able to nod, then he stumbled back the way he'd come.

Gyan keyed his throat-mike. "Bridge, the science team members are all dead."

Li's voice could barely be heard by the others. "Acknowledged. Can you bring the bodies back to the ship?"

"We'll need to use the sealed body bags on the shuttle but, yes, we can do it."

While a private stepped out to get the bags, Brod studied the room. Immediately, he noticed a small piece of metal lying on the carpet beside the chair in which one of the bodies rested. The robot had joined the group and scanned the room, recording, from several different vantages. The ship's computer would be using the full array of the robot's sensors and would be able to provide an almost molecule-by-molecule reconstruction. Brod waited until the robot had finished examining the room, then drew its attention to the artifact.

After a moment, the speaker on the robot said, in Able's voice, "A button from a Valek dress uniform."

Gyan assisted the men who wrestled the bodies into the body bags and he and Brod carried two of them to the shuttle. When Brod returned he found the robot again scanning the compartment from different angles, recording what might have been revealed by the removal of the bodies. Within a minute he'd gone through the entire station—what remained of it— recording everything, then Able's voice said, "Captain, besides the Valek button and the obvious signs of violence, there are no other anomalies on this vessel—no other foreign objects of any sort."

Face grim, Gyan gestured to the rest of the party. "Return to the shuttle."

Brod was the last to board the shuttle. The ride back to the *Krishna* was a silent one. When they'd returned and seen the bodies taken to the infirmary, Brod and Gyan stripped off their lifesuits and strode to the lift.

"Bridge level," Gyan said, then glanced at Brod. "You were a little hard on the new man, weren't you, Commander Brod?"

"Captain," Brod's voice, even to him, sounded like a low grumble, "if you dispute my methods of command, you may report any violations to our superiors."

Gyan blinked at the words and tone and stared intently at the door.

When they reached the bridge they saw the familiar image of Able and heard him say, "Yes, Commodore, I can possibly follow the ship used by the ones who did this. The Liang drive and its alien versions do leave a sort of ripple effect in time. It's a different sort of measurement but it is possible to discern. The ship of those responsible for this was moving toward Valek space."

Li studied the screen, absently stroking his chin with his index finger. "Send a report by ship's bottle to Liu station giving the coordinates and disposition of the *Copernicus*. They'll decide whether they want to retrieve what's left of the station. We haven't room for it in the cargo bay, and we can't haul it around after us. After you've sent the message, set a course following the trail you detected, and I want the command staff of first and second watches to assemble in the command room."

When Brod strode into the command room he was nearly the last to arrive and was mildly surprised to find Lieutenant Commander Moreno seated near the end of the table. He took his own chair beside Captain Singh and across from Commander Feng.

Li nodded to Commander Able at Brod's left. "Please record

this meeting, Commander." He glanced around the table. "Have any of you any observations or suggestions?"

"It was not the Valek who did this," Brod said.

Li raised an eyebrow. "That is a rather remarkable assertion, considering the only clues are a Valek button left with the dead and a trail leading us into Valek space."

"Sir, the Valek are warriors. Those people on the station were tortured to death. The Valek would only torture to extract information, and the scientists on the station had no meaningful military information, something any Valek would have known. When the Valek take prisoners they either release them, trade them, or dispose of them efficiently. This was not the work of the Valek."

Li apparently considered the argument for a moment. "Lieutenant Commander Moreno?"

"From what I know of the Valek, Commander Brod's analysis seems correct. There are three reasons for torture." She raised her index finger. "To extract information. These people had no information of value." A second finger joined the first. "To humiliate the enemy. While some warrior cultures have practiced torture for this reason, it doesn't fit the Valek mind-set. The pride—arrogance if you will—of the Valek is quite sincere. They need not humiliate their enemies because they believe their enemies to be intrinsically inferior. It would be like a human torturing a dog or cat to make it less human."

"There are always sadists," Li observed.

"But not in Solar League command levels, nor I suspect among the Huer commanders either. From what we know, the Valek command candidates are as carefully screened as ours. The reason is obvious. Even a small ship is too dangerous and too valuable to entrust to an unstable commander. And there is still the other reason." Moreno raised a third finger. "To terrorize, and the Valek have had enough experience with humans to know torturing prisoners would have the opposite effect. All these reasons point to someone other than the Valek. The first supposition I can provide is that someone wishes to provoke the Solar League, to cause it to take action against the Valek.

Li had folded his hands; now he opened them and stared down at them. "I seem to have assumed the role of 'Devil's Advocate,' so I will play it out. The only real clue we have is a Valek button. Commander Able, isn't it probable it was left by a Valek?"

"While it's possible, Commodore, it is hardly probable. One must think in terms of degrees of possibility," Able replied in his dry, precise voice then offered an experimental smile with his analysis. "It's also possible the known laws of physics could be repealed in the next few moments and we and the universe would be reduced to subatomic particles. While it is possible the button was left by a Valek, that possibility is of a very low magnitude.

"Consider, Commodore, that the one recognizable anomaly on the *Copernicus* is so obvious a clue and left in a place where even the most cursory examination would find it. Would it not be reasonable that anyone leaving so obvious a clue wouldn't leave others? And, so far, I have detected no other clues."

"But if they were in a hurry…?"

"I would remind you, Commodore, the members of the science team were tortured, probably tortured to death, a time-consuming occupation. If whoever did this had been hurried, they would not have taken the time to torture and, if they'd been interrupted, would have left more evidence behind. Remember, we found none of the implements."

Li's cheek twitched as he clenched his teeth then he tapped a code on his comcard. "Doctor Zhang, have you had time enough to examine the bodies?"

After a pause, the doctor's voice, sounding flat and subdued, said, "Yes Commodore."

"Can your render a preliminary report?"

"Yes, Commodore. We were able to identify the bodies of the Observatory team; Doctor Akan Sar was head of the project. Doctors Estaban and Marie Ayala were the astronomers, the elderly couple. The younger couple were Nils and Katrina Karlson, the pilot and navigator. Ling Kuofeng was a graduate student assistant."

* * *

Li glanced around the room. If Dr. Zhang's face was as pale as her voice, she must look almost bloodless, he thought. "Have you determined the causes of death?"

"Doctor Sar and Esteban Ayala were flayed alive and finally killed by electric shock. Nils Karlson and Ling Kuofeng were treated with a caustic solution that eventually burned them alive, then also finished off with electric shock. Both women were burned with acid and slashed with edged weapons. Doctor Maria Ayala died of her injuries while Katrina Karlson was suffocated."

"That is quite sufficient, Doctor Zhang." Li again scanned the table. Moreno seemed very pale and she was swallowing hard, as though to keep herself from being ill. Brod's eyes seemed to be trying to burn holes in the bulkhead behind Lieutenant Commander Feng while Gyan appeared to be concentrating deeply. Eyes glared and cheek muscles stood out clearly on almost all of them. Only Able seemed able to maintain his composure.

"Have you any further analysis to offer, Commander Able?"

"Yes sir. The button found on the *Copernicus* is from a Valek dress uniform. It is difficult to imagine a Valek officer wearing a dress uniform to such a scene of carnage. It would suggest we are dealing with a species which makes no distinctions between dress uniform and battledress.

"Given the xenopological and xenopsychological arguments presented by Commander Brod and Lieutenant Commander Moreno, the possibility these atrocities were committed by the Valek drops several degrees of magnitude to almost negligible."

"Captain Singh, do you concur with your fellow officers?"

Gyan looked at the others and nodded. "I do. I hadn't really thought about it but it felt wrong, like what, in a detective story, is called a frame-up." He paused, as though listening to some sound the others couldn't hear, then said, "Come to think of it, all the ChiTseTsi wear are their carapaces."

Li had already thought of the ChiTseTsi, if only because of the viciousness of the incident but he reminded himself that as a ship's commander he must be impartial and simply follow the trail. "We should be able to learn who is responsible when we catch the vessel we're following," Li said. "Commander Able, is there any way we can overtake that ship?"

"The idea I have has elements of risk, Commodore but I believe so. As ships engage their Liang drives they create a sort of ripple effect in time. Some of my sensors are capable of determining that time ripple effect. By following the ripples, we can follow the ship. This would involve very carefully plotting the other ship's course. An error of less than a degree would, at light speed, quickly take us beyond recovery of the trail, as would a change of course by the vessel we follow, but if we remained at a speed that would allow our sensors to constantly follow the trail, we would never gain on the other ship. I propose that I carefully plot the course, then advance in dashes. We will record our position after each jump so if we lose the trail we can return to a previous location to reacquire it."

"Does that create a problem for Engineering?"

Able gave an almost imperceptible nod. "It'll be more of a strain on the ship's systems than a light-speed marathon—the frequent jumps and shut-downs will degrade the relays and contactors and make the damper effect more critical. It would be better to have the engineering crew work in two shifts instead of three so we can have more of the staff available. It will be difficult but we can do it."

"Very well. Alert the engineering staff."

As the rest of the command staff filed out, Gyan remained seated. As Brod closed the door after himself, Li waited briefly before he leaned back in his seat. "Do you have a problem with the analysis or the method of the pursuit?"

"No, sir. It's a personnel matter." Gyan paused, then plunged in. "It's Commander Brod, sir. One of the boarding party threw up when we found the bodies. I almost did, too, but Brod dressed the man down very harshly. And when I mentioned that I thought he might've been too hard on a new man he cited regulations and chain of command. He's been different since we visited the Liu station and I can't put my finger on what it is. Something is bothering him."

"Do you trust him?"

"I'm not certain. If he won't come to us with his problem, we can't help him and until he resolves the problem, he becomes, perhaps, a problem for us."

"Part of my responsibility is to review disciplinary actions. If Brod's report is too harsh I can resolve the matter at the administrative level. Brod's service, so far, has been exemplary." Li paused, considering, then added, "As for Brod's personal problem, I realize you'd begun to regard him as a personal friend as well as a superlative officer, and that's the very reason we should respect his privacy and trust his judgment."

"Yes, sir." Gyan's agreement was obviously reluctant and he left the command room still frowning.

Li sat scowling at the table. Something else needed to be dealt with. He stared into the camera lens above the door. "Commander Able, I need to see you in the command room." In less than a second a bright swarm of colors coalesced into the image of Able, who saluted. Li waved it away. "Not needed here. I just recalled that before we investigated the science station, you said something about another anomaly. What was it?"

"I'd observed that there seems to be a tiny black hole within two hundred thousand kilometers of the *Krishna*. It did not appear to represent a danger but it was something I hadn't expected."

"Do you have any speculations about what it is or what caused it?"

"No, sir. I have insufficient information to hypothesize."

"I'm afraid we won't have time to investigate it, Commander Able. We have a far more urgent matter to deal with—the pursuit. Are you ready to begin?"

"I am, sir."

"Then let's commence. Dismissed."

* * *

Brod strode into the small Marine ready room. Four of the Marines were seated at terminals, writing reports while another man had disassembled his autorifle and was cleaning it. Private Rivera sat stiffly in a chair.

Brod crossed the room to the small office. "Lieutenant Jeroskaya, may I use the office briefly for a personnel matter?"

Jeroskaya nodded, turned off her computer, and walked out the door.

Brod pivoted. "Private Rivera, to the office."

The Marine stood and marched into the office, halted when he was within a pace of the desk behind which Brod had seated himself, and saluted. The man seemed almost frozen in the rigid 'attention' pose and Brod returned the salute before leaning back in his chair, his arms crossed, and said, "At ease," still finding the order ironic.

Rivera shifted to the slightly less rigid position but remained stiff. "Private Rivera," Brod said, "have you any excuse for your behavior aboard the *Copernicus*?"

"No excuse, sir," the private replied.

Brod was pleased by Rivera's sense of discipline. "You weren't with us in the battle with the Chadanor. Was this the first time you'd seen a fresh body?"

"Yes sir."

"If you remain in the Marines it will probably not be the last time." Brod gave the human a moment to absorb the implications. "Do you wish to transfer to another branch of the service?"

"No, sir."

Brod studied the Marine for a long moment. If the expression on his face were to be believed, he was determined to redeem himself. "Then you will have opportunities to prove you've learned. Dismissed."

Rivera pivoted in the correct military fashion and left the room, closing the door behind him. Brod stood and paced after the private until he reached Jeroskaya. "The office is yours. I'd like to be sure the troops are on alert, ready to assemble in moments."

"Do you expect trouble?"

"One always expects trouble, Lieutenant. That's how it's best avoided."

* * *

Kee greeted him in their rooms and Brod felt his mood

lifted. Kee looked up from her terminal. "I'd heard you had some trouble. I was sent a message to keep the door to the class closed for a quarter of an hour."

"Just a precaution," Brod replied. "I doubt they moved the body bags down your corridor. The station we were to reprovision was…invaded. We're now following the ship of those responsible."

Kee gazed at his face, a searching look, then looked back at the monitor. "Something's been troubling you, Brod. Would you care to speak of it?"

"I would if I could." He made the palms-up gesture. "Perhaps later."

Kee studied his face then made the gesture for "I understand."

Brod prepared the dinner, which took only minutes. The humans had processed most of the flavor out of their food to make it easy to store and simple to prepare. As he set the rations down on the small table they shared he asked, "Are you adjusting to human hours?"

Kee joined him at the table. "They're a remarkable species. Not enough time for work and not enough time for a real rest. One has to wonder what they do with the rest of their day."

Brod repeated the gesture with his hand. "On a ship, very little, I suspect. After dinner I'll go to the exercise room and probably go to bed early. Would you like to exercise with me?"

"If you can wait half an hour. I still have some reports to grade. I think teachers work hardest of all the castes, and without the exercise."

They ate in silence and Brod waited for Kee to finish her work. He couldn't tell her what was bothering him for several good reasons. The first was he hadn't realized it himself until she'd mentioned it. Another reason was because he didn't want to add to her burden. Yet another was because he couldn't trust the privacy of their rooms, or even anyplace on the ship. The ship's computer was ubiquitous. Even the computer itself was spread throughout the ship and its sensors could be anywhere.

He could at least take satisfaction in not having been a spy. He'd told the humans nothing about the new Huer attractor and he had told the Huer nothing about Commander Able. He had kept faith and secrets for both races. In some ways it was easier because the humans and the Huer were not at war and he wondered, if they had been, whether he could have kept his silence. Honor led one way and his core took a different path. He looked down at his three-fingered hands. His hands were Huer but he wondered if some part of him weren't becoming softer, more human. That had been the source of his anger with Private Rivera. The private was supposed to be a warrior but he was too human. To a Huer Warrior, death was an old acquaintance, somewhat shabby and disreputable perhaps, but a known quantity.

He wondered whether he felt better or worse now that he'd understood the source of his feelings.

"Are you ready?" Kee asked, as she turned off her monitor and stood.

* * *

Brod strode onto the bridge a quarter of an hour early. Captain Wu still sat in the captain's chair but Gyan was conferring with Able. He glanced at the door and, after a moment's pause, motioned for Brod to join them.

"Please repeat your information to Commander Brod." Gyan said.

"The ship we're pursuing is approximately six hours ahead of us. They executed a course change and finding and plotting the new course required some of the time we'd gained on them by making the jumps. We also seem to have acquired a pet black hole."

"Explain, please," Gyan said.

"I'd mentioned to the commodore that shortly after we reentered normal space near the *Copernicus* that I'd observed a very small black hole. It wasn't a threat or a danger to us before, nor is it now, but it's a fascinating anomaly. I'd very much like to study it but the time it would take from our present mission might prove crucial. It seems to be following us."

"Is it possible it's something being created by the *Krishna* itself," Gyan asked, staring at the array of readings from the sensors. "I don't see it being detected by any of the instruments."

Able moved his hand over one of the readings and greatly magnified the scale to show an extremely low-level reading. "To a human it would not be significant but it's very pronounced to me. One of the problems with creating instruments for humans to read, particularly when dealing with the scale of the universe, is that the smallest readings are unnoticed. I doubt even the crew of *The Long March* would have detected it because of the minimal levels of the changed readings and, because they couldn't notice it, wouldn't request more information from the computer. The difference between an AI and a computer is that one has to know what questions to ask a computer, while an AI asks its own questions."

Brod stared at the reading. "Is there anything different about the Krishna that might cause something like this?"

"Not to my knowledge, Commander Brod, and if it were some phenomenon created by the ship, I'd have detected it on our voyage from Earth. I can assure you its first appearance coincided with the visit to the *Copernicus*."

Commodore Li entered the bridge and took the command chair, and the ship hiccupped twice more before the chime sounded announcing the tiny jump. Brod took his place at his console then glanced at Able, as the AI said, "Commodore Li, the trail we've been following has been intersected by another trail, and no more than two hours ago."

"Interesting coincidence that we should find this. Considering the volume of space, how likely is it we'd find this intersection?"

"Not likely at all, sir, but once I knew what we were looking for I programmed the sensors to pick up a higher level of ripple effect and to stop there. Normally, instruments don't register while the Liang drive is in operation but since the ripple effect also disturbs the function of the Liang drive itself, it wasn't difficult to program an alarm and killswitch. It's entirely possible that the new trail was left by the ship we're following, which means that the commander of the ship is intelligent enough to anticipate possibilities and use them to advantage. It also follows that such a ship's commander would have a reason for us to find the new trail. If that commander anticipated that we might follow them, they also had the foresight to plan. Our present position is very near the space claimed by the Valek."

Li clenched his fists. "Can you determine whether this new trail was left by the ship we're following?"

"Only to a degree. There are different ships' signatures, I believe. I could possibly answer with approximately sixty percent certitude."

"How long would it take for you to make the analysis and plot the new course?"

"Approximately half an hour."

"Do it," Li snapped and glared at the screens. "Helm, slow to a stationary position relative to the position Commander Able will designate; where the trails cross. We want to be prepared to follow either trail as soon as the analysis is completed. If the new trail was likely left by the same ship, then the four hours we've gained on the vessel we're chasing will be well worth the gamble."

* * *

The slow advance of minutes seemed interminable and Brod scanned the flow of information from the ship's sensors. Whether the Valek had been responsible for the attack on the *Copernicus*, they were now at the enemy's border. If he'd been worried about boredom on a human ship, this chase should compensate for a year's tedium. The instruments were now his eyes and ears and he studied them intently, for the hunter could suddenly become the hunted.

The silence on the bridge grew heavier and the crew became aware of their position and Brod recognized that sense of a coordinated crew working together until the ship became an almost living entity.

"Ship emerging at four-thirty by seven-thirty-five," Able announced, then Brod picked up the image on his instruments.

His small screen showed stars veering drunkenly as the detectors swung to focus on the new element. "Commodore," Brod snapped, "ship at sixty thousand kilometers and closing fast."

The same image appeared on the large central screen; an oval-section body with curving bearers for the engine pods. Brod examined the image and the readings. The vessel was small, about the size of the *Challenge*, but from its power signature it could be a formidable enemy.

The klaxon hooted for "action stations" and Brod was intensely aware Kee and her students were sealed into their section of the ship.

"Permission to assume a defensive posture," Isharra said.

Li nodded. "Do it."

Isharra deftly brought the *Krishna* around, exposing only minimal area and making it easier for Brod to bring most of his weapons to bear. To Brod, it seemed the move of a fencer or a duelist.

"Repulsors active, Commodore?" Brod's attention was fixed on the expanding shape. "It appears to be one of the new Valek Stormbird-class ships. For its relative size, it is almost as powerful as the *Krishna*, and designed as a dedicated battle vessel, with almost no boarding complement."

"Does he have his repulsors on?" Li asked.

"No, sir."

"Activate our repulsors only if he activates his. No repulsors," Li mused. "This Valek seems to have nerve enough for a fleet. Open hailing frequencies."

"He's hailing us, sir," Able said.

"On screen."

The two side screens still showed the oncoming vessel but the central screen was focused on a Valek in the short, dark green jacket of their navy. He seemed very young to have such responsibility but had a commanding presence with piercing eyes. "Captain Rasak of the Valek cruiser, *Tercel*."

The computer translated and Brod's conditioning was sufficient to bring an image to mind. A tercel was a small, fierce predatory Earth bird.

The Valek smiled, the expression looking more predatory than amused. "Commodore Li, of the *Krishna*, I believe. Your reputation precedes you."

"You have the advantage of me, Captain Rasak."

The Valek's faint smile broadened fractionally. "Perhaps." He turned to one of his off-screen crewmen and asked, "Was that maneuver as easy to execute as it looked?" After another Valek replied in the negative, Rasak stared at Li. "Beyond a... commendable maneuver, you have taken no offensive action. I am curious as to reasons for your presence near Valek space."

"We're in pursuit of a ship, the crew of which attacked and murdered the science team of an unarmed research station. The ones responsible left a button from a Valek uniform."

Rasak's left eye became a slit and his right eye widened. Had he been a human, he'd have raised an eyebrow. "And you assume the Valek are responsible?"

"No, Captain, I do not. My command staff and I consider it highly unlikely the Valek were involved in the attack."

"Interesting. Very interesting." Rasak paused, apparently considering and choosing his words with care. "A Valek freighter was attacked and the crew killed. Some of them did not die quickly. An object was found by our search team. Do you recognize this?" He held up a small object, then held it closer to the camera. A human comcard.

Li gazed back into Rasaks' eyes. "Do you assume we're responsible for an attack on a Valek ship?"

"No, or we would not be having this conversation. While I am loathe to let slip a chance for combat with such an illustrious ship and crew, I prefer not to fight for the amusement of scavengers. We have followed the attackers' trail to here and our instruments detect it beyond this point."

"We may be following the same trail, Captain Rasak. Perhaps a combined effort would be to our mutual advantage."

"Well said, Commodore Li."

* * *

Li studied the Valek, who seemed very young to command such a capable vessel, which meant he was either an exceptional leader or well-connected to someone high in the Valek command, possibly both. Rasak had already demonstrated both boldness and good judgment, so he wasn't just a political favorite. This Valek could be a dangerous enemy or an excellent—if touchy—ally. "If you agree combining forces would be mutually beneficial we should share some plans." He looked at Able. "Give the *Tercel* a wider view of our bridge."

Within seconds the screens changed. The left screen kept the long view of the Valek ship, the center screen showed the close-up of Rasak, and the right screen showed a very Spartan but efficient bridge.

Rasak gazed around the humans' bridge with the studied detachment of an experienced haggler in a new bazaar. The arrogance common to the higher classes of Valek had apparently, in the captain's case, been translated into an air of amused superiority. "Your bridge is most spacious, Commodore Li." It was impossible to tell from either his expression or his tone whether the remark was a simple observation or intended as an exercise in irony.

Li chose to accept the statement as a compliment. "Thank you, Captain Rasak." He glanced around the room, observing the reactions of his crew. Brod was staring intently at the Valek like a warrior evaluating an opponent while Moreno simply watched. Able gave no sign he needed watch anything but the sensors. The stiffness in Isharra's back and shoulders spoke eloquently of her disapproval as well as her intention to remain coldly professional.

"Commodore, the trail grows colder," Rasak said. "Do you have any suggestions?"

"Yes, Captain. My science and navigation commander has developed a pursuit pattern that seems to have the best chance of overtaking the ship we're after. It involves plotting the predicted course of the ship, a sudden dash using the Liang drive, and dropping back into normal space to verify we're still on the trail. With two ships working together we should be able to 'leap-frog' our pursuit. If this plan is acceptable to you, I will instruct my officer to prepare a list of coordinates to transmit to your navigator. I suggest we stop every two hours to confer if necessary and to rest the ships and ships' crews for a quarter-hour. If either of us lose the trail we will return to our previous coordinates and rendezvous."

"Very good, Commodore," Rasak said. "This still leaves three matters to be dealt with. If the trail leads into human space, you will claim to be escorting us, while if the trail doubles back into Valek space, we will be your escort.

"The other problems involve the conclusion of the chase. When we close in on the other ship I will expect you to take every precaution, as will I. We are in a unique situation and if either of our ships are destroyed, those trying to create an incident between our races will have succeeded. The final difficulty is in determining the fate of the prisoners, if any. The penalty for violating Valek space and killing Valek citizens is death."

Li permitted himself a smile. "I have heard there is a Valek saying; 'The first step to enjoying a balur dinner is to catch the balur' I suggest we catch the balur before arguing about how it best be cooked."

Rasak's answering smile contained little humor and no warmth. "And I recall a human saying; 'We agree to disagree.' Whatever our immediate solution, Valek honor will be upheld and Valek justice will be served." The Valek stood. "I believe this conference is concluded." He paused. "Have you any idea who we might be pursuing?"

"Most of my command staff thinks it's most likely the ChiTseTsi."

"Very interesting," the Valek said again. After a moment he added, "There is a ChiTseTsi delegation in our capitol presenting a mutual-defense pact. If your staff is correct, we may send their heads back in blocks of Lucite. The Valek are neither a toy nor a tool to be manipulated." After a glance at one of his officers he said, "I'm transmitting images of both sides of the comcard we found."

"Thank you, Captain. Commander Able, please transmit to them the image of the button we found as well as the coordinates for our chase pattern."

Rasak turned to his right, probably to stare into a small screen then at another of his crew. "My navigator will require some few minutes to input the coordinates into our system." He looked around the bridge of the *Krishna* again and, for a moment, locked gazes with Brod. "We will contact you before making the first jump." The images of Rasak and his bridge both disappeared and all three screens were filled with the picture of the *Tercel*, which was almost nose-to-nose with the *Krishna*.

"Helm, bring us around to the new course."

Isharra's fingers flew across her console, stroking the keys and tabs and the *Krishna* backed away from the Valek ship until they were far enough apart for either to engage their Liang drives then slid smoothly around and beside the *Tercel* as smoothly as the arms of a dial face so both ships were parallel.

"Nice work, Lieutenant." Li had been impressed by the maneuver which had been as elaborate and graceful as a ballet move but he knew it had been performed more for the benefit of the Valek helmsman than for him. It was the mark of a gifted helm that they were always ready to display their talents, especially to other helmsmen, but too much praise could spoil them.

Li glanced at the screen, then at Moreno. "How do you judge Captain Rasak?"

"He's very much what he seems to be, Commodore. He is young, aggressive, and self-confident. From observation, I'd guess his self-confidence is well-earned. If he has a weakness, it's the lack of the sort of compassion and mortal identity that comes with enduring failure, but do not think less of him for that. While it limits him as a leader of his race, it does not detract from his qualities as a purely military leader. In that role, his weakness is an advantage in that the missing compassion is replaced by a greater ruthlessness."

Li watched the Valek ship, caressing his chin with his index finger. "The most important question is; can he be trusted?"

Moreno stared at the Valek ship. "Yes, Commodore, I believe he can within the parameters of his cultural mores. He is temperamentally honest, if only because of his self-confidence. Because he perceives himself as at least the equal and probably the superior of any adversary, he would readily announce his intentions."

Li glanced at Brod. "Commander Brod, you and Rasak seemed to recognize each other."

Brod paused, trying to precisely phrase his response, groping for words with which to explain an essentially emotional response. "In a sense, sir, we did. We both knew the other has stood to battle, although I don't believe he's ever been overmatched. Captain Rasak is a new blade; he's very bright and keen and he's been well-forged but it's difficult to know how well the steel has been tempered. He has been heated but not quenched."

"That's a very interesting description, Commander. Could you explain the last part of that comment?"

"Yes, sir. He's been heated in battle but, as Lieutenant Commander Moreno has pointed out, he hasn't been quenched by personal defeat, and that is the true test of the temper of a blade. Until he's felt some kind of defeat, we cannot know whether the steel will be brittle or soft or whether it will have been toughened."

"Commodore," Able said softly. "all systems are prepared to resume the pursuit."

"Thank you, Commander Able. Can you use the image of the comcard to find out to whom it had been issued?"

"Already done, sir. The card had been issued to Nils Karlson, the pilot of the *Copernicus*." After a glance at his screens he said, "Captain Rasak is hailing us, sir."

"On screen."

The Valek stared at them with his predatory eyes. "Our course is set and we are prepared to commence the chase, Commodore."

"Captain, the device you found had been issued to one of the crewmen of our research station. There's no further doubt the crew of the ship we're following was responsible for both atrocities." After a pause he said, "Since we're both ready to engage drives, my navigator can transmit a signal for both ships. Screen off."

The dizzying shifts in the starfield as the ship rapidly jumped in and out of the time wrinkles left Li feeling faintly nauseous. "Command staff, please report to the command room. Commander Able, please notify the officers of the third watch. I doubt they've had time to get to bed. Also, record the meeting for the second watch command staff. Lieutenant Commander Moreno, I'd like you to attend as well. Commander Able, you have the bridge but please notify me immediately if anything requires my attention."

"Done, sir."

After reaching the command room they had to wait only minutes before the third watch officers jointed them. Li took his position at the head of the table and concisely reported the arrangements with the Valek to the staff. As he finished his report he stared at each of the others in turn. "Did anyone else notice something remarkable?"

Gyan cleared his throat then said, "Yes, sir. The Valek were following the trail of the ship. No other Solar League ship could do that, as far as I know. This means that, in some fields, they are our superiors."

"Very good, Captain Singh. Commander Able, could you explain how the Valek got the jump on us in that regard?"

"I believe so, sir. I'm still not familiar with Huer physiology but let us assume you entered a dimly-lit room and a hypothesized alien who is normally able to see into the infrared bands was also in the same room. You would each see something different, and if you needed to enhance your view you might turn on a light, while the alien might do something very different. Even an alien with the same sensory equipment might try some other approach. Given the diversity of the known intelligent species, there will likely be different solutions to the same or similar problems, and it's likely problems and opportunities will be perceived in very different ways."

Li leaned forward in his chair. "Captain Singh, what is your evaluation of the Valek ship and its crew?"

"Commodore, the ship looks new but well broken-in. Watching their bridge crew, they all seemed familiar with their systems. I had the impression they were an elite crew. If they aren't, they think they are and they might as well be."

"Commander Able, how is the engineering staff standing up to the rigor of the chase?"

"There've been no problems—yet. I can detect a slight degradation of some of the systems but any loss of performance is minor. Commander Brod, you seem uncomfortable. Could you explain why?

"Every time the ship activates your long-stride drive I sense it. It's only an annoyance."

Able cast a significant glance at Li. "Is Kee also aware of it?"

"Perhaps. She doesn't complain but it is not in her nature to do so."

Able's image looked at the others around the table. Do any of you detect the energizing of the Liang drive?"

They all looked at each other and finally Moreno said, "Perhaps. I'm not sure. I feel something when the Liang drive is activated but I was never sure if it was related. It's so minor it's not even a physical sensation, more an emotional state, like a fleeting regret."

Li frowned. "How do you feel it, Commander Brod?"

"It's a little like a hiccup. It seems to me the ship is hiccupping."

"Very interesting," Able said in his driest academic voice. "Were you given an intensive physical examination when you reported to the academy?"

"They took a little of my blood and some rather personal and embarrassing samples and the doctor mentioned that both my close and distant vision were better than that of most humans. That's all."

"Does the ship's lighting seem harsh or dim to you?" Able asked.

"No, Commander."

"Unfortunately, I haven't the equipment aboard to test for other differences. Commander Brod, would you allow me, at the end of the cruise, to run some tests on you?"

Brod made the palm-up gesture.

"Unless there's anything else," Li paused then stood. "It's

time for the first watch staff to return to the bridge and the third watch staff to get some rest. I anticipate more tense times ahead."

As they left the room together, Moreno fell into step beside Brod. "Commander, might I see you in my quarters after the watch ends?"

Apparently caught by surprise, Brod paused before replying, "Very well."

* * *

Rasak took his place to the right of the head of the table. It rankled him that despite his command of the ship the head of the table was reserved for the Security Officer. Across from him sat Satar, his second in command, and Starkad, the Chief Engineer. To his right Taran, the Captain of the second watch sat forward in his chair, his nictitating membranes half covering his sleepy eyes. Finally, Batagar, the Security Officer, entered the room. A year younger than Rasak, he was short, with heavy shoulders and jowls.

Batagar took his seat at the head of the table, set down a stylus, and announced, "I'm calling off this hunt after ghosts, Captain Rasak. I demand to know why you didn't destroy the human ship on sight."

His voice icy, Rasak replied, "In the first place, I might've been able to defeat the *Krishna* but it would have been heavy work for a fighter—"

Batagar raised his hand, fingers clenched and both thumbs at right angles, and shook it, the gesture for contemptuous dismissal. "The humans are soft and their bloated ship an easy target."

"I presume you've read the reports of Ambassador Velnik." Rasak tried to keep the annoyance out of his voice. "Theirs is a large ship and is as formidable as its size indicates, with numerous weapons stations and it is commanded by a human who survived five of our years as a prisoner of the ChiTseTsi."

Batagar repeated the dismissive gesture. "A bloated ship and a broken commander. You should have attacked it immediately."

A trilling sound interrupted Batagar before he could say more and the engineer removed his speaker and glanced at it, face grim. "We have had an incident in Engineering and it appears to be sabotage. Will you assist me, Security Officer Batagar?"

As soon as Batagar had left the room Satar leaned forward and growled, "That one—"

Rasak chopped the air with his right hand then picked up the stylus and broke it. Electronic gear spilled out of the barrel. Looking under the table, Rasak found the second microphone. Always trust a Security Officer to leave at least two. He detached it from the bottom of the table, tossed it to the floor, and ground it under his boot heel.

Satar grumbled, "If that little used chamberpot ever gets command of a ship, I hope I don't know any of the crew. He's going to get a lot of good fighters killed."

"He'd never have gotten as far as he did had his uncle not been the Leader of Security," Taran snapped.

"Speak well of him," Rasak said. "He's walking to his fatal accident." He stared into the eyes of the other two. "He was about his uncle's business. The Leader of Security was unwise enough to invite the ChiTseTsi to send delegates to the Council. He lost his eldest son in the war with the humans and never learned not to mistake a grudge for good judgment."

"What are we going to do, Captain?" Satar, who'd taught Rasak, was now the one learning.

"We're going after the ship that killed our brothers. I am not pleased to be working with humans but Valek blood and pain must demand a heavy price or it's worthless. If, as I'm beginning to suspect, it's the ChiTseTsi who did this, a dead nephew may be the least of the Security Leader's concerns. He's likely to have an appointment with a strangling post."

The door opened and Starkad returned to his chair. "You may as well sit in the honor seat, Captain."

* * *

For Brod the rest of the watch was spent either in scanning his instruments or ignoring them, since few of them functioned with the Liang drive engaged. Brod monitored the power flow to the weapons and the repulsors, almost hoping for some problem that would give him the opportunity to improve them but they remained perversely functional in normal space.

When Feng came to replace him at the console he left the bridge feeling more weary than if he'd fought a battle. Tension and tedium could exist together and they were more draining than combat. He'd almost forgotten his promise to visit Moreno but found her waiting for him at the door.

They walked together to her rooms. Like Brod and Kee, she had a tiny sleeping compartment, a very compact kitchen and dining area, two chairs, and a computer terminal. She gestured toward one of the chairs and turned the other away from the computer monitor.

"I hope I don't make you nervous, Brod, but we've never actually had a chance to talk. When you mentioned being so aware of the functioning of the Liang drive, I realized how little I actually know about you. For instance, I don't even know if the Huer feel fear the same way humans do."

Brod found the chair a little small but still comfortable. "I mean no offence, Lieutenant Commander, but there are things I don't wish to speak of on board this ship. I am not trying to hide them from Commander Able but they are things that don't concern him or the Navy."

Moreno's brow wrinkled then her face smoothed again. "There are no sensors in this room, nor in any of the living quarters. I determined that much before I agreed to serve on the *Krishna*. Anything said in this room will not be repeated or overheard. You may decline to answer any question you choose and you may leave at any time."

Brod studied Moreno's features. While he still had trouble interpreting human facial expressions, her face seemed—serene was the only word he could find to describe it. "Very good. You asked a question. By fear, I assume you mean the knowledge your personal world could end, that events indicate you are at least at risk of losing your life." At her nod, he said, "Of course, there is some fear. That is nothing to be ashamed of. Shame only comes when you let the fear keep you from doing your duty." After a moment's thought, he added, "A little fear can be a good thing. It is the father of tactics and why we don't simply rush headlong into every confrontation."

Moreno stared into Brod's face and he wondered what she was searching for. "How do you feel about being allied with a Valek ship?"

Brod scowled. "It would be more correct to say we have common purposes, at least for the present."

"Do you respect Captain Rasak?"

Brod considered the question before answering, "Yes, I do."

"But you don't like him," Moreno said in a tone that was almost a question.

"No, I do not, but one need not like an enemy to respect him. The Valek are warriors. It has been my experience many of them will fight to their deaths. They will try to kill you, even as they die. That is the warrior's way and I can respect it, but respecting someone is not the same as allowing him to kill you."

Moreno leaned forward and asked, "Will you have any problem working with the Valek?"

"No," Brod replied. "That was the decision of my commander. While we Huer may not wear our command positions on our sleeves or shoulders, we still have discipline, perhaps even a stronger discipline than the humans."

"But you are working with humans," Moreno said, "and we were once an enemy. Did you respect us?"

"Most of the humans the Huer fought were brave. Yes, we respected them."

"And you respect the Valek. Why do you hate them?"

"Hatred has nothing to do with my feelings toward the Valek. We have a truce with them, but they are still an enemy. The Huer can learn many things from the humans but no one needs to, or can, teach a Huer how to deal with an enemy. Humans do not lack courage but you cling to the idea a defeated enemy is no longer an enemy, or an enemy who has not been defeated but assured you of their good intentions is no longer an enemy.

"As you said, we were once your enemies but we both changed. It is possible that someday the Valek will change, but for now they are enemies. A truce is not peace."

"How do you know when an enemy has changed?" Moreno

offered Brod a cup of tea and at his shake of the head sipped at the cup.

"By his actions. Words are only words; only actions matter. I have not seen Valek actions change except we no longer attack each other on sight."

"Perhaps our cooperation with Captain Rasak will be a beginning of change you can see. I'd like to speak with you again, Commander Brod and, if she agrees, to Kee. You may have things to learn from humans but I think we humans have things to learn from the Huer as well."

Brod stood. "I will mention it to her."

Returning to his quarters, Brod felt more relaxed. Some of the conversation had helped him say things openly he hadn't realized had even been disturbing him. With more sunlight, mists grew thin and dissipated and one saw more clearly. When he opened the door to the rooms he shared with Kee he found her preparing dinner.

"I could have done that," he said.

"Not necessary. When the call to action stations came the children were too excited to study so I let them choose projects and work on them and I was able to grade their reports. I've heard we were communicating with a Valek ship."

"We were. The same ship that attacked the *Copernicus* also attacked a Valek freight ship," A sudden thought struck him but he decided to wait until he could discuss it with the commodore and Commander Able. "The Valek's ship's captain is cooperating with us in the search for the ones responsible. Apparently, someone is trying to foment trouble between the humans and the Valek."

"If you catch them, the end of the chase is likely to be the most dangerous part of the hunt." Kee sat and began to eat.

Brod sat and also began to eat, considering Kee's comment. He knew she hadn't been talking about a possible battle with cowards who attacked unarmed ships and tortured victims who couldn't resist. He was familiar enough with the Navy regulations that required Commodore Li to request and accept the surrender of the cowards and he could guess Captain Rasak had regulations, too, and they were far more realistic.

When he'd finished his meal he leaned back in his chair. "I also spoke with Lieutenant Commander Moreno. She seems very interested in the Huer."

"To what end?" Kee's tone held a hidden but hard edge.

Brod stared at the air just over Kee's head, trying to put his perceptions into words. "I think, just to understand us better. I have the impression she believes understanding others is, to her, an end in itself. She said she'd like to speak with you, as well."

"We will invite her to dinner here, so we can be more comfortable. I hope you told her nothing you didn't want the ship's computer to hear."

"I'd been worried about that, too, but I was given to understand none of the living quarters have sensors." He paused, searching for something to say that would let Kee know he cared about her. "What are your lessons like?"

"There are several sets. In the morning I teach children aged three and a half to ten years old. I have seventeen students, so I have to challenge all of them. The novelty of my being a Huer has worn off and now they regard me simply as a teacher, meaning someone to be ignored or outsmarted. I do try to make it as challenging as possible. My afternoon classes have fifteen students and I teach them mathematics as well as a smattering of other disciplines. Their ages are from fourteen to eighteen, so I assign different levels of work to them, and I have two who are remarkably intelligent. They're ready for advanced mathematics."

Brod watched Kee's face. She seemed animated by her work and its challenges but he still felt nagging doubts. "Do you ever regret you left Huerda?"

Kee apparently considered the question before she turned her hand down. "I sometimes miss our cubs or the sept, but, no, I think I made a good choice coming here. I learn from my students, as they learn from me and I'm learning from you." His face must have betrayed his surprise. "The bond of the sept is that we all think much alike, but that's also the weakness of the sept. You and I are very different, so I can appreciate our similarities—they're likely the things that make us Huer—even as I treasure our differences because they make me see things differently.

"I did not choose you as my mate because you were a Warrior, I chose you because you're Brod. Had you chosen some other caste, I would've chosen you just the same, but I also perceive that some of your best qualities are what led you to be a Warrior. That was something I'd never really understood before."

Chapter 11

When Brod reported to the bridge a quarter hour before his watch he found Commodore Li slumped in the command chair, his chin resting on a cradle of his thumb and index finger, staring at the blank screen. "Are we any closer to catching them?"

"I believe we're within an hour of them." Li hardly moved in the chair. "Unless they take evasive maneuvers, we should catch up with them in the next four or five hours."

Brod felt the change from the Liang drive and scanned the instruments, wondering what Able could see that he couldn't.

"Commodore," Able said, "we've lost the trail."

Li leaned forward in his chair. "Commander Able, is there any chance we can intercept the Valek before they make their next jump?"

"Not if they've followed the schedule."

"Helm, stop forward speed. We're going to have to engage the Liang drive and return to the Valeks' point of departure. Commander Able, set the course."

After the *Krishna* had reentered normal space, Li said, "Hold position. Commander Able, how hard is it going to be to pick up the trail again?"

"Not very difficult, Commodore, but time-consuming. The trails left by the *Krishna* and the *Tercel* will, of course, obscure the older trail, which will be fainter. Also, we'll be unable to engage the Liang drive until we've found the new trail."

Li frowned and stroked his chin. "Commander Able, do you think they know they're being followed?"

"That would be a logical supposition, Commodore. It is also logical to assume they had hoped to be followed into Valek space by a Solar League ship. If they had not been followed, they'd have done what they did—leave damning evidence at both attacks so the humans and the Valek would be primed to fight each other. If they were followed, they apparently hoped either the human ship or the Valek would fire on the other, thus creating an even greater incident."

Li absorbed the information with the suggestions, then asked, "How long before the Valek ship returns here?"

"Most likely, within the next twelve to sixteen minutes."

The time dragged as though crippled. Brod tested the controls for the sensors and the weapons and verified all systems were operating at or very near peak efficiency. After fifteen minutes, Able announced, "Ship preparing to enter normal space, twenty thousand kilometers, bearing one six zero by one eight three."

Brod directed the weapons to the designated area but left them unarmed.

"They are hailing us, Commodore."

"Respond." They all stared at the image of the *Tercel* and, on the central screen, Captain Rasak.

Rasak scowled. "We've lost the trail." His tone was almost accusatory.

"Captain Rasak, my navigator will give you position and heading for finding the trail."

Able's voice issued clearly from the speaker. "Captain Rasak, I suggest you take up a position one hundred thousand kilometers to your bearing three one four by one six three, parallel to the trail we've been following. The *Krishna* will take a position the same distance on the opposite side of the trail. This will leave us in mutually supporting distance and easy communication range. If your instruments are sufficiently sensitive, I suggest point two lightspeed on your mass-effect engines."

Rasak glanced to his left, apparently at a crew member out of the screen. "I'll do as you suggest," he said, and the screen went dark.

"Cooperation with us is still fresh enough to annoy them," Gyan observed.

Brod watched the Valek ship move away to its course. "It is for some of us, too."

Li pressed a key on the arm of his chair. "Engineering."

"Lieutenant Chaviere here, sir."

"Lieutenant, we're going to be running on our mass-effect engines for quite some time. This will give you an opportunity to perform maintenance on the Liang drive and its components.

How are the mass-effect engines holding up?"

"Well enough, sir. We're seeing no degradation of function."

Li looked a question at Able, who simply nodded.

Brod prowled his work area, making a hundred tiny corrections to his instruments, none of them necessary. Commander Able would be the first to detect anything but his own instruments were the only eyes he had in that vast night and he wanted to use them to help stalk the enemy.

Li ran his hand over his shaved head. "Commander Able, can you estimate the speed of the vessel we're following?"

Able tapped one of his instruments and a series of numbers appeared on the left side of the screen. "Actually, fairly slow. They seem to be cruising at only about three times light speed. Either they're conserving their energy or they're not finished playing with us. A high-speed jump to a homeworld would be too obvious. They want to make sure they're not being followed before they return to their base."

Gyan shifted in his seat. "But we're following them at sub-light speed. We can't catch them this way."

"Whoever we are following must have a goal," Able replied. "Eventually, they'll stop maneuvering. Once they've set a course, we should quickly overtake them unless they make a run at an incredible speed." Within minutes he announced, "The trail is stronger here, which means they changed course in this direction. Shall I hail the Valek ship?"

"Please, do so," Li said.

Able sent a new set of coordinates to the *Tercel*. As he finished, Rasak appeared on the central screen. "We've received your coordinates and change of course."

After the screen had gone blank again, Li asked, "Why didn't the ship we're following make the turn tighter?"

"Because they can't." Able appeared to be looking at the instruments for a moment before elaborating, "Do you remember the analogy of the hose in space? The idea that a ship is a bubble in the hose? Just as a hose is stiffened by the water pressure, the 'wrinkle' is very tightly bound. In almost all cases, the course plotted is simply a straight line. The ship we are pursuing is plotting a curving course, which is difficult in the first place and, except for evasion, inefficient. Normally, the Liang drive moves a ship from one place to another but in what amounts to a straight line. If the course plotted creates too tight a curve, the hose would be likely to rupture, with disastrous consequences for the ship."

Using the readings from his own instruments, Brod tried to plot likely courses but because the curve continued he was faced with an infinite series of possible courses. He deleted the proposed courses and simply studied the plotting line Able had established to show the trail. It had already passed thirty-five degrees from the original course. Brod watched as it approached forty-seven degrees before it flattened into another straight line. Again, he plotted the probable course but found nothing likely.

"Commodore," Brod said, "there's no clear destination on their present course."

Li studied his own small display. "No, there isn't. I have the feeling they haven't finished their evasion games." He tapped the key on his chair. "Engineering, is maintenance completed on the Liang drive?"

"Yes, sir. The system is on standby."

"Very good, Lieutenant Chaviere. If we need to engage it, it will be on Commander Able's orders."

Again Brod detected a signal from the Valek ship just as Able announced, "Commodore Li, the *Tercel* is hailing us again."

At Li's nod, Captain Rasak's predatory features appeared on the central screen. "Commodore Li, we have lost the trail again. This is becoming tiresome."

Li leaned forward. "Commander Able, has the ship we've been following executed another turn?"

"Yes, sir. Just detecting now." Able's image seemed to fade for a moment as the computer used nearly all its power to detect the new course. The image steadied. "Interesting. I find the fleeing ship diverged from its course and that the trail curves in all three dimensions. If the curve continues, it can be intercepted again...here." He shot coordinates to the Valek ship and engaged the Liang drive for fifteen seconds. As they re-emerged he said,

"And there it is, Captain Rasak…" Rasak reappeared on the screen. "Captain Rasak, if you follow the series of coordinates, speed, and times I've given you, you should detect the trail again in fifty-three seconds. I've also given you the coordinates we're following so you can rendezvous with us."

"Done," Rasak snapped, and disappeared from the screen.

"What did they do, Commander Able?" Li demanded.

"They spiraled out of their original course. It was what might be described as a corkscrew maneuver. It cost them time but a single pursuer would be forced to follow it and, at sub lightspeed, this would take the pursuer even longer. With two ships, bracketing the original course, we could detect the maneuver and cut across the gaps."

"Good work, Commander Able," Li leaned back in his chair. "They seem very inventive."

The Liang drive engaged for twenty seconds. "If the spiral is widening we should intercept the trail—here. And there it is. I'll be engaging the Liang drive in rapid spurts."

Gyan stared at the screen through narrowed eyes. "Was there any other advantage to their maneuver?"

"Sir, if a single ship were following as closely as we are, they'd lose time having to follow the spiral maneuver. A ship following more than two hours later would likely lose the trail completely. Because the trail we're following dissipates, just as the waves caused by the passage of a boat dissipate, a ship following the trail directly would be confronted with a huge, thinning cone. There would be no way to detect a trail leading away except by chance, since the possible lines of departure would be infinite, seen from the mouth of the cone.

"The time spent following the corkscrew would allow the trail to thin to the point it would be undetectable and, by that time, the exit would also have dissipated beyond detection."

When they emerged into normal space there was no longer a trail. "Commander Able, take us to the Valeks' last position."

Brod prepared himself for the ship's hiccup and they emerged within thirty thousand kilometers of the *Tercel*. Even as Li hailed the Valek ship Isharra maneuvered the *Krishna* alongside and matching speeds with the *Tercel.*

Rasak's feigned indifference was gone as he said, "My navigator has found the point of departure! He believes we've gained about half an hour on the other ship."

"Thirty-seven point six minutes, Captain Rasak," Able said.

Again Rasak's face registered the expression that, for a human, might've been a raised eyebrow. "Whoever you are, you are not the commodore but, I suppose, given your competency, you've earned the right to speak. You have an exceptional crew, Commodore. I could only raise the morale of my helm by mentioning your helm is a Walawi. Our navigator is now establishing settings for another leap-frog relay. We're sending them to you now."

The chase continued to narrow the lead of their quarry, but slowly, and they lost another hour when they lost the trail again and had to slow to sub lightspeed to acquire it again.

The chime sounded for the end of the first watch and Li stood. "I am going to order all the first watch off the bridge. If we haven't caught the other ship by the beginning of the next first watch, I will want the command staff in the command room thirty minutes before the watch change. I know you all want to remain but we chose the people on second and third watches because we could trust them. Captain Amin-Madini, you have the bridge."

Seeing Li leave the bridge, Brod turned his instruments over to Feng. Not wanting to prepare a meal, he used his comcard to call Kee. "We've just been dismissed from the bridge. Would you meet me at the mess hall?"

"No," Kee's voice replied. "I'll finish up here and eat later. I've invited Lieutenant Commander Moreno for dinner tonight. She should be at our quarters at eighteen hundred."

Two hours. Brod decided to stop at the mess hall for a light meal then exercise to get some of the stiffness out of his body.

The mess hall of the <u>Krishna</u> was not divided into an officers' mess and an enlisted mess. With so many civilians aboard it would have been impractical as well as, to Brod, scandalous. He only took small servings of half a dozen foods and found a seat at the end of a table. While eating almost mechanically, Brod considered the probable courses he'd laid out. It seemed to point to a planet the computer identified as a Chadanor colony world.

He wasn't sure whether he simply did not believe the Chadanor were the ones they were pursuing or whether it was hope they might find a more worthy adversary.

He began to review the possible threats against the *Krishna*, evaluating each. Unfortunately, he really couldn't form an estimate of the degree of threat posed by the fleeing ship. From what he could guess from comments overheard, Able had extrapolated it was likely a relatively small ship with a crew of one hundred twenty to a hundred fifty. The Valek ship was about that size with about the same crew complement. He could only hope they weren't reaching into a burrower's den, an easy way to draw back a badly bitten hand.

There was always the possibility they were being drawn into a trap but the chances of that seemed remote, since the ship leading them into an ambush would hardly have taken such pains to obscure its trail.

He could form a very good estimate of the danger represented by the *Tercel*. The Stormbird class warships were a dangerous departure from standard Valek ship design. The Valek had, in the past, built their ships large with high ceilings and much wasted space. From what he could see of the Valek bridge on the screen, it was about the size of the *Challenge*, with even larger engines which were probably as efficient as the Huer designs. The crew accommodations would be Spartan, more like the Huer vessels, and any other space would be for weapons, air-tight bulkheads, and multiple control systems in case of battle damage. As Gyan had said about the *Challenge*, the *Tercel* was all business.

To add to the danger, the Valek were more noted for efficiency than patience, which increased the chances of a battle between the *Tercel* and the *Krishna*.

Unlike the *Krishna*, the Valek ship carried little, if any, scientific equipment other than the required sensors—some of which were apparently better than human or Huer equipment— and no excess crew. There would be no families aboard, no one not needed to operate the ship or fight. He wondered how many hours their crew operated in watches. Depending upon their endurance, they might have to fight tired, a small but real advantage to the *Krishna*.

After he'd finished eating he strode to the exercise room. Lieutenant Isharra had already arrived and, wearing her mask, was practicing on two rings hanging from the ceiling by straps. She was holding herself erect, her arms at her sides, and the rings didn't tremble. Slowly she drew up her legs, holding them straight in front of her, forming an L with her body, then she leaned forward, swinging her legs back until she had performed a forward roll, ending it by holding herself erect, feet up, legs straight, her arms bearing the weight of her vertical body.

Slowly she extended her arms out to the sides until her body and arms formed an inverted T. Drawing her arms in, she again pivoted on the rings to vertical, then again extended her arms, forming a T, which she maintained for nearly a minute before sagging to a vertical position, her arms drawn up. She executed another maneuver, almost too quick to follow, in which she released the rings to spin twice in the air before alighting on her feet, her arms raised. It was an amazing display of skill and strength and several of the humans clapped their hands together. Taking it as a form of accolade, Brod did the same.

The corners of Isharra's eyes wrinkled, then she walked to the showers.

Brod changed to the exercise clothing in his locker and found one of the machines that would allow him to increase the resistance enough for him to have to strain to use his arms and legs. He worked at the machine until he'd raised a good sweat, then he walked to the showers. After cleaning himself he oiled his body and dressed again in his uniform.

Returning to their quarters, he met Kee in the corridor and opened the door for her. "Why are you late?"

"I had a disciplinary problem with one of the boys. We talked and I contacted his parents and kept him until they arrived. After I spoke with them I doubt I will have any more problems with him. And I managed to do most of my other work while we were waiting. Then, after they'd gone, I finished the work. The surroundings seemed to make it easier for me. And you?"

"Waiting is more draining than fighting would be. I had a light meal, then exercise. Waiting also stiffens the body more than does battle." He thought a moment. "I saw the Walawi in the exercise room." He tried to describe her performance. "I would not want to practice combat with her. I could win, I think, but I would have to kill her."

Kee smiled. "Beyond the other consequences, it would make it very difficult for you to find someone to practice with." She gestured to show she was about to make an admission. "I was curious, so I looked up her open file. She is surprisingly heavy. She weighs almost seventy kilos. Her body must be very dense."

Brod helped Kee prepare the meal, noting she was using many spices. While it was a feast to a Huer palate, a human might find it very hot to the taste. At almost exactly eighteen hundred hours they heard the door chime and Kee opened it to admit Moreno.

The table was too small to hold the entire meal so Brod or Kee carried each course in turn to the table. Despite his earlier meal, Brod ate well and Moreno surprised them by eating what, for a human, constituted a full meal. When she'd finished she leaned back in her chair and smiled. "That was excellent. I've seldom found anyone whose cooking reminded me so much of my family's meals. Thank you very much. May I help clean the dishes?"

"You are a guest," Kee said. "It would be unseemly to expect you to work." She stared a moment into Moreno's dark brown eyes. "I was told you were curious about the Huer."

"More curious about you and Brod. When one shares a ship with others you become friends or irritants." She smiled again, creases forming in her cheeks. "Besides the fact I like what I see of you, becoming an irritant to you could have painful consequences."

Kee laughed and, after a moment, Brod joined her. "We are larger and stronger than humans but we would not do you a hurt unless you could find a way to threaten us."

"There are other ways to hurt some humans than physical harm. Some of us are very sensitive to being disliked and we find it as unpleasant as physical discomfort. The two of you tend to be very private and privacy is your right. If I invade that privacy in any way, please remember I know very little about the Huer and tell me if or how I've offended you."

"Fair enough," Kee replied. "And you will extend us the same courtesy, I hope."

"Do you and Brod have children—that is, do you have young?"

"We have three sons and a daughter; Lagobrod, Shkogar, Kral, and Yrta."

Moreno's brow wrinkled. "Does 'Lagobrod' mean 'son of Brod'?"

"No," Brod replied. "In my family the firstborn son is named Lagobrod if his father is Brod. If the father's name is Lagobrod, then the son is Brod. It's a family custom. I named my second son Shkogar because he is the greatest Warrior I know, while Kral is Kee's father's name. Yrta is named after Kee's mother."

"Don't you miss them terribly?"

Brod blinked, then considered his answer. "Am I sorry I'm not there to give them encouragement, to see their success, and help take away the sting of a loss? Of course. But I know their sept-brothers and sept-sisters will do that." He paused, trying to sort his perceptions of human customs. "From what I've seen, you humans place great emphasis on 'love.' As I understand it, it is a pleasant emotional state. When I look into the faces of my sons and daughter I see the faces of my father, my mother, Kee and her father and mother, and it is a pleasant thing but it has no value beyond being a comfortable sensation. It is only self-gratification. Most of you humans do seem to understand the concept of duty to their young, usually doing their best to provide their young with what is needed and to prepare them for adulthood.

"For a Huer, that preparation is most important for each cub must become a worthy Huer, bringing honor to his or her family and sept. This is not only for the good of the cub but for survival of the family and the race. To a Huer, action is all and the most pleasurable sensation is dust compared to the agony felt if a cub were to face disgrace and dishonor the family. Families have been known to change their names in shame."

Moreno drew a deep breath. "That seems very harsh."

Kee made the palm-up gesture. "We are all the Huer. If our sons or daughters turn against the Huer, they turn against us all. The family is drawn together by blood, and no worthy Huer would bring shame on his or her family."

Moreno sat absorbing what she'd been told and the implications and Brod wished he could see the thoughts behind her eyes.

"Who decides whether someone has—offended against the Huer, and who punishes them? And how are they punished?"

"The septs judge their own and punish their own, for the honor of the sept is also at stake," Kee replied. "If the offense was against someone outside the sept, they may ask an Administrator to judge, but I don't remember hearing of such a thing happening. The ultimate punishment is death. That is only used in cases of hidden murder. The next most severe punishment is banishment, for a set length of time or for life. At one time, all those banished were sent to an island. We now have a colony world for that. There they live with other outlaws. Other punishments might confine someone to work and to separate quarters. It's to show they have cut themselves of from the brothers and sisters of their sept. Among we Huer, that is a harsh punishment. But what would be more harsh, to punish those who offend against the race or to allow the Huer to become divided?"

Moreno's smile was wry and a little rueful. "You will excuse me. I was making a human error. I had been idealizing the Huer. To be honest, it's almost a relief to learn not all Huer are as honorable and as competent as the two of you."

"Are all humans as pleasant and competent as you are?" Brod asked. "We must all remember the crews of starships must be exceptional members of their races. Just as Captain Rasak is an exceptionally able Valek."

* * *

The chiming of Brod's comcard reached into his sleep and dragged him out. He pressed the comcard and said, "Brod here."

"I need all first watch command crew to meet in the command room half an hour before your shift begins." Brod recognized the recorded voice as that of Commodore Li.

Brod checked the time on the card. He would still have time enough for breakfast, a good shower, and to get into his uniform before he needed to be on the bridge.

* * *

Li stared at Rasak's image. The Valek seemed to be showing signs of fatigue. Li suspected Rasak was observing the same thing about him. "Commodore Li, my navigator has plotted the course we are following. It leads to a Chadanor colony world. If we simply accelerate, we can reach the world and be waiting for the ship unless it increases its speed."

Li observed the very slight shake of the head as Able turned toward him. "It could be another false trail and, if it is a ruse, we could lose the trail. I'm meeting with my officers in—" he glanced at his comcard—"less than forty-five of our minutes. Let's follow the trail until after the meeting. If I don't learn anything there, we'll either do as you propose or split our forces."

Rasak glowered but finally said, "Agreed. And if anything convinces you jumping to the Chadanor world would be a bad idea, you might share the information."

"You have my word on it."

Rasak looked as though he were considering a retort but simply switched off the screen.

Li sat staring at his instruments, knowing that, to him, they were useless. Only Able and the Valek seemed to find anything to follow. The right hand screen still showed the sleek but functional lines of the *Tercel* and he knew Able was monitoring it constantly. If power were routed to the repulsors or to the weapons, Able would take instant action, too fast for him to follow.

He marked time until he stood to walk to the command room. A record of the meeting was to be kept, not only to satisfy Naval regulations but so the command staffs of second and third watch could see and hear the discussion. When he arrived he found Captain Singh and Commanders Able and Brod already sitting at the table and the others filed in as he took his seat at the head of the table.

Li let his gaze go around the table to rest for a moment on each officer. "The Valek navigator has extrapolated the present course of the ship we're following to a Chadanor colony world. Does anyone have any reason why we shouldn't simply jump ahead of the ship we're following and be waiting for them?"

"Yes, sir," Able said. "I believe that course of action would be ill-advised."

"Why so, Commander?"

"Commodore, I find it no more reasonable to believe a Chadanor course-heading than a Valek button. From past behavior, the commander of the ship we're pursuing is extremely wily. The dispersion maneuver he used earlier tells us he assumes he's being followed. Anyone so suspicious is unlikely to believe he has eluded all his pursuers and anyone so devious will probably lay a false trail. An incident between the humans or the Valek and the Chadanor could have possibly disastrous consequences."

Li turned to Gyan. "What about you, Captain? Your first assumption was, I believe, that the ChiTseTsi might have been responsible for the outrages. Isn't it possible the Chadanor were involved?"

Gyan smiled. "No, sir." He paused a moment, then spoke slowly. "I suppose it's possible but, as Commander Able would say, highly improbable. Commander Able, didn't you say almost nothing was missing from the *Copernicus*?"

"That is correct, Captain, with the exception of Nils Karlson's comcard and the panels that were simply blown out."

"Meaning it wasn't the Chadanor who attacked the observatory," Gyan said. "As you know, the Chadanor have almost a religious taboo against not taking anything that can be carried away. Had it been a Chadanor ship involved, they probably wouldn't have left so much as the station's metal framework." He leaned forward, arms on the table. "I still think it's most likely the ChiTseTsi."

Li nodded. "Good point, Captain. I only hope the Valek are as easily convinced as I am. Lieutenant Commander Moreno, what's your assessment of the benefits and risks of our cooperation with the Valek?"

Moreno placed her folded hands on the table then opened them. "The benefits are obvious. Working together, we have a much better chance of catching the ship we're after. And working together makes us and, I hope, the Valek less hostile, more accepting. On the other hand, Captain Rasak presents two problems. He is eager and aggressive, which increases the likelihood of an incident with an uninvolved ship. And I do not believe he intends to capture those we're pursuing to turn them over to a Solar League tribunal. The Solar League has no death penalty."

Li nodded again. "And do you have any suggestions for dealing with him?"

Moreno turned her opened hand palm-up. "None that haven't already occurred to you, Commodore. All we can do is keep it constantly in his mind that our mutual antagonist's main goal is to create an incident between us. I have no advice about dissuading him from either destroying the ship we're following or taking its crew back to the Valek homeworld."

"Commander Brod," Li's smile was thin and flavored with irony. "I presume you've given some thought to the threat represented by the Valek."

"Yes, sir. If there is a battle between the *Tercel* and the *Krishna* it will be between two well-trained warriors. You must be prepared to kill with the first stroke. The least hesitation or mischance could mean the difference between survival and defeat."

Li leaned back in his chair. "And how do you evaluate our relative strengths and weaknesses?"

"I believe the *Krishna* is faster with the Liang drive engaged but that has no part to play in a battle. The *Tercel*, in normal space, is probably faster and has better acceleration. The *Krishna* is fractionally better-armed but the *Tercel* is going to be a small, fast target, hard to hit. Our crew may be better rested; I know nothing about Valek endurance but I believe the crews work in two watches, each of about ten and a half of your hours. That advantage, if it is one, may be countered if we're dealing with an elite crew, which seems might be the case. There is another factor to consider; our crew will be fighting for their families on the ship but the Valek are all Warriors, who can afford to be more daring."

"So," Li leaned back, digesting the information. "The ships and crews are fairly evenly matched. It seems that, as always, it comes down to leadership."

"Yes, Commodore," Brod replied, "but that, too is very close. You have the greater experience but audacity may prevail over wisdom. Do not dismiss Rasak because of his age. He is a trained Warrior who has stood to battle. I would judge him to be ruthless and resourceful."

"How is he most likely to attack?"

"Commander Able should be able to detect an energy build-up in the seconds before a Valek attack. Rasak is most likely to launch a massive attack with all weapons, hitting us hard enough to overwhelm our repulsors and inflict serious damage. He's unlikely to use his own repulsors until we survive his first attack—if we survive it."

"Do you have any recommendations?"

"Yes, Commodore. Captain Rasak will want to fence with us sword-to-sword. We must find a way to make it a knife fight. Since they will probably not use their repulsors, we must strike hard immediately. If we can damage them enough, we should close in to use our autocannon to finish it."

Li raised an eyebrow. "Commander Brod, your suggestion is noted but I'd like as many options as possible and I would prefer to avoid a confrontation. If Captain Rasak is to be reminded that conflict between his ship and ours would play into the hands of our mutual enemy, we should remind ourselves as well." He paused, considering. "Captain Rasak advised we approach the other ship with repulsors active. I suspect he'll do the same."

Li turned to Able. "How are the engines holding up?"

"The engines are holding up, it's the slave systems we have to be concerned about. The forces of the Liang drive and the ME engines are behaving predictably but, like any reaction, they have to be controlled by the electronics systems, which are, in turn, controlled by relatively primitive mechanisms. To those mechanisms, the frequent openings and closings cause the same sort of wear as months of normal functioning.

"The down time when we lost the trail let us maintain the systems but all the slave systems will need maintenance performed at least every fourteen hours, preferably every twelve hours."

"How long will the maintenance take?"

"No more than an hour, perhaps as little as half that time. The Valek ship is going to almost certainly have the same problems, Commodore."

"I'll take the matter up with Captain Rasak at our next rendezvous, at the beginning of first watch." Li looked at each of the officers in turn. "Does anyone else have anything to discuss? No? Then you're all dismissed except for Lieutenant Commander Moreno."

Li watched his command staff file out of the room, Captain Singh closing the door behind himself, then looked at Moreno, who sat back in her chair, her arms crossed. "I have and will continue to give it thought but I still have no idea how to reach Captain Rasak," she said.

Li waved the statement aside. "I wanted to discuss Commander Brod." He stood and walked around the table to take the seat opposite Moreno's. "Lieutenant Commander Moreno, I feel some misgivings about Commander Brod. The situation with the Valek is a very delicate one. Do you think Brod might become…unstable?"

Moreno's brow furrowed as she obviously concentrated, trying to express inchoate emotions and intuitive perceptions into precise words. "No, Commodore, I do not think that at all likely. I sense some emotional turbulence but some of that seems resolved. I observed yesterday when he was describing Captain Rasak he spoke metaphorically, comparing Rasak to a new blade. It was a warrior's metaphor but the Huer always seem to speak more bluntly, without embellishment or—poetry, perhaps."

Li studied her face. "Do you know what might be causing this…upset?"

Moreno shook her head. "No, but I feel he's coming to grips with it. He seems almost to be trying to become more Huer than the Huer. And the other metaphor he just used—the Valek wanting a swordfight and proposing a knife fight is aggressive, a warrior's response."

Almost to himself, Li mused, "There's no love lost between the Huer and the Valek."

Moreno again shook her head. "I don't believe that was the source of his motivation, Commodore. I didn't perceive hatred as much as a desire to do what he thought was his duty. And I believe I detected an element of insecurity. It was as though he felt a need to prove himself."

"So, you believe he is fit for duty and still capable of being objective. Thank you," Li said, "you are dismissed." He followed her out of the room and paced to the bridge and took his command chair but he still frowned, feeling something had been missed. He wished he'd asked Gyan the name of the Marine Brod had dressed down on the *Copernicus*, but he could wait and get the information later.

* * *

Brod watched his instruments as though they were ill-trained animals, as though they'd misbehave if he ignored them for a moment, but another part of his mind was still dealing with the threat of battle with the Valek. He'd have suggested, in the heat of battle, using a shuttle to let a small group assault the relatively small Valek crew but there was no way to make such an effort anything but a suicide mission. If the ships could be brought close enough together, using the repulsors as attractors to capture the Valek ship and use weapons to break through both hulls would allow a similar assault, but the chances were too long.

He had to remind himself power and courage might be where the honor gleamed but craft was sometimes needed to snatch bright victory.

Li had been frowning but now he smoothed his face and leaned forward in his chair. "Hail the Valek ship, Commander Able."

Rasak instantly appeared on the central screen. "If you have words to persuade, Commodore Li, you may save them. My navigator has found another curve in the trail and we're following it now. We lose time now but will make it up as the trail steadies again. Somehow, I doubted the Chadanor could summon backbone enough to anger either of us, much less both." The Valek broke the connection.

"Commander Able?"

"It's just as Captain Rasak said. I'd just detected the change in course before he hailed us."

For most of the watch they followed the trail, which turned back the way it had come. "Perhaps the ones we're following hoped to hide their trail among his and our old ones but the newer trail is easier to follow," Able said, and they again began the series of dashes.

Nearing the end of the first watch, Li jumped the *Krishna* ahead to catch the Valek ship. "Captain Rasak, we must stand down an hour for maintenance on our ship's system,"

Rasak's face had grown weary lines. "Agreed, Commodore." His reluctance was plain in his voice. The screen returned to the starfield.

"I want all the first watch off the bridge," Li said. "The command staff will meet again thirty minutes before first watch and I'd like Doctor Zhang to join us." He stood and strode out the door.

Brod turned the weapons over to Feng with a mixture of regret and relief. In time of danger, his place was on the bridge but the mixture of tension and tedium had again drained him. He found himself wanting to see Kee, to talk with her, to forget weapons and threats he couldn't fight until his next watch.

* * *

During the watch Li had learned the Marine Brod had dressed down was a Private Mario Rivera, that he served on first watch, and he was in the mess hall. He also noted there had been no disciplinary note added to the man's record, nor had he requested a transfer. He studied a picture of the man then strode to the mess hall, selected a light meal, and glanced around the room. He noticed several Marines sitting together and walked toward their table.

As soon as he approached, the Marines sprang to their feet and saluted but he merely nodded. "There's no rank in the mess hall. May I join you? I hate eating alone."

With a little shuffling they made a place for him and he sat down. "I wanted to thank you all for your service" He nibbled at his food and sipped his tea. Rivera seemed comfortable with the rest of the Marines, not like someone in disgrace.

"How many of you are new to the service?" Li asked.

Rivera and another man both admitted to being first-timers and a corporal grinned. "Don't worry about them, Commodore, we'll make real Marines out of them if it kills them both." Most of the Marines chuckled.

"How did you come to choose the Marines?"

The other new man grinned at the corporal and replied, "In my case, because their standards are so low I knew that even I could meet them."

Li looked at Rivera. "And you?"

Rivera paused before he answered. "It was a challenge. I wanted to be more than I was."

"Have you succeeded?"

Rivera nodded. "I'm on my way. It's not always easy. If I'd wanted it easy, I'd have joined the Navy." This brought some real laughter.

"Do you have any regrets?"

"Sir, everyone has regrets, but becoming a Marine is not one of them. This is a first-rate team serving on the best ship with the finest officers."

Li smiled a little self-consciously. "Those are words every

ship's commander wants to hear." He finished his last morsel and the last sip of tea. "Thank you, ladies and gentlemen. Carry on." He stood, carried his tray back to the end of the line and strolled back to his room.

Sitting by the holographic aquarium, he watched the graceful movements of the images of fish. He'd developed a favorite. A small red-tailed black shark had apparently come to enjoy riding the bubbles to the top of the 'water' and leaping upward. Had it been a real aquarium he suspected he'd, sooner or later, find the fish flapping on the floor. The other fish, swimming in elegant dignity, ignored the thrill-seeker but he'd become Li's favorite.

It was a relief to know Brod had dealt fairly, probably even generously, with Rivera. Perhaps Gyan had overreacted, and he felt even he had been less even-handed to the Huer than Brod had to a human.

The long hours on the bridge were beginning to catch up with him. Even Gyan was a little old for some of the hours they'd been keeping. He undressed, lay on the bed, and let sleep overcome him.

* * *

Aware of the tramp of many feet around him, Brod looked around and found himself part of a marching host, clad, like the others, in leather armor. Even on metal-poor Huerda there had always been enough good steel for blades. Many of the figures around him carried wooden shields bound with leather and billhooks, like heavy claws set on staves. He recognized Shkogar marching beside him, wearing armor like his own, and a leather helmet. "Where are we marching?" Brod asked.

Shkogar laughed and replied, "It doesn't matter. In this place, all paths lead to battle."

Looking around him, Brod saw a human among the Huer but wearing the same battle armor and carrying the same weapons.

And all about them lay a heavy mist, so dense they could not see all their own army. Pressing ahead, Brod could see only fog as thick as fleece and when, in the advance, he could discern shapes ahead they were only blackened, gnarled trees and misshapen shrubs. If he could not see the enemy, he could hear them; war cries, and the roars and howls of beasts.

He realized he was in a legend, and he wondered if he and those beside him marched in the doomed army of King Hvald or in the host that avenged him. Not that it mattered. This was a good day for either victory or death and he wouldn't try to send his friends back while the bloodbirds waited to feast. Like him, they were willing to live or to die for a worthy cause.

The sounds came closer and he gripped his shield tighter and drew his sword.

Shapes appeared in the mist and he and those with him started to break into a run toward the enemy, then he heard a voice. "Let death wait awhile. Don't wear yourselves out running when there's fighting to be done." He thought it was Chattuck's voice.

They slowed but still strode forward to the shields and weapons facing them. Steel sang and crashed and rang and they made their way forward through that press of fighters. Using his own shield he drove against the shield of an enemy and cut at his leg with the sword. As the fighter went down, Brod prepared to strike a killing blow then had to use the sword to parry a cut at his own head by another enemy. The blades shrieked and he freed his first, to split the head of his attacker.

He forced his way forward, leaving the wounded man to be finished by the ones who followed him. He grinned broadly, showing his teeth but with his jaws clamped shut. He could hear some of the wounded screaming and he chose not to die dishonored or give his enemies the least victory. Shkogar, beside him, carried no shield but swung a sword with one hand and an ax with the other and it seemed neither of them fell without killing an enemy.

Finally he was through the line and moved to his right, opening the hole they had carved wider then Shkogar shouted, "Rest a moment, brother. We have a day's worth of trimming ahead of us," He pointed with his sword at armed giants who trod toward them.

A streak of blue-gray flashed past him and he realized it was Isharra, wearing only her furred pelt and with a claw in either hand. She shot into the forest of moving trunks and began slashing the tendons at the backs of the knees, felling the trees. Brod and Shkogar roared a war cry as they rushed ahead and began to finish the wounded giants. Brod dropped his battered shield to use both hands to wield the sword. The giants' hides were like leather, or harder, and soon dulled his blade.

Within moments the surviving giants broke and ran. Brod approached Isharra, reaching her just before the mists thickened until they could hardly see where they placed their feet. Brod shouted for Shkogar but the fog seemed to steal sound as well as sight.

He gestured with the sword in a direction he hoped led back to the battle but within fifty paces he realized they were following a track leading upward, with stone walls on either side. Perhaps the mist thinned or perhaps their way led them above it but he could see the path continuing upward. After another sixty paces he could see the path led to a clearing that held the tumbled stones of a ruined building.

"When we reach the clearing," he said, "move to the right. I'll go left."

As the level ground widened, Brod sidestepped to his left. A figure, almost as tan as the stones, sprang to the top of a low wall to Brod's left. The figure appeared to be as tall as Brod but with most of its mass in the lower half. It had powerful legs ending in two long shanks, each with two digits armed with talons and another spur or claw jutting from each knee. Its arms were small and thin and its face built around a jagged gray beak.

Directly in front of Brod a bone-pale thing with a black fleshy crest atop its head stepped from behind a boulder, a knife in either hand. Another pale figure rose from the base of the wall, swaying atop a serpentine body largely hidden by the rubble through which it slithered. It had two pairs of upper limbs like tentacles, each ending in a mass of tendrils. A fourth demon, which looked like a misshapen Huer, its scales or fine feathers the dark red-brown of rust, moved to Isharra's right, swinging a club studded with sharp bits of stone.

Brod growled as he stalked forward, displaying his teeth,

using a soft focus to observe all four of the demons, not allowing his attention to be fixed on a single opponent. As he and Isharra approached the heap of stones he pretended to slip.

The tan thing launched itself at Brod, springing at him with its legs drawn up to slash. Brod leaped to the side and struck with the sword at the small of its back. The dulled sword failed to bite and snapped at the guard, leaving Brod with only the hilt. The thing shrieked, a high-pitched sound that hurt the ears then leapt back to the wall.

Brod tried to analyze the demons' strengths and weaknesses as his whipped out his claw. The knife-wielding demon facing him was probably the less dangerous of the two. The other one probably used only its legs and its beak to fight, since the arms were so small as to be almost useless. Because of the structure of its legs—he watched it shuffle to his left—it walked awkwardly but could apparently leap surprising distances.

The serpent-like demon facing Isharra began a startling threat display, swelling to a third again its former size and shades of black, red, and violet rippled across its skin in strange patterns.

Isharra had allowed herself to be distracted and Brod saw the rust-colored demon rush her. He shouted a warning then the pale thing darted toward him, waving its knives then side-stepped and Brod leapt forward just in time to spoil another leaping attack by the tan monster. Replying with an attack of his own he drove a kick, again catching it in the lower back. Its scream was not as loud as before and it seemed staggered. Brod had recovered before his second enemy had reached him and, as the demon thrust with the knife in its left hand, Brod slashed back with his claw and cut its arm to the bone.

Brod also felt the bite of a blade across his belly as the demon slashed with its right-hand knife. Brod caught the right arm and, sidestepping, twisted it up behind the monster's back, driving the blade in just to the left of the spine, then kicked at the backs of its knees, knocking it down

At the edge of his vision Brod saw a flash of movement and sprang to his right. The tan demon landed beside him and lunged at him, beak gaping, the jagged edges as dangerous as any cutting weapon. Brod drove his left forearm against its neck and slashed with the claw but hardly marked the demon as it sprang several meters away.

Spinning, he saw the pale monster with the black crest stumble to its feet then it reached back with its right hand and plucked the knife from its own back. It seemed to feel no pain at all, at least while it was in the grip of battle-rage and, while it had been slowed and weakened, its left arm hanging useless and blood as colorless as water ran down its arm to its left hand, it displayed grim determination as it stalked him.

Brod knew he must be prepared to face a double attack. He sprang at the crested demon, then threw a side-kick into its lower body, using the length of his leg to come in under the knife while keeping his body beyond the reach of the blade. As soon as the kick landed he threw himself back, narrowly avoiding the slashing talons of the other demon. This time he was ready and slashed just below the beak with his claw then leapt back as it slashed at him with its beak. It tried to shamble around to face him but he continued to circle it, dodging its weakening attacks.

He sensed the crested thing stalking him again and spun, blocked the knife slash with a parry of his claw, caught the thing by the arm and flung it toward the dying tan monster. Desperate to kill before it died, the demon caught its former ally's head in its beak, then both legs shot up and it ripped into its victim, disemboweling it. Brod slashed again and the demon toppled, its head at an odd angle.

Brod staggered back, suddenly aware of his own panting and weariness. He caught up one of the knives the pale demon had dropped and turned to face Isharra. The rust-colored thing lay face-down, great black slashes in its body, and Isharra faced the snake-demon with the studded club in her hands. She'd avoided the tentacles but still hadn't been able to hurt the monster. Ducking one of the tentacles she raced up the tangle of rocks and brought the club crashing down on what seemed the thing's head. The blow smashed the club but hardly seemed to stun the creature and she leapt down past the demon to recover her knives.

Isharra apparently saw the tail whip toward her and ducked under it but, before she could recover, the tail swung back toward her at knee level and swept her legs from under her. As Isharra fell the demon struck, its upper limbs tangling around her, pinning her arms to her body.

Brod leapt upon its back, slashing at the protruding hemispheres at the top of what he took to be its head. The blades grated over the bulges and Brod realized they couldn't be eyes. He stabbed at what he thought was its neck and slashed open one of the bladders that inflated as part of its threat display. The stink, a smell as of dead things, was almost enough to throw Brod off its back. The monster writhed under him and two of the tentacles reached back for him, the tendrils probing.

He slashed at the tendrils, saw the tentacles recoil, and saw Isharra had freed an arm. He tossed the knife he'd taken from his enemy to her then, using the claw, aimed his strongest blow at the base of the upper right tentacle and, as his blade sank in, sawed at the limb.

The thing roared as he cut off a tentacle then screamed as Isharra sank her blade into its underbelly. The demon thrashed and Brod struck at the tentacle that had been clutching Isharra, cutting it deeply enough it was useless. The other tentacles whipped back at him and the tail flailed but he'd locked his legs around the thing's body and slashed until the demon shuddered and fell limp beside Isharra.

Brod stumbled free and limped to where Isharra still lay. He had to slash away a few of the tendrils to free her but she lay motionless, her eyes staring upward, spots of blood in the foam at her mouth. Pressing his ear against her chest, he could hear her heartbeat slow, from almost as rapid as his own to a weak throbbing a second apart until it stopped. He could not guess whether she'd been badly wounded or whether her body had simply burned itself out from lack of food.

Lurching to his feet, he looked down at his own wound, which had begun to burn. The leather armor had been ripped from side to side but only a little blood flowed. He wiped the ichor off his claw on the moss and sheathed the weapon, then looked around. The fog had lifted and all the demons here were dead. He started to pick up Isharra's body, found it weighed more than he'd thought, bent at the knees and raised her from the ground and limped back down the path.

Within a hundred paces he saw Shkogar's body, torn by a dozen wounds, although he still grinned. He was surrounded by a hand and a half of dead monsters. Brod placed Isharra's body beside his brother's and had to draw several deep breaths before he could howl their spirits to the afterlife.

Shkogar's sword was broken a forearm's length from the point but the ax, though blunted and notched, was still whole. Brod picked it up and stumbled to where the dead lay in windrows. Commodore Li, Captain Singh, even Lieutenant Commander Moreno all lay dead, along with Chattuck and his sept brothers. From the dead enemies around them, some of them demons, they hadn't died easily. He raised his voice in another long howl for all of them and heard the howl answered.

From the ranks of the dead rose a double handful who were only wounded; Kee, Lagobrod, and Lagobrod, Brod's father among them. Another figure joined them. His armor was as bloody as any and he limped badly, but he still held a sword. The face was hidden by a sort of mask at the lower edge of the front of the helmet that protected his eyes, but Brod could guess this was King Hvald.

Hearing a sound like thunder, they turned to see another army running toward them.

"We've done a day's work," King Hvald said, "but the day isn't over. Goodbye my friends until we meet in the afterlife." And they made ready for battle.

Chapter 12

Brod woke gasping for breath. Stumbling to the small kitchen he poured a glass of water, trying to wash the taste of the dream out of his memory. Huer did not believe in omens nor did they take counsel from dreams, but he wondered why this one had been so vivid and clung to him like a burr.

The setting had been one of the great legends of the Huer, and it was the story of the first of two battles that had led to the deaths of the gods of Huerda. King Hvald was the greatest and most worthy of all the old kings, and he'd been betrayed by a kinsman who had offered much to the gods and invoked the giants and the demons. King Hruk had been an unworthy Huer and an even worse king. After the second battle, when Hvald's distant kinsmen and the families of his companions had avenged Hvald and his army, King Hruk was captured and flayed alive then buried, still screaming, in a bag made of his own skin. Hruk had been so dishonored his name was only remembered at naming time, so no Huer would ever again bear the name and even the predatory bird after which he'd been named was called a *chakar*.

Hruk's queen, who had urged him on, was drowned in a midden pile and the two of them buried in a desolate corner of their stolen kingdom and the place forgotten.

Those two battles had brought an end to demons and giants as well. Almost all were killed in the two battles and those who escaped always fled the light of day. For many years after the war they could almost be seen—strange shapes in the darkness or movement at the corner of a Huer's vision, but they seldom left even tracks of their passing. Perhaps their restless spirits still walked, but they had no more substance than a puff of breath on a cold day.

And after the battle the gods began to die. Their temples were laid waste and no offerings made to them. Because they had supported an unworthy Huer against a worthy one, they became despised rather than honored or even feared. Whether they aided Hruk because of greed or vanity, for offerings or for deeper reasons of their own, they'd shown themselves unworthy. No Huer would acknowledge a being who could be bought or cajoled or who regarded the Huer only as toys or tools or counters in a game, and every Huer was taught to count only on his own strength, skill, and luck.

If the crops failed or plague broke out, some might cry out the gods were angry, but it was not a call to placate them with gifts but to strive against them.

Perhaps, Brod thought, he'd had the dream to remind him that worthy Huer and worthy humans, and others besides, stood together against the unworthy.

Glancing at his comcard he saw it was time to rise and prepare for another long day of duty.

* * *

As Li showered and ate he tried to examine his feelings about Brod. He'd begun to think of the Huer as a friend. As he raised a cup of tea to his lips he was struck by a realization; Brod was alien. He set the cup down without sipping. Li had understood the Huer were aliens but in his intense study of them he'd forgotten that. He probably understood them as well as anyone human, with the possible exception of a few academics, but he did not truly know them. He was capable of understanding human feelings, because he shared them with the rest of his race, but Huer were not merely large humans of a warrior culture. They were born of different air, fire, water, and…earth was not an appropriate word. Their chemistry was different; even their perceptions were different. Their hearing went deeper into the subsonic and might extend into the high range better than humans and, perhaps, they could see further into the infrared than humans.

Li raised the cup again and drank the tea. It seemed the best course was to trust Brod.

His comcard chimed and Li saw the call was from Gyan. "Li here."

"Commodore, might I have a word with you before the meeting?"

"Of course, Captain." Gyan's tone had told him this was an official matter.

After dressing carefully, Li strode the short distance to the command center and found Gyan waiting for him. Taking his seat, Li touched a pad on the display before him which locked the door and lit the red marker above it. "Captain Singh, have you any objection to his meeting being recorded?"

"No sir." Gyan paused. "I mean no disrespect to you or any of the crew but I'd like to transfer to another watch."

Li blinked. "Accepting your statement that you mean no disrespect at face value, I have to ask what prompted this decision."

Gyan stared into Li's eyes a very long moment before he replied. "Commodore, I believe I've served well, but I wanted to become a captain to command a ship. I understand that you're the commander of the ship and the mission and that you are ultimately responsible for both, but I feel my place on the bridge could be taken by an empty chair. I realize part of my function is also to learn from you and your experience, but the other captains on board could profit the same way. I believe I've earned your trust enough to request a command role."

Li continued to stare at Gyan but his mind was in another place entirely. While he'd manipulated Prime Minister Xo, he still had some reservations about his own ability to deal with some situations and if, as so many of his staff believed, the ship they chased were crewed by ChiTseTsi, he couldn't completely trust himself not to freeze at a crucial moment. He wondered how much of this he should share with Gyan, decided the less elaboration the better.

Li leaned forward. "Captain Singh, until the present crisis is resolved I need you beside me. I need someone I can trust. If, for any reason, I fail to act, if I hesitate when action is desperately needed, I want you to assume command. After that, well, watches are like engines and the parts are not truly interchangeable. Is there someone else on first watch you find difficult to work with?"

"No, sir, and I don't find it difficult to work with you, I just have trouble finding work to do."

"Very well. Then I propose a different solution. Since it would be a great inconvenience to transfer the command crew of an entire watch, and transferring a captain to new staff is awkward, I will transfer my own schedule to the different watches, rotating the watches I work with. Will that be satisfactory, Captain?"

Gyan looked a little stunned and Li couldn't suppress a grin. Gyan finally said, "Yes, sir, that would be more than satisfactory. Thank you, sir."

Li's grin widened a bit. "Don't thank me too effusively, Captain. You'll still have to put up with me for a third of our voyage."

Gyan grinned back. "I think I can manage that, sir."

"Very good. Now," Li touched the pad again, "let's let the rest of the command crew in and see if we've narrowed the mystery ship's lead."

Commander Able appeared as Brod opened the door and strode to his seat. Within minutes Lieutenant Commander Moreno and Doctor Zhang and the third watch staff joined them.

"How close are we to the ship we're following?" Li asked Able.

"We are now within two hours of them. After their last maneuver they increased their speed, which limits their ability to take evasive action, and both the *Krishna* and the *Tercel* are capable of higher speed with their Liang drives."

"Do you think they're doing it because they think they've lost their pursuers or because they think they can outrun us?"

"I haven't sufficient information to formulate a hypothesis, Commodore. Their course still takes them to no known destination."

Li pursed his lips. "So, the mystery continues. Have you arranged another rendezvous with Captain Rasak?"

"Yes, sir. We'll confer at the beginning of first watch."

"Does anyone else have anything to discuss?"

"Yes, Commodore," Commander Able replied. "At the end of the first watch yesterday I realized I'd have time to send a probe to the black hole that's been following us."

"Is it still following us, Commander?"

"Yes, sir."

"Please explain to the staff what we're talking about, Commander Able." Li leaned back in his chair and wished for a cup of tea. When Able had finished his explanation, Li said, "Did Captain Amin-Madini agree with sending out a probe?"

"Yes, sir. I suggested the idea to him and mentioned I felt you'd approve and he concurred. I sent a message to the Valek ship letting them know I was firing a probe at an anomaly. They could detect no anomaly but gave permission for us to send out the probe. As soon as the probe had left the ship the black hole disappeared. It was gone for approximately twenty-two minutes, then reappeared in a different place some one hundred thousand kilometers away. Since it would take too long to launch another probe and get back any information before we needed to be underway again, I chose not to try again."

"Has it, in any way, threatened either the *Krishna* or the *Tercel*?"

"No, sir, it has not. By the time Captain Amin-Madini had finished his watch he was referring to it as 'our pet goat.'"

"Very good, Commander Able. Since no one else has anything to add, I'll make an announcement. Following the conclusion of our present mission, I will be assigning myself to the various watches on a rotating basis, beginning with the second watch. Dismissed."

Li followed his staff to the bridge and had just taken his seat when Able announced, "The Valek is hailing us, sir."

"On screen," Li said, and sat straighter in his chair.

Rasak appeared wearing the same air of superiority he'd exhibited earlier. "Commodore Li." He glanced around the bridge until his gaze settled on the scowling Brod. "I see at least one member of your crew is not pretending neutrality. I approve of the honesty."

His attention returned to Li. "Commodore, we cannot maintain this sort of pursuit much longer. My crew grows impatient. And we have yet to make arrangements for the conclusion of the matter. The Valek will require live prisoners to stand trial or bodies to be exhibited—unless, of course, the cowards we pursue grow a spine and choose to make a fight of it."

"If the ship we're following does choose to fight, it seems there will be no problem," Li replied, "other than that of survival. If the other ship surrenders, I'm bound by the terms of the Solar League charter."

Rasak snorted in disgust. "A scrap of document put together by a collection of toothless old crones mumbling platitudes. I don't believe your league even provides for the death penalty."

"And the Valek, it seems, have nothing else," Li riposted.

"Vermin like these we pursue have no claim to protection," Rasak said, a hissing in his voice. "Several of the Valek on our freighter were burned alive by some sort of acid. What of their lives? The ones who have done this seem to have done it to cause an incident between your race and mine. What of all the lives that would have been lost in such a war. No, let the pirates' values be placed on their own lives."

"If we kill them, how will we know who gave the orders?" Li asked. "This is certainly not just a rogue ship we follow. Its crew are only the hands. Would you give up the chance to get at the mind behind the hands?"

"To do what, Commodore Li? Stamp your feet at them? Frown and send moralizing messages? Your league has about it the odor and softness of decay. If an assassin were to strike at me, I would cut off his head and his hands. The league will do neither. It will purse its lips and accomplish nothing but to provide amusement for the renegades." Rasak had half-risen from his chair and seemed to hover over Li, like a hawk preparing to strike. Controlling his passions, the Valek sat down, resuming his manner of dispassionate amusement.

"I observe, Commodore, that your helm is a Walawi. Why not ask the Walawi about the strength or compassion of the league? The league allowed the ChiTseTsi to nearly destroy the Walawi as a people, to leave them with no land of their own, then the league sat down with the ChiTseTsi and accepted the new borders rather than fight for non-humans. So much for league strength and justice. The Walawi were hauled away to be dumped like rubbish on worlds your people found nearly uninhabitable, and given your cast-offs and your uncertain 'compassion.' You had 'compassion' for the 'rights' of the ChiTseTsi because they were willing to fight but your 'compassion' for the Walawi seems strained at best. We Valek are not Walawi."

Rasak's voice dropped, becoming almost soft. "The Valek have not always been warriors but it is a lesson we have learned well. We have, in our past, been invaded by others. None fought for us, none raised their hand in our defense. Our only ally betrayed us. You will excuse us, Commodore, if we choose to protect Valek interests ourselves rather than trust a league incapable of defending its allies or itself."

Li's eyes narrowed. "You've oversimplified Solar League history and principles but even I will admit the league is not perfect. We have, in the past, made our mistakes and I have no doubt we shall make more. Perfection is a goal, not yet attained, but something we must strive for." He paused, disliking the taste of the next few words he must utter. "As commander of a Solar League Naval vessel, it is my duty to uphold League Naval directives and to implement League policies."

Rasak leaned back in his chair, his disagreement obvious in his posture. "Then we understand each other. As a Valek Captain I also have my duty to the Valek people." He leaned forward staring into Li's eyes. "Would you accept, Commodore, that if this ship is captured in Valek space, its crew must be subject to Valek law?"

Reluctantly, Li nodded. "If you will accept that a capture in human-claimed space will result in League Naval control of the vessel and its crew."

Rasak's mouth was set in a grim line but he said, "Agreed."

"And in unclaimed space?"

"Then, Commodore, we will again have a problem. And we have not yet addressed the question of how to proceed with the pursuit. My crew deals better with battle than with tedium."

"As does mine, Captain. Unfortunately, neither my navigator nor I have come up with a better solution than the method we're using now"

"I should tell you, Commodore, that the only reason we're cooperating with you is because the open enemy who faces you is less dangerous than an assassin hiding in the dark."

"Very sensible, Captain, but we are not your enemies and we are not confronting or threatening you."

For a moment Rasak's eyes looked much older than the rest of his face. "Sometimes, Commodore, the absence of an enemy is a greater threat than an enemy at one's gate. Without a common enemy, a common cause, a people fragment. Selfishness and greed replaces selflessness and duty so, when an enemy appears—as one always does—that enemy finds a people soft and divided against itself.

"To be honest, Commodore Li, I would relish the opportunity to do battle with you but our duties have made of us temporary allies. 'The next best thing to a good friend is a good enemy.'" The last remark was delivered in the manner of a quotation.

Li inclined in head, a brief nod. "I would prefer to believe the next best thing to a good friend is a good ally, and it seems to me the mark of great leadership is the ability to lead a people into the future without any enemy other than that people's baser natures."

Rasak returned the nod. "We have agreed on some matters, which is probably the best we can achieve at this time." His gaze swept across the screen, obviously staring at each member of the bridge crew, stopping when his attention fell on Brod. "Brod, is it not? I served under Flightleader Falk when he had his... incident with you and your brother, but I wouldn't have made the great mistake he did. I would not have allowed so formidable an enemy to live."

Rasak looked away from the screen for a moment then said, "We are preparing to resume the hunt. We will speak again in two of your hours." Rasak disappeared from the screen and the Valek ship disappeared into time.

"That was interesting," Li observed, "but nothing was accomplished that required Rasak's presence."

"Commodore Li," Able said, "I believe the Valek has

succeeded in what he set out to do. While he was on the screen, the Valek ship was running on battery power. I believe he was doing what humans call 'saving face.' He bought time for his engineers to perform maintenance and, possibly, some repairs."

"That seems likely, Commodore," Gyan interjected. "With our screen drawn close on Rasak we couldn't see how many of his crew were on the bridge or what they were doing. With a smaller ship and a limited crew, more of their complement would be needed for repairs."

Li smiled at the screen. "So, Captain," he murmured to himself, "you do have a weakness—vanity." He glanced around the room as the *Krishna* engaged her Liang drive. "I want the command staff in the command room in five minutes. Commander Able, please relay that message to the third watch command staff and to Doctor Zhang. Commander Able, you have the bridge."

* * *

When the command staff assembled Doctor Zhang was the last to arrive. As she took her seat she said, "I'm not sure why you want me here. This seems like a command problem, out of my area of expertise."

Li inclined his head to her. "I should be grateful for any ideas and often the best ideas are those from a fresh perspective. Captain Rasak and I have agreed if the ship we're chasing is captured in Valek space, the ship and its crew will be his prisoners while if they are taken in human-claimed space they will be ours. Lieutenant Commander Moreno, could you predict his commitment to abide by our agreement?"

Moreno's hands, which had rested flat on the table before her were raised and she studied their backs, as though she were trying to read an answer there. "Commodore, I feel the captain is, within the bounds of his customs and culture, honorable."

Gyan leaned forward to look down the table at Moreno. "I'd like to point out that, while deceit and manipulation are not exclusively Valek traits, the machinations of the Valek court have made them almost an art form as well as a necessary survival trait."

Moreno's voice and erect posture revealed an uncharacteristic annoyance. "Captain, you are only giving voice to prejudices, which are beneath you. The various races have different talents and abilities but none has an exclusive claim to a higher morality and there are frequently greater differences between members of the same race than between members of different races. Individuals are just that—individuals. The captain impressed me as too self-confident to waste his time with dishonesty. I'd believe him to be a Valek of his word—for good or ill."

Doctor Zhang frowned at Li. "How could you make such an agreement with the Valek? You know what will happen to the crew of the other ship if we find them in Valek space."

Li sighed. "In the first place, our agreement is in accord with maritime regulations, which precede and supersede any League authority. In the second place, I find myself in some sympathy with Captain Rasak. The crew of the ship we're pursuing is attempting to create a conflict between the Valek and the League, and they've done it by torturing both Valek and humans. You examined the bodies from the *Copernicus*. It's very difficult for me to overcome my very human desire to avenge them."

Zhang pressed her lips tightly together but said nothing.

Gyan glanced at Brod. "I heard the remarks Rasak made to you. He seems to have a special dislike for you."

Brod smiled, lips closed. "It was not meant as a threat or insult, Captain. He was merely acknowledging me as another warrior. If anything, it was a compliment, one I would be pleased to return. He is a true Warrior, that one."

Doctor Zhang opened her mouth as if to speak then apparently bit back whatever she'd meant to say.

"This still leaves us with the problem of the proper course to take if the ship we're following is captured in unclaimed space or space claimed by some other race," Able said.

Li nodded. "Precisely. In that event, Captain Rasak and I will require another discussion. We are at the edge of known claimed space so this will be likely the case. To be sure there is still a captive ship about which to confer, I propose that we try to keep the *Krishna* between the Valek and their intended prey, unless the ship we're after opens fire. If that happens, we will assist the Valek in destroying the other ship."

Gyan raised an eyebrow. "Interposing the *Krishna* between the *Tercel* and the other ship is a difficult and dangerous maneuver, Commodore."

"Do you think Isharra can do it?"

Gyan grinned. "If there's a helm in the Navy who can do it, it's Isharra."

"Very good."

Gyan's grin vanished as quickly as it had come. "I don't believe I need to point out to you, Commodore, this maneuver could succeed too well and the Valek might try to get to the other ship through us."

"I'd thought of that, Captain Singh. Commander Brod, you must be prepared to use deadly force on either the *Tercel* or the other ship, but do not fire on either without my order."

"Yes, sir."

Glancing around the table, Li noticed an unusually unreadable expression on Able's face. "Is there another solution to the problem I may have missed, Commander Able?"

"No, Commodore. I was just trying to reconcile your orders with your earlier admission. I find it interesting that though you have some desire for vengeance you are willing to risk the *Krishna* to protect those who have offended you. Humans, despite their emotional responses, are obviously bound by ideals. A quick examination of history reveals this was seldom the case. A most interesting observation."

Li smiled, although it was bleak. "We will try to make it the case on this ship. You are all dismissed but Doctor Zhang."

Zhang frowned at the table as the rest of the staff filed out of the room.

As the door closed behind Gyan, Li nodded to her. "I appreciate your diplomacy of a few minutes ago but I would also appreciate hearing what you wanted to say."

"I don't believe you will, sir, but you can have the thoughts for what they're worth. I find the posturing of the 'warrior cultures' disturbing. They seem to regard war as a game, not caring who or what they destroy. Most of the 'warrior cultures' are only a rationalization for aggressiveness. Their real aims are conquest, rape, and pillage; the very antithesis of civilization. They're nothing but barbarians with technology, which only makes them more dangerous."

Li nodded. "Doctor Zhang, I agree with many of your points but I also believe many of their societies inculcate some excellent values; a sense of duty, loyalty, and, yes, even ruthlessness. Isn't it possible your distaste for the warrior cultures is because you, yourself, are a warrior with those same values?"

Doctor Zhang shook her head. "No, I work to save lives, not take them. I see no possible parallel."

"Doctor, I needn't remind you of your exemplary record for a sense of loyalty or duty. As for ruthlessness, you constantly display it in your battle against disease, crippling trauma, and even death itself. Tell me, when you have a patient with a disease, do you concern yourself with the well-being of the microbes? No, you ruthlessly exterminate them. You've had to perform triage, so you know there are times when you must largely ignore someone injured too badly for you to save in order to devote your time, energy, and skills to a patient who might live. That, Doctor, is ruthlessness. Necessity may be the mother of invention but she is also sister to ruthlessness."

Li stood and began to pace. "Almost all of the warrior cultures with whom I've come in contact have been one of two kinds of people. The Huer culture is the result of a people living on a harsh land, a place where to simply live another day is a battle, not only against enemies but against the very world, where conquest simply means getting enough to eat and keep warm. The other sort are like the Valek, defenders of society. It is inevitable, or seems inevitable, that a society which requires warriors for its survival will, in turn, become a warrior society.

"This is not to dismiss or excuse acts of aggression by these warriors but to point out warrior cultures evolved in answer to a need and the warrior's primary role is defensive. The best of these cultures tend to attempt to teach their warriors the ideal of protecting the weak, those unable to protect themselves. Think of the order of knighthood in Earth's European Middle Ages. All too often the knights were only thugs or bandits in armor but the rules of chivalry, although all too often ignored, were an attempt to instill civilized values.

"Look at Commander Brod. For all his ferocity, he's willing to lay down his life for anyone on this ship." Li returned to his chair, sat, steepled his fingers, and leaned forward. "Let me assure you, Doctor Zhang, that in this vast and uncaring universe, it is often comforting to have a warrior at one's side—or working in one's infirmary."

Almost reluctantly, Zhang smiled. "You're very persuasive, Commodore Li, but my sickbay is my battleground alone. All other battles stop at the entrance."

"I certainly hope so, Doctor." Li smiled and stood. "Dismissed."

* * *

To Brod, the day seemed like the day before, and the pursuit, seemed to have gone on for months. Each time they arrived in a new sector of space his attention went to his instruments. It chafed him he couldn't see with his own eyes but must look at the universe through the display of the ship's sensors. The repulsors seemed to be operating smoothly and he made a few changes to the power flow to the weapons. Again it was a sense of guilty relief when he heard the chime for the second watch to take over.

He decided to visit the classrooms where Kee taught. The teachers' hours were longer than the watch hours so first-watch parents could accompany their young to and from the classrooms.

To Brod, the concept of being off-duty was a foreign one. To be a Warrior was not only a function, it was a way of life, and he could no more not be a Warrior than he could not be Huer. He understood his friends on the crew were able to put aside the responsibilities of command, each in their different way, but Brod could not truly understand the ability. Their pleasures seemed empty, without purpose. He didn't respect his friends less because of their incomprehensible activities—he'd learned to accept such differences—but neither could he appreciate those activities in the sense of being able to see himself enjoying them.

For Brod the greatest joy lay in the satisfaction of carrying out his duties. Apparently this was not a common trait among humans. The nearest any human came was, surprisingly, Lieutenant Commander Moreno, whose function was not of command but of support. And, Brod admitted to himself, he'd come to deeply enjoy those times with Kee, even when they said nothing to each other. He wondered if this enjoyment were a weakness. Sharing quarters with the only other Huer on the ship smacked of retreating from the humans. It was, he finally decided, a matter of kinship and he wondered how Lieutenant Isharra felt about being the only Walawi on the ship.

He reached the door of the classroom just as it was shoved open and a flood of young humans poured out into the corridor, surging around and past him like an ocean around a stone and making as much noise as a river in flood stage. The voices of human children were pitched just below the level of inaudibility to Brod. They laughed and shouted, running to waiting parents or apparently too engaged in conversation with each other to even notice their parents.

One of the children stopped just before running into Brod's legs. Slowly the boy tilted his head back, staring upward, as though Brod towered a kilometer tall. He swallowed, then, in the thin, reedy voice of young and some very old humans, he asked, "Are you Ms. Kee's husband?"

"I am." Brod had seldom wondered how his voice sounded to humans but he did so now.

The boy's face registered awe, then he said, "She's a great teacher."

Kee had reached the door just as the boy spoke and Brod saw her smile. It made her almost radiant.

The boy extended his hand in the manner of some humans. "I'm Xuan Van Nguyen. I'm very glad to meet you." The child's manner was formal.

Brod gently took the boy's hand and shook it. "I am Brod and I am pleased to meet you." He watched the child walk around him and away, amused to see a trace of swagger in his stride.

Kee approached him, arms spread. "That was well done," she said, as he spread his own arms. "I've accepted an invitation for us to dine with Lupe this evening at eighteen hundred hours. I hope you don't mind."

"I'd be pleased but I need to exercise before the meal. Another day of watching numbers and waiting for something to happen. I need to exert my body because my mind is already exhausted."

"I'll go with you. I need a little exertion as well."

* * *

Brod touched the chime on Moreno's door and she opened it immediately, waving them into the room. Brod noticed she'd added another chair and a low table as he caught the scent of human food. It seemed different from the smells of most human food.

"Please, make yourselves comfortable." Moreno gestured at the chairs. "The dining area is too small so we'll eat here." As Moreno prepared the plates Brod glanced around the room. Some framed sheets with pictures and human writing hung on the wall above the computer. He'd noticed those before but the hologram was new and caught his attention. It depicted a narrow street lined with building of some smooth, tan substance with dull red corrugated roofs. At the second level of what were probably homes, many of the buildings had a door and a metal framework, almost like lace, apparently designed to let humans walk out of the house and stand above the street.

"I'd noticed your computer before. How can you be sure Commander Able isn't capable of reading what you input?"

Moreno carried in a tray with three filled plates and three large glasses. "Because that is a closed system. It is in no way connected to the ship's computer." She set the tray on the table. "I'm sorry I can't serve beer, which is more traditional but I hope you enjoy the juices." She handed a plate and a fork to Brod and another to Kee.

Brod looked down at the heaps of food and some sort of pastry roll. Seeing him hesitate, Moreno sat and picked up her own roll and bit off the end of it. Copying her action, Brod found the roll was some very thin flatbread wrapped around meat, cheese, some vegetables and something he didn't recognize, although it was pleasant. It was also heavily spiced, deliciously hot to the taste.

For a time they simply ate and drank until the plates were bare. After a final drink, Moreno set her glass on the table and said, "I'd become curious about Huerda. What sort of world is it? Do you think it might be possible to visit sometime?"

Brod smiled. "If you don't mind being the center of attention. Few humans have visited Huerda and none outside of Huerdahan, our capital city. As for what sort of world it is, what is Earth like? I saw only a small part of it. Huerda is larger than Earth, so the world has many faces."

Kee glanced at him. "I've always lived in cities and one city is very like another. Brod, you've been posted to some of the wild parts. Perhaps they would interest her."

Brod leaned back and fixed his gaze on the line where wall met ceiling. "I was last on one of the most restful. The plains are seas of waving grass. The most common animals there are the three-horns—they are about the size and general appearance of your northwestern elk but with three horns—and the plainstalkers, about the size and general appearance of your extinct dire wolves, although the plainstalkers are almost hairless. There are also small burrowing animals and a few herds of beasts we catch and train as mounts. They're rather like some of your larger breeds of horses. Besides a few snakes and, of course, bugs, those are the most common.

"My first posting was more of a challenge—it was actually part of my training. It was in the northern highlands, a craggy place with many basalt pillars that looked like the bared black fangs of an angry world. The wind there is very cold and dry. I remember a river of mist that fell from a rock wall, like the ghost of a waterfall, the moisture making the rocks glisten as it fell until it disappeared, sucked dry by the arid air. It seemed the world was all black and white and shades of gray, lit by an orange sun." For a moment he lost himself in the memory, drinking in again the wild, sere beauty of the place.

"Here, you only find small animals unless you cross the mountains. There the land is also craggy but the air is moist, carried off a sea. Here the rocks are covered with patches of pale green lichen mottled with violet, and bushes, silvery green, dark green, gray-green. You have to avoid the silvery green bushes. Do not touch one or let it touch you. Hidden in its leaves are pods with barbed tips and poison. First the poison itches, then it burns. It can cause an adult Huer to become very ill, and it eventually kills small animals. They die with the pod still caught in their body and their body becomes food for the seeds in the pod.

"There are also grayish spring trees with heavy, flesh-like branches with thorns but no leaves. You cannot approach within five meters of one of them—they're sensitive to vibration and shoot the thorns, which are also poisoned, and this poison kills much more quickly than the other, so the body dies near enough to feed the tree. We're not sure whether they're plants or some very basic sort of animal, or even both, but no lichen grows on them.

"The most common animals on this side of the mountains are sure-footed quadrupeds which graze on the lichen and some of the bushes. They're about half the size of a plainstalker and they are prey for the great bloodbirds and a stealthy predator only a little larger but powerfully built. The predator's flesh is the tastiest meat I've ever eaten, even better than that of the three-horns.

"Another place I was sent was barren. Only the hardiest plants, with very deep roots, could live in that place of sand and heat. Earth has two huge oceans but Huerda has nothing like them, only small seas, some of them heated from the core of the world. In most places, days are hot, nights cold, and if the wind is blocked from a sea by mountains, it's arid. The only moving creatures there were small, spiny, and venomous."

"And I understand it's poor in metals," Moreno said. "You had to carve a civilization with wood and stone, horn, leather, bones, and clay. I'd guess it took you longer to do it but, with what you had, you built a road to the stars."

Brod turned his hand palm-up. "We found enough. The worlds you humans granted us have metal enough but we still use as little of it as possible. We can do wonders with ceramics but, unfortunately, one cannot build starships out of bricks but we have other riches. The lack of metals helped tie us together. The best stones for making edges are in the highlands, the best leather is from the plains, the best woods from several other places. We had to trade to survive."

Moreno nodded. "You are a wealthy people indeed, and I'd very much like to see your world."

Brod turned his palm up again. "Perhaps, someday. I believe you'll have six months' liberty after this cruise."

"What do you think the Valek homeworld is like?"

Again the palm-up gesture and a grin as Brod replied, "A bad place for a Huer to visit." He stood. "We thank you for the very fine meal. We have over six of your years to get to know one another."

Kee also stood. "Yes, thank you for the food and for getting Brod to talk of places he's been. It's something we've never discussed, something of value to me."

"That seems strange," Moreno said, "that you've never talked of your world."

Kee also made the palm-up sign. "I have always lived in or near cities. I never thought to ask what the rest of the world was like. Oh, I knew, in some dim, academic sense, it was different but never thought to ask."

As Moreno walked with them to the door she said, "Next time I shall have to ask you about your cities."

* * *

As Brod and Kee strolled back to their quarters, Brod's comcard rang with the deep note he'd chosen. He glanced at the screen and saw he was being called by Gyan.

"Brod here."

"Brod, I'd like to meet with you at your convenience."

"Where?"

"Wherever you'd be most comfortable."

Brod frowned. He'd treated Gyan with the same cool

professionalism Singh had shown him but the message suggested Gyan was uncomfortable with the situation. It was possible he might request Brod transfer to another watch but his manner was conciliatory. If that were the case, he had no desire to embarrass the captain by meeting where they could be overheard. "Your quarters are the third door forward of mine, are they not?"

"They are."

"When?"

"As soon as you wish."

"I should be there in about five minutes."

"Very good." The glowing screen darkened. He told Kee, "Captain Singh wants to meet with me. I'll leave you at our door and continue to his quarters."

Kee looked at his face. "Do you think it's important?"

"It would seem so to the captain."

"Are you angry with him?"

"No." He saw the answer did not completely satisfy Kee's curiosity, so he added, "We had a disagreement."

The answer satisfied Kee more than it did Brod. It was, after all, only a disagreement and Gyan had begun to be a friend. To a Huer, a disagreement seemed a small thing on which to break a friendship but humans might be very different. Part of the problem, he realized, was the hierarchy humans made. It was much harder for them to make a disagreement or misunderstanding right, because not only their pride but the hierarchy stood in the way.

He left Kee entering their quarters and paced to the captain's door and pressed the chime.

Gyan opened the door wearing an exercise suit and stepped aside to let Brod enter.

Gazing around the room, Brod saw the quarters were the same size as his own. Across from the door stood a small case with crystals which might be for music or video, flanked by a long, curved sword in a black leather scabbard. On the other side of the case stood a pillar of dark wood on which rested a metal representation of an older human ship.

Noting Brod's scrutiny, Gyan said, "The sword belonged to

one of my ancestors. It's almost a thousand years old. The ship was my first ship as a commander. It was called *The Glorious Light*."

"Did you have a reason for wishing to meet with me?" The question came out harsher than Brod had intended. It was perfectly proper for a Huer but humans seemed uncomfortable with directness.

Gyan nodded. "Would you care to sit down, Com—Brod?"

"Thank you." Brod took the chair away from the door. Gyan settled into the other and stared at the model ship for a long moment before he spoke. "I'd like to clear up a possible misunderstanding. Brod, like you, I'm concerned for each member of the crew under me but I would not want you to think I would question your abilities or your leadership."

Brod gazed at Gyan for a very long moment. The human had come as close to apologizing as was proper, something even a few Huer couldn't have done, and Gyan was a proud man. To acknowledge the statement directly would further wound Gyan's dignity while to ignore it as though nothing had been said would be an insult. He reached a decision. He turned and looked at the metal piece on its pedestal. "*The Glorious Light* looks a worthy ship. Obviously it was well-commanded."

Gyan leaned back, relaxing, in his chair. "She had a great commander, Commodore Sauvage."

Brod smiled, lips closed. "Better than Commodore Li?"

"Not better," Gyan replied. "Different. It was a different ship and a different mission. It was during our war with the ChiTseTsi."

"What are they like; to fight?"

"They're dangerous. They're very cunning. They'll never make an approach on you in an attack vector unless they believe you won't be able to fire at them." Gyan shook his head. "Very dangerous but not like a Valek or, from what I've heard, a Huer. They want to kill, they do not want to have to fight. At least, that's true of their commanders. We've never dealt with just a soldier."

Brod considered what he'd heard before he said, "Not a

worthy enemy, but one well worth killing."

After a pause, Gyan asked, "As a Huer, how do you feel about serving in the human Navy?"

"It's different," Brod admitted, managing a weak smile. "I understand your weapons, your instruments. I even, sometimes, understand you humans but we are a different blood and bone."

"There are human legends," Gyan said, "of creatures who must rest in or on their native soil. I think we all carry that native soil here," he tapped his chest.

Brod smiled more broadly, lips closed. "A Huer would have said here," tapping his upper belly. "We believe the spirit resides in the liver. But you're right. Wherever we go, we carry some of Huerda in our centers. You humans and the other races are like us in that. If Earth were destroyed as a planet there would still be an Earth as long as one human lived who carried the memory of Earth."

"You were very brave to do it—to become a crewman on a human ship. I'm not sure I'd have the courage to serve on a Huer vessel."

"I think you would serve and serve well, but you would have some of the same doubts I have. Sometimes I wonder if I am truly Huer. I couldn't fire on a Huer ship, but I couldn't let a Huer ship attack the *Krishna*."

After a moment's thought, Gyan replied, "You're right, I'd have the same doubts. You seem to be searching for what is truly Huer and separate it from things that are only temporary features of the culture. All cultures change. Some change very slowly but they all evolve or die."

"You need to understand, Gyan, that all cultures are manifestations of something central to the beings who create them."

"I'm not sure I'd completely agree with that, Brod. There's no universal culture on Earth, even now. What is central to being human? Cannibalism? Feudalism? What about slavery? I think to determine what is truly human, one would have to find a common element in all human cultures."

"But there is only one Huer culture now." Brod stared at the ancient sword but not seeing it. "The foremost thing, it seems, is loyalty to the pack. First to the race, then to the sept and family." He stood. "I should leave. You've given me things to think about, things that require reflection."

Gyan rose from his chair. "I admit to being prejudiced. I'm proud to call you a friend and, if you have any doubts, I think you're as Huer as your claw," he pointed at the weapon on Brod's belt. "And I trust you." He extended his arms, fingers straight, and remained that way until Brod extended his arms and lowered them. "Good night."

* * *

Brod woke feeling refreshed. Something seemed subtly different, as though the world around him had grown clearer. Or, perhaps, what had grown clearer was his place in the world. He glanced at Kee's sleeping face and smiled, then dressed for exercise.

He limited himself to a quarter of a human hour and when he returned found Kee doing her morning exercises, performing the elaborate maneuvers with grace and strength. He attended his toilet, dressed, and, after Kee sat across from him at the table they shared the meal and the budob, a sharing of silence rather than simply the quiet that can come when two Huer merely occupy nearby spaces. He wondered if any of the human languages had a word for it but he guessed the sensation was also known to humans.

Brod finished his meal and drew a deep breath. He still felt the sense of focusing for several minutes and he enjoyed the feeling, trying to identify the source of the perception of well-being, then he left for the bridge.

Gyan met him at the door to the bridge, wearing a faint smile. "Good morning, Commander Brod. I have a good feeling about today."

"I, also, Captain Singh. We Huer don't believe in omens but perhaps this is a good sign."

Together they entered the bridge where Gyan assumed his command chair to the right of the Commodore's. Li was already seated in his chair and Able stood in front of a bank of instruments. Brod took control of his station and checked the instruments. According to the information, the ship and its systems were near peak condition. The door to the bridge opened again and Isharra took over the helm. Within moments the watch change was complete.

Seeing the first watch at their stations, Li said, "Commander Able, what is the status of our hunt?"

"We have narrowed the lead of the ones we're pursuing to perhaps three quarters of an hour. According to my readings, the *Tercel* is showing some degradation of function but nothing below Naval parameters."

Li smiled. "If you'll forgive my saying so, an able ship and an able crew."

"I believe we've already established that, sir," Able replied in his driest tones. "Our next rendezvous with the *Tercel* is scheduled in seven minutes, fifteen seconds."

"Has the ship we're following tried any other evasive maneuvers?"

"No, sir. Ironically, by speeding up, they're also leaving a clearer trail. We're still easily capable of catching them. Their version of the Liang drive seems limited, or is at least less powerful than those of the *Krishna* and the *Tercel*."

"Is the black hole still following us?"

"It is indeed, sir. When our present task is concluded, I hope to have a chance to run some tests and launch another probe."

All the crew studied their instruments and controls and it was almost startling when Able announced, "The *Tercel* is hailing us, Commodore."

"Central screen."

Rasak looked composed. He took a deep breath through his nose and smiled. "The scent is stronger. Our prey is near. Will you need to take time for maintenance?"

Li stared at Rasak's hawk-like features and Brod could guess he was remembering Able's observation of the *Tercel's* condition. Now the Commodore was deciding whether the time lost chasing their quarry was worth helping Rasak 'save face.' "Yes, Captain Rasak, we will need to stand down for one quarter of our hours."

The Valek vanished, although the screen showed the *Tercel* clearly visible in the darkness of space. Gyan smiled. "I wonder whether Captain Rasak is going to get his own hands dirty working with his crew."

Brod turned back to his displays. He found himself warming to the Valek. He had not been honest when he'd said he didn't hate the Valek. Some part of him hated them with a deep and abiding passion since he'd learned they'd killed his father, but he was developing a respect that verged on affection for Rasak. Brod had long since discovered Huer and humans were not all the same, and now he was learning some Valek might have something of the true warrior's spirit. Rasak reminded Brod of his brother, with his wild and fierce honor and loyalty that made Brod proud to call him "brother."

Rasak was not the organic fighting machine he tried to seem but vulnerable, mortal, and armored only in his aspirations and his honor. Brod could appreciate the reality even more than the appearance, for it was the manner of a Huer Warrior.

For the first time he began to hope he would not have to fight the Valek. If battle came between the *Krishna* and the *Tercel*, Brod would fight ruthlessly and would not hesitate to deliver the killing stroke, but he would regret having to kill Rasak and his crew.

Even as he wanted Rasak to live, he wanted the Valek to keep his honor. There seemed only a limited measure of honor in the universe and it would be a great loss if, in the desperation of combat, Rasak were to forsake honor for something as common as survival.

"The *Tercel* is hailing us again, sir."

At Li's nod Able routed the image to the center screen. Rasak appeared, smiling again, a smudge on his cheek. "Is your maintenance completed, *Krishna*?"

"Yes, *Tercel*."

"Very good. We have our coordinates. Good hunting. On your mark, *Krishna*."

"Engage," Li said and the last thing they saw on the screen

before it went blank was the *Tercel* also vanishing into time.

Chapter 13

Within an hour the ships had recovered the time they had lost on maintenance and Brod was running a steady weapons analysis. The lasers were fully charged, the missiles were in the tubes or in the bays, ready to be loaded, and the gauss cannon were fully functional. The repulsors were at full power and the sensors, when they emerged into normal space, were performing at the upper limits of their capabilities.

Able had begun to count down, in minutes, the lead of the ship they were following and had just announced, "Ten minutes," then his dry, precise voice said, "Commodore, the trail is gone."

Gyan leaned forward, staring at the screen as though willing the ship into it. "Is it possible we've simply overshot them?"

"No, sir. By my calculations it would have retained a lead of at least nine minutes, twenty-nine seconds."

Li frowned at the screen. "Time to rendezvous with the Valek ship.

When the *Krishna* reached the coordinates for the last Valek jump they found only empty space. "They've probably gone to our previous coordinates, which means they lost the trail before we did. Able, take us to those coordinates."

* * *

Even as the *Krishna* dropped again back into normal space the screen flickered and Rasak appeared. The Valek's face had been transformed; it was even more intense and predatory. We have them, *Krishna*! Within minutes we'll be able to engage them!"

Brod had hardly noticed the Valek, instead concentrating on the ship's sensors, letting them be his eyes, ears, nose, and probing fingertips, almost wishing he could be as totally a part of them as was Able.

For nearly an hour the ships ran at sub lightspeed until the trail disappeared and they slowed. "Within range, I can only detect one star and its associated orbiting bodies," Able said.

"After subtracting the star and its satellites, our sensors show no bodies of sufficient mass to be a ship." Able's voice came as near as possible to expressing surprise.

"Could they have fled beyond sensor range using their mass-effect engines?" Li asked.

"No, Commodore, because we came in using sensors and we've allowed them time to gather data from several light-minutes of space, they could not have been able to escape detection."

* * *

Li stared at the star, twenty degrees to their starboard and nearly at their horizontal. If they'd followed the trail as well as they thought, this was where the other ship had emerged. "Commander Able, could you run a simulation of the escaping ship as it returned to normal space to discover the most likely heading?"

"It will be quite difficult, Commodore Li. There are a number of variables, including the mass of the ship and its residual velocity, but we can try."

"Have the simulation displayed on the screen." Li leaned forward, as intent as a cat watching a fly. "Have the display use the starfield as we see it. That will simplify establishing a course."

"Program running, Commodore." The screen showed a large white globe as it entered the screen on their course. The globe shot ahead, curving slightly as if affected by the star's gravity, and all but disappeared into the void.

"Increase magnification."

The screen seemed to rush forward until the globe was visible but continued to dwindle, with no destination apparent.

"Have you examined the sector the ship fled into?"

"Yes, Commodore, but there is no ship in that sector nor any object of sufficient mass to hide one."

Li glared at the screen. "Something is escaping us, something besides the ship." He snapped his fingers. "Run the program again but this time with the stars and the planets in the position they were in when the other ship dropped into normal space."

"Yes, Commodore."

This time the star blazed at sixteen degrees to starboard and perhaps a degree above horizontal. The globe appeared again but this time the course plotted took the form of an ever-widening ribbon as it swung much more sharply around the star as Able allowed for differences in mass and velocity. "Increase magnification," Li said.

The ribbon widened until it was almost a white roadway in the blackness of space but Li now saw what he was looking for. The ship had used the slingshot effect to move out of sight. "Helm, give us a course for a safe distance around that star. Able, end the program and hail the *Tercel*. Repulsors at full power, Commander Brod."

Rasak responded immediately, his face stark on the screen, all pretence of amusement gone. "What have you found, *Krishna*?"

"Follow us, Captain. I believe I've found the hole our hare has run to."

He waved to Able to break the connection and asked, "Has the *Tercel* powered up its repulsors?"

"Yes, Commodore," Able replied before Brod could. "They are running on a course parallel to ours at twenty thousand kilometers, and they're hailing us again."

Rasak appeared on the screen, his fists on his hips. "Commodore Li, it would seem our problem remains. This sector of space is unclaimed. I propose if the ship is captured, we each take half the prisoners. To be scrupulously fair, I am offering you first choice. You may take the top half and leave us the bottom half or take the right half and we will be satisfied with the left." He smiled.

Despite himself, Li returned the smile. "A Solomonic decision, Captain. Unfortunately, it is not acceptable. My counter-proposal is to demand the surrender of the ship and see if there is anything to decide."

Rasak's smile never wavered. "If there is to be an agreement, it had best be made speedily." Rasak broke the connection.

"Helm, slow and make your turn around the star as tight as

possible. Commander Able, how many planets orbit this star?"

"There are five planetary bodies, as well as a string of asteroids between the orbits of the second and third planets which appear to be the remains of a sixth planet. The projected heading of the ship will nearly intercept the second planet, which is hidden on the other side of the star."

"Very clever. Someone is familiar with this part of space and has given considerable thought to it. As soon as you can get readings from the planet give me an analysis."

"Readings on the planet are coming in now, sir," Able announced. "The atmosphere is largely methane. The liquid masses that appear to be ocean are ammonia. The planet is an explosion waiting to happen, and no readings indicate the presence of any lifeforms."

"How many satellites does the planet have, Commander Able?"

"Two, sir. One is approximately the mass of the *Krishna*. The other has an average diameter of one thousand, six hundred kilometers. Both are composed primarily of iron ore with a high concentration of nickel and carbon."

"If I were going to hide," Li said, as though to himself, "I believe I'd choose a small orbiting body to limit the stress on my vessel and to make escape easier. I'd also prefer a place with a higher metallic content to mask my ship from a scan. Helm, full stop relative to that moon. Commander Able, hail the unknown ship."

"Hailing, sir, on all available frequencies."

"Continue the hail and, on all hailing frequencies, announce we are going to destroy the larger moon with a barrage of missiles."

Brod looked up from his instruments, baring his teeth in a ferocious grin, as Able said, "Message coming in now, sir. Audio only."

"Hold your fire, human ship." The oily voice caused Li's scalp to stir and his blood seemed to have been changed to icewater.

"This is the *Krishna*, commanded by Commodore Li Wing Hua." Getting the words out of a constricted throat cost effort. "Identify yourself."

"Yes," Rasak's voice cut in. "Identify yourself so I can tell my superiors whose body I'm presenting."

"On screen, split view," Li said. The right screen showed Rasak glowering into the camera while the center screen presented a view of the rugged face of the moon, a confused pattern of sun-lit surfaces dappled with dark shadows. "Identify yourself and your vessel, and on visual."

The central screen was suddenly occupied by a head largely hidden by a chitinous helmet but with a short, sharp nose, lipless mouth, and eyes like beads of obsidian. Patterns had been carved in the carapace and painted a pale yellow.

"I am Rippled Surface, commanding the *Dream of Wealth*, a privately registered research, exploration and mining vessel of the ChiTseTsi authority, and I object to this unwarranted attack."

Li was rendered momentarily mute by the depth of the emotions wracking him. Some animal part of him reacted on a totally emotional and physical level at the sight of the ChiTseTsi. He couldn't even recognize the feelings that overwhelmed him—fear, anger, hatred, revulsion, or, perhaps, all of them. For a moment the face seemed to be the face of his torturer, who'd tried to break him.

Rasak leaned toward the screen. "ChiTseTsi, prepare to surrender your ship and crew to the Valek ship *Tercel* and the human vessel *Krishna*."

The ChiTseTsi's eyes widened and Li recalled that seemed to be their form of laughter. "By what authority?"

Rasak was still smiling but with an intensity in his eyes that was almost a physical force. "By the authority of superior weaponry." The computer translated the next word as "cockroach." "I'll see your envoys are returned to their ships. At least their heads will be. While I'd prefer to have more conclusive proof of the complicity of your government, we Valek are used to doing without luxuries."

The ChiTseTsi's tiny eyes narrowed. "You have no right to attack my ship. The ChiTseTsi are not at war with the Valek or the Solar League and, since we are in unclaimed space, your attack is unprovoked aggression."

Li was still struggling to bring his body and his emotions under control and clamped his jaws shut but Rasak continued smiling. "Commodore Li, this thing's courage is matched by its honesty." His eyes shifted as he spoke directly to the image of the ChiTseTsi on his screen. "There are many enemies more dangerous than a ChiTseTsi opponent but none as dangerous as a ChiTseTsi speaking peace. You are an inept liar. There is no peace between the Valek and the ChiTseTsi, only the absence of war, and your treaty with the humans is not peace, only time for you to prepare for the next war.

"But Commodore Li and I are not speaking of war; we are speaking of murder and piracy. For such crimes, even the Solar League might dust off some old regulations and find the death penalty."

Rasak's voice and face made his contempt plain. "Cockroach, you fancy yourself cunning. You bore me with your transparent duplicity. You could not last an hour at the Valek court. Either surrender, come up and fight, or die where you are." He turned his head slightly. "Weaponsmaster, prepare to fire on my signal."

The ChiTseTsi's eyes widened again but there was nothing of amusement in the expression. "Do not launch. We are coming up to surrender."

The left screen displayed the view of the moon's surface. From a patch of shadow cast by a crag, the manta-shaped ship slowly rose on steering jets.

"You are not," Li rasped. "You will immediately put down

your vessel and you and your crew will wear lifesuits and abandon your ship. We will send down a shuttle to pick you up. Your ship will be awarded to the Valek."

The oily voice replied, "I surrender to the *Krishna*. As a former prisoner himself, her commander will no doubt observe all the protocols governing the treatment of prisoners. But we cannot abandon ship."

Li was surprised to find himself standing, drenched in sweat, his fists at his sides so tightly clenched that his nails, trimmed short, still dug into his palms. "Helm, put the *Krishna* between the *Tercel* and the ChiTseTsi vessel."

"Yes, sir." Despite her own detestation for the ChiTseTsi, Isharra put all her skill into the maneuver and the *Krishna* leapt between the Valek ship and the ChiTseTsi vessel.

"Rippled Surface, put your ship down or I will simply let the Valek destroy you."

"The ChiTseTsi have powered up their repulsors," Able said.

Li could feel his heart pounding, could almost hear the flow of blood in his ears. "Rippled Surface, you will immediately turn off your repulsors and accept a boarding party."

The ChiTseTsi's computer-generated voice replied, "I regret, Commodore, that it is not possible to comply with your request at this time." The ChiTseTsi swaggered two steps toward the camera. "I cannot expose my ship and crew to hostile vessels who have not agreed to accept our surrender under reasonable conditions. And we request the presence of a neutral observer."

The demands of the ChiTseTsi came like a blow to his head. Blackness swept into the edges of Li's vision until he seemed to be watching the screen through a tunnel, until he could only see the screen in which Rippled Surface stood. Details became clearer; the thing's cruel, lipless mouth, its reptilian eyes glowering from beneath the heavy ridges above and below them.

Li was reminded, painfully, that man is more than a rational creature, that his emotions and body existed apart from the mind and all his will was directed to quelling the rebellion inside himself. His rational self had put his captivity at the hands of the ChiTseTsi behind him but his nerves and muscles, rage and pain, remembered all too clearly. But Li Wing Hua had earned command of the *Krishna* by virtue of his mind and will, and these now reasserted themselves. "We accept your surrender, and I accept responsibility for your treatment as prisoners. Set your vessel down and power down your repulsors."

* * *

Brod understood some of what his commander was experiencing. He'd seen Li's hands curl into fists at the sight of the ChiTseTsi. Brod was prepared to fire lasers and launch missiles until the small moon was only another belt of pebbles and it was only his iron discipline that kept him from launching an attack before receiving an order to fire.

With a shock he realized he'd been concentrating too much on the ChiTseTsi, and cursed himself for committing an apprentice's error.

Rasak glared from his screen. "As the Commodore says, power down your repulsors and prepare to be boarded, or keep them up and prepare to die with them."

Rippled Surface's bravado seemed to desert him. The oily voice was tinged with something like desperation. "I have already offered my surrender to the humans."

"And kept your repulsors on," Valek snapped. "A prisoner who refuses to submit to boarding is hardly a prisoner. Commodore Li, our weapons can destroy their space-drive engines and, if anything is left to board, you may do so at your leisure." Rasak disappeared from the screen and the image showed the *Tercel* springing toward the ChiTseTsi ship.

Isharra reacted instantly but Brod could see the *Tercel* had moved more quickly than any pilot could react. There was no time for orders or requests, barely enough time in which to act.

He threw the repulsor power to the repulsors on the side between the *Tercel* and the ChiTseTsi, extending the range of the repulsors, just as the Valek launched a missile. The repulsor deflected the missile by only a few degrees but at thirty kilometers even the minor deflection was enough to cause a miss. A small sun burned for a moment, its glare washing over the jagged rock, then vanished.

"Commodore Li," Rippled Surface said, the oily voice pleading. "We have surrendered but I must keep my repulsors on. I am prepared to follow you to your nearest hub."

Valek laughed. "There's no way to control another ship in passage. Are we to accept the word of a proven liar?" He vanished again to be replaced by the image of the *Tercel* thrusting itself like a fencer's blade and firing another missile. This time Isharra was better prepared and the *Krishna* shuddered as the repulsors detonated the warhead.

Rasak reappeared on the screen. He was no longer smiling and his eyes glittered like blades. "Commodore Li, are you preparing to do battle with us?"

"No, Captain, only protecting my ship and my prisoners. This is what the ChiTseTsi want, isn't it—for us to fight each other? Why give them what they want when we are on the verge of success?"

Rasak lowered his head slightly, glaring at them from under the brows. "It will not be a success if these vermin are laughing at us from the comfort of a Solar League prison. They have incurred a debt in blood and justice requires they pay it in the same currency."

"Captain, you—"

The *Krishna* seemed to reverberate to the hooting of the klaxons.

"The black hole," Able reported, "is moving toward us at great speed. I am going to enhance the image so it can be seen on the screen."

"Could it be a ChiTseTsi weapon, or some way to let their ship escape?"

"It's impossible to theorize—" Able began.

The image of a black mass outlined in white vanished behind the moon then, from the other side of the moon flashed the *Challenge*, executing a high speed turn that must have left the inertia dampeners howling and smoking and the frame of the ship to groan. A string of glowing beads shot from the front of the ship followed, in less than a second, by a laser beam. The ChiTseTsi ship and its crew were suddenly transformed into a globe of light that expanded then dissipated.

From his instruments, Brod could tell debris was impacting on the *Krishna's* repulsor field but not penetrating it.

Before Li could order open a hailing frequency another face appeared on the left screen. Shkogar stood grinning, his bridge crew beside him. "Shkogar of the Huer vessel *Challenge*. You two may disengage from each other. There is no longer anything for you to fight about."

The sudden appearance of the Huer vessel had changed Rasak's expression to grim satisfaction tinged with rage that his enemy had been taken from him. He glared from side to side, apparently observing both Li and Shkogar on a split screen. Slowly his insolent smile returned. "Well done, Huer. It is rare to find two such worthy adversaries. We will meet again, Commander Shkogar.

"Commodore Li, our differences have been concluded, if not in a manner entirely satisfactory to either of us." He disappeared from the screen, his image replaced by that of the *Tercel* turning away toward Valek space. Her mass effect engines carried her a safe distance from the primary and she vanished.

Li faced Shkogar, who now occupied the central screen. "Your arrival wasn't expected, Captain Shkogar."

Shkogar laughed as though at a bawdy joke. "We followed you from your hub. From your assignment, I could sense something not right, so I followed. Then I detected the transmissions between the *Tercel* and your ship and I decided to monitor the situation. I thought it best to remain hidden while we followed you, in the event the Valek attacked you. As for our appearance, you have your own history to thank. I'd become interested in human Warriors. There was one called 'Alexander'"—his mouth stumbled over the human words— "and I learned how to cut Gordian knots."

Commodore Li's manner became formal as he stared at Shkogar on the screen. "Captain, your actions have violated several Solar League regulations."

Shkogar laughed again. "Then it is a good thing I am a Huer, is it not?"

Li allowed himself to smile. "A good thing for both of us." He stared at the screen a moment. "I understand the Huer do not overprovision their vessels. With your permission, I will send a shuttle with one of my officers to the *Challenge* with some supplies."

"Very well, Commodore Li." Only the image of the *Challenge* remained on the screen.

Li turned to Brod. "Commander, I would be grateful if you'd take some supplies I'll provide to the *Challenge* for me." He stood. "Captain Singh, you have the bridge." He led Brod to the Commodore's quarters and handed him two bottles of Scotch. "And if you find anything else in the stores that appeal to a Huer palate, take them, too."

* * *

When the airlock opened Brod found almost the whole crew of the *Challenge* waiting for him. After greeting his brother, Brod handed him the two bottles and a case of freeze-dried peaches.

Shkogar poured a little of the Scotch into each Huer's cup and started to pour a cup for Brod. "Just a little," Brod said. "You and your crew have earned it."

Shkogar tossed back his drink and growled with contentment. "My helm was obviously trying to impress his Valek and human counterparts with that turn. Maybe even the Walawi. I would have had his hide for it but for the fact he's probably the best helm in the fleet."

"And the fact he was carrying out your orders."

Shkogar gave a quicksilver grin. "Sometimes it's better to let our enemies, and even our allies, see the flash of our blades. It makes for better understanding."

Brod gestured at the empty bottle. "As a Solar League officer, Commodore Li had to express condemnation for your actions but, as a man, he wished to show his appreciation."

"You didn't need to tell me that, brother. A Huer judges actions, not words. Your Commodore Li is at least a little Huer here," He tapped his lower chest.

"I was rather surprised you'd studied human Warriors."

"Only a little. I have little time for dead Warriors, human or Huer. My interest is in today's Huer, and tomorrow's. Besides, we are all the same and all different. It is important to honor the past but not to be bound by it. The universe is changing and we must grow with it. We need to keep our honor, of course, but we must extend it to the other races as well."

"If one of my cubs," Brod said, "chooses to join the Warrior caste, I would be proud to have him or her serve under you."

Shkogar laughed. "Talk to me about it again when the time comes. A good Warrior may not live so long." He became serious again. "I would be honored." He stared at Brod with open affection then, as though embarrassed, picked up one of the empty bottles. "It's unfortunate Captain Rasak couldn't share a drink with us. He was a Warrior worth fighting."

* * *

Commodore Li sat in the chair beside the holographic aquarium but not looking at it. He'd managed to compose himself but the adrenalin released by both the external and internal battles had finally burned out, leaving him exhausted and with a bitter taste in his mouth. His comcard chimed and, noticing the message was from Able, displayed it on his large screen. "Commodore Li here."

Able gazed into the screen. "Commodore, do you wish to have me send the recording of the past eighty-four hours by ship's bottle?"

"Yes, please. Also send them the message we are returning to the Liu station to await further orders, and direct Captain Singh to return there. It needn't be at high speed. It'll take time for the bottle to arrive and at least as long for us to receive a reply. Has the shuttle returned from the *Challenge*?"

"It has just left the Huer ship, sir."

"Then ask Captain Singh to set out for the hub as soon as the shuttle's secured. Have you anything else to report, Commander?"

"Yes, sir. During the transmissions to and from the CheTseTsi ship I was able to access their databank. I have positive links between the ChiTseTsi authorities and the actions of the ship. I also have the location of their homeworld."

"Weren't the files protected?"

"Of course, sir, but I have rather more experience in electronic data storage and retrieval than a human operator." Li seemed to hear a shadow of disappointment in Able's voice that Li might think he could be denied access by a mere machine.

"Include that with the recordings. Is there anything else, Commander?"

"Not at this time, sir." The screen returned to a pale blue.

Before he could rouse himself from his chair his door enunciator chimed. "Enter," he said, abandoning the resolve to get to his feet. Lieutenant Commander Moreno entered and closed the door behind her.

"Please, sit down." He gestured at a chair facing the one in which he sat.

Li glanced up at Moreno's face. "I was actually glad Captain Shkogar destroyed the ChiTseTsi ship. Not all my training nor my humanitarian ideals nor any commitment to Solar League policies were sufficient to keep me from being relieved—even glad—that Rippled Surface and his crew were dead."

Moreno allowed a moment of silence to pass before she replied, her voice soft. "Commodore Li, we must all strive toward impossible ideals. It's what makes us greater than we are, and impossible standards are the only ones worth having, but we must also accept our humanity. You are not responsible for your feelings; only your actions. You would have done everything you could to defend the ChiTseTsi ship, despite your own feelings.

"To borrow a phrase from Brod, I believe we have all been quenched. Now we learn the temper of our characters and I believe we've all been made stronger. I sensed it in Captain Rasak before he left. Your example, as much as he might dislike admitting it, impressed him deeply, and I think he's gained some measure of compassion. As for you, the quenching was abrupt and you're still feeling the shock of it, but I know you won't abandon your ideals and principles. Just remember, sir, discouragement is not defeat.

"I think that's the greatness of all of us—that while we are imperfect and realize we're flawed, we still strive to the ideal." She waited until she perceived that her words had reached him then stood and walked out.

He hadn't particularly wanted a war with the ChiTseTsi, but it was very likely. There would be a change in the government and, probably, changes in the Navy. Unfortunately, some incompetents would be replaced by other incompetents. Captain Singh would probably get his own ship to command but it would be a warship. He wondered how many of his crew he would lose to a Navy rebuilding its strength, and how many he would lose in the war.

While the *Krishna* would be a formidable warship he hoped it would remain an exploration vessel, even one crewed by unseasoned officers. With luck, the change in political leadership might result in Earth discarding her pretentions and becoming part of a true league made up of Huer, Valek, and Walawi as well as humans. Perhaps even the Chadanor might join. The Walawi might recover their world, or what was left of it, and rebuild. If so, Isharra would probably, for her part in it, become a major figure.

All this was in the future and so imponderable. All he knew now was that Moreno was right; he'd done his best to serve his professed ideals. He took a deep breath, let it out slowly. He was at peace with himself.

About the Author

James K. Burk has been writing almost all his life but just started being published in the last dozen years or so.

James has a checkered background. He has worked with almost every building material known to man and was even a stone-plainer. His favorite job was being a Sunday gunman at an amusement park where he fell over hitching posts, out of wagons, and even off roofs. Sometimes it was even intentional. This latter job was very useful for his weird western novella, "The Ghoul of Socorro," number four in the Night Marshal series. He has also written fantasy, HIGH RAGE and TAKING HOPE and science fiction, REDEMPTION and HOME IS THE HUNTER. His short stories have appeared in several of the Bubbas of the Apocalypse series, and he has two chapbooks of short stories, STRANGE TWISTS OF FATE and ILLUSIONS OF SANITY.

When asked which is his best book, he usually replies, "The next one."

Books Published by Sky Warrior Books

Purchase them through online resellers and better independent bookstores everywhere. Visit us at www. skywarriorbooks.com for news, upcoming books, and promotions.

Alma Alexander

2012: Midnight at Spanish Gardens (E-book, Trade Paperback)

Embers of Heaven (E-book, Trade Paperback)

Gift of the Unmage (E-book)

Spellspam (E-book)

Cybermage (E-book)

S. A. Bolich

Firedancer (E-book, Trade Paperback)

Seaborn (E-book)

Windrider (E-Book, Trade Paperback)

L. J. Bonham

The Debt (E-book)

Shield of Honor (E-book)

Wolves of Valhalla (E-book)

M. H. Bonham

Daemons and Shadows (E-book)

Prophecy of Swords (E-book)

Runestone of Teiwas (E-book)

Samurai Son (E-book, Trade Paperback)

Serpent Singer and Other Stories (E-book)

The Spirit Wolf (E-book)

Robert W. Brady Jr.

Indomitus Est (E-book)

Indomitus Vivat (E-book)

Bob Brown

The Dragon, The Damsel, and the Knight (YA E-book)

The Lost Enforcer (E-book, Trade Paperback)

James K. Burk

Redemption (E-book, Trade Paperback)

John Dalmas

Signature of God Volume 1(E-book)

Signature of God Volume 2 (E-book)

Soldiers! Part 1(E-book)

Soldiers! Part 2 (E-book)

The General's President (E-book)

The Second Coming (E-book, Trade Paperback)

Deby Fredericks

Seven Exalted Orders (E-book, Trade Paperback)

Valorie Hein

The Burden (E-book, Trade Paperback)

Carol Hightshoe (Editor)

Zombiefied: An Anthology of All Things Zombie (E-book, Trade Paperback)

Gary Jonas

Acheron Highway (E-book)

Modern Sorcery (E-book, Trade Paperback)

One-Way Ticket to Midnight (E-book)

Quick Shots (E-book, Trade Paperback)

Frog and Esther Jones

Coup de Grace (E-book, Trade Paperback)

Grace Under Fire (E-book)

Pat MacEwen

The Dragon's Kiss (E-book)

Rough Magic (E-book)

Christie Meierz

The Marann (E-book)

Michael J. Parry

The Oaks Grove (E-book)

The Spiral Tattoo (E-book)

Phyllis Irene Radford

Healing Waves: A Charity Anthology for Japan (Editor) (E-book)

How Beer Saved the World (Editor) (E-book, Trade Paperback)

Gears and Levers 1: A Steampunk Anthology (Editor) (E-book, Trade Paperback)

Gears and Levers 2: A Steampunk Anthology (Editor) (E-book, Trade Paperback)

Gears and Levers 3: A Steampunk Anthology (Editor) (E-book)

Lacing Up for Murder, A Whistling River Mystery (E-book)

So You Want to Commit Novel (E-book, Trade Paperback)

Dusty Rainbolt (Editor)

The Mystical Cat (E-book)

Deborah J. Ross (Editor)

The Feathered Edge (E-book, Trade Paperback)

Laura J. Underwood

Ard Magister (Book One of Ard Magister) (E-book)

Ard Magister: Demon in the Bones (Book Two of Ard Magister) (E-book)

Dragon's Tongue (Book One of the Demon-Bound) (E-book)

The Hounds of Ardagh (E-book)

Steven E. Wedel (Editor)

Tails of the Pack (E-book)

www.ingramcontent.com/pod-product-compliance
Lightning Source LLC
Chambersburg PA
CBHW031101260626
47172CB00001B/156